CHRISTOPHER'S GHOSTS

CHRISTOPHER'S GHOSTS

CHARLES MCCARRY

This edition first published in the UK in 2008 by
Duckworth Overlook
90-93 Cowcross Street
London EC1M 6BF
Tel: 020 7490 7300
Fax: 020 7490 0080
inquiries@duckworth-publishers.co.uk
www.ducknet.co.uk

A catalogue record for this book is available
from the British Library.

ISBN 978 0 7156 3765 4

Book design and type formatting by Bernard Schleifer
Printed and bound in Great Britain by
Creative Print & Design, Blaina, Wales

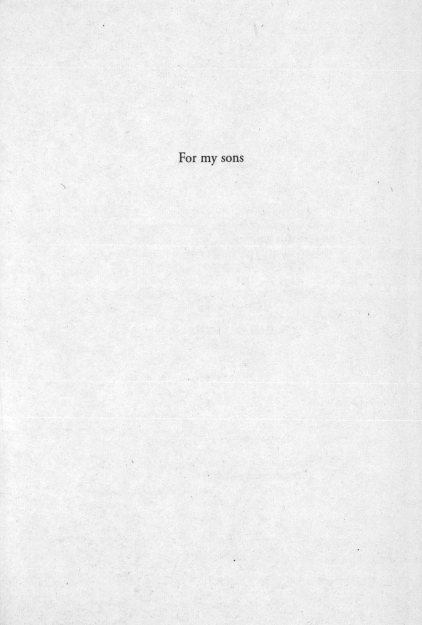

For my sons

PART ONE
1939

ONE

1

In the summer of his sixteenth year, in the last weeks before the second World War began, Paul Christopher kept seeing the same girl in the Tiergarten. She was about his age—maybe a little older. She was slender, dark-eyed, pale, and even in sunlight her hair was black with no hint of brown. She wore it in a long plait. She dressed in blue—a short coat, skirts that swung as she walked, white knee socks, sometimes a beret. She never smiled or made a gesture. She seemed to be watching him, just as he was watching her. Paul, dribbling a soccer ball or sailing a model boat or reading in the sun, would look up and there she would be, close enough for him to see her face but too far away for conversation. They would catch each other's eyes, blue gazing into brown. It was always Paul who looked away first. When he looked again, she would be gone like a ghost. Once or twice he took a step toward her. She immediately turned around and walked away without so much as a look over her shoulder. She was sad, or so Paul thought from a distance. He was reading Balzac that summer. The girl reminded him of Victorine in *Le Père Goriot*. She was pretty. If she had been happy, she would have been beautiful.

Like Paul, the girl was always alone. He had no friends his own age in Berlin. Until he was ten he had gone to school with other boys, but when the dictatorship came to power his parents sent him to school in Switzerland. His father was an American. Paul traveled on an American passport, but because his mother was German and he had been born in Germany, his nationality was an open question to the authorities.

Twice this summer—it was now early July—the secret police had summoned all three Christophers to its headquarters at No. 8 Prinz-Albrechtstrasse to inquire about Paul's case.

A major named Stutzer recorded their answers in the three thick files containing the information that the secret police had gathered on them so far. Because he asked the same questions over and over again, as if they had not already been answered, it took Stutzer more than two hours to cover three or four questions. Why was Paul not a member of the Hitler Youth as all German boys his age were required to be? Did he associate with the decadent Jews and communists who frequented his parents' apartment? Was he allowed to listen to their treasonous talk, to their insults to the Leader? Why had he been sent to a school where French was spoken, where hatred of the Reich was taught as part of the curriculum, where history was falsified, where decadence was the order of the day? Why was he not attending a German school?

Paul's father refused to answer these questions on grounds that they were not questions but provocations, and that they were irrelevant because Paul was an American citizen who could not, under the laws of his own country, take an oath to serve and obey a foreign potentate— that was the term he used—without automatically losing his citizenship. Hubbard Christopher's mannerisms were American, and worse than that he had acquired them at an Episcopalian prep school and at Yale College. He exuded untouchability. He looked amused when being questioned by Stutzer, as if he had bought a ticket to a play that was so bad that it was interesting. It was hard to imagine a more dangerous look to have on your face when visiting No. 8 Prinz-Albrechtstrasse.

The last time they were interviewed, Stutzer had lost his temper. "Whatever your theories on nationality," he shouted, "you must not assume, Herr Christopher, that you can laugh at our questions and not be asked harder questions that will bring you under even deeper suspicion. Remember that."

The Christophers were suspected of crimes against the Reich, and they had in fact helped several enemies of the dictatorship to escape from Germany. There was no real need for the secret police to prove these charges. On his own authority Major Stutzer could send them to a concentration camp or even summarily execute them, but for reasons of his own he wanted to prolong the questioning, to maneuver them into full confessions. His interest in the Christophers, especially in Paul's mother, was deeply personal. They had a history. Always Stutzer's eyes were fixed on her, staring hard, when he fired his questions and threats, as if he was deeply interested in the impression he was making on her. He rarely looked at Hubbard or Paul.

The Geheime Staatspolizei, or secret state police, abbreviated as Gestapo, have been imagined by later generations as a collection of freaks, but in fact they looked like any other Germans. Stutzer was a recognizable type—bony, erect, triangular face, long nose, thin wet pink lips, quick mind. He spoke educated German. He was not, however, educated in the sense that Lori Christopher was educated. She spoke German, French, and English with equal fluency. She knew Latin and ancient Greek and had read the greatest books in all those languages, she recognized almost any European musical work immediately and played the piano expertly, she knew painting and sculpture as well as she knew music, she had memorized the poetry of Goethe and other giants of German letters, she remembered mathematics through calculus. Stutzer had no need for such a body of knowledge. As Hubbard said, secret policemen were like all tribal peoples—they might not know a lot, but they all knew the same things. The Christophers called Major Stutzer Major Dandy because Dandy was what his surname meant in English and because he was almost comically dapper.

Because the questions asked by the secret police were always the same, even when they seemed different, Paul thought of other things while they were being asked and answered, or not answered. Mostly he thought about the girl in the Tiergarten. Why was she always there? Why was she always alone? In his experience, girls traveled in pairs, one of them pretty, the other one plain. Why was she watching him? Why did she always wear blue? Why did she never give him a sign apart from her entrances and exits? Who was she?

A day or two after an interview at secret police headquarters, Paul was flying a kite in the park when a half-dozen Hitler Youth appeared.

They wore campaign caps, brown shirts, neckties, ornamental belt buckles, shorts, knives on their belts. Paul was in a large open space. He saw them coming a long way off. Because there was nothing else to do except run, he went on flying his kite, a large box kite that he had made himself. The Youth advanced in a column of twos, led by their section leader, marching in step, ankles turning on the rough ground, apprentice soldiers on serious business.

Just then, at the edge of a grove of trees, the dark-haired girl appeared. One moment she was not there and the next moment she was, as if someone had turned on a magic lantern and projected her image onto a screen. She stood beside a large linden tree and watched. The section leader, whose shoulder boards bore a single crosswise narrow stripe instead of being plain like the other boys', shouted orders to halt, make a left face, and stand at ease. He then marched over to Paul.

"Papers!" he shouted. He had a voice that had recently broken, grave blue eyes under thick smudged eyebrows, a large straight nose, shiny patches of healed acne, a thin neck. Behind the bully stood his audience. Paul ignored him. He had met others like him in three different countries. He had his own instructions on how to deal with the type. "Don't argue, don't hesitate," his American boxing instructor, Fighting Jim Cerruti, had advised. "Feint with the left and then hit the bum on the nose with a straight right hand. Hard. You gotta break his nose with the first punch, understand?"

"Papers!" the leader said again, louder this time, and with a pinker face.

Again Paul ignored him. His kite was climbing. He paid out string. The wind was strong at the kite's altitude and the taut string quivered. The leader made a movement. He had a knife in his hand. He cut the string. The kite escaped and climbed rapidly, blowing east toward the River Spree. With the severed string still in his right hand, Paul faked with his left, then punched the leader on the nose with a straight right.

It was a short, hard punch, delivered with a lot of force because Paul's feet were already set as a result of his work with the kite. He felt the cartilage split under his fist, saw blood fly, saw the leader's cap fly off. The knife spun away, nickeled hilt glinting in the sun. The leader fell to his knees, hands to his face, blood flowing onto his brown shirt and neck-tie. He shouted a strangled command, his voice breaking. The others attacked. There was nothing to do but fight. Paul had no chance against six attackers even if they were unskilled. He knew this, but he also knew that he could not escape, so he stood his ground. He landed a few punches, drawing more blood, before he was subdued. Two of the boys held his arms behind his back while the others took terms punching him in the face and stomach. Paul kicked his attackers until they threw him to the ground and began to kick him. With no adult present to call them off, Paul thought they might kill him, but before that happened they wore themselves out. They were short of breath, panting.

The leader, nose still bleeding, delivered several kicks of his own.

"Next time obey orders!" he said. "This will teach you to answer questions."

The Youth fell into formation and marched away. Paul knew that his beating had not lasted as long as it seemed. He understood, vague-ly, that the leader and his detachment had been messengers from Stutzer. Deputizing for the secret police was a great honor for these boys. Paul lay on his back and looked upward into the cloudy sky, won-dering where his kite was now. Far to the east, he thought, perhaps over Hellersdorf or even beyond. He had been kicked in the stomach, in the groin, in the back, in the kidneys. Every bruise throbbed. He realized that he was losing consciousness.

Fingertips touched his face. The girl was kneeling beside him. He revived a little. The pain was worse. She said, "You're conscious. Good. Is anything broken?" He thought, How would I know? but said noth-ing. He didn't want to say the wrong thing and frighten her away. Up close she had a wonderful face—dark liquid eyes, full lips, perfect teeth, pale skin that was nevertheless faintly brown, as if another complexion lay beneath the one on the surface. She was speaking English, not German. She had an accent like his mother's, barely detectable and unmistakably Prussian. She had gone to good schools.

In German Paul said, "I don't think anything is broken."

In English she said, "I speak no German."

Paul said, "Why not?"

"Look at me, then think about it," she said. "Stay here. Don't move."

She leaped to her feet and ran. After a moment she returned with a water-soaked handkerchief and began cleaning his face. Her touch was gentle but efficient. She concentrated deeply on what she was doing. Paul smelled blood, wet linen and the water it contained, the girl. Especially her hair. He put a hand in front of his face to stop her from continuing the first aid and said, "Thank you, but I should go now."

"Go where? No one will help you. They will take one look at you and know you have been beaten up and think you're a Jew or a Bolshevik."

"They can think what they like."

"My father is a doctor," she said. "I'll take you to him."

Paul got to his feet. Standing up, he was overcome by dizziness and nausea. When he leaned over to vomit, it seemed to him that he was falling into a bottomless abyss. His legs would not obey him. He lost his balance and fell. He tried to get up again but couldn't. He felt the girl's hands on his arm, guiding him.

The girl said, "You have a concussion. That's a serious matter. Let me take you to my father."

"Does your father speak German?"

"He wouldn't dream of speaking anything else," she replied.

2

The father who was a doctor determined that none of Paul's bones had been fractured. However, four lower ribs had been broken. Paul, stoic up to that moment, shrieked when the doctor poked each of them with a stiff forefinger.

Better the lower than the upper ones, the doctor told Paul. The upper ones, when shattered, could pierce the lungs or the liver or the spleen. "The ribs will be painful for a few weeks but there is no treatment, they must heal themselves," the doctor said. "Try not to make sudden movements. No sports for a month. You must make yourself cough fifty times every day." He demonstrated the deep, phlegm-clearing cough that he was prescribing. "Now you," he said.

Paul coughed. The pain was excruciating. This showed on Paul's face. He gasped and seized his side. The doctor said, "Yes, it will be painful at first. But it is absolutely essential to clear the lungs. Otherwise they can become congested and that could be fatal. You could drown from the fluid in your own lungs. Drown! So cough! Ten times when you wake up, ten times at mid-morning, ten times at noon, ten times in the afternoon, ten times before you go to bed. Do you ever wake in the night?"

"Sometimes, not often."

"If you do, put your face in the pillow and cough ten more times before you go back to sleep."

The doctor found no other sign of internal injury. The ribs had not splintered and punctured the lungs. The spleen seemed to be intact. The liver felt normal.

"Nevertheless you must be watchful," the doctor said. He spoke very rapidly, as he did everything else. He spoke in a mumble, something rarely heard in the old Germany where everyone was exhorted to speak to strangers at the top of their lungs. "If you notice blood in your urine or stool," he continued, "or if you cough up blood or bleed from your anus, penis, nose, or ears, you must go to a doctor immediately. At once, without delay. Do you understand?"

"Yes, Herr Doktor."

"Herr Professor Doktor. Your family has a regular doctor?"

"Yes, Herr Professor Doktor."

This doctor was a small lean man with a bald crown with two puffs of graying black hair growing on either side of it. He was sure of his skills, unsmiling, abrupt in his speech. It was obvious that he expected meek obedience from his patients. Paul thought that he was angry about something—an injustice, an insult—at the center of his being. Whatever it was, he quivered under the weight of it. Paul had seen this condition in some of his parents' friends and in certain of the brainier masters at his school.

"Sit up," the doctor said.

Paul obeyed.

The doctor cut several long strips of adhesive tape, then taped Paul's ribs, sternum to spine, on each side. He pulled the tape very tight. It was a painful process. Paul did not make a sound or a face.

"It's all right to gasp," the doctor said when he had finished one side. "We're alone here. I know it hurts."

Paul nodded.

"You're good at hiding your feelings," the doctor said, cutting tape for the other side of Paul's chest. "That's a useful quality in life, as you will find."

Paul could think of no answer to this that would not be disrespectful, so he said nothing.

The doctor said, "Did you cry when you were a baby?"

"I don't know."

"Your parents didn't tell you?"

"No."

"Then you must have cried. Or maybe you didn't but they thought it would be bad for your character for you to know that. Do you think the Leader cried when he was a baby?"

"I never imagined that he ever was a baby, Herr Professor Doktor."

"Ah, a wit! Do you think it wise to make such jokes, young man?"

"There's nothing funny about the Leader, Herr Professor Doktor."

The doctor looked up. He was enjoying this conversation. "Then you are a loyal German even if you are a wit?"

"I'm not a German, sir."

"You're not? You certainly sound like one. And look like one. They could paint you in the uniform of a hussar and hang you in a museum. If you're not German, what are you?"

The pain of having his ribs strapped made it difficult for Paul to hear what the doctor was saying, much less answer.

"American," Paul said.

"What luck. How did that happen?"

"My father is an American, my mother German."

"Your mother doesn't mind your being an American instead of a German?"

"She and my father decided before I was born that I would be an American." Paul did not know why he was telling this strange little man about whom he knew nothing things that no one outside the family had a right to know.

"Why did they make such a decision?" the doctor asked.

"I wasn't there."

"But maybe a fortune teller was and she saw the future."

Paul said nothing. In fact there was a fortune teller in his family's life, a friend of his mother's. She lived with the Christophers when she was in Berlin. Perhaps the doctor was collecting tidbits for the secret police. Living in the Reich made you think such thoughts even when you hadn't been beaten within an inch of your life in the last half-hour.

The doctor finished taping. He had already put iodine on Paul's skin where it had been broken. "There," he said. "Done. Your parents will be surprised when they see you. You live nearby?"

"Not far," said Paul, cautiously.

The doctor sat down at a desk, unscrewed the cap of a thick black fountain pen, and wrote for a minute or two with great speed. When he finished, he blotted the paper, folded it, and handed it to Paul.

"This is for your parents," he said. "It describes your injuries and the treatment. If you have severe pain, not twinges but pain, take one aspirin dissolved in water every four hours."

"And your fee?"

The doctor waved away the clumsy words. "No need."

"Thank you, Herr Professor Doctor."

"Since you're an American you can dispense with the honorifics. In your country, I understand, you call doctors 'doc.'"

"That's true, doctor. I will say goodbye now."

"Let me ask you a question before you go," the doctor said. "Why did they do it?"

"Who? Do what?"

"Have you forgotten? The Youth. Why did they beat you up?"

"They didn't explain."

The doctor bit his lower lip, nodded his head. "Then all is in order," he said. "Nothing has changed."

3

After Paul told them the story of the beating and his medical treatment, his parents read the doctor's letter, written on plain stationery. It was unsigned.

Lori said, "What is this doctor's name?"

"It was never mentioned."

"No diplomas on the wall, no name on the door?"

"His office was small, too small for the furnishings."

"What did his daughter look like?"

"Dark hair, pale skin, pretty. My age, I think. She was alone."

"Anything else?"

Lori knew that there must be something else. And there was—or was there? He had seen the girl at a distance. He saw no need to mention these sightings, or to list the small details of her appearance that he had memorized so that he could reassemble her in his imagination when she was not present.

He said, "She spoke English to me."

"Why?"

"It's against her principles to speak German, she said."

"Her father must be a Jew, hiding his professional life," Lori said. "We have put the poor man in danger."

Under the Nuremberg Laws dealing with the legal status of Jews in the Reich, Jewish doctors were permitted to treat Jewish patients only. Treating an Aryan patient, even in an emergency, was a serious offense.

"The girl should not have taken you to her father," Lori said.

Hubbard said, "Let's not assume too much. They may not be Jewish at all."

"She had a reason," Paul said. "She told me that no one would help me if they saw me beaten up, because they would think I was a Jew. Or a Communist."

Lori looked steadily at her son for a long moment. "Sensible girl," she said. "I'd like to meet her."

Paul told himself that he would never let that happen. His parents would be a danger to her. The authorities knew too much about them

and wanted to know more. The thought of the girl being questioned in
No. 8 Prinz-Albrechtstrasse by Stutzer, just the two of them alone in
that airless cubicle, was already unbearable, though he did not even
know her name.

Hubbard called the novel he was writing *The Experiment*. No matter what happened on any particular day, he sat down at his writing
desk and recorded the whole experience as fiction. The result was a new
kind of novel in which nothing was made up—a truth novel. Its action
consisted of the minutiae of his daily life, the characters were his family and friends. It was a lampoon of the National Socialists and the
world they were creating. It was a supremely dangerous document to
have lying about the house but it was his work. It was art.

Hubbard did not write about Paul's beating in that day's chapter of
his novel-in-progress. It was too dangerous. Even Hubbard in his zeal
to sacrifice everything for art understood this. Stutzer had made it plain
that he intended to frighten them, to break them, to ruin them by
threatening Paul. Hubbard said, Secret police work is not complicated:
find the weakness, get your finger in it, make notes.

Hubbard and Lori and everyone else they encountered appeared
in Hubbard's manuscript under their own names, including even certain National Socialists they ran into while out on the town or at dinner parties given by conservative friends. Lori was distantly related to
some of them and she might as well have been related to them all.
They had grown up together, they did not judge each other, at least
not yet. To them, Lori's political passions were an eccentricity, like
her marriage to an orphaned American who wrote novels because he
had no property and no prospect of ever having any. Lori was a
romantic. It was in her blood. She was forgiven almost everything by
those who knew her family because she was beautiful and intelligent
and her heroic father had been killed by political fools. Her weakness
for the dregs of society notwithstanding, she was a member of an
ancient family, descended from ancestors who had fought and dined
with Charlemagne during the First Reich. Her friends thought that
she was immune from the dictatorship no matter how foolishly she
behaved. They believed that they were all immune. People like them-

selves always had been. But both Hubbard and Lori knew by now that nobody except the Leader himself was immune from the new justice.

Hubbard had friends of his own in Berlin, American friends. His connections to them were pretty much the same as Lori's to her own cohort. That evening Hubbard and Lori were dining at the house of a friend, O. G. Sackett, who was the first secretary of the American embassy. With his dark suits and white shirts he always wore a pink necktie. He and Hubbard were connected by the long-ago marriage of great-aunts and -uncles. They had been roommates and team-mates in boarding school, they belonged to the same secret society at Yale. They were as much bound together by a web of blood and oaths as any two Germans ever had been. Hubbard's friend was called O. G. because these were the first two initials of his given names, Osborn George, and because his strongest cussword was "Oh, golly!" Later in life, when he commanded thousands of Americans and others during the Cold War, the initials would come to mean "Old Gentleman." He was an honorary godfather to Paul Christopher, a duty he took seriously.

"O. G. is our best hope," Hubbard said.

"A very faint hope," Lori said. "They'll never let Paul out of the country now. He has assaulted the Hitler Youth."

"They assaulted him first."

"True but meaningless."

"There are ways to deal with these matters, Lori."

"You think they don't know all about us? All about Paul? Their noses are everywhere."

This was also true. Hubbard did not understand why they had not yet been arrested. Lori understood only too well, but the secret was not one she could share with her husband.

O. G.'s house was not far away, so they walked from their apartment in Charlottenburg. They did not trust taxi drivers or people who rode on streetcars, or even their own car in which they were alone, because it might be wired by the resourceful technicians of the secret police. Only in the open air, speaking in whispers, could they talk freely. Lori was convinced, in fact she *knew*, that microphones had been hidden in the walls of their flat. She had heard the sounds of them being installed in the walls they shared with the loyal Germans who lived in adjoining apartments. Germans who always before had been delighted to know and say hello to the charming Frau Christopher now passed her on the stairs in silence, with eyes averted. She had not confided this information to Hubbard, either. It could only lead to questions that would be overheard by the listeners. Hubbard was irrational about life, liberty, and the pursuit of happiness. He thought that the Declaration of Independence and the Constitution applied to him no matter where he found himself in the world. He had a right to say, to write, to publish anything that came into his head. No one had a right to eavesdrop on him, especially no foreign government. Damn their microphones.

Rank and lineage notwithstanding, several of Lori's ancestors, some quite recent, had been beheaded. Until recently the guillotine had still been the punishment of choice for treason in Germany, and she knew that many people, including some no older than Paul, had lost their heads for less serious crimes than punching a Hitler Youth on the nose when he was on official Reich business. Outwardly Lori was the picture of confidence and calm. But she dreamt of the guillotine. In her heart she did not believe that any of her family, not herself, not Hubbard, not Paul, not the uncle and aunt who had raised her, were likely to live much longer. She knew as realities things that Hubbard could not imagine. Paul knew some of the same things, having learned them by accident.

But Lori did not know that he knew.

4

The dinner at O. G.'s house was a black-tie party, which in Berlin meant dress uniforms and medals. There were the usual army, navy, air force, and SS uniforms, but also several different types of party uniforms, the SA in dromedary brown, others in coats of many colors. The foreign office had its own uniform. So did other government departments, the government of Prussia, and many others. Hubbard was virtually the only guest in a dinner jacket.

"Dear Lord, O. G.," Lori said, shaking her host's hand. "Don't you know anyone who can afford evening clothes?"

"Imagine what it was like in the kaisers' time," O. G. replied with his gay Rooseveltian smile. "Every regiment designing its own dress uniform. All those different kinds of swords and hats stacked up in the hall."

It was his job to entertain the ruling class, to get to know them and their minds, to encourage them to like him, if not necessarily trust him. The men and women with whom he chatted and joked gave every sign that they did like him. As an American he was a racial grab bag, of course, and besides that a bachelor, which was an iffy state of being at a time when homosexuals were being sent to concentration camps, but he had excellent manners and he spoke German just well enough to be taken seriously rather than resented. In the reception room, Lori took a glass of sparkling wine from a waiter and gazed into the middle distance, hoping that she would be shunned, as sometimes happened to her at these affairs. However, she was soon joined by a man she knew. He was the only man in the room besides Hubbard who wore evening clothes—in his case, a tailcoat and white tie, as if he were going to play the violin after dinner. He clicked the heels of his gleaming patent leather shoes and snapped his narrow head forward, then back.

"Good evening, Baronesse!" he said. "Your husband and I seem to have the same tailor. But then we have always had similar tastes."

He was blond, long-faced, tall, though not as tall as Hubbard, with military posture and, except for broad womanly hips, quite slim. The tailcoat drew attention to his large behind. On other occasions, so did the short skirt of his belted SS uniform jacket, the clothing in which Lori usually saw him.

"Good evening," Lori said. She did not address him by his rank, major general. This was a grave breach of manners. He was the chief of the SS intelligence service and also the Prussian secret police, who controlled Berlin. These two offices gave him the powers of freedom or confinement and life and death over everyone in the Reich. He was thirty-five years old.

But he ignored Lori's slight, in fact showed by subtle signs that he was amused by it. "I had not intended to come tonight," he said with another smile—white but uneven teeth, eyes that challenged Lori's idea of herself. "But then I read the guest list, saw your name on it, and realized that I was far too weak to stay away."

Across the room, Hubbard was talking to the plump wife of a Wehrmacht general who was one of the few people in Berlin or anywhere else in the world who had read every one of his books. She liked his work—adored it, in fact, to the point where Hubbard feared that she would drag him to a sofa and have her way with him despite the difference in their ages. But even as she paid Hubbard fulsome compliments, holding his right hand in both of hers, her eyes worked the crowd.

"Oh my," she said. "Your wife has bagged the star of the evening, Reinhard Heydrich himself. Why would he be here when we are all so far below him? Watch out, dear man! The major general has a terrible reputation, and Mrs. Christopher is so very attractive."

One of O. G.'s assistants was passing by. Hubbard seized him by the arm. "Timberlake, what a coincidence," he said. "I was just telling Mrs. Halder, here, about your wonderful poetry."

"About my what?" said Timberlake. But it was too late for him; the lady was already asking him the first of a hundred questions.

"Ah, we have been spotted by your watchful husband," Heydrich was saying to Lori. "He is rushing toward us, he will be here in no time, and there will go our conversation out the window. May I see you tomorrow?"

Lori gave him a cold stare.

"No response?" Heydrich said. "How delicious. I must find a way to make you be kinder to me. Otherwise I will have no tomorrow."

"Go!" Lori said.

"She speaks!" Heydrich replied. "She fears embarrassment. The husband draws ever nearer. What will he suspect? I hold her fate in my hands."

Hubbard was now close enough to make out their words above the babble of the party. Heydrich smiled, snapped his head forward an inch or two, but did not offer his hand to Hubbard.

"You have interrupted us too soon, Herr Christopher," he said. "Your wife and I have been discussing Bach. Do you not agree that the E major concerto for violin is dazzling in its key changes? Six different keys in the fifty-two opening bars! Those astonishing dissonances, those diminished sevenths!"

"My wife is the musician."

"She plays an instrument?"

"The piano."

"Beautifully, I'm sure. One day perhaps I will have the pleasure of hearing you play, Baronesse."

Baronesse was the title of an unmarried daughter of a baron. The title, by which Heydrich always called her when he called her anything at all, erased her husband.

Lori said nothing.

Heydrich said, "Perhaps we could even play together sometime, though I am a mere amateur." The whole Reich knew that Heydrich came from a musical family. It was said that he played several instruments.

Again, silence from Lori. She looked straight at Heydrich, but as if he wasn't there.

Heydrich clicked his heels and headed straight for the front door.

"He does admire you, that dancing partner of yours," Hubbard said. "You hurt his feelings just now, you know." Last year she had danced with this man at a tea dance in a hotel, not knowing who he was. Heydrich had flirted with her ever since. This was permitted if a woman was married. It was regarded as gallantry, reassurance, a harmless form of flattery. No one actually believed this. It wasn't true even in operettas. But Hubbard's tone was light. He feared nothing from other men where Lori was concerned.

"Or do you actually like him a little?" He teased. "He makes you blush."

"I loathe him," Lori said.

At her elbow O. G. murmured, "Maybe you should try not to let it show quite so plainly, my dear."

5

At dinner Lori was seated next to a one-armed Wehrmacht brigadier general who had served under her Uncle Paulus in the World War. He wore the Knight's Cross of the Iron Cross at his throat and told her tales about Paulus's feats of arms and merry pranks in the regimental mess. Like many of the soldiers Lori had known, this one was frozen in boyhood. He was too much the gentleman to frighten a lady with descriptions of the horrors of combat. "The battle line is less gory than people think," he said. "The smoke hides those awful sights you see in Bolshevik films."

"But when the smoke clears?"

"By that time you have advanced a kilometer or two and all you see are cows in green fields and the backs of the enemy."

In the brigadier's stories the war had been fun—Lori's Uncle Paulus chasing a Russian in a horseback duel during the Battle of Tannenberg that ended with Paulus lopping off the Russian's hand with his saber and then, noblesse oblige, dragging the vanquished enemy to a burning house and thrusting the stump into the flames to cauterize the wound. The brigadier had known Lori's father, too—he and Paulus had been in the same regiment of lancers—and would have told her stories about him, too, if he had fallen in battle instead of being beaten to death by a gang of Bolshevik rabble. On the day of his death, her father had gone for a stroll from the hospital in Berlin where he was recovering from wounds received in the last battle on the western front. Because of his injuries he had been too weak to defend himself. No one ever spoke of his death—a German officer must always go down fighting—but Lori had often imagined it, and she imagined it again now, except that it was Paul's death she envisioned while surrounded by the smiling people, now gorging on food and the latest gossip, who were most likely to kill him.

She was obsessed by the possibility—in her heart, the inevitability—of Paul being murdered by the politically insane. One side or the other would slaughter him, then march on, singing "The

Internationale" or "Die Wacht am Rhein." She had felt this in her bones even before she conceived her child. She knew then that she herself was somehow going to be responsible for her son's death. The fact that she would devote her life to trying to save him from his fate would make no difference. She listened to the brigadier, who was now talking about his schooldays with the irrepressible Uncle Paulus. If Lori's photograph had been taken at that moment the image would have been that of a gently smiling, perfectly composed woman. What was going on in her mind was another matter.

After the sherbet she escaped, making a graceful excuse to the brigadier and the person on her right, and locked herself in the library. Two or three times someone rattled the doorknob, once or twice somebody knocked. Then she was left in peace. Conclusions had been drawn. Someone, more likely two someones, required privacy. Lori was not at the table, Heydrich was not at his place. Everyone had seen them talking, had seen Heydrich's outrageous flirting. What could be more obvious? This man could order the immediate death of anyone in Germany and beyond. What woman could resist such power?

Lori read Dickens while waiting for the guests to leave. O. G. owned the complete works, bound in leather, so she read passages from several novels. She did not like Dickens, did not like the way he made the monstrous entertaining. She resented happy outcomes that could not possibly have arisen from the hopeless circumstances in which the author placed his characters. She disliked the palimpsest that was his style, so that all the sentiment was in the ink and all the truth was between the lines.

The last guests departed, the last peal of laughter faded. Hubbard's frisky American knock, shave-and-a-haircut-two-bits, sounded. She turned the key and let him and O. G. in. Hubbard gave her a searching look. She was distraught, head thrown back, eyes red, throat ligaments taut. In earlier days he would have smiled at her, but he had long since learned how much she disliked this American reassurance when there was nothing to smile about, so he kept his teeth beneath his lip. O. G. locked the door, then poured scotch whisky from a decanter, added to each drink a squirt of seltzer from a siphon, then handed the glasses around. Lori put hers down on the table beside her chair.

"Drink, my dear," O. G. said. "You look like you need it."

To the surprise of neither man, Lori did not obey.

To O. G. she said, "You know what happened to Paul today?"

"I've heard a version of it," O. G. said. "Heydrich told me."

"Heydrich?" Hubbard said. "He knows?"

"I'm afraid so. He takes an interest in the Christophers. Speaks of you as if you are dear friends."

Lori's eyes were wide, her body rigid. A quick pulse beat in her blushing chest, above her décolletage. Hubbard avoided looking at her, as if he could make things worse by noticing what was happening to her.

He said, "But why on earth should Heydrich know?"

"Because charades are his business," O. G. said. "Also, they are his nature. He plays games."

"He sent the Youth to attack Paul?"

"It's not impossible. Everyone knows what he is capable of doing, but who knows for sure what he actually does or orders to be done? He's a man of mystery. That's why he has risen so far so fast."

"But why Paul?" Hubbard said.

"He wants something from you."

"What could he possibly want from me, for heaven's sake?" Hubbard asked.

O. G. shrugged. "Does it matter? Whatever it is, he's licensed to take it whenever he wants."

He drank, his mild gaze fixed on Lori's face. Hubbard drank. Lori remained as she was, staring at nothing, rigid in her chair, silent, face averted, heartbeat visible. Hubbard had never seen her so withdrawn. Her genes and her upbringing discouraged displays of emotion, but now her face was a map of her fears, whatever they were.

Suddenly Lori said, "It is not safe to discuss these matters."

"It's perfectly safe to talk here. . ." O. G. said.

"Ha!" said Lori.

". . . so I will come to the point," O. G. continued. "I think we should get Paul out of Germany as quick as we can, and then get the two of you across a frontier as soon after that as possible."

"How?" Hubbard said.

"In two weeks' time I sail home on the *Bremen* for consultations in Washington. Paul can go with me. He can stay with Elliott in New York."

Lori said, "They'll grab him at the passport control."

"Not if he's under my protection."

"What protection?" Lori said. "Do you think they care about diplomatic immunity? You just got through saying there is no immunity from them."

"They're ruthless, but there are rules just the same," O. G. said. "I have a plan."

"What plan?"

"It's better that you don't know the details."

"He's our son!"

"Yes, he is," O. G. said. "And what if the next time you are invited to the Prinz-Albrechtstrasse they decide to get rough? If they beat Paul—I'm talking about grown men, trained thugs, taking turns with fists and feet and clubs—which secrets will you decide not to tell them?"

6

By now Paul was in love. This had not happened to him before, but he was a reader and an observer; he knew the signs. Nevertheless the power of the thing astonished him—the feeling that he never had enough breath in his lungs, the long hours and days of anxiety, the longing, the suspicion, the raw craven fear of loss, punctuated by fleeting moments of happiness when the girl appeared: She was more apparition than human. Except for the moments she had knelt beside him, bathing his cuts and bruises, he had always seen her at a distance. He still did not know her name.

Having one's wounds treated by a beautiful female is a powerful aphrodisiac. Paul was beginning to feel symptoms that had little to do with the pure love between man and woman about which he had read so much. Until he had felt her fingers on his battered face, smelled her skin and hair, seen the light in her eyes, she had been like Rima the Bird Girl in his favorite novel, W. H. Hudson's *Green Mansions*—free, innocent, unattainable, a child of nature. But when he thought of her now, he visualized the thing that he remembered best about Rima—that she was naked in her rain forest (at least in Paul's imagination) when the hero first caught sight of her. Recalling those passages had a physical effect on him. This troubled him. He wondered if he had a dirty mind; he apologized to both of the lovely wraiths who had somehow become one in his imagination.

Haunted by the girl and tormented by his injuries, Paul slept fitfully on the night after he was beaten up by the Hitler Youth. He heard his parents come in late after their party. They were awake for a long while, speaking in whispers in the sitting room, his father pacing. Finally they went to bed and Paul drifted into sleep—dreamless sleep, to his surprise. When he woke soon after dawn, he could tell by the feel of the house that his mother had gone out and that his father was writing. This was their routine. Hubbard rose at five every morning, and after drinking a bowl of coffee and milk and eating toasted bread and cheese, began to write the latest passage of *The Experiment*. This morning he had a great deal to write about. He finished, usually, in time for lunch at one-thirty. During the hours he spent at his writing table, Waterman fountain pen in hand, he was in another dimension. Time dissolved, he had no thought or perception of the real world. Paul knew this because he had seen his father in this state nearly every morning of his life, and also because his parents joked about it all the time. When he was writing, Lori said, Hubbard was *andeswoher*—elsewhere, unreachable. That was why she did her shopping and other womanly chores in the morning. Her husband did not even know that she was gone. And when he came back up the rabbit hole she was always present, saying something new to his ears, the table set, food ready to be served, that day's bottle of wine, his reward for outstanding industry, open and breathing or chilling in an ice bucket.

When Lori was happy or upset, she went riding. Paul had never seen her so upset as she had been since he came home after his beating. Last night's whispers told him that she hadn't recovered. Their elderly hors- es —Lori's Lipizzaner mare and his father's elderly hunter—were sta- bled near the park. Hubbard had bought them and their elegant tack during the great inflation of the nineteen-twenties. He had arrived in Berlin at a moment when one American dollar was worth two trillion Reichsmarks and a single egg sold for eighty billion marks. Now that the Reichsmark was four to the dollar once again, keeping the animals was a foolish extravagance, but Hubbard refused to give them up. His trust fund yielded enough to live on, and—always a surprise—he some- times made a little money from writing. He dipped into his meager cap- ital, a sin against which he had been warned all his life, so that they could have their horses and their yawl, *Mahican*, which was docked at Lori's family home on the island of Rügen on the Baltic Sea.

By the time Paul got out of bed, the clock told him that his moth- er had already departed. There was no possibility he could join her, even if his injuries had not prevented it. His entire body ached where it had been punched and kicked, especially his insides. The mere thought of being in the saddle, riding at a trot, was agonizing. Paul had not been forbidden to go back to the park. His parents never forbade him anything. They had trusted his judgment ever since he was old enough to go out on his own. He had crossed busy streets by himself when he was barely able to talk. Nevertheless he felt that he might be doing something that they had trusted him not to do when he decid- ed to go to the Tiergarten. He went anyway. He had no choice in the matter. He usually caught his first glimpse of the girl in the morning. This time, if he saw her, he would walk up to her, look her in the eye, shake her hand, thank her. He would take the second step now that she had taken the first. Or so he told himself. In minutes Paul was dressed and on his bicycle, eating bread and butter with one hand and with the other steering around streetcars and automobiles and steaming heaps of horse manure. The Christophers lived in Gutenbergstrasse, only a few blocks west of the park. He was through the gates of the Tiergarten in no time, drifting on his bike down a gentle hill that led to the meadow where the girl usually appeared.

He locked his bicycle to a rack and continued on foot. It was a sunny day in June. A breeze from the west and the horses on the bridle path (Paul could feel hoof beats in the turf beneath his feet) had stirred the dust. It hung like gauze in the slanting silvery light that shone through the trees. Such birds as were still singing this long after the sun had risen seemed far away and muted. In the distance—everything seemed distant—someone played "My Blue Heaven" on a harmonica. Paul sang along, silently. It was one of his father's favorite shaving songs. Hubbard woke up every morning with a song on his lips. In an off-key baritone, he sang all his songs as if they had been written about him and Lori and Paul: *Yes sir, she's my baby/ No sir, don't mean maybe.* Paul wondered what yesterday's leader would have done about these decadent songs, written perhaps by Jews, if he had heard them. Taken names and reported them to No. 8 Prinz-Albrechtstrasse? Thrown the harmonica into the Neuer See? He smiled. He knew that there was nothing funny about National Socialists, but he could not help it. They were so serious, so absurd, so numerous.

Then he saw her. She stood on a slope above him, the hazy sunlight in her face. Behind her stood a line of trees. He expected her to move back into them as usual and for an instant, before he smothered the image, he thought of the innocent nude Rima in her Venezuelan fastness. Then the girl came walking down the hill. She moved like an athlete and looked like one too, long-legged, erect, natural, unselfconscious. Not marching at all, just walking like a natural person. Paul let her come to him. When she reached him she did not offer to shake hands, nor did she smile. She looked him over with minute attention. His face was still a mask of iodine and bandages.

"You don't look quite as bad as I expected," she said. She spoke English, as before.

Paul said, "Nothing serious."

"Yesterday I thought they might have killed you."

"As you can see, I survived," Paul said. "Thanks to you."

"What did I have to do with it?"

"A lot. The first aid, taking me to your father, taking me home."

"I did it for my own sake. You owe me nothing."

"That's not true."

She ignored the protest. She looked behind her, then behind Paul. The park was all but deserted at this hour. "We shouldn't talk now, not here of all places," she said.

"But I want to talk," Paul said. He smiled at her. He was tall for his age, but she was too, and she stood slightly above him on the hillside, so that they looked directly into each other's eyes.

"There are things that you should tell me," she said.

"I agree," Paul said. "And vice-versa. Can we start with names?"

"I know your name. I have known it for a long time."

"How? We've never seen each other before."

"I have my ways."

"Which are?"

"We used to live around the corner from each other. I have always known who you are, Herr Baron."

"My name is Paul. I'm no baron. What shall I call you?"

"That's up to you."

"You don't have a name?"

"I want a new one."

"You want me to baptize you as well? We can use the lake." Where did this lame witticism come from?

"Nothing so religious as that," she said.

Paul wondered if she felt as awkward as he did. Her face was grave, but for the first time he saw a smile—a tiny one that lifted one corner of her mouth and changed her eyes. She was flirting with him, but doing so in a way no girl he had ever known could have imagined flirting.

Paul said, "Okay, but first I'll have to know you better. What should I call you in the meantime?"

" 'Miss' will be fine."

"No. It doesn't suit you." He paused, then said, "Rima. Do you like that name?"

"Yes," she said. "I do."

"Then Rima you are."

She looked at her watch, not a wristwatch but a round gold lavalier pinned to her blouse. "We've been out in the open long enough," she said. "Meet me tomorrow at half-four in the ice cream place in the Ausburgerstrasse."

Half-four. It was the first mistake in English she had made. Paul didn't correct her.

7

Paul rode home by way of the stables. As he pedaled, horses moved apart. He rode through them, and after a couple of hundred meters, to his delight, saw his mother. She was mounted but she had stopped her horse to speak to somebody on the other side of the railing that enclosed the bridle path. This was no surprise. The morning ride was a social occasion and Lori had many equestrian friends. The person she was talking to had his back to Paul. He wore a brown fedora, cocked slightly to one side, and despite the warm weather, a long black leather coat with a belt. A second man, stumpy and stolid and clearly a subordinate, stood by. Lori's Lipizzaner shied. The man turned, keeping eye contact with Lori, and Paul saw that the man was Stutzer. He was speaking to Lori in an unsmiling way, and he was doing all the talking. She was perfectly silent, but Paul, who knew her every expression, could tell that she was resisting whatever suggestion the man was making to her. Paul thought that he understood what was happening. Her beauty created embarrassing situations. Paul had been a witness to this all his life. For his mother, this encounter with a man she loathed was hateful. Paul did not want to make it worse by interfering, but he had a duty to protect his mother. Why did she not just ride away? Then Paul saw that the smaller man, the assistant, had hold of the Lipizzaner's bridle. The horse, a coal-black animal, obeyed him; he must know about horses. Anger rose in Paul's chest. A uniformed Berlin policeman stood on the sidewalk on the other side of the railing, watching the scene. Not far away, another policeman loitered. They did not interfere as they would have done if anyone else was bothering a respectable woman. Paul looked more closely and saw two other men, both young and both dressed in identical fedoras and belted leather coats. An SS trooper in uniform stood beside a gleaming Daimler. A second uniformed trooper sat behind the wheel. Paul had seen this tableau before in the streets of Berlin, and he knew what it signified— a secret police operation.

Suddenly his mother dismounted, ducked under the rail, and walked toward the Daimler. No one touched her or spoke to her. There was no sign that she was being arrested. She seemed to be acting of her own free will. The SS trooper opened the rear door of the Daimler. A man in uniform sat inside on the leather upholstery. Paul could not see his face, just his lean long legs in riding boots, crossed at the ankles. His mother got into the car. The man inside lifted her hand, rolled back the top of her riding glove, and kissed the inside of her wrist.

The SS trooper closed the door and the big car with its curtained windows moved away. The policemen stopped traffic for it. The fellow who had been holding the bridle of Lori's Lipizzaner mounted the animal and rode off toward the stables. He brought the animal to a trot, its best pace. He rode competently, back straight, head erect, eyes straight ahead. He must have been a cavalryman at some point in his life, before Germany changed.

8

Next day, on his way to the ice cream shop, Paul was accosted by brownshirts—big jovial political street-fighters with bony fists and wily eyes who made jokes about his battered face. Had he run into a door, a husband? Ah, he could smile, he was a good loser! They were collecting for yet another National Socialist Party charity. There were many such charities and new ones were being invented all the time. The contributions were in reality a political tax levied by the party. Everyone understood this, and knew that refusal was unwise. The brownshirts specified the contribution they wanted from Paul, one mark. Paul handed it over and they gave him a tin swastika pin to show that he had contributed.

The day was sunny and warm, ice cream weather, and the shop was crowded. The usual notice, *No Jews*, was posted in the window. Rima was already seated at a tiny table for two. When Paul joined her she ordered chocolate ice cream with chopped nuts and whipped cream. Paul asked for the same. They ate in silence. This was no place for private conversation, not that there was any such place in Berlin.

Rima had dressed for the weather. Instead of her usual blue wool she wore a light green dress that showed her knees when she walked, or so Paul imagined. He also pictured her chiffon scarf floating as she moved. Her long ebony plait was wound round her head. She wore pumps with high heels and white socks, as was the fashion all over Europe that summer. She wore bracelets on both wrists, and on her left hand a modest ring with a red stone that might have been a ruby. She looked more like a woman than a girl. They finished their ice cream.

"What now?" Rima asked.

"A walk in the zoo?" Paul suggested.

"No thank you. I hate the cages. I hate the smell. Imagine what it would be like if you had a lion's sense of smell and all you could smell was captivity."

"And never fresh blood."

"Not funny."

The tables were very close together here. It was impossible to talk without being overheard. Their English attracted the attention of two women at the next table. One of them leaned closer and listened. Outside the shop window the brownshirts lingered.

"How much did you give them?" Rima asked.

"What they asked for, one mark."

"Not enough, in my opinion," Rima said. "Good German boys out in all kinds of weather, helping the poor and the unfortunate and the families of our men in uniform. Give them another coin for me on the way out."

The eavesdropper looked suspicious, but went back to her conversation with her friend.

On the way out, Paul dropped a coin in the brownshirts' collection box. "Ah, the good loser!" one of them said, handing Paul another swastika pin and throwing a mock punch at his jaw.

When Paul and Rima were out of sight, he put the pin into his pocket with the other one. Now both he and Rima had pins, and if they wished to put them on they could walk in the city without being accosted for more contributions. There was no possibility of either of them wearing a swastika, but unless they did so they could not stay on the streets without being bankrupted. There would be other brownshirts on every street corner. Without the pins, there would be questions, taunts, and worse.

"I have an idea," Paul said.

The ice cream shop was just south of the zoo, near the boundary with Schöneberg, called the American quarter of Berlin though few Americans lived there or anywhere else in the city. They took a streetcar to Nollendorfplatz and paid out another mark to the brownshirts who were collecting tolls at the trolley stop. The American church was only a few steps away, in Motzstrasse, a quiet little street. The doors were unlocked. The nave, which smelled faintly of soap and wax and dust and candle smoke, was deserted. The silence inside was so complete that it seemed that even the stones had no memory of voices or music. They were alone. They sat down together in the back pew.

Rima pointed at the large wooden cross that was the only décor apart from the stained-glass windows.

"What cult is this?"

"It's for all Protestants, I believe."

"You come here often?"

"Only once when I was an infant, to be baptized. I don't remember it."

"Then your parents are Protestants."

"They don't practice a religion. They wanted a baptismal certificate as one more proof that I'm an American."

"Why?" Rima said.

"In case they ever needed it."

"A lot of Americans must be nonbelievers. There's nobody here."

"Vespers at five," Paul said, reading a sign. "We have almost an hour."

"Then I'd better begin," Rima said. Paul started to speak. Rima put a finger on his bruised lips. "No," she said. "No questions now. I will speak. Then, if you wish, you will speak. Then, if we both wish, we will discuss what happens next." Rima handed Paul her identity card. "So that you'll know my original name," she said. "And certain other facts."

Her baptismal name was Alexa Johann Maria Kaltenbach. She was born in Berlin on 21 December, 1923, so she was six months older than Paul. No "J" was stamped in red ink on her papers, which meant that she was not considered a Jew under the Nuremberg laws.

Paul was surprised. She saw this. "Don't be deceived," she said. "I have one Jewish grandparent, my father's father, so I'm not officially a Jew. My father, however, had three Jewish grandparents, so he's a Jew under the law even though he's a Lutheran and has been one all his life. Two of his three Jewish grandparents were Lutherans also. My mother is of pure Aryan blood, according to the official investigation. She lives in Argentina."

"Why?"

"My father drove her to France for a vacation, gave her bank drafts for all but a few thousand of the Reichsmarks he had saved, and told her to go to Buenos Aires, put the money in a bank, and wait there until the madness was over."

"What about you?"

"I am still here. Stop asking questions."

Dr. Johann Kaltenbach, Rima's father, believed that the present political situation, as he called the dictatorship, would pass. In his own mind he was a German like any other. He had been born in Germany of German parents, attended German schools, loved the kaisers while they reigned. In the World War he had bled for Germany on the western front. Since childhood he had gone to church every Sunday and on all Christian holidays. He prayed as a Christian at meals and before he slept. He sang *Stille Nacht* on Christmas Eve. He had no consciousness whatsoever that he was Jewish because his parents had never told him or his brothers any such thing. He had chosen medicine as his profession because he believed that easing the suffering of the sick was a Christian calling. When the war started he interrupted his studies in order to join his reserve unit on active service. He rose to *Oberleutnant* in the Reichswehr and served for three years as an infantry officer on the western front. He was wounded twice and was awarded the Iron Cross first class for bravery.

After the war he completed his medical education and learned surgery as an apprentice to one of his professors. In a matter of a few years he was one of the most respected surgeons in Germany. He specialized in the lungs and heart at a time when tuberculosis was rampant. His practice flourished. Patients came from all over Germany and beyond to be treated by him. Often he was their last hope, and he saved many from death. His fee for a successful surgery was one year's income of the patient he had saved. He charged nothing if the patient did not recover. He married a pretty, spirited, loving girl whose father was a learned professor of philosophy. Her Christian family accepted Kaltenbach without question. He was happy, he grew rich, tears formed in his eyes when he heard the bugle call "*Ich Hatt' Einen Kameraden*," the German equivalent of "Taps," played at memorial services. He tithed his earnings to his church. He had a soldier's contempt for politics. Germany was being killed by politics. He disliked the National Socialists but loathed the Bolsheviks, and in 1932 he voted for the National Socialist candidate for the Reichstag because he was one of his patients and because he knew for a fact that the man was not a traitor to Germany, while all Bolsheviks everywhere were traitors by definition. It had never occurred to Dr. Kaltenbach that his Germanness could be questioned, let alone taken away from him.

"And when this happened just the same and they stamped a big red 'J' on his papers and then confiscated his property and his medical practice and forbade him to treat any patients except other Jews, he thought it was a mistake that would soon be rectified," Rima said. "He still thinks it will be rectified, that everything will be rectified. I think he believes that the clock of existence has struck the wrong hour or something, and that the people who now rule Germany are men from Mars who somehow got lost in the universe and ended up on our planet.

One day God, the supreme clockmaker, will notice this mechanical error and send them back where they came from and all will be right with the world again."

Paul said, "Doesn't everyone believe that, even the Nazis?"

"Maybe. But in the meanwhile Father has no patients because he doesn't know any Jews. He never knew any Jews except for some of his patients."

"Jews are informing on your father to the secret police?"

"People who say they're Jews. Maybe some of them really are Jews. Please let me finish."

It was at this moment that Paul conceived the idea of rescuing Rima and her father. They could sail to Denmark aboard *Mahican*, as many others had done when they had no other recourse than arrest and death. He did not hear the next few words of Rima's story because he had started to remember what he had seen two days before on the bridle path of the Tiergarten. Memories came to him like newsreel images—pictures that were quicker than the actual events, with the sound slower and louder. When a memory was unwelcome he stopped it from forming in his mind by thinking about a sport, some good moment when he had scored a goal in soccer or made a hard shot in tennis or skied through fresh snow and looked back on a turn to see his own tracks. Now he slammed a door in his brain because he had begun to see the Daimler and the booted man in its backseat and then his mother in her riding clothes, getting into the car.

It was almost five o'clock. The stained glass window closest to Paul and Rima depicted Jesus's entry into Jerusalem on a donkey. Its rich colors glowed in the bright light of the sinking sun. An old bald vestryman lighted candles. Worshippers began to arrive, grandmothers mostly. Some of them prayed while they waited for the service to begin. The church bell rang. The organ played soft music. Though he was not especially musical, Paul recognized a many of the pieces. He had heard his mother play them all his life. The effect was peaceful, affirmative, a tidy little compliment to the Almighty. It made Paul feel at one with the strangers around him. The throaty emotion he experienced was not so very different from the one that Rima evoked in him.

Rima was whispering now, directly into his ear. She held his hand in her own hands. Paul found the warmth of her breath on his skin and the heat of her hands on his flesh almost unbearably arousing. Having such feelings in church made the experience more intense. Rima's scent changed, too, as she whispered. They were in the last pew. No one could see them except the vestryman, who gave them a long look, then disappeared, carrying the staff with which he had lighted the candles. The organist changed composers. Paul recognized the melody, unmistakable even to a heathen, of "Jesu, Joy of Man's Desiring."

"Paul," Rima whispered through the music, "I know they are going to kill me. They'll invade another country soon and close the Reich to foreigners and do whatever they like. That's the intention. It cannot be otherwise. And I can't bear the thought of dying before I have known love—everything about it. *Everything.*"

Paul did not know what to say.

Rima did. She said, "Will you please be my love before it's too late? Please."

Paul replied, "I already am."

TWO

1

Paul and Rima could promise each other love, but the practicalities were another matter. Where would they meet? How would they communicate? How would they find privacy? How could they keep their secret? These are questions for all clandestine lovers. For Paul and Rima, they were questions of life and death. Everyone in Berlin was an informer—housewives in an ice cream parlor, the street car conductor, someone you passed on a stairway, your closest friend, your teacher. Their love was a danger to Rima's father, to Paul's parents, to themselves. By falling in love, these children had become fugitives. There was no safety for them. Rima knew in her bones—she had just said so—that she would be lucky to be alive at age eighteen, and Paul knew that she was right. The machine—she imagined the secret police apparatus as an enormous clanking tank that obliterated everything in its path—could take her long before that. Her father could disappear at any moment. If that happened, she would become a ward of the government and would herself vanish. No one would ask where she had gone or what had happened to her. She would cease to exist in the mind of any living person.

The same could happen to Paul, no matter what kind of passport he carried. The United States of America was not going to declare war on Germany over a missing boy. So far the secret police had taken no official notice of his scuffle with the Youth, but by defending himself from the power of the dictatorship he had committed a serious crime.

Stutzer knew every detail. Paul had given him what he needed to black-mail his parents, to make them confess to their all-too-real crimes against the Reich. The secret police knew all about the *Mahican* and its nighttime sails. The Christophers knew that they knew. The secret police were attacking Paul's mother because they thought the woman was the weak link. They wanted something from her. They thought that Lori would break, that she would do anything to save her son. Even though she was the strongest of the three of them, Paul knew that they were right.

At supper that evening, the menu was normal—an omelet with mushrooms, ham, bread, cheese, apples, no wine because alcohol drunk in the evening gave Hubbard bad dreams. The conversation was normal. Lori had received a letter from her Aunt Hilde, who wanted to know if they were coming to Rügen for midsummer, which fell on the next weekend.

"Are we going?" Hubbard asked.

"Of course," Lori replied. "I'll write to her tonight. We always go to Rügen for midsummer night."

"Good," Hubbard said. "Maybe we can sail."

After supper, each under his own reading lamp as if God were in his heaven and all was right with the world, Lori wrote her letter to Hilde while Hubbard read the three-week-old *Saturday Evening Post* that O. G. had saved for him. He laughed at the *Post's* cartoons, devoured every word of fiction in every issue, especially the serialized novels of James Warner Bellah, but never read the articles. Hubbard did not trust journalism, did not believe that it could ever approximate the truth because everyone lied to journalists. Paul held a volume of Balzac, his summer reading assignment, in his lap. The book might as well have been print-ed in Sanskrit. The type swam away. He could not concentrate. He was still in the American church with Rima's breath in his ear, her leg against his, his hand in her hand.

"Paul," Lori said, "time for Schatzi's walk."

The Christophers had no servants. When the cleaning woman, who also did the laundry, came on Wednesdays, Lori locked up her hus-band's manuscripts and sent him out for a long walk while she stayed home and supervised. Otherwise they did their own chores, with Lori as maid of all work, Hubbard as dishwasher, and Paul in charge of odd jobs. One of these was to take the family schnauzer for a walk. The little dog was one of several thousands in the city whose name was Schatzi —"Sweetheart." It had belonged to a dog-loving Social Democrat who fled Germany and left it in their care. At nine-thirty Paul took Schatzi out on its leash as usual. The nearest public grass was six blocks away, in a small wooded park with gravel walks and a fountain at its center. Paul had arranged to meet Rima by the fountain at ten o'clock sharp. They had decided in the American church that they must always behave as if they were under surveillance. The streets swarmed with dog walkers and cigar smokers. Paul noticed no one following him, but it was impossible to be certain in this sea of potential informers that he was not being watched.

Rima waited by the fountain as arranged. To Paul's surprise, she led a dog of her own, another kind of small terrier. She wore a head scarf, ends tied under her chin. She walked slowly away down one of the wider gravel walks. He waited until she was far ahead and then, keeping his distance, he followed. She turned onto a narrow path, then into the trees. Here there was no artificial light at all apart from the distant glow of street lamps beyond the park's spiked iron fence. They were alone. The earth beneath their feet was spongy, damp. He smelled ferns, rotting vegetation.

"Whose dog is that?" Paul asked in a whisper.

"It belongs to a neighbor, an old lady," Rima replied, also in a whisper. "I'm doing a good deed."

With a few deft movements, Rima leashed the dogs to trees. Then she took Paul's hand and walked him a few steps away from the dogs. She took his face in her hands. She whispered, "Can you see me?"

"No."

"Nor I you. It's all right. We have four other senses. Wait. I'm going to take off my scarf."

After a moment, she shook her head. Her hair, no longer braided, fell free. It was perfumed. He smelled her skin. He did not move.

Rima said, "I look different now."

"I wish I could see you."

Rima said, "There are other ways to see."

Paul could barely talk. He said, "What?"

"Do something," Rima whispered.

Paul groped in the darkness and put his hand on her hair. He stroked it, put his nose into it, put both hands under it, touched her cheeks, lifted the hair, which was thick and silky but less heavy than he had expected, and much longer. It fell to her waist and below. His arms were around her now. Her body moved inside her clothes. They were very close. She put her arms around his neck and moved even closer. Their bodies brushed. She kissed him on the lips, her own lips fluttering. He imitated this. She took his lower lip between her lips. Nothing like this had ever happened to him before. Rima touched his tongue with her tongue. He had had no idea that such techniques existed.

Rima pulled him closer, pasting herself to him. She was a strong girl, slender and muscular. She made no noise. She was in a state of total concentration, he could feel it. Suddenly she stopped kissing and turned her face away. She was crying. He touched the tears and whispered her name.

She said, "Ssshhh."

She clung to him, arms around his neck, the length of her body still against his body, but now she seemed relaxed. Many moments later she stepped back. He let her go. By now he could see much better in the dark. Her face was almost visible. He saw her pale hands twisting her long dark hair and realized that she was braiding it. She wound the plait around her head, pinned it, and re-tied her head scarf. She took his face in her hands. She kissed him, a chaste affectionate kiss.

He felt her put a note in his hand. "Tomorrow afternoon," she whispered. "This will tell you where."

Paul kissed her again, this time making the first move. He was a little ashamed that he had not acted first when they entered the trees, that Rima had been obliged to do it. He was still too young to know that a man can almost never be quick enough to make the first move when a woman has made up her mind to make love to him.

In a normal tone of voice, Rima said, "Go first."

When he walked back into the light he realized that he was leading the wrong dog. He turned around and walked back. He and Rima met in the path, switched leashes and dogs as smoothly as veteran secret agents, and walked on in opposite directions. In the instant that this maneuver took, Paul saw that Rima's face was different—softer, with a different light in the eyes.

Balzac had been right about pretty girls. When they were happy, they were beautiful.

2

The next morning at five o'clock, even before Hubbard had started to write, two of Stutzer's men came for him and Paul. They were young fellows, fresh-faced and correct. They were dressed alike in versions of Stutzer's civilian wardrobe—brown fedoras, black leather trench coats, highly polished shoes. Hubbard called them the apprentices.

Standing calmly in the doorway in his dressing gown, Hubbard said, "What is it you gentlemen want?"

"Papers."

Hubbard handed American passports and German identity documents to the apprentice who was doing the talking. He put them into his coat pocket without looking at them.

Hubbard said, "I ask you again. What is this all about?"

"Get dressed, you and your son," the other apprentice said. "You have five minutes."

"We are under arrest?"

"You now have three minutes," said the first apprentice. Apparently it was part of their technique to take turns as spokesman of the arrest. Paul saw that his father loved this detail. Hubbard said, "Paul, get dressed. Bring a sweater. Use the bathroom." As the Christophers knew from earlier arrests, the refusal of toilet privileges for hours on end was one of the features of secret police interrogation. It was an effective technique. Who knew what the punishment might be for wetting on Major Stutzer's floor?

Lori, who somehow had managed to appear with her hair combed and fully dressed in a gray frock, stockings, and low-heeled black shoes, said, "Why are you doing this?"

One of the apprentices said, "That is not your concern."

"My husband and son are not my concern?"

"Today they are our concern. You are expected to go riding in the Tiergarten this morning at seven-thirty exactly. No later."

The apprentice was perfectly proper, his face expressionless. So was his companion. But Lori saw in their eyes that they wanted her to understand that they knew what they knew. They seemed to be suppressing lascivious smiles. Paul emerged from his bedroom, fully clothed. He overheard the conversation. As he listened, he looked into his mother's frozen face. There was nothing there for the apprentices, or for him.

In rapid English Lori said to him, "Be polite, Liebchen. Keep your head. Be calm, always calm. Answer only the questions they ask, not the ones they don't ask."

"German only!" an apprentice said.

"*Jawohl*, Mama," Paul said. He took a step toward his mother, as if to kiss her.

"No touching allowed!" said the other apprentice.

At No. 8 Prinz-Albrechtstrasse, Hubbard and Paul, standing up in a locked room with no chairs, waited until noon, when two men in uniform, not the same ones who had arrested them, came for Paul. Hubbard cried, "Just a moment!" They took Paul, slammed the door in Hubbard's face, and locked it.

The guards marched Paul to another room where Stutzer was seated at a desk. There were no chairs for visitors in this room, either. Stutzer was reading a file, his pink lips pursed. He went on reading it for many minutes more, ignoring Paul. All German bureaucrats did this. They had done it under the Weimar Republic. No doubt they had done it under the Holy Roman Emperor and Barbarossa and Bismarck. The purpose was to show that the bureaucrat could ignore you, but you could not ignore him.

At last Stutzer made a note on the file he was reading, blotted the ink, then closed the file and placed it in a drawer. He took a key from his pocket and locked the drawer. He put the key back into his pocket. In one corner of the room stood a small sink. Stutzer got up, turned on the faucet and washed his hands. He left the water running when he sat down again at his desk. Paul had never in his short life had to urinate so badly.

Stutzer retrieved his key, unlocked the drawer, withdrew another file, and studied it for several minutes. Without looking up from the file he said, "Section leader Schulz of the Thirty-eighth Hitler Youth whom you viciously attacked in the Tiergarten on 16 June, 1939, suffered a broken nose, a cracked jawbone, two broken teeth, cuts on his face, and injuries to his testicles, which were driven out of the scrotum and into his body by a vicious and treacherous kick. At the time of the attack, he was on official duty. Therefore the assault is considered an assault on an official of the Reich. The penalty for assaulting an officer of the Reich while on official duty is death."

Paul did not speak. He did not need his mother to remind him that it was a mistake to say more to these people than was absolutely necessary.

Stutzer said, "Do you agree that you inflicted the injuries I have just described?"

"No, Major."

"'No?'"

"I hit him only once, on the nose. The injuries you describe could only have been inflicted by several blows."

"So you admit that you struck this boy who was wearing the uniform of the Reich and was on official duty."

"I didn't strike him because he was wearing a uniform and I had no way of knowing he was on official duty. I struck him because he cut the string on my kite for no reason."

"How did you know that he had no reason?"

"What reason could anyone possibly have for walking up to a total stranger, drawing a knife, and cutting the string of his kite?"

Stutzer tapped the file. "You provoked him."

"I was minding my own business, flying a kite."

"Then why did you punch him without warning?"

"As I said, he cut my kite string. He still had the knife in his hand. I didn't know what he might do next."

"Why should he do anything else, supposing that what you say about the kite string is true?"

Paul had had conversations like this with his headmaster, who did not like to see French boys lose a fight to an American any better than this man liked seeing a member of the Youth have his nose broken by one.

Paul said, "He was behaving in an unpredictable way. I thought it prudent to protect myself."

"From what?"

"I thought he was going to attack me."

"Why would you think such a thing?"

"Because he was not the first bully I had ever encountered, and the others were his friends. In fact they did attack me a moment later, six against one. They beat me until I was unconscious."

"I remind you that after you attacked their leader, who was wearing the uniform of the Youth, a young man who had sworn an oath to protect the Leader with his life. In your mind you were actually attacking the Leader, is that not so?"

"No."

"What do you have against the Leader?"

"Nothing whatsoever, Major."

Stutzer knew perfectly well that this was a lie. "Then why are you not a member of the Youth? You have repeatedly refused to join."

"That has been explained to you, sir. It is impossible for me to join. Only Germans of pure Aryan blood can belong. I am an American citizen."

"You are the son of a German mother. You were born in Germany. Under American law, the child of an American father born abroad takes the nationality of the mother. Therefore you are a citizen of the Reich."

Paul was silent. He knew he had already said too much. This was how the secret police were going to proceed against him and his family; this would be their argument. Whether or not it was true was irrelevant.

This was the pretence on which they proposed to act. There was no escape from their pretences. Nearly everything men like Stutzer held dear was a pretence, a substitute for a known fact—that they were Aryans, that the Jews were their secret enemies, that Germany had deserved to win the World War, that they were the party of peace, that Adolf Hitler was their savior. Even at sixteen, Paul knew that there was no exit from this wilderness of pretence, that Stutzer could draw his pistol and shoot him dead right now and then go on with his day and his life as if he had crushed a fly. They would tell the Christophers that their son had been shot while trying to escape. Or that they had let him go with a stern warning (he was only a boy, after all) and he had vanished— sailed away to Denmark, perhaps, or gone to France—and not even the secret police could find him.

3

O. G. knew quite a lot about Stutzer.

"Franz Stutzer, son of a Munich policeman, an early member of the party," he said. "Recently promoted to major and awarded the Iron Cross first class for work he did in the Sudetenland, where he commanded a special SS unit of some sort. As you know, he was formerly the head of the secret police office in Rügen. He works in secret police Department A, which deals with enemies of the Reich."

"Then he's not small fry," Hubbard said.

"Not at all. Stutzer is a high muckamuck, no question about that. He's good at the work. Trusted by his superiors, admired by his men. One of Heydrich's boys."

They were seated in O. G.'s large office in the American Embassy in Parisierplatz. Tall windows filled two walls of the room. In June in another country, or even a more southerly part of this one, it would have been a sunny office, but it was raining in Berlin and the light was feeble. Tea was served by O. G.'s secretary—sugar cookies, cucumber sandwiches, Uneeda saltines spread with deviled ham, a delicacy to Hubbard and O. G., inedible for anyone who did not grow up on it and even for some who did. At his father's request, Paul had just told O. G. about his conversation with Stutzer. He and Hubbard had been released at three in the afternoon. They had stopped at the apartment to collect Lori, then came straight to the embassy.

O. G. said, "Let me ask you something. Does this man Stutzer have some personal reason for pursuing you?"

Hubbard and Lori exchanged a look. She said, "You tell him, Hubbard."

"Well," Hubbard said, "Lori did slap him in the face in front of twenty witnesses in the Kursaal Café in Putbus, on Rügen."

All expression drained from O. G.'s face. "He was a member of the Gestapo at the time?"

"Oh, yes. This was in the summer of 1936, shortly after he arrived on Rügen as chief of the local secret police."

"May I ask why you did this, Lori?"

"A drunk was crawling from table to table, stealing cream from the little pitchers in which it was served. This was a habit with him. He meant to amuse. He was shell-shocked from the war, everybody knew that. When he stole Stutzer's cream, Stutzer kicked him in the face and broke his jaw."

O. G. nodded. "So you slapped him."

"Socked him, actually," Hubbard said. "Backhand. Hit him hard enough to knock his hat off and give him a shiner."

"You were among the witnesses, Hubbard?"

"No, but Paul was."

"I see," O. G. said. "Stutzer didn't arrest you on the spot, Lori?"

"No. But I don't imagine he has forgotten."

O. G. said, "No, probably not."

"So what do you suggest about Paul?" Lori said to O. G.

"What I've been suggesting for a year even without knowing what you just told me," O. G. said. "Leave the country. Now I would add, In the name of God. That may be all they want."

"I don't think so," Lori said.

"Ah," said O. G. He did not ask why she said what she had just said. Hubbard was less discreet. "Why? Because you socked Stutzer?"

"That may be Stutzer's motive, but it isn't the reason," Lori said. "They're more serious than that. They'll never let me go."

"Why you, in particular?" Hubbard said.

"Because I am a German citizen who has helped Jews and what they call communists. Therefore I am a traitor. Who knows what they imagine you are."

"They don't have to do much imagining," Hubbard said.

Lori said, "Paul is also involved. They may be lunatics, gentlemen, but I say it again, they're serious."

"Please don't think I'm being facetious," O. G. said. "But if they get any more serious you'll all be in Dachau, Paul included. They don't give a hang about age or nationality or anything else when they think they're dealing with the enemies of the Reich."

"Well, that's what we are, aren't we?" Lori said.

"Ssshhh," O. G. said. There were things he did not wish to know, even if he already knew them.

Paul knew what was coming next—the plan to get him out of Germany. In his opinion no one, not even O. G., had the power or the guile to manage this. Besides that, he, Paul, would not agree to go. How could he leave his mother, how could he leave Rima? How could he save himself and leave them to their fate? He knew what that fate would be. The secret police would do to them what the Hitler Youth in the Tiergarten had done to him, but they would do it to the death. He had begun to see that these matters were very simple. Everyone talked about how serious the National Socialists were but as he walked along the corridors at No. 8 Prinz-Albrechtstrasse, he had heard them laughing uproariously behind closed doors. They were like policemen everywhere. They enjoyed each other's company. They were good fellows doing what had to be done. They liked talking over the day's work. They thought that the people they arrested were funny, that their fates were comical, that their hopes of outwitting the secret police were laughable.

O. G. said, "As I've already suggested, I really do think, now more than ever, that Paul should go home with me. The *Bremen* sails for New York on the sixth of July."

"That's very soon," Lori said.

"Let's hope it's soon enough," O. G. replied. "They have enough on Paul right now to arrest him. They might do it just for the effect it would have on the two of you. Today might have been a rehearsal. It certainly was a message. Your son, alone in their hands—imagine. They'd really be in the driver's seat."

Paul said, "Excuse me, but do I have anything to say about this?"

"Of course you do, Paul," O. G. said.

"I won't go anywhere without my mother and father."

"Then you should discuss the matter with them," O. G. said. "You have until the fourth of July to talk it over, assuming the secret police don't move sooner. Nobody's going to abandon your parents. I couldn't let that happen. I've made promises to the gods that I'd never let it happen. The idea is to get each of you out by the best available means. Then you can all get together at the Harbor and let the rest of the world go by."

"How will you get them out after I'm gone if you're in America, too?"

"The embassy won't be closed while I'm away," O. G. said. "Others can execute the plan. The plan is, first you, then them. Those fellows on Prinz-Albrechtstrasse will be looking for a party of three, so with any luck they'll be looking the other way at the vital moment."

"We hope," said Hubbard.

"Can't travel far in this world without hope," O. G. said.

Or with it, Paul thought. He looked into his mother's eyes and saw that she agreed.

4

Lori went riding in the Tiergarten almost every day. She came back, most days, in time for lunch. Rima saw their opportunity when Paul told her about his family's morning routine—Lori absent, Hubbard present in physical form but so completely elsewhere mentally that he might as well have been underwater. After their moments in the darkness of the park they were desperate to be together. But they had no privacy and none seemed possible. They met as if by accident in shops and museums, but never in a place where they could touch.

Finally they tried the obvious—a cinema. But when they kissed, a watchful customer reported them to the management. They were ejected. The head usher—he wore a badge of office on his uniform—demanded their names and addresses so that their misconduct could be reported to the authorities. They told him nothing, but learned a lesson. Even if the secret police had not been watching Paul, even if Rima had not been the daughter of a Jew who had no rights, it would have been next to impossible for them to be together. The entire adult world was a vast secret police force charged with keeping an eye on young people. They met sometimes at night when walking the dogs, but this was furtive. It made them feel guilty. It was dangerous for Rima to be alone in a park, alone on darkened streets.

On the streetcar, Rima said, "Then you're alone in the morning?"

"My father is home."

"But oblivious. Do you have a back door?"

Paul said, "Yes. In the kitchen."

"This door locks with a key?"

"With a bolt on the inside."

"There's a back stairway? You take the dog for its walks by the stairway?"

Paul nodded.

"So if someone forgot to bolt this bolt, on a typical morning a burglar could come up the stairs, sneak inside and tiptoe through the house and no one would be the wiser?"

Rima explained the plan. She too was free and unobserved in the early morning. Her father slept until noon—in fact he slept beyond noon. He slept whenever he was alone. This would have been an unimaginable weakness had he still been a German. But he was not. The theft of her father's identity and property and career, the shock of suddenly ceasing to be the man he had striven all his life to be, had driven him into a stupor.

"It's as if he's already in the afterworld," Rima said. "The world of the living is still visible to him. He looks out the window and sees people going about their business. Every now and then he sees someone he knows on the street, but they don't see him or hear him. If they do, if they used to be his friends, they don't know him. He's a phantom."

All this Rima whispered to Paul as they stood together on a streetcar. No matter where they were, the two of them conversed in whispers. They told each other everything. They hardly knew each other, after all—glimpses in the Tiergarten, minutes in each other's arms in the pitch-black night in the park, an hour in the church, a kiss in a cinema. Not only was Rima Paul's first love, she was also his only friend. Otherwise, he lived in quarantine and so did she.

Now, however, Rima had a plan. They would be together, alone. "We will become each other," Rima said. "We will have time. It will be wonderful."

That word, as she spoke it in English, meant what it had originally meant, full of wonder. All of her words about love sounded as if she had just invented them. She would come early in the morning, Rima said, while it was still dark. The window of Paul's bedroom overlooked the courtyard at the back of the building. If his mother was absent and his father was writing, he would turn on a light in his room, then go to the kitchen and unlock the door on the back stairway. Rima would run up the stairs, he would let her in, they would be together in his room until eleven o'clock. Then she would leave by the front entrance.

"You will be seen," Paul said.

"It won't matter," Rima said. "I have a plan."

By mistake or as a sign of their contempt for him—what harm could the former Professor Doctor Kaltenbach possibly do now that he was nothing but a Jew?—the authorities had left her father's medical records with him. Rima had examined them. She had found the file of a rich German woman on whom her father had operated several years before.

"He saved her life, or anyway cured her pain," Rima said. "Afterward, in her gratitude, she kissed every one of his fingers."

"How do you know that?"

"You're not the only one with a father who writes everything down."

"So how does this affect the plan?"

"She lives in your building. Miss Hulda Wetzel."

Paul knew the woman, had always known her. She lived in the apartment below the Christophers. She had been the companion to her sickly mother before the old woman finally died; now she was alone. She was deeply shy and nervous, never married. She had told Paul many times, but Lori never, how beautifully his mother played the piano, especially Liszt.

"Miss Wetzel is part of the plan?" Paul said.

"She is essential to it," Rima replied. "Miss Wetzel has a dog, a Pomeranian. I have observed her walking the dog. Miss Wetzel doesn't like poop. I will volunteer to walk her dog. She will be overjoyed. I will then have a reason to be on the back stairway."

"What if she says no?"

"Why would she do that? I'll tell her who I am—the daughter of the famous surgeon who saved her life."

"Does she know what has happened to your father?"

"It doesn't matter."

"Miss Wetzel is a timid person. She may be frightened to be involved."

"No, my darling. She'll remember Papa as he used to be. As long as we leave her in innocence she'll understand. Not everyone we ever knew is a hateful wretch."

Paul longed to kiss this beautiful girl with the electric mind and the wide-open brown eyes in which he saw his reflection, but on the streetcar such behavior was strictly forbidden.

5

The plan did not work out exactly as Rima had designed it. Miss Wetzel wanted her snow-white Pomeranian, Blümchen, walked for an hour three times a day—at seven in the morning, at noon, and at dusk. She and Rima discussed this over cups of chocolate in Miss Wetzel's apartment while the dog sat on Miss Wetzel's lap and nibbled treats.

"How is your dear father?" Miss Wetzel asked.

"He is less active than he was."

"I'm very sorry to hear that. So many people need his genius."

Rima smiled, sipped her chocolate, and ate a butter cookie. She wanted to wander no farther down this path. They talked about the dog and
the deal was struck. Rima would walk Blümchen three times a day,
seven days a week, for a weekly fee of ten marks-fifty, or fifty pfennigs
per walk, plus a Sunday bonus of one mark.

"That's pretty good money," Rima said to Paul, reporting the conversation as they walked through a museum. "We can buy Benny
Goodman records and dance. Do you have a gramophone?"

"An American Victrola," Paul said.

"Benny won't disturb your father?"

"Nothing disturbs my father. The secret police may come and arrest
us for listening to decadent music."

"How will they know?"

Paul explained about the microphones in the walls. Rima's eyes
widened as they always did when she was told something interesting.

"Dear God, they do hate you," she said. "What have you done to
deserve this?"

Paul loved Rima, but he could not trust her or endanger her with a
truthful answer to this particular question.

"It's just one of those things," he said.

"Ah, you Americans," Rima said, snapping her fingers. " 'Just one of
those things, baby.' We'll go on whispering."

They were in a room full of classical sculptures. In a whisper Rima
sang a bar of "And the Angels Sing." Hearing Benny Goodman, they
danced a few steps among the marble nudes. Rima's English had become
much more idiomatic since she had been speaking the language with
Paul. She had learned it from books and from a succession of young
English tutors who had been expelled from the country one after the
other on morals charges. Her accent was a mixture of the accents of
these tutors, Londonian in one part of a sentence, Etonian in the next,
West Country in the third. This was because her ear was so keen. What
she heard, she spoke. She sounded more like Paul every day.

Rima began her duties as a dog walker the following morning. Because the Tiergarten was close and because there were lots of other dogs there to keep Blümchen company, she walked in that direction. She set out, as her agreement with Miss Wetzel specified, at exactly seven in the morning. At that hour there were already a good many people in the streets. Some were dog walkers like Rima. Most were dressed for the day—men in suits and felt hats, women in frocks and sturdy shoes. There were few workmen in this neighborhood, but some whirred by on bicycles. Yesterday's horse manure had been cleared during the night by Berlin's efficient street-cleaning force so that Rima as she walked could smell flowering shrubs and trees rather than the overpowering scent of animal scat. She was lost in a daydream of Paul, imagining their first morning together in his room. She saw them dancing, talking, listening to music, dancing again. As she danced in her daydream she wore a sheet wrapped around her body, like a toga. She hummed as she dreamed, American songs that Paul had taught her—"Flat-Foot Floojee," "Oh, Look at Me Now."

She was inside the park before she knew it. She woke from her daydream on a path that ran between the bridle path and the sidewalk. Blümchen barked shrilly at everything and everyone. Long ago her breed had been large working dogs. The fact that Pomeranians had been bred down into lap dogs over many generations evidently had not registered on Blümchen's brain. She thought that she was as large and ferocious as her ancestors. Though she was actually no bigger than a ball of yarn, she barked at the horses, at other dogs, she growled and showed her teeth. She yapped at squirrels and leaped against the leash, trying to chase them. Well-dressed matrons picked up their own small dogs and carried them safely away from this shaggy little bundle of noisy aggression.

The sun strengthened. Workmen watered the bridle path to keep down the dust. Miniature rainbows formed in the spray. When horses came by, the men turned off the hoses and the big lathered animals cantered or trotted by. Rima had never ridden, but she liked the sight, the sound, the scent of sweated horses. She walked along the bridle path, Blümchen barking all the while. The dog was tremendously excited. Rima wondered if it was the smell of the horses. What a treat for Blümchen's Pomeranian senses, Rima thought. It must be the equivalent of a person, born like herself in the twentieth century, being dragged across a savannah and suddenly smelling a herd of mastodons.

"Suppose dinosaurs were covered with feathers, like birds," she said to Paul later on, when they were together. "Suppose they sang like birds when they woke in the morning. Imagine the sight of that, the sound."

In the moment itself, however, something broke this chain of thought. Standing at the curb was a woman whom she knew, though she had never met her. She knew at once that she was Paul's mother. The woman, wearing jodhpurs and boots and a tweed hacking jacket, looked like him—the same face that Rima had thought was unlike anyone else's, the same bottomless eyes, the same musician's hands.

The woman stood beside the open door of a black Daimler. An SS trooper in uniform held the door. Another sat at the wheel. A large beautiful Alsatian dog lay on the floor of the backseat at the feet of a man wearing burnished black riding boots. Blümchen barked frantically at the Alsatian. The woman, lovely but profoundly sad, looked for a brief moment into Rima's eyes, as if she recognized her, too, and then got into the car.

Rima was farther away from the Daimler than Paul had been when he had witnessed a similar scene a few days earlier, so she was able to see inside and recognize Reinhard Heydrich, the head of the entire secret police apparatus, as the man who lifted Lori's hand, peeled off its glove, and kissed the palm.

6

After dropping off Blümchen at Miss Wetzel's back door and declining a cup of chocolate and a bun, Rima ran up the back stairs, pushed open the Christophers' unlocked kitchen door, and slipped inside. Paul awaited her. They kissed. For long moments, all was silence. Then, in the middle of the kiss, Hubbard uttered a loud guffaw. Rima leaped in her skin.

"I warned you," Paul said. "He does that when he's writing. But if we walked into his room he wouldn't know we were there."

They were whispering as always. Paul led her through the reception rooms—strange misshapen sculptures, a grand piano with music open on the rack, bright upholstery, Persian carpets that looked very old. Expressionist paintings and drawings that looked like cartoons hung on every wall. A large studio drawing depicted a young nude, a girl not much older than Rima, who looked boldly at the artist and seemed to be in the very early stages of pregnancy. She was the woman who had gotten into Heydrich's Daimler.

"My mother when she was nineteen," Paul said. "And me before I was born, I'm told. Does it shock you?"

"No. It's beautiful." She went closer and read the artist's signature. "Who is Zaentz?"

"He was well-known in Berlin not so long ago. Most of these pictures were made by friends."

"But these friends no longer come here?"

"No, they've all left Germany."

"So the Christophers are alone."

"Not quite," Paul said, touching her.

They walked down the hallway to Paul's room. He had turned off the electric light and closed the curtains, so it was dark.

"Can we have a lamp?" Rima asked. "I must be able to see you."

He switched on his reading lamp. The room, half in shadow, took form—shelves of books, stacks of magazines, record albums, photographs taken in America, in France, in the Alps, in Rügen, all showing Paul in the company of his parents and what Rima took to be other relations. The stuffed head of a wild boar hung over his desk.

"What in the name of God is that?" she asked.

Paul explained. Schloss Berwick, the house on the island of Rügen in which his mother's Uncle Paulus and Aunt Hilde lived, stood in a grove of beech trees. When Paul was twelve, his great-uncle had taken him on his first boar hunt. They rode out before dawn, hoping to catch the unawares as they fed on the beechnuts that had fallen to the ground. They found half a dozen pigs feasting on the nuts and, on

Paulus's command, charged them at the gallop through the morning mist, smooth gray tree trunks whizzing by. A boar charged Paul's horse as he charged it. He killed it with a lucky thrust between the shoulder blades. Paulus dismounted, bled the trophy, and smeared Paul's cheek with the blood of his first kill.

"Charming," Rima said. "And this is the lucky boar?"

She inspected everything, then wound up the gramophone, chose a record, put it on the turntable, and lifted the needle onto the spinning wax record. This time the band was not Benny Goodman's but Tommy Dorsey's, playing "Getting Sentimental Over You." They danced in stocking feet so as not to make Blümchen, whose play room was directly below, start barking.

When the song ended, Rima took the pins from her hair and shook it out, then took Paul firmly by the hand and led him to the bed. Sex was not a mystery to him. His parents had always been frank with him and he had read descriptions of the act in novels and looked at the cartoons and photographs that were passed around at school. Rima, however, had technical knowledge. She had read her father's medical books, and of course she knew her own body as no one else, not even Paul, ever could. She was the initiator, the guide. She was nimble in bed as in everything else. She had no shyness. She asked for what she wanted. She made rapturous noises that astonished Paul as much as the pleasure of the act itself, but not as much as the way in which the passionate love he already felt for this girl expanded within him until he felt nothing else, thought of nothing else, wanted nothing else, and finally was aware of nothing else. Rima trembled, she wept, she cried out. She amazed him.

All morning they lay in bed, whispering. They completed Rima's daydream by dancing, but in this perfect real world with no sheet wrapped around her body. She drew Paul back to the bed. They made love. They fell asleep, awoke, they made love again. They were enclosed in an atmosphere of their own mingled scent, each other's skin, each other's senses.

"Nothing like this will ever happen to us again," Rima said.

Had anyone but Rima uttered these words they would have sounded to Paul like a line from the movies, but he knew that what she said was true, that he would never make love again, no matter how far in the future, without remembering Rima. Whatever happened, this hour would haunt him for the rest of his life. He wept. Rima, dry-eyed now, smiled down at him. She said softly, "Oh, my love."

At noon precisely, Rima knocked on Miss Wetzel's kitchen door and heard a volley of soprano barks on the other side. Miss Wetzel threw open the door. "See her little tail wag?" she said. "Blümchen is waiting for you. Already she likes you."

Rima followed the same route to the Tiergarten as before, and as before, Blümchen scolded every living thing she encountered. Rima did not try to stop her. She was wrapped in contentment. Her heart was peaceful, she had never been so happy, she saw no end to this overwhelming bliss as long as she and Paul could be together. To feel like this every day—imagine! She had been warned by women and by books that the first experience for a girl was painful, ugly, bloody, and brutal. They had lied.

7

Just as she reached the park, at eleven minutes after noon, Rima was arrested. She was standing on the sidewalk near the bridle path, more or less on the spot where she had observed Lori getting into the gleaming Daimler earlier in the day. Blümchen attacked the Berlin policeman who took Rima into custody, yapping and nipping at his boots and wrapping her leash around his ankles. The portly cop lifted his feet as if stepping out of somebody else's underwear and cursed loudly.

"Under arrest?" Rima said. "For what?" It was a pointless question. Everyone knew that no one in the Reich had a right to know why he or she was being arrested. But for a moment, snatched so rudely from her reverie, Rima thought that the policeman might be taking her into custody because he had been attacked by Blümchen.

"Control your dog!" the policeman said.

She gave the cop an astonished grin. Ear-tips to toes, Blümchen was no more than seven inches tall. The policeman took Rima by the arm and set off down the sidewalk. Blümchen continued to dance around the two of them, barking incessantly and lunging at the policeman. The policeman kicked at the dog. Blümchen counterattacked, sinking its needle teeth into the burnished leather of his boot. Despite the desperation she felt, or maybe because of it, Rima was overcome by giggling. She was only sixteen, after all, and whatever she had said to Paul in the American church, she did not really think, especially on this particular morning, that she was going to die. Not at her age, not when she had just learned that human happiness was so deep, so sweet, such a surprise.

At the police station Rima was booked and made to hand over the contents of her bag and pockets, and also Blümchen. "That dog belongs to Miss Wetzel of number eleven Gutenbergstrasse," she said. "I am only the dog walker. If the dog is not back on time, the owner will be frantic." No one in the police station seemed to hear anything she said.

In another room, Rima was stripped and searched by a gaunt unsmiling female with a man's gruff voice who smelled of decaying teeth and strong antiseptic. This woman put a finger between Rima's legs, shook it disgustedly and washed her hands. Then she pointed to the sink and shouted, "Wash yourself!"

After Rima was dressed, the woman marched her back to the booking room. To the elderly policeman in charge she said in a loud voice, "No contraband discovered! Evidence of very recent fornication noted!"

Every sentence this woman uttered ended in an exclamation point. The elderly policeman, silent and expressionless, dipped his steel pen in an ink well and entered her words in his log.

Rima expected to be locked in a cell, but she was told instead to sit at a table in classroom posture—feet flat on the floor, knees together, hands folded, spine vertical but not touching the back of the chair, head erect, eyes straight ahead. Holding this position required strength, alertness, stamina. It made the mind as well as the body ache. It made the urethra burn. It had kept generations of children in order. It had been invented by an evil genius.

After a long time, much more than an hour, the gaunt female, now wearing a wide leather belt from which a truncheon dangled, told Rima in ringing tones to stand up. She then placed her in handcuffs, took her by the arm and marched her to a back door. Outside, an Opel sedan waited. It was black like the Daimler and gleaming with wax, but smaller. A man in civilian clothes sat at the wheel. Rima got into the backseat as ordered. The woman got in beside her. The windows were curtained. There were no inside door handles. Rima's hands were cuffed together behind her back. The thick cloth upholstery was dappled where it had had been spot-cleaned over and over again. Like the woman beside Rima, it smelled of strong disinfectant.

They drove through city streets to another back door. Her handcuffs were removed. Another woman, this one broad and muscular, took custody of Rima. She walked her down a corridor, unlocked a door, and pointed a finger. Rima walked into a small windowless room. It was no larger than a closet and devoid of furniture apart from a bulb inside a wire cage screwed to the ceiling. The woman said, "After the door is closed, remain standing." Rima said, as if to a teacher, "May I please go to the lavatory?" The woman did not answer. She closed the door behind Rima and locked it. The light went out. The darkness was complete.

Rima walked around the room, feeling the walls with her palms, counting her steps. She had no idea why she did this, but when she was done she knew that the room was three and a half steps long and a little more than two steps wide. This knowledge seemed important; at least she knew something about her situation. She wondered what time it was. The police had taken her lavalier watch along with her other belongings and she would not have been able to see the watch even if she still had it, but she missed it. She tried to remember how many times she had looked at her watch that day. The answer was many more than usual. She had checked the time at least once a minute while waiting for the hour of her rendezvous with Paul. After that she forgot about the invention of watches. She put a hand over her mouth, afraid that she might sob with the giddy joy of the memory of that morning. She was sure that this little black room was equipped with hidden microphones, almost certainly with a judas hole through which prisoners could be observed.

Rima was bone-tired. She lay down on the floor. A loud knock at the door awakened her. A voice shouted, "Remain standing at all times!" She stood up, expecting the door to open, the light to go on, for whatever that was going to happen to start happening. But nothing happened. She leaned against the wall, hoping for sleep. Again, just as she was drifting off, came another knock on the door. It was earsplitting. Obviously her keepers wanted Rima to know that they could see her in the dark.

8

By the time the light came on again, hours later, Rima was barely able to stand. Her entire body trembled, she was sweating. Her bones, her entire skeleton, ached. Her head throbbed. She had a stomachache. She was desperately thirsty and at the same time frantic to urinate. The combination of remaining upright, remaining awake, trying to make saliva, and preventing herself from emptying her bladder had numbed her mind. She was having great difficulty thinking about anything except urination. The hours in the dark literally had unbalanced her. She staggered, and now that she could see her own body again she had to remember how to stand upright. She could not tell which way was up, which down, which sideways. She was nauseated.

A woman in uniform whom Rima had not seen before opened the door. Like the others before her she was unsmiling, but she was younger. She was slim, nice-looking, sisterly, with large blue eyes with a light in them that might have been kindness.

"Come out," she said.

Rima did as she was told, catching hold of the doorjamb to keep herself from falling. Trembling, she looked into the woman's eyes and said, "May I please use the lavatory?"

The woman's kindly eyes did not change expression, but she snorted as if Rima had asked for a glass of champagne. In the same harsh tone as the other women, she said, "March! You're lucky you weren't given a liter of water to drink and ordered to stand with your arms above your head!"

Rima and her custodian walked rapidly down a long corridor, lighted every two meters by bare bulbs in cages like the one in her cell. With every step Rima expected to lose control of her bladder. If she did, what would happen? She knew that she would have to clean up after herself, but what else? The silence in this place was deep, as if Rima were the only prisoner. She wondered what had happened to Blümchen. If the little dog were here and alive Rima surely would hear her. There were no clocks, no pictures, no bulletin boards, no brush marks in the neutral gray paint on the walls, nothing to see except locked doors.

At last they turned into another corridor and stopped before a door. Rima's guard unlocked it and gestured for her to go inside. "Touch nothing!" the guard said. "Remain standing at attention at all times!" The door closed; she heard the lock turning.

This room had a window, small and high and barred. To Rima's surprise, it was still light outside. A bare desk and a wooden chair stood in the middle of the room, a small white sink in the corner. Rima wondered if she dared use it, but she was sure that she was being watched through some sort of spy-hole, and what would the punishment be for urinating in a sink in which members of the secret police washed their hands and drew themselves glasses of water? Rima had never before in her life thought so much about punishment as she was now doing. Until noon on this day she had hardly thought about it at all. Now she thought of nothing else. Not even Paul.

The lock turned, the door opened. Rima was standing with her back to the door, rigidly upright, heels together, hands by her sides. She did her best not to tremble, but her body would not obey her commands and she shook from head to toe. She was deeply frightened. She feared that she would at any moment wet the floor like a puppy. She did not know whether to remain as she was or turn around, but what she had learned already about this place and its rules told her to do nothing that she was not told to do.

A man in a gray civilian suit, swastika in his lapel, sat down at the desk. He was younger than she expected. He was extremely well-groomed, self-possessed, quick in his movements. His clothes fit him perfectly. His starched shirt was snowy white, the knot in his dark-blue necktie was expertly tied. He placed a file in the exact center of the desk, opened it, and read with complete absorption. Rima remained at attention. This was a much more fatiguing posture than merely standing up. In the dark she had slouched, shuffled, shifted her weight from one hip to the other. None of this was possible now. She did not know how much longer she could control herself. She pressed her thighs tightly together. In spite of herself she drew a sharp wet breath through her teeth. Without looking up from his reading, the man rapped on the desk three times. Rima felt that she might faint. Who knew what this signal might mean? The slim woman appeared almost instantly. The man behind the desk pointed at Rima. The woman said, "Come!" She led her down the corridor to another door and put her key in the lock. She had only one key, but it seemed to fit all doors. Rima though that she was going to be put back into the dark, but when the woman pulled the door open she saw a lavatory inside. It was spotlessly clean.

The woman said, "Be quick! Do not keep the major waiting after he has done you such a kindness."

Information! Rima felt a spark of triumph and a rush of fear. She was in the hands of the secret police, she knew the rank of the man who held her fate in his hands. It was a high rank. He wore the same medal her father had won in the World War. She knew that he had the power to lock her up forever or let her go free if he wished, and the authority to impose any of the many possible penalties that lay between freedom and standing upright in a dark room for the rest of her life with her arms above her head.

Rima already had some information about this man. From Paul's stories, she recognized the major as the man the Christophers called Stutzer. He was writing in the file when Rima was returned from the lavatory. Without being told—she was already trained a little—she stood at attention before him. He went on writing for some time. Then he closed the file, recapped his black-and-gold fountain pen, and placed it precisely in the center of the file. The pen was embossed with a swastika, gold on a red enamel button.

He said, "You are aware that sexual intercourse between Jews and Aryans is forbidden by the laws of the Reich?"

"Yes, H. . ." The *H* sound escaped her before she could stop it, so she did not make the cardinal mistake of calling him major, thus revealing that she knew something about him, however small the detail. She changed the form of address to the all-purpose sir.

He gave her a knowing look, as if he knew precisely what she had just prevented herself from saying. He said, "Your age?"

"Sixteen."

"How do you know so much sexual intercourse at the age of sixteen?"

"I know very little, sir."

"Until you were tutored by some Aryan with whom you went to bed last night?"

"No, sir."

"You do not deny that you copulated with an Aryan this very morning?"

Rima's heart beat harder. Her breath came faster, she felt sweat on the palms of her hands. How could even a major know such a secret? How could she answer his question? If she lied and they did know about her and Paul—had they planted cameras in the Christopher's apartment as well? had someone spied on them?—she would be entirely in their power. The result would be the same if she betrayed Paul and told the truth. They would never let go of her. They would take him.

Stutzer did not wait for her answer. The look on his face, the careless way in which he turned a page of the file, were meant to tell her that he already knew it.

Without pausing, he said, "Your father is the Jew Israel Kaltenbach?"

"My father is the surgeon Professor Doktor Johann Kaltenbach, sir," Rima replied. "The name Israel was given to him recently."

Under the Nuremberg laws, all male Jews were required to have the name Israel added to their papers. All Jewish women were Sara on official documents. This made it possible for the authorities to determine their race at a glance, as if the red "J" already stamped on these papers might be overlooked.

Stutzer said, "Do you yourself have the name Sara?"

He knew perfectly well that she did not. He knew the details of her identity card. It was in his hands.

Rima said, "No, sir."

"Why not?"

Rima answered respectfully. "Because I have only one Jewish grandparent. . . ."

He interrupted. "Which?"

"My father's father, who married a Christian. . . ."

"Married a what?"

"Excuse me, please. An Aryan. My mother is an Aryan. So were both her parents, of course. Under the laws of the Reich I am therefore not considered a Jew."

"Correct. But in your own mind are you an Aryan like your mother or a Jew like your father and grandfather?"

"I don't know, sir."

"But you consider that you are entitled to engage in sexual relations with an Aryan because the Jews in your family have always done so?"

"I don't understand your question, sir."

Stutzer said, "I don't understand you, Sara. You don't know whether you're breaking the law by fornicating with an Aryan, but you do so anyway. Why are you so reckless?"

Rima saw that this man was implacable, that he did not care how stupid he seemed, that he would keep on asking the same question until he had the answer that he wanted. If she gave him what he wanted, she was lost. If she betrayed Paul and herself, she would be lost in a larger sense, and lost forever. She remained silent.

Stutzer said, "It must be love. Yes, that must be the answer. I ask you this very simple question: How do you see yourself? Are you an Aryan or a Jew? I mean in reality, not according to a technicality of the law."

Rima said, "This has never been made clear to me, sir."

This was a risky but truthful answer. She did not know and, as far as she could tell, no one knew where she stood in the official directory of races. In limbo, she supposed, like an unbaptized child wandering outside heaven in the next world. The Reich was itself a next world—the party itself kept saying so—in which the rules were made by an inscrutable, all-powerful father who knew the secrets of every heart. The secret police were his angels.

Stutzer said, "But what in your own mind do you *think* you are?"

"Truly I do not know," Rima said.

"Then I will inform you of the facts," Stutzer said. "You are a Jew who for legal purposes is not considered a Jew, but is a Jew just the same."

Stutzer gazed benevolently across his desk at Rima. He had just stated an evident truth. His face told her that he hoped for an argument so that he could refute it with ease. Rima was shaken by his calm assurance that he knew everything. No one who came before such a man had any hope at all.

He said, "It must be difficult for you, who looks something like an Aryan, who believes in her mind that she is an Aryan, to realize that in fact you have always been a Jew and nothing but Jew. Did you know this? Did your parents tell you?"

"No, sir."

"Then what did you think you were?"

"A German, sir. A Lutheran. A human being."

His pink lips curved in a tiny smile. He knew that Rima's words had slipped out, that she regretted them, that she had frightened herself. He said, "But now you discover that you are none of these things and never were, that it was all a fraud perpetrated by a Jew, your father, on his own child."

Again Rima was being invited to betray someone she loved. First Paul, now her father. Who next? She had no one else except her mother, and she was far away and safe, and an Aryan. Rima remained silent.

"No answer?" said Stutzer.

"I do not wish to argue with you, sir."

Suddenly he was like an uncle. "Oh-ho!" he said. "About what? Argue! Perhaps you can persuade me."

"I don't think so, sir."

"So you won't even try? Why not?" Suddenly he was human, smiling, arching a thick eyebrow. He was almost flirtatious. He looked at her as a man looks at a pretty girl. She knew the look. Every day a hundred men looked at her in that way.

Rima said, "Because I am afraid of you, sir. That is the truth of the matter."

"Afraid of me? Why?"

"Because I have done nothing wrong, yet here I am."

"You have done nothing wrong?" Stutzer said. "You can't be serious. You have stolen a valuable dog from Miss Hulda Wetzel and you have consorted sexually with an Aryan male. That is not the end of the list of your crimes. Far from it."

"Miss Wetzel paid me to walk her dog," Rima said. "I would certainly have returned it safe and sound if I had been able to do so."

Stutzer showed her a look of exaggerated surprise. "You are arguing, therefore you are making a mistake," he said. "True, you only argue about the dog. We don't care about the dog. It is the other matter, the violation of the racial laws, the illegal fornication, that you must answer for. Also an even more serious matter we have not yet discussed."

Perhaps half an hour had passed. Rima was still standing at attention in front of Stutzer's desk. Up to now she had experienced tremors in her knees and hands and a backache. Suddenly she developed a twitch in her cheek. She could feel it, but not control it. It must certainly be visible to Stutzer. He would be amused by it. It was a sign of his mastery, a sign of her weakness. Her entire body began to tremble. Her brain was powerless to stop this. She was, she knew, the picture of guilt and fear.

Stutzer gazed at her in mock astonishment. He asked no questions because it was obvious that Rima was in no condition to speak or even think. He offered her no help, no encouragement. He gazed at her face, her body. It was a slow, methodical, openly sexual examination—a human moment, the last thing she had expected from this man.

"Ah, you're beginning to dance," he said.

In a powerful voice, not at all like the almost soothing one he had been using up to now, he called out a name.

"Fleischer!"

The young female guard with the sympathetic eyes came in immediately. She must have been standing right outside the door, waiting for a command.

"Into the dark with this one," Stutzer said. "And then coffee for me. And a large drink of water for Sara, here."

Before she was locked into a cell, Rima was given a liter of water to drink. It was served in a heavy glass beer-garden stein, difficult to lift. Rima drank slowly, gripping the stein in both hands.

"Quick, quicker!" Fleischer said. Again her wide sky-blue eyes seemed sympathetic, but Rima realized that this was a trick of the light or her own imagination. This woman's eyes would brim with kindness and understanding even if she were beating someone with a whip. When Rima finished the water, Fleischer ordered her to face the door, come to attention, and hold her arms above her head.

"The hands must not touch," Fleischer said. "The feet must not be moved. Under no circumstances, not even if you pee pee like a stupid little bitch, will the arms be lowered. Do you understand?"

She shut and locked the door behind her as she left. The lights went out. Rima held her arms above her head as ordered. She had expected this to be uncomfortable, but she discovered in less than a minute—she counted off seconds in her head—that it was painful, then excruciating, then insupportable. Her brain sent urgent messages to her nerves and muscles to cease doing what they were doing. When its warnings were disregarded, the brain sent more warnings—pain, tremors, tears, involuntary sobs. Rima kept counting seconds. After counting to three minutes, she knew that she could not possibly continue to hold this position. Suddenly the lights went on. The judas hole opened, Fleischer's eye appeared—filled, no doubt, with what would appear to be compassion. The lights went out. Rima began to feel faint. The urge to urinate was much stronger than it had been before. She clenched her teeth to keep from sobbing, she wrapped one leg around the other to control her bladder. She lowered one arm and gripped her crotch. The lights went on. Whoever was watching her through the peephole hammered on the door. Rima felt warm water running down her legs, soaking her stockings. She fainted.

After Rima had cleaned up the floor—with a mop, not as she had feared with her tongue—she was given another liter of water to drink and told to resume the position. She was not allowed to remove her wet garments. In the dark, she smelled her own urine. Again she timed the intervals between moments when the lights were switched on. This happened every 180 seconds precisely. When in darkness, she held her arms above her head in a dancer's O, fingers entwined, and one after another assumed the ballet positions she had learned as a child. Her movements were clumsy; she hadn't danced in years and she had never been interested in ballet. Every few seconds she lowered her arms one at a time and let the blood rush back into them. Every 175 seconds she resumed the torture position and held it until the lights came on and then went off again. She understood that she might be caught and knew that she could not possibly predict the consequences if she was. In her mind, the worse had already happened when she emptied her bladder. As she danced, she formed a picture in her mind—she and Paul together in America, in a forest of very old trees with deeply creased bark. There was much more light in this vision than she had ever seen with her own eyes, even in Italy, and she commanded her brain to make it brighter and brighter, so that in the end Paul and his primeval trees seemed to exist in an overexposed photograph.

After a time—Rima had no idea how long a time—Fleischer came for her.

Back in Stutzer's office, Rima again stood at attention before the bare desk. Her need to urinate was intense. Her stockings and underwear were still damp. She could smell them. She wondered why she had not been ordered to take them off. Now the major would be subjected to an unpleasant odor.

He did not seem to notice. His manner was different this time, brusquer, more businesslike, perhaps because he had changed into a uniform. He now wore a pistol on his belt, the Iron Cross itself pinned to his tunic.

Without preliminaries he said, "There are two charges against you so far—the theft of a purebred Pomeranian bitch which has a value of one hundred-twenty-five Reichsmarks, and contravention of the sexual laws concerning miscegenation between Jews and Aryans. These charges have already been proved. Their disposal is in my hands. If I were to sign an order for imprisonment, you would go to a camp to be rehabilitated. There would be no specific term of years of imprisonment. All would depend on the recommendation of the camp commandant. He could release you in a few years, certainly not less than two or three years, or keep you for the rest of your life. What do you have to say?"

"I do not know what to say, sir."

"Address me as Major."

"Yes, Major."

"The charges are serious, as I have explained," Stutzer said. "But there is another matter that is even more serious. We will discuss that now. On 16 June you were an accomplice in a vicious and unprovoked physical attack on a member of the Hitler Youth. This boy was seriously injured by his assailant, a foreigner who is a trained pugilist. You sympathized with the assailant and assisted him, true or false?"

"He was injured in the fight. The others marched away. I helped him as best I could, as I have been taught all my life."

"We know that you took him to your father's office and your father treated his wounds," Stutzer said. "Your father is a Jew. The assailant is not a Jew. For a Jewish doctor to treat anybody except a Jew is strictly forbidden under the laws of the Reich."

Stutzer stopped speaking. He was awaiting an answer, a confession. Silence gathered.

Rima said, "My father is a doctor, Major. It's his duty to treat the injured."

"He's a Jew. He has violated the law. This will not be tolerated. For him there will be no interview, no courtesies, no opportunity to apologize and atone, as there has been for you even though you are a quarter-Jew. Do you understand what will happen to him? I order you to reply."

"No, Major."

"He will go to Dachau. He will have no hope. He will never be released. His fate will be your fault."

Rima began to sob. She could not control it. She understood what this man was doing to her. She knew what he wanted. She knew that if she wished to see the light of day again, to see her father and her lover again, she had no choice but to agree to whatever he wanted.

Stutzer said, "Earlier in this examination, when I asked you what you thought you were all your life, a Jew or an Aryan, you said you were a German, a Lutheran, a human being, in that order. Why did being a German come first?"

"Because that has always been the first true thing about me. The fact that I am a German above everything else is what I have always been taught by my parents, my family, my minister, my teachers."

"And at this moment, you are still a German above all?"

"Yes, Major."

"Good," Stutzer replied. "Then we can go ahead."

He rapped sharply on the desk—twice, this time.

Fleischer entered instantly, carrying a chair and a cup of soup.

"Sit down, eat a little something," Stutzer said to his prisoner. "Then we will talk."

THREE

1

While Rima was learning what Stutzer wanted of her, the Christophers were driving to Rügen. Hubbard had been saving gasoline for months for this journey. Their old Horch phaeton, olive-green with black fenders, crimson leather upholstery, and gleaming chrome headlights and trim, moved smoothly over narrow country roads. Hubbard loved this machine, the baritone purr of its engine, the mellow *ah-OO-ga*! of its horn, the many smells of it. He liked also the look of the world as the Horch rolled through the Prussian countryside with the top down. To Hubbard, always ready to transform nature into art, this automobile was a time machine bearing them past peasant villages and fields in which women with stout chapped legs were yoked to cows and helped pull the plow or cultivator through ruler-straight rows of potato plants and cabbages and turnips that grew in the chilly black muck.

"Gustavus Adolphus saw these same folks three centuries ago when he marched through Pomerania during the Thirty Years War," Hubbard said. He possessed the gift of enthusiasm. Every single thing in the world interested him, and despite his agnosticism, not a few things beyond it. At this point in the journey, Hubbard always made the same remark about Gustavus Adolphus of Sweden. In fact, he had a familiar saying for nearly every crossroads. Paul smiled fondly, happy to hear the well-worn words. In the backseat, Lori, her auburn head resting against the red leather upholstery, did not open her eyes. She was pale, inert. She seemed to lack the energy to smile. Hubbard had been watching her face ever since they left Berlin. Now he stole another glance at her in the rear-view mirror. Her expression had not changed all morning long, nor had she smiled or spoken a word. When they stopped by a lake to picnic, she ate little—half an apple, a bite of cheese—and said less. Hubbard was unbothered by his wife's withdrawal. Lori was entitled to her moods.

After lunch Hubbard let Paul drive the Horch. Paul had been driving since he was twelve, and now that he was bigger he handled the machine almost as easily as Hubbard. He kept an eye on the mirror, checking to see if they were being followed. Hubbard noticed this.

"On the lookout for the enemies of mankind?" he asked.

"Yes."

"That's always a good idea, but they have no need to follow us. They're everywhere. All they have to do is sit in a window and watch us drive by, then phone the guy who's sitting in the next window a few kilometers up the road. The minute we arrive in Rügen they'll call Stutzer in Berlin."

In this flat country the roads, mostly unpaved, ran straight, and there was little traffic apart from farm horses hauling wagons. These were huge chunky animals. Hubbard identified them by breed— Rhenish, Westphalian, Schleswig-Holstein. He told his son, not for the first time, that eight million horses belonging to the German army had been killed in battle in the 1914-18 war.

"The astonishing thing," he said, "is that two and a half million wounded horses were treated at the front in German veterinary hospitals and returned to duty."

Hubbard had gotten this information from Paulus, the old lancer. Today's Wehrmacht boasted of its modernity and its mechanization, Paulus said, but if there was another war, horses would drag guns and ammunition and rations into battle just as they had always done and be blown to smithereens by enemy shells, exactly as before. They would die in even greater numbers, unimaginable as it seemed that more living things, human and animal, could be possibly killed in a new war than were slaughtered in the last one.

A dozen or so interesting facts later, the family arrived on the island. Hubbard had grown up among mountains and he had always thought that Rügen needed a more dramatic landscape. Granted, the island itself was a prominence, with chalk cliffs rising hundreds of feet above the leaden Baltic. But the place needed some reworking, nothing major, but why not add a knob or two, as in a landscape by Giotto, to put it in perspective? Instead of sheltering in its beech groves, Paulus's house, Schloss Berwick, should stand on a hill, with lines of sight from its windows taking in all the rest of the island and the panorama of the sea. True, the wind would be an inconvenience, but wouldn't it be wonderful to hear it moaning and howling in the night and see ships and sails and whitecaps?

Paul steered the Horch up the drive "Look, darling, it's just the same," said Hubbard over his shoulder. Lori gave him her first faint smile of the day. It was mid-afternoon. Among the pale gray beeches with their pale green foliage, Schloss Berwick floated in watery light, feeble sun twinkling in its window glass. "On the first day I saw this house and this grove, coming down the path from the cliffs, I thought it was the most romantic sight I had ever seen," said Hubbard. He reached behind him with his long arm and took Lori by the hand. "And then, Paul, I saw your mother and knew what romance really was," he said. Lori lifted Hubbard's large hairy hand to her lips and kissed it. Watching in the mirror, Paul remembered her own gloved hand being lifted and kissed by a different man in the back seat of a Daimler.

Paulus and Hilde came out of the house. Hilde carried a bouquet she had picked from her garden for their arrival.

"So, Paul," said Paulus, eyeing the boy's half-healed injuries. "You've been wounded. Did you make the rascal pay?"

Paul knew that no reply was needed. He leaped from the car, shook his great uncle's hand and bowed like a Prussian, a silent click of the heels, a snap of the head. No hugging for Paulus.

"You should see the other fellows—seven of them, no less," Hubbard said. He offered no details, Paulus asked for none.

"Favorable odds," Paulus said. "Strike first, strike hard. That's something to write on your shield, as long as the enemy understands it's a warning, not friendly advice."

It was four in the afternoon. The sky was bright and at this latitude would remain so well into the evening. Lori went immediately to her bedroom and shut the door. Hubbard and Paulus went for a walk along the cliffs. Paul was not invited, so he supposed they were going to decide his fate between them. He carried the bags upstairs, then drank the cup of chocolate and ate the cakes that Hilde offered him. From the kitchen window he saw suits and overcoats and Turkish carpets airing in the backyard on taut wire clotheslines. Like the Christophers, Hilde and Paulus had no live-in servants, but two ruddy sisters with Popeye arms came once a week to clean the house. This was their day and Paul could hear them upstairs, shouting to each other in the hard-edged local dialect he had learned from them. Paul had known these women, Lena and Philippina, all his life. They had cared for him when he was an infant. Their cousin had been the midwife who delivered him. Their chief interest in life was village gossip, not national politics. However, this was the new Germany and he wondered what gossip about the family they passed on to the police when their day's work was done.

Certainly they would be expected to report. "Oh, Paul, I forgot," Hilde said. "There was a phone call for you." She pinched his cheek. "So grown up now, receiving phone calls from young ladies. *Bold* young ladies. From Berlin!" Hilde had to search for the slip of paper on which she had scribbled the number. She found it at last in her sewing basket, pinned to a scrap of cloth. "She gave no name," Hilde said. "She spoke proper German, which was a surprise considering that she seems to have had no upbringing. Did you give her this number?"

"I gave it to no one, Aunt Hilde."

"Then I wonder how she got it. Our last names are not the same. How could she know whose number to ask for?"

Paul said he could not imagine. But he could, and the sour taste of suspicion rose in his throat. Paul asked permission to use the telephone. Hilde granted it, but by the look on her face it was plain that she did not approve of this business of young girls calling her great-nephew, and cared even less for what such a breach of modesty implied. Hilde did not like supernumerary females. Paulus had always had girls hanging on him, so had his brothers, especially Lori's father. So had Hilde's sons, all of them so good-looking but all of them dead now. Was Paul going to be another one?

Even though the doctor was a Jew, the Kaltenbachs still had a telephone. It was not for personal use. The authorities had made that clear. It was for use in connection with Dr. Kaltenbach's medical practice, and only that. If all of his patients were Jews, did this mean he could not speak to Aryans on the telephone? Dr. Kaltenbach did not know; this had not been explained to him. Perhaps his tormentors hoped that he would make an innocent mistake that would turn out to be a crime punishable by worse humiliations than he had already suffered. Whatever the explanation, it was better to assume that something was forbidden than to assume that it was not, so the doctor never touched the receiver unless he was sure that a Jew was on the line. It was Rima's job to answer during office hours and make sure that this was the case before she called her father to the phone.

Paul had expected it to take a couple of hours for the call to go through to Berlin. However, the Kaltenbach's number rang almost immediately. On hearing her voice, Paul said, "Rima."

"My love. You are safely there?"

"No broken bones. It was an easy drive. We hardly saw another car."

After a pause—for a moment Paul thought that the connection had been broken—Rima said, "I want to come to you, Paul."

"Here?"

"Yes, I must. Tonight. On the eleven-forty train."

Paul didn't hesitate. It was too late for hesitation. His curiosity was too great. Besides, he longed for her. And whoever was listening had heard enough. They should hear no more.

"Of course," he said. "I'll be at the station to meet you."

"Your family will not be upset?"

"They'll understand. Take the train. What about your father?"

"He doesn't know. I'll leave a note."

It was not love but deathly fear that Paul had heard in Rima's voice. He felt what she was feeling as if he were the one who was afraid. But he was not afraid—not for himself, anyway. He had never in his short life been afraid—not of bullies even before he learned how to fight them, not even of Stutzer. His father said that he got this from his mother and her family—look at Paulus—but Paul had never seen his father show a sign of fear, either. Hubbard watched, he listened, he smiled. Then he wrote everything down and this act seemed to cure everything, even the instinct for self-preservation.

When Hubbard and Paulus returned from their walk, they were silent and withdrawn, rare behavior for either of them. Paul had planned to tell the family his news one at a time, Hubbard first, Lori last, so as to give them the opportunity of consulting each other and making a decision. However, Hubbard and Paulus seemed determined to remain together, and Paul needed time to stop Rima if the answer was No. In that case he would take a train to Berlin. He would go to her.

Paul told the two of them about his phone call. As usual, Paulus's taut face showed nothing. Hubbard absorbed Paul's words, then smiled—but faintly. Paulus let Hubbard, the father, ask the questions. There was only one.

"This is the girl who helped you in the Tiergarten?"

"Yes."

"Then of course she can come," Hubbard said. "Paulus, is that agreeable?"

"Certainly. Is she pretty, Paul?"

"More than that, Uncle."

Paulus gave him a long look while his smile, beginning in his eyes, peeled off the expressionless mask that he had been wearing since his walk with Hubbard. More than pretty? More evidence that Paul, this splendid boy, was like his maternal grandfather, like Paulus himself, like all of his Prussian forebears. "*Wunderbar!*" Paulus said.

Hubbard had similar manly feelings. He threw a heavy arm around Paul's shoulders and squeezed. His eyes glowed. Paul could see that his father was imagining the meeting of Paul and Rima at the station—Paul waiting on the platform, Rima alighting from the train, their proper public hello, the longing in their eyes. Hubbard was not, however, imagining the watchers in the shadows. He saw no evil unless it tapped him on the chest.

2

It was well after midnight when Rima arrived at Schloss Berwick. Hilde greeted her at the door with a heart-chilling demonstration of old-fashioned good manners. She was kind but distant, hospitable but not welcoming. She spoke all the right words without uttering a kindly one. The girl had brought her overnight things in a rucksack, as if she were on a Wandervögel hike. Her large, intelligent, and beautiful brown eyes—Hilde immediately admitted these obvious qualities to herself—touched everything in the entrance hall. As if on tiptoes, Rima looked from object to object as if checking an inventory, which in fact she was doing because Paul had told her about the Arras mille-fleurs tapestry with its unicorn at the turning of the stairway, the suits of armor, the stuffed boars' heads, the giant-size swords and spears, the huge Kilim rug that one of Paulus's brothers had sent home from Turkey before being killed by a British shell at Gallipoli while advising the Turkish infantry.

Notwithstanding the telephone call and the rucksack, the girl seemed perfectly proper. She radiated good health and good nature. Her smile was enchanting. With her creamy complexion and thick black hair she was different from the blond, blue-eyed ideal of the moment. Still, she was altogether lovely. Hilde thought so, and Hubbard and Paulus were stunned by Rima's face and figure. They called her immediately by her actual baptismal name, Alexa. Hilde called her Miss and nothing else.

Lori did not even know that Rima was in the house. She was in a deep sleep and had been for hours. Hubbard believed that she must have taken a sleeping pill. He thought that a good long sleep would do her good. He left her undisturbed.

Rima had eaten on the train. No, she wasn't thirsty. But she was very tired. Might she be permitted to say goodnight? Hilde showed her to her room. It was exactly what Rima had expected—turned-down bed, chair, wardrobe, writing table with pen and ink and crested stationery, a vase of spring flowers, a bowl of apples, a pitcher of water for washing, a carafe of water for drinking, a washbowl, a chamber pot. In all of Schloss Berwick with its sixteen rooms, there was only one bath-room, one lavatory. Hilde did not mention this, but Rima already knew it, thanks to Paul's detailed briefing on the schloss.

As soon as the door closed behind Hilde, Rima undressed and got under the featherbed. She had brought a nightgown but she did not put it on. She had come here to make love and her first experience of lovemaking had taught her that removing twisted clothes was an awk-ward process which wasted moments that might be better spent. She blew out the candle by her bedside—only the ground floor of the schloss had electricity—and waited.

On the station platform, during their only moment alone, Paul had said with a smile, "I'll come to you tonight. I know the house, and what if you got lost?"

Rima really was exhausted. She was asleep when Paul arrived. She heard the lock click. She opened her eyes immediately. Rima felt that she had been deep in sleep and that it had taken her a long time to climb out of it. No clock struck. She had no idea what time it was. A fat moon lit the room. They could perceive if not see each other in the dark—eyes, teeth, hints of skin. Paul relit the candle.

"What if someone comes?" Rima said. "Not that this scene would surprise your great aunt, judging by the looks she's given me."

"No one will come," Paul said.

"Can you open the window? This featherbed is like a steam bath. I'm swimming in sweat."

Paul did as she asked. It took all his strength to lift the sash. It squealed, wood on wood. Cold air and the brackish smell of the Baltic Sea came in with the draught. When Paul turned around Rima put a finger to her lips and beckoned him closer. They lay down together, face to face.

Whispering, Rima said, "I have something to tell you."

Paul said, "Wait. I have a question. Why did you come here? It's dangerous. They'll find out, if they don't know already."

"That's what I have to tell you," Rima said. "They sent me."

"Who?"

"Who do you think? Stutzer. He gave me money for the ticket."

"Why?"

"To spy on you. So please don't tell me anything you don't want them to know." Paul started to speak. Rima put a finger on his lips. "Listen," she said.

Omitting no detail, she told him about her arrest, and then what had happened to her at police headquarters and later at No. 8 Prinz-Albrechtstrasse. However, she left out all mention of Lori's meeting with Reinhard Heydrich. She described the proposal that Stutzer had put to her: Watch the Christophers, ingratiate herself with them, report to him everything they said and did.

"What did you say to that?"

"I agreed, of course."

"Agreed to spy on us?"

"Yes. Otherwise my father will be sent to Dachau. It will kill him and I'll never see him again. Stutzer made that plain."

"Did they beat you?"

"No, just the things I've told you about."

Paul remembered the way in which Stutzer stared at his mother. How had he looked at Rima? He cleared his throat. His voice shook. "They didn't. . . ."

"No. They're serious about being Aryans. They fear pollution from such as me. That was obvious. Besides, I wonder about your man Stutzer."

"Wonder what?"

"If girls even interest him. He dresses the way a woman dresses, for the affect. We must make plans if this is going to work."

"If what is going to work?"

"Our deception."

Paul said, "How can it possibly work?"

"We'll fool them," Rima said.

"Have you lost your mind?"

Rima nodded and whispered on. She believed that they could fool Stutzer, lead him in the wrong direction.

"Tell him harmless scraps of the truth but keep the real secrets to ourselves?" Paul said. "He'd know. He'd take revenge."

"What's the alternative? Shall I betray you? Or go back to Stutzer and tell him I've changed my mind? Or what?"

All this in whispers.

"But what could they possibly want to know?" Paul said. "My parents hide nothing. I'm not old enough to have secrets."

"What about me?"

"They must know all about you, and all about you and me. Who do you think Stutzer thinks your Aryan lover is if not me? Otherwise why would they even think you could be their spy?"

In the flickering light of the candle, Rima gave him a long, steady look. Then she looked away. "What answer to that question do you want?"

"The truthful one."

"That's the answer that frightens me, the truthful one."

What was she saying? Their eyes locked. Something strange had happened. He was lying in bed beside the loveliest creature he had ever seen, and she was his at the price of a gesture. But his flesh was not responding.

"Tell me what you're afraid of," he said.

She described what she had seen near the bridle path in the Tiergarten. "The man inside the Daimler was Reinhold Heydrich," she said.

Paul said, "How do you know it was him?"

"I saw him. I've seen his picture. He's at the bottom of this. He wants something from your mother, and everything that's happening results from that."

"But he can just take anything he wants. Kill anyone he wants, put them in prison."

"Nevertheless, I think he's blackmailing your mother."

Paul leaped to his feet and walked to the window. Rima thought that she had lost him. He would think that she was lying, that she really was a spy, that she was in league with Stutzer, that Paul would remember how she had spied on him in the Tiergarten and think that even then she was on duty. That the love she offered him was a lie, too. How could he not think these things?

But he knew better. Rima had seen nothing more than he himself had seen, but somehow she had seen more. She had seen that the man who waited for Lori was Heydrich. The hangman. The man in charge of assassination, torture, imprisonment in four countries now and who knew how many more yet to come. If Lori Christopher was paying blackmail for something, what else could that be besides Paul's safety? She was buying his escape from this country, from those people.

Why would Stutzer, holder of a lofty rank in the secret police, personally interrogate a couple of children like Paul and Rima? *Stutzer is a high muckamuck, no question about that*, O. G. had said. *One of Heydrich's boys.* These thoughts were difficult to bear. Paul put his face in his hands. Rima, nude, still stood behind him with her arms around his waist. He shuddered. She placed her lips against his bare back.

This was the candlelit scene that met Hilde's eyes a moment later when she threw open the bedroom door without knocking. She gasped, but she was not surprised by it. It, or some variation on it, was what she had expected to find. Paul was not in his room. Given the blood that flowed in his veins and the incorrigible nature of the human male, where else could he be but bewitched in the arms of this girl, what else might he be doing? Why else had Rima come here? This was by no means the first such living tableau that Hilde had stumbled upon in her forty years in this house.

In frigid tones she said, "Please don't turn around, Miss. Paul, your father needs you. Come at once."

Rima released Paul. He ran from the room as he was, in pajama bottoms. He found a commotion in the hall. Hubbard and Paulus held Lori between them. She wore one of her knee-length nightgowns, a pale blue one this time with yellow flowers embroidered on the bodice. Paul had seen her ready for bed many times before, but never when she was not quicker and more alert than anyone else in the room. It appeared that the men were trying to make her walk, but she was unconscious. Her legs dangled, her head fell forward, her hair hung in her eyes. The transition between the painful thoughts Paul had just been having about his mother and this incomprehensible scene shocked him to the core. It defied the laws of experience, but it was all too believable.

Now that Paul was here, he was ignored. Neither his father nor his uncle offered an explanation for Lori's condition. Neither seemed to have any idea what to do about it. They were not talking to Lori or even to each other. The did not shake her or call her name or throw water in her face. They simply carried her back and forth, up and down the hallway, hoping apparently that she would suddenly wake up and start walking. This was as likely, Paul thought, as that a doll should wake up and walk. Hubbard and Paulus asked for no help or advice. Perhaps, Paul thought, they had summoned him to witness his mother's death. Lori might be dead already. Paul couldn't understand what the grownups thought they were doing. Hilde had vanished down the stairway. She must be calling a doctor, he thought. But then he heard her rattling pots in the kitchen.

Paul said, "She's unconscious. What's the matter with her?"

Hubbard said, "We know she's unconscious, Paul. We think she's taken too much of something by accident."

"Too much of what?"

"Sleeping pills. We don't know."

Lori's eyelids were closed, long thick lashes against her cheek. She was deathly pale. Paul could not tell if she was breathing. He realized that Hubbard was not sure, either. Hubbard fell to one knee and placed his ear against Lori's lips. For once no smile lingered just behind his long bony face, ready to break out.

Paul knew this: someone must act. "Car keys!" he said.

"I don't know where I put them," Hubbard said. He seldom did; the family spent hours looking for things he had misplaced. He was always writing, always in his trance, even when he did not have a pen in his hand. But he was not writing now. He was within this moment in this world and nowhere else.

Where was Lori? Paul wondered. Was she thinking, dreaming, was her mind empty for the first time in her life, did she know where she was or what was happening or how far gone she was? No more than a minute had elapsed since Paul had rushed from Rima's room. Now Rima appeared, barefoot and barelegged but otherwise fully clothed. Without asking permission, she walked past Paul and between the two men. She took Lori's face in her hand. She was not gentle. She peeled back an eyelid and looked into the eye, took a pulse in the neck, listened and then smelled at the mouth. She took Lori's lower lip between her finger and thumb and squeezed it hard, then twisted. Lori uttered a sound and recoiled from the pain.

"There is no time for the car," Rima said. "How long has she been like this?"

Hubbard did not reply. His face was slack, his hands trembled. It was obvious that he could not think, let alone speak. Paulus answered Rima's question. "She was still awake at nine. I heard her coughing when I walked past her room."

It was one-thirty in the morning now.

Rima said, "What did she take?"

"Something to make her sleep, we think. Only she knows what or how much."

Rima said, "Paul, get a bowl. Be quick."

He was back in an instant with a heavy china wash basin. "Bend her over," Rima said to Paulus. "Paul, hold the bowl. She's going to vomit."

Rima opened Lori's mouth, holding the jaw with one hand, and thrust her forefinger down her throat. Watery vomit shot into the bowl. Lori threw back her head and gasped for air. "Don't let her do that," Rima said. "She could inhale her own vomit and suffocate. Keep her throat straight." Rima said. Paulus complied. Rima wiped the inside of Lori's mouth with a forefinger, snapped it clean over the bowl, then with the same finger massaged the back of Lori's throat again. She vomited once more, less explosively. She was breathing visibly now, gasping for air, and moving in small ways—her face changed expressions, her head jerked, her limbs twitched.

Rima said, "Paul, run a cold bath. Lots of water. Be quick. Gentlemen, please take her to the bathroom."

Hubbard lifted her into his arms. The bathroom was downstairs, off the kitchen. Cold water, tinted with rust, gushed from the big iron faucets.

Rima said, "Into the water, on her back." The men hesitated. "Now," Rima said. Hubbard and Paulus did as they were told. Lori moaned, thrashed, tried weakly to escape from the freezing water.

"Someone bring towels and blankets," Rima said. "Make coffee."

"She hates coffee," Hubbard said.

"Tea, then."

The water was now up to Lori's chin. Her blue nightgown wafted around her legs in the water as if stirred by a current.

"She's shaking like a leaf," Hubbard shouted. "She'll catch her death of cold."

He made as if to lift Lori from the tub. Rima said, "No. Not yet. First she has to wake up."

Lori's eyes opened, as if she had heard Rima's words. Rima said, "Look at me."

"I don't know you," Lori said, coughing.

"No, but I'm trying to help you."

They were speaking German. Rima held up three fingers. "How many fingers, dear lady?"

"Three."

"What is the name of your son?"

Lori did not answer.

"Good girl," Rima said. "You're being careful. You're awake. But now you must stay awake. Do not go back to sleep. It is strictly forbidden. Do you understand?"

Lori glared at her but did not answer.

To Paulus, Rima said, "Get her out of the water now. The baroness—where is she?—and I will get her out of that nightdress and dry her and wrap her in blankets. After that she must get dressed and walk until she is completely awake. That may take hours. We will take turns, Paul and me first, then you and Herr Christopher, Herr Colonel Baron. Do not let her go back to sleep. And, Paul, get rid of the sleeping powders immediately."

"At your orders, Miss," Paulus said. Rima smiled at him, a small polite smile. He said, "If ever I need resuscitation, my dear, I will call on you, if I may."

Hilde appeared, bearing teapot, sugar bowl, milk pitcher, and cup and saucer on a silver tray. The china was paper-thin, with blue Chinese scenes painted on it. Rima's mother had had dishes very much like these. Rima, kneeling by the tub, held Lori's head above the water. "Wake up, Lori!" she said over and over. "Stay awake!"

Lori's large gray eyes stared at her with hatred, then closed. Rima shouted at her, "Open your eyes at once!" Lori lifted a hand to strike this impertinent stranger, but her muscles would not obey her and her arm fell helplessly into the water.

"Baroness, please help me," Rima said. Hilde looked for a place to set down her tray. Paul took it from her.

To the men Rima said, "Out, please, gentlemen."

When the women emerged from the bathroom, Lori was dressed in slacks, a turtleneck sweater, a headscarf, and stout shoes. She staggered as she walked. By turns her eyes were empty or suspicious or burning with anger, as if controlled by a switch. Her jaw was slack. She still breathed through her mouth. Despite her elegant clothes she was a shocking sight to Paul. In the fifteen years of his life he had never before seen his mother when she was not in complete control of herself and everything around her.

Paul said, "Does she need a jacket?"

"You're not taking her outside?" Hilde said. "It's dark, it's damp. Her hair is wet. It is dangerous to her health. This is a sick woman."

"The moon is out," Rima said. "The night is warm. Breathing fresh air will be good for her."

Hilde said, "You don't know our sea air, young lady. Nor is the moon a healthy influence."

Hilde had taken enough orders from this impertinent stranger who was hardly more than a child. The tea that Hilde had made for Lori had gone cold while she carried out one incomprehensible instruction after another. Now Lori would have nothing on her stomach. She needed something hot to drink. She needed a doctor.

Paulus said, "The girl is right. Lori needs fresh air. Exercise!"

"How do you know she's right?" Hilde said. "We don't even know who she is."

Paulus lifted his eyebrows. Did Hilde think that Rima was deaf? However, Rima, her arm around Lori as if she had known her for years, seemed unaffected by what had just been said about her. She waited for a decision, her eyes on Paulus.

Paulus said, "She's been right about everything else so far. Also, she is a guest in this house and she is a friend of Paul's."

"A very *close* friend," Hilde said.

Paulus had been married to this woman for two-thirds of his life. He knew exactly what she was saying, and now he understood why she was so angry. He had seen her in this state before, for similar reasons. Hilde must have caught these children in bed. Paulus was tremendously pleased. He himself had not had his first honest girl until he was twenty.

"If she and Paul are close, all the more reason to regard her as a friend," Paulus said.

Hilde knew that she had been overruled—another betrayal. She sniffed, turned on her heel, and left Paulus with the female he preferred on this particular night. Paulus opened the front door.

"Ring the bell when you wish to be relieved, children," he said.

3

For the next hour Rima and Paul walked Lori up and down the gravel drive, under the beeches. The gibbous moon provided more than enough light. The night was tart, a bit damp but not chilly. Lori was not yet fully conscious. Sleep was calling to her. Or perhaps, Paul thought, it was death. In either case Lori was trying to answer. When her head bowed, Rima shook her hard and shouted into her ear: "WAKE UP!" From time to time Lori stumbled or coughed convulsively and as if talking in her sleep, muttered nonsense to herself in a voice so choked that Paul and Rima could not make out the words. Paul recognized the tone; there was no mistaking it. She was furious, she was arguing with some invisible presence. Paul did not even try to understand what his mother was saying. He was afraid of what he might hear. When she lost her balance or coughed, he wrapped her in his arms, kissed her cheek, murmured her name.

"She'll be all right," Rima said, at the end of one long coughing spell.

"Has she caught a chill?"

"Maybe, from the cold water, but she's strong."

Paul said, "You have no idea."

His mind teemed with images of the last hour. Mostly what he remembered was Rima. In her certainty, her competence, her instinct for command, she reminded him of Lori. Paulus was right—without Rima they might have lost his mother. Certainly Lori had been fighting hard to die. He had seen that in her eyes in the tub when she glared at Rima—this perfect stranger who was interfering with her will—and tried to strike her. She would slip away again if she could. He knew that as well as if his mother had whispered her plans into his ear. She wanted to die.

To Rima Paul said, "Your father taught you how to do what you did tonight?"

"In a manner of speaking, yes," Rima replied.

Paul waited for her to go on. Even at sixteen he believed, as he believed for the rest of his life, that nothing useful could be learned by asking questions.

"Actually," Rima said, "I learned it from his medical books. They always fascinated me. I read them on the sly. Also I had some practical experience. My father did this same thing."

"When?"

"A year ago, when they took the last thing from him, his house in Charlottenburg and everything in it, and gave it to someone who's important in the party."

"He took sleeping powders?"

"I think so. If it had been poison he would have died."

"You were alone with him when this happened?"

"I found him when I came home from school. He wasn't quite unconscious yet. The stuff took longer to work than he thought. He fought with me. He had a pistol in his hand—his officer's Mauser from the war. I couldn't understand that at the time. Why take poison and also shoot yourself?"

"Weren't you afraid?"

"Of the gun? No. I knew my own father wouldn't shoot me. For him? Yes. Terrified. You now know as well as I do what it feels like to see something like this happening."

"But in the end you saved him, just like tonight."

"Saved him? I wouldn't say that. I prevented him from succeeding in what he wanted to do."

A silence followed. Lori broke it. In a clear voice she cried, "I will not permit this!" She stopped in her tracks and struggled to free herself from Paul and Rima. She was strong, violent. After a moment Rima said, "Let her go. She'll hurt herself."

Paul said, "The cliffs are nearby."

"In her condition how can she run away from you?"

Freed of restraint, and of support, Lori lurched forward, ran two or three steps, then fell. She cursed in German, coughed convulsively, cursed again. Paul fell to his knees beside her, "Mama, it's Paul. Everything is all right. Let me help you."

Rima stood back, watching, silent, not interfering. Her face was in shadow. Paul remembered her as she had been when she got out of bed an hour ago, her tumbled hair. Under the circumstances, it was an incongruous thought. It was absurd to be thinking of what had not happened between him and Rima rather than this ugly thing that had happened to his mother. It was worse than absurd to have a heart full of love for Rima, to feel blood rushing in his body for her, to think of nothing but her, while his mother might be dying. He was overcome by guilt, but the blood still rushed. He helped Lori to her feet. She stood still, submissive, while he brushed dirt from her clothes. Rima took her other arm. They walked to the end of the drive, then turned around and started back.

"I think," Rima said as if her story had not been interrupted, "that my father had his pistol because he intended to shoot anyone who got between him and death. Except me, of course."

Lori was silent now. She seemed to be walking more easily. She looked at nothing, said nothing. She was breathing normally. Paul wondered what would make a person want to die so badly that he would kill to defend his desire. But in the case of Lori, he knew, or thought he did.

Later, while the house was sleeping—Lori, too, now that it was safe for her to close her eyes—Rima went to Paul's room. She went back to her own bed just before dawn, the moment at which Paulus habitually snapped awake and went for his morning march along the cliffs. She saw him from the window, head high, stepping out toward the sea, walking stick in hand, a large wolfhound keeping step at his heels. His head turned left and right, he inhaled the morning air to the bottom of his lungs. He was like a stag in a state of alert. The maleness of him made Rima smile. How much like Paul he must have been when he was young.

4

Next morning Rima and Lori were first down for breakfast. With a brisk handshake Lori introduced herself as if she and Rima were laying eyes on each other for the first time. In Lori's case this may have been true. Who knew what she had seen or heard the night before? Today she was perfectly self-possessed.

"I must thank you for your help last night," she said.

"I did very little," Rima said.

"That's not quite the truth, as I understand it, but you have my gratitude."

Perhaps that's not quite the truth, either, Rima thought, looking into Lori's steady eyes. The pupils were still dilated from whatever over-dose she had taken. Because of the enlarged pupils her eyes looked almost black and so cold that it was hard not to think that Lori was making them so by an effort of the will.

"I'm glad we're alone," Lori said. "We must get to know each other."

Breakfast was laid out on a sideboard. Lori helped herself to butter and jam, bread, a piece of cheese, a slice of ham, a boiled egg. Clearly she meant to fill her empty stomach. Rima took bread and butter and a cup of coffee.

They sat down on opposite sides of the table, looking into each other's faces. Rima was surprised by Lori's youthful appearance. Take away the bruised eyes and the shadow of misery and she might have been a girl of twenty. She ate like a teenager—silently, greedily, everything on her plate.

"Now I must interrogate you," she said when she was finished.

Rima said nothing.

Lori said, "It's my duty as a mother, you understand."

"Of course."

"You are a nurse?"

"No, a student. A former student."

"But you are Professor Doctor Kaltenbach's daughter?"

"Yes. Do you know him?"

Lori switched to English. "Your father is a fine person and a great surgeon," she said. "But you know that. I knew your mother, too. She played the viola very nicely. She is getting along all right in Argentina?"

"I believe so. Her letters don't always come through."

"And when they do they have been opened."

"Sometimes it seems so."

"You're circumspect, I see."

"Everyone in the Reich should be circumspect."

Lori examined her, as if answering her own question before asking it. "You are what age?"

"Sixteen."

"You seem older."

Rima spread her hands—whatever you say.

"At your age that's a compliment. Seeming to be older at your age may not be a good thing in every way, but it's an advantage. It's difficult at sixteen to get people to take you seriously. Especially if one is as pretty as you. How did you learn English?"

"From tutors. My mother thought it would be an advantage. She always hoped to go to America."

"And now she's there, in Argentina."

"Not that America. New York City is where she wanted to be, because of the gaiety and the skyscrapers. She thought that my father could work there and be as well known as he was in Berlin and we could live in peace."

"So she saw it coming, what we have now in Germany?"

"Maybe not the entire reality, but she guessed enough to realize what it would mean for my father."

"And your father?"

"If you know him," Rima said, "then you know the answer to that question."

Lori nodded. "I'm curious about how you met Paul."

Rima took a moment before she answered. This was not because she had to summon memories. Those were always with her—not as memories, but as the most vivid things in her mind in every moment of the present. She could not get Paul out of her head. She had never before understood the entire meaning of that cliché, but now she did. Clichés, she realized, were clichés for a reason.

"I saw him for the first time last summer, in the Tiergarten, near the Neuer See. He was just standing there in the middle of a lawn, looking at the world."

"A figure in a landscape."

"No, a boy in the midst of life. He was very still but entirely alive. That's what I noticed."

"And you decided that he was the one for you?"

"Yes. At that moment."

"You're very frank. I admire that. Did you approach him then?"

"No. The authorities were in the midst of ruining my father, taking everything away from him. It wasn't possible to know where this process would end."

Lori interrupted. "You didn't want to involve Paul?"

Rima said, "I decided to wait and see what happened to my father."

Lori said, "So you set your cap for him, you spied on him, you became a mystery woman in his eyes, you made him grateful to you, and at last you captured him."

"I would not have chosen those exact words to describe what happened," Rima said. "But yes, those are the essentials."

Lori said, "I see. And why exactly did you come to Rügen yesterday?"

"To be with Paul."

"You love him?"

"Of course I do."

"He loves you?"

"He has said that he does."

Lori paused, eyes locked with Rima's. "And there is no other reason that you came here yesterday?"

"Yes, but I can't answer your questions about that. I'm sorry."

"You are not pregnant?"

"No."

Lori coughed into her napkin—deeply, almost consumptively, as she had done the night before. Her bruised eyes watered; she dried them on the napkin. "I may understand your reasons better than you think," she said. "I've seen you before, you know. You were watching me by the Tiergarten the other day. You were walking Miss Wetzel's little white dog."

"Yes, Mrs. Christopher, and you were getting into a black Daimler."

"You identified everyone in the car?"

"I recognized the man, Mrs. Christopher."

"Whom have you told?"

"Only Paul. He had seen the same thing happen on another day."

Lori bit her lower lip, the first visible sign that her emotions were engaged by this conversation. Her pupils had grown smaller while they talked. She said, "You realize that I should hate you for all this, do you not?"

"As a woman, I understand such a feeling. But I think it is wrong."

"You consider yourself a woman?"

"Didn't you at my age?"

This made Lori pause, even smile briefly with her fierce eyes. "Perhaps a year or two later than sixteen," she said. "And if as a woman you think what you think, then what is your opinion as an intelligent human being?"

"I think I should not have been in the wrong place at the wrong time, and I am afraid—very much afraid, Mrs. Christopher, that it's going to cost me everything."

Lori looked at Rima without expression, then shook her head as if to rid it of a notion or an impulse. "Perhaps not, or at least not yet," she said. "They saw you too, you know. They may well think that you can be useful to them."

Rima was taken aback. What did this woman know? She said, "I am prepared for that possibility."

"Are you indeed, Miss? Be careful. Many others have thought the same thing and most of them are dead."

Lori folded her napkin and drew it into its silver ring, then rose from the table. She touched Rima on the shoulder. Rima looked up at her.

"You are gorgeous," she said. "Paul is a lucky young man, but he is very young, younger than you. Take precautions when you're with him. You know what to do?"

Rima nodded. "May I ask you a question?" she said.

"Fire away."

"Do you hate me?"

"Of course not," Lori said. "I'm all booked up in that department."

5

Better than anyone else, Lori knew that Rima had saved the family from the embarrassment—and in the Christophers' case, something worse than that—of letting the secret of Lori's suicide attempt out of the house. Had they called a doctor, he would have been obliged to report his visit and the particulars of the emergency to the police. They would have investigated and passed the information on to higher authority. There would have been another detention, another interview. Heydrich himself would have interrogated Lori the next time he abducted her from the Tiergarten, drove her to his confiscated hunting lodge in a wooded section of Berlin, and entertained her at lunch with his theatrical conversation, his painful manners, his learned appreciation of her piano playing. He had perfect pitch just as Lori did or so he claimed, he was hopelessly in love with her, the most perfect Aryan female he had ever seen.

"You are from folklore, from art!" he had told her, kissing her palm on the day that Rima saw her getting into the Daimler. "You are the eternal German beauty, do you wonder that I love you?"

He kept Paris clothes for her in a closet at the hunting lodge and required her to change into them when, as he put it, she called on him. He gave her gifts of jewelry and perfume, once a Julius Blüthner grand piano that had belonged to Franz Liszt and later to a famous Berlin pianist who—how should he put it?—no longer played in Germany, just as the former owner of his hunting lodge no longer lived in Germany. Lori could not touch the keys of this magnificent instrument without nausea, but during her hours in captivity she played it for Heydrich, who preferred the romantics and also, though he was slightly ashamed of this, the operettas of Lehár and Strauss. To Heydrich, their love, as he called it, was, as he put it, a sublime operetta, tuneful and gay and sometimes (he admitted it), marked by foolish misunderstandings.

In fact, Lori did not misunderstand her situation in the least. Her trysts with Heydrich were the price for his staying his hand against Paul, Hubbard, Paulus, Hilde and everyone else to whom she was connected by blood and friendship. The secret police knew the identities of the people she loved. None of them was safe. Heydrich really did have the power to do whatever he liked in Germany. His popular nickname was Der Henker, the hangman. In her own mind Lori called him Die Spinne, the Spider. The entire German people was caught in his web. He could, if the whim took him, sentence them all to death and in their enthusiasm for obedience they would shoot each other down to the last two men alive, who would thereupon enter into a murdersuicide pact.

When he wanted to be alone with Lori without the possibility of interruption—to spare her worry, as he put it—he would order the arrest of Hubbard, and now that Paul was home from school, of Paul, too. This was the reason for their detentions, for the endless, pointless interviews with Stutzer. Even though he knew all about them, Heydrich never referred to the crimes of which the Christophers were undeniably guilty—the smuggling of a large number of fugitives out of the country aboard the *Mahican*. Nearly all of these people had been Jews, a few had also been Social Democrats, some really were or for fashion's sake had pretended to be communists. Some of them even managed to take their money, or some of it, out of Germany with them. Helping such people—enemies of the state, enemies of the people, racial and political scum—to escape justice was treason. A capital crime. Heydrich knew all the names, all the dates, all the details of the Christophers' nighttime rescues. Lori knew that he knew. On his whim she could be shot or tortured and then shot. Or beheaded or impaled on a meat hook. So could Hubbard, so could Paul because he had stowed away on a couple of their night sails to Denmark. Heydrich was capable of shooting Hubbard and Paul or tripping the guillotine himself and requiring Lori to watch. And then, sentimental fool that he said he was, not shoot her because he could not kill the thing he loved.

Lori was not glad to be alive on Midsummer Day. The lingering effect of the opiate she had taken the day before clouded her mind and still struggled with her brain for control of her body. She did not know which opiate it had been. She had thought that so-and-so many grams of the stuff would kill her, which was all that mattered. The dose she swallowed had not been enough. Her body had saved her by being stronger than the drug. Now, the morning after, she was chilled, she shuddered, her legs were weak and made small involuntary kicking movements. She had vomited the huge breakfast she had eaten almost immediately after she ate it. She tasted vomit, she smelled it for hours afterward.

She had never in her life been so angry at herself, so ashamed, so furious with her own stupidity, her own weakness. How could she have let herself be driven to this by mere humiliation? What had she been thinking? Her death would have been a death warrant for the others. Had she died, Heydrich would have avenged the insult of her escape by charging her jealous husband with murder. Everybody at Schloss

Berwick this weekend would now be lying in a cellar with bullets in their brains or their heads in baskets.

"Stupid!" she said to herself. "Stupid!" It was the worst insult she could imagine.

These thoughts passed through Lori's mind as she sat in a strip of sunlight in Hilde's sewing room. She had no one to whom she could speak of such matters. Nor would she ever have anybody, no matter how long she lived. Hilde stayed near, slyly watching Lori over her flying knitting needles, on the lookout for another suicide attempt. But in reality she was as disinterested in Lori as a cat in some other cat's kitten. She had always been kind to Lori, the orphan who grew up in her house, because it was her duty to be kind to her and because Paulus, who adored his brother's child, commanded her to be kind. But Hilde had never had feelings for Lori. By the time the child came to live with them, Hilde's sons, every one of them, had fallen in Russia or France. Hilde had no feelings left.

A shaft of sunlight fell on Lori's legs. Perversely, she shivered again. Hilde looked up from her knitting, alert for any sign that she could tuck another coverlet around Lori or fetch the hot-water bottle that Lori had so far refused. Lori was already wearing a sweater and a shawl and her lower body was wrapped in an afghan.

"I'm not cold," Lori said quickly, to forestall more wrappings. "I just have the shakes."

She gave a foolish smile as if what she suffered from was too much red wine the night before. For the first time in her life Lori, who had never believed in the supernatural, wished that she was a Catholic. She would then have someone to talk to. But would even a priest believe, let alone understand the confession that would spill from her mouth? If he told her she was forgiven, would she believe that? What right did any human being have to forgive her? One of the most evil men in the history of the world was in love with her. Her beauty, her personage, which had always given her such pleasure, had brought about this horror. She loved her husband, she had loved him from the moment she saw him walking into this very house sixteen years before. The sight of him—tall, horse-faced, absurdly sure of himself, delighted by everything, foreign in every possible way—had made her laugh so hard within herself that the only way to conceal the joy he gave her was to be harsh with him, to be distant, to show no interest in this oversize boy who fascinated her. Now, she knew, he was upstairs at his writing table, recording everything that he had witnessed the night before. This was as necessary to him as morphine to an addict. When he was done, everything would be recorded, nothing about Lori would ever be forgotten. He left nothing out, except what he didn't know.

"Dear God, Lori," Hilde said. "You're crying."

She was truly alarmed. The old woman had never seen such behavior in this dry-eyed girl. Lori, as a child, had not wept even when her father was murdered. Hilde gave her her own handkerchief, one of the scores she had embroidered with tiny thread replicas of every flower ever known to Germans.

6

By the time Paulus returned from his morning march, Midsummer Day had turned sunny and warm. Paulus's pocket thermometer gave him the exact temperature. By Rügen standards it was subtropical— 25.5 degrees centigrade at eight in the morning. What would noontime bring? he asked Paul while they ate their morning sausages and toasted cheese and Paulus drank his breakfast beer. Whatever the weather was, blistering heat or blinding light, Paul must take advantage of it.

"Right after breakfast you must take your charming little nurse for a long walk in the forest," Paulus said. "This is the day for young people. Then in the afternoon take her to town. Buy her ice cream. They'll be wearing costumes in the villages and dancing in the streets. Tonight, bonfires for you two to leap through, shadowy places for lingering. Nothing to worry about. All the priests and ministers and even some of the policemen are locked up until dawn tomorrow."

From across the table Hilde said, "Kindly stop such talk. A child is present."

"A child, ha!" said Paulus. "He's exactly the right age, Paul, you may not see another Midsummer Day like this one in your lifetime. Take advantage."

Under the indigo sky the Baltic was calm and almost blue. The wartime ban on sailing had been lifted for the holiday, and pleasure craft were permitted inside a three-kilometer limit. Amateur sailors raced one another, tacked too hard and overturned or collided. One or two boats were blown ashore. Rima and Paul watched this higgledy-piggledy regatta from the cliff tops. The Christophers' yawl *Mahican* bobbed at its mooring a few meters offshore.

Rima said, "When will we sail?"

Paul had promised her this. "Later," he replied. "Too many Sunday sailors now."

"After dark, maybe?"

Rima looked up at him with dancing eyes to make her meaning plain. She was as spontaneous as an American. Paul had never known anyone remotely like her, except on summer vacations in the Berkshires. When among themselves, his Hubbard and Christopher relations and their children said whatever came into their heads, they swung from ropes over river gorges and let go at the apogee, plummeting feet-first into swimming holes surrounded by great gray rocks.

Paul told Rima all this as they strolled along the cliff path. She said, "Tell me about your mother."

Paul said, "They say she's always been the way she is."

"And how is that?"

Paul smiled. "Wonderful."

"Because why?"

"The way she is, the way she looks. She's afraid of nothing."

"Really, of nothing?"

"Of nothing. Paulus is the same, so is the entire family."

Which must be why so many of them are dead, Rima thought. "Not long ago I saw an example of that family characteristic in the Tiergarten," she said.

Paul looked puzzled. Rima read his face and saw her mistake. She said, "The Youth. Were you afraid?"

"There wasn't time."

"Angry?"

"No."

"Then why did you attack seven enemies single-handed?"

"I've been taught to hit the other fellow hard before he hits you," Paul said. "It works, usually."

"Taught by your American relations or the Germans?"

"Both, actually. They think alike about most things."

"Including beating the stuffing out of the Leader's followers?"

"I think so. Neither family ever talks about him, or them."

They were out of sight of the house, on a walking path crowded with other hikers. One of the walkers, a stout man wearing lederhosen, knee socks with garters, and a Tyrolean hat with a large brush of deer's tail-hair sewed to its braided hatband and a large swastika badge pinned next to it, heard this exchange and stopped in his tracks.

"What was that about beating the stuffing out of the Leader?" he asked in English. He had a ruddy beer-drinker's face, skin stretched tight over fat.

Rima looked puzzled. Paul said, "We were practicing our English, sir."

"And talking treason!"

"I'm sorry, but you are mistaken."

Now that Paul was speaking German, the man placed his accent. "Do you talk treason in Berlin?" he asked.

He himself was from Munich. Paul could hear it in his vowels. He was not shouting, but his voice was loud. Other hikers hurried past, eyes averted. No one wished to get involved in this. Paul did not answer. The man from Munich produced a pencil and a notebook. "Names!" he said. "Addresses!"

Rima said, "We were talking about our dog, Schatzi. She's very naughty."

The man said, "You are lying. I understood every word you said."

"I'm sure your English is perfect, sir," Paul replied. The sun was shining and the sky was cloudless. Paul was happy. He held hands with the girl he loved. He had slept with this wonderful creature the night before and he was going to sleep with her again tonight, if not before. Paul put a hand on the man's shoulder. "March on, sir," he said in German. "Enjoy the beautiful day. You have made a mistake. Let's part as friends."

"I've made a mistake, have I? We'll see about that, you snot. I have your descriptions."

Paul bowed. "And we will always remember you, sir."

Paul led Rima to the edge of the cliff. It was more than one hundred feet high at this point. "Follow me," he said. He swung over the edge. Rima followed. There were many handholds and footholds in the chalk, and in moments they were on the beach.

"You're mad," Rima said. "How do you know he's not the Gauleiter of Bavaria?"

"That's exactly who he is," Paul said. "You can tell by the hat."

She laughed. They embraced and kissed in full view of scandalized people who were walking along the beach. The chalk on their hands came off on each other's clothes.

"Not only do you insult the flower of the great National Socialist party," said Rima, leaning back in his arms. "Now there is this immoral behavior."

7

Under Frederick the Great and earlier princes, Paulus's ancestors had possessed a large part of Rügen as well as lands in Pomerania and Prussia, but over the generations bad luck and bad management reduced these holdings to a few hectares. Among the remnants of the family's prosperity was a small, shallow lake called the Borg—a pond, Hubbard said—with an island in its center. On the island stood a circle of flat rocks, some of them tumbled, others tilted, one of two still upright after hundreds, perhaps thousands of years. The circle was believed by Hubbard to be an artifact of a druidic cult that flourished before the time of Christ. Little Stonehenge, he called it.

"According to Julius Caesar, the word druid meant wisdom in old

Celtic," he said. "Caesar also tells us that druids believed in the immortality of the soul, and that the soul passed from one person to another on the death of the body."

Rima, who had never before encountered a walking encyclopedia like Hubbard, or an agnostic either, smiled demurely. This encouraged him to go on.

"Midsummer must have been the druids' great day," he said. "The sun's longest shining of the year, imagine. Lady Flavia Anderson, an amateur scholar we met at a dinner party in London, had a theory, based on a lot of research into ancient sources, that the druids lit their Midsummer Day fires by focusing the rays of the sun through a glass ball filled with water. She believed that this burning glass was—pay attention, now—nothing other than the Holy Grail."

"Fascinating," Rima said.

"Yes, isn't it?" Hubbard said, delighted by her interest. "Lady Flavia also believed that Joseph of Arimathea brought this object to England not long after the Crucifixion. Of course its existence immediately became the greatest secret of the realm, not to mention the world. Thus *Le Morte d'Arthur* et cetera."

"Who was Joseph of Arimathea?"

"Didn't you go to Sunday school? He buried Jesus, which of course gave him first dibs on worldly belongings. According to Lady Flavia, the glass ball probably started out as Thummimm or Urim, the sacred dice used by the ancient Israelites to ask God questions."

Rima said, "But. . ."

Lori said, "Don't ask him questions, dear. It only makes things worse."

They were building a bonfire. The island was the safest place to have such a fire, being surrounded by water, and in Hubbard's opinion the circle of stones added mystery to the ceremony. The pond was no more than knee-deep in any one place, and Hubbard and Paul, feet sinking into oozing muck, had spent an hour wading back and forth between the shore and the island, carrying armloads of fallen beech limbs. They built an enormous heap of dry beech wood and fir to make the fire and, to replenish it, laid up more twigs and branches and logs nearby. The result looked like a huge beavers' lodge, but more unkempt.

"Fir on the bottom, beech on top," Hubbard chanted in druidic tones. "May the fire of the sun never stop."

It was late in the afternoon. The sun was sinking but the day was still bright. "Most people light their bonfires after dark, which comes very late today," Hubbard said. "But that eliminates the burning glass, which is the whole point of the thing. Besides, light made by man answering light made by the gods must have been the basic druidic idea. Sir Perceval, the grail!"

Paul produced a small magnifying glass marked with the fleur-de-lis of the Boy Scouts of America. Like many of the things Hubbard treasured, it was an heirloom. He knelt and focused the rays of the sun into a pinpoint. Tinder smoked, glowed red and then, when Hubbard breathed on it, burst into flame. Hubbard fed it twigs until it was a considerable fire in its own right, then pushed it into the brush pile. In minutes the whole brush pile was aflame, sending smoke and sparks upward and with its heat driving Rima and the Christophers back to the water's edge.

From a silver bucket Hubbard produced a bottle of sparkling wine and popped the cork, which splashed in the lake.

"This is actual French champagne, rather than good old Schaumwein like the druids drank," Hubbard said with a wink, filling glasses. "Krug 1929, courtesy of Uncle Paulus."

"Actually the druids drank mead," Lori said wanly. She was not yet recovered from the night before. Her hand shook, spilling wine from the glass.

They drank the wine and watched the fire burn itself out. After supper, at which Paulus flirted chastely with Rima like an uncle with a niece and Hubbard held forth on Celtic folklore, the two young people went for a walk.

"Your family is very jolly," Rima said. "Are they always this way?"

"My father and Uncle Paulus, yes. My mother too, usually."

Rima said, "Look, northern lights."

Suddenly the northern sky was irradiated with color—the whole spectrum, from horizon to horizon. Rima had never seen such a display. Gigantic brushes might have been dipped into lakes of paint by the gods and wiped across the heavens.

"Oh, beautiful," she said.

"Solar wind," Paul said, "mixing with the earth's magnetic field."

"You are your father's son," Rima said, but she threw her arms around Paul and pasted her body to his. "It's the druids, you fool."

Clouds of pink, plumes of green, columns of orange, swaths of purple. Rima gasped as each appeared.

"Where is the sailboat from here?" she asked.

"Not far."

"Then let's sail, Paul. Imagine seeing this from the surface of the sea with no other light, no other people. Just us."

The wind was brisk. Paul took the yawl out to sea with the jib and the mizzen sail. In the after-daylight they ghosted through small boats that still stood offshore, sails lowered, crews and passengers transfixed by the aurora borealis. When they were a couple of miles from shore, out of sight of the other boats, Paul dropped the sails and let the yawl drift. The aurora continued to explode. When he was a small child his parents had taken him to the studio of an eccentric painter. This man made his art by throwing whole buckets of paint onto a large canvas, then energetically shoving the colors around with a push broom. The flying paint, the vivid splashes, the joyful artist had been delightful sights for a child.

"How far are we from the Arctic circle?" Rima asked.

"I'm not sure," Paul replied. "You can ask my father when we go back."

"Go back? Who said anything about going back?"

Sails down, they sat in the bow with their arms around each other. The northern lights were sometimes visible from Berlin, but this was unlike anything Rima had ever seen before. It was a white night on the Baltic, at this hour not so much light as pale darkness. Had the earth tilted, had the solar wind blown itself out?

"I feel as if someone has painted cataracts on my eyes," Rima said.

The display began to fade. "Look, the lights going out," she said. "How can such a thing happen so fast?"

Mahican pitched gently in the low chop, water thumping against the hull. They couldn't see the shore or any evidence of its existence. Rügen did not have enough electric lights to make a glow in the sky and the moon had not yet risen.

"Where would we go if we put up the sails and just went?" Rima asked.

"The wind is from the west," Paul replied. "We'd end up in Danzig, maybe."

"Not Danzig, please."

"Lithuania, then, if we used the helm or started from farther out to sea. Maybe Sweden. Or Helsinki."

"Helsinki sounds good. Can you ski?"

"Yes, but it would take a long time to get there, we'd be hungry and thirsty, and it would be a long beat back."

"Beat?"

"We'd have to sail against the wind. Lots of zigzags."

Rima drew him closer. "Can we go farther out and just let it sail? Can you lash the helm? I don't mean all the way to Finland."

"Why?"

"To make the lights come back on," she said.

"The aurora borealis?"

"Something similar."

Paul did as Rima asked. They were lying together on the deck, Rima's hair unbound, their clothes scattered around them, when the searchlight of the S-boat hit them an hour or two later. This light was so intense that it seemed to make a noise like a huge captive insect. There was just the light—no siren, no loud hailing. Also laughter from the darkness. The sailors were enjoying what they had discovered.

Rima grabbed her clothes and scurried below. As she ran, the searchlight followed her. The siren sounded. Then the loudhailer blared.

"Heave to!"

Only the mizzen sail was rigged. Still naked, Paul brought the boat about into the wind and dropped the sail. Someone aboard the S-boat tossed him a line. He made it fast, then put on his trousers and shirt and the American sneakers he had been wearing.

"What boat is that?" the man on the loudhailer asked.

"*Mahican*, out of Rügen."

This was a magic name to the secret police, who were aboard all coastal patrol boats and also had boats of their own. Paul knew that many questions would be asked, that none of his answers would be believed. The episode could go on for hours, or that there might not be an end to it. It was strictly forbidden to sail this far from land at night.

The S-boat launched a small boat. The boarding party consisted of an overage navy lieutenant with a stomach and a petty officer with a submachine gun. A third man wearing a uniform with the blank collar patch of the secret police came down the rope ladder. As the small boat came alongside *Mahican*, the searchlight switched off. The secret policeman was in shadow. Paul could not see his face.

"Papers!"

Paul had no papers to show the boarding party. Neither he nor Rima had brought them. The papers for the boat were kept in a locked drawer in Hubbard's desk. He told them this.

"No papers?" said the navy lieutenant, amazed. This was a serious infraction.

Rima appeared, fully clothed. Her hair was braided. She was composed—frozen would have been the better word.

"Explain," the lieutenant said.

"We sailed on an impulse, without bringing documents."

"An impulse." The lieutenant's face was stony, but his tone let Paul know that he knew what sort of impulse he was talking about. He snapped his fingers. "Like that?" he said. "That was your impulse?"

"We saw the aurora borealis," Paul said. "We decided to sail out and look at it. We didn't think. We apologize."

"Names?"

Paul and Rima supplied the information the lieutenant needed. This included the usual dates and addresses and the names of their parents and grandparents. The lieutenant wrote them out by the light of a flashlight. He spelled Christopher with a K. Paul corrected him.

"That's not a German spelling," the lieutenant said.

"I'm an American citizen."

The lieutenant was surprised. "You sound like a German. You look like a German. This girl is also an American?"

"No," said the secret policeman in a voice of authority, breaking his silence. "She is a quarter-Jew. We know all about her. You, Christopher, where were you taking her?"

The voice belonged to Major Stutzer.

"Nowhere," Paul said. "We were just sailing."

"You were just sailing along," Stutzer said, "boy and girl enjoying the evening, is that it?"

"That is correct, Major."

"And merrily breaking the laws of the Reich as if they do not apply to Jews and American citizens. Is that also correct?"

"We had no such intention," Paul said.

"We will see about your intentions," Stutzer said. "You, Jewess. Did you steal this boat?"

"No, Major."

"Before this is over, you may wish that you had." To the navy lieutenant Stutzer said, "Take them in tow. I will stay aboard the sailboat."

The navy lieutenant said, "You want to stay aboard this sailboat while it is under tow?"

"Absolutely."

"Very well, Major."

The navy lieutenant's face was expressionless. "Make it so," he said to the sailor, who fastened a line to *Mahican*.

FOUR

1

The S-boat did not finish its patrol until dawn. Long before that, Rima was desperately seasick and so was Major Stutzer. The heavily armed patrol vessel, more than a hundred feet long, was driven by two engines capable of making forty-five knots. It spewed diesel fumes that were breathed in and vomited out by the three people aboard the yawl. In the S-boat's twin boiling wakes, *Mahican* yawed and pitched and shipped water. Paul had observed many S-boats under way in the Baltic and had never before seen one moving this fast unless it was in pursuit of a high-speed target. Stutzer knelt in the stern, retching. His tight, tailored uniform was soaking wet. He had lost his cap with its death's head badge. His brilliantined hair stood up in spikes. Paul had already lashed Rima to the main mast to keep her from being catapulted overboard. Now he secured Stutzer to the mizzen mast. It occurred to Paul that Stutzer may have become the first member of the secret police ever to be tied up by someone he had just arrested. He was too sick to protest. Paul checked the knots and made sure there was not so much slack in the line as to make it possible for Stutzer to fall overboard and be dragged behind *Mahican*. The last thing he and Rima needed was to dock at the navy pier with a drowned SS major in tow.

Paul, queasy himself, was afraid that *Mahican*'s wooden hull, which was at least twice as old as he was, might break up under the stress of being towed at high speed. Stutzer could not command the S-boat's captain to slow down because he had no means of communicating with

him apart from shouting into the slipstream, which was useless, or ges-
ticulating, which was hopeless because he was aft of the S-boat and all
its lookouts were gazing forward or to port or starboard.

As soon as the S-boat was tied up at the navy dock, Stutzer scram-
bled ashore and demanded that the gangplank be lowered. As soon as
it was he dashed aboard. Rima and Paul heard him screaming at the
lieutenant. His voice was shrill. He threatened investigations, interro-
gations that would reveal the hidden reasons for this outrage. At the
very least, a long term of imprisonment was inevitable. Execution,
even. The middle-aged sailor who brought mugs of sugary coffee to
Paul and Rima grinned happily as he listened to this tirade.

The apprentices, wearing civilian clothes, had been waiting on the
dock for the S-boat. They too listened as their chief berated the captain.
As yet they had no orders regarding Paul and Rima, therefore they
ignored them. Stutzer went on and on, and although Paul could not see
him, the memory of an enraged Stutzer uttering screams filled with spit
formed in his mind. He had seen Stutzer in this condition once before,
on the day when Lori slapped his face in the Kursaal Café. Had Paulus
been captain of this vessel instead of the plump lieutenant, Paul thought,
Stutzer would long since have been marched below in manacles if he had
not walked the plank.

At last Stutzer came ashore. He was still wet and it was clear that salt
water and bile had ruined forever the fine wool of his beautifully tailored uniform. He was still furious. The captain of the S-boat had had
his joke. Now he had an enemy. In a shout, Stutzer gave orders to his
men, then disappeared. The apprentices conferred. The sailor who had
brought the coffee was still with Paul and Rima on the dock.

Paul said, "What happens to our boat?"

"We may want to keep it, it's such a nice one," the sailor said.

"I mean really."

"You'll probably get it back from the navy, if the navy holds onto it.
After all, what have you done that's so terrible?"

The apprentices approached, expressionless, marching in step. The
sailor took back the empty coffee mugs and made a face. He acknowledged no authority but the navy's.

At secret police headquarters in Bergen, Paul and Rima were taken not to separate cells as they had expected, but to a small room with a window, and told to sit in chairs at opposite ends of a table. When Stutzer returned, more than an hour later, he wore civilian clothes—a blue double-breasted pinstripe suit with a white shirt and a silk polka-dot tie the color of red vermouth. Exactly the right amount of starched shirt cuff, fastened by an opal cufflink, protruded from the sleeve of his jacket. The handkerchief in his breast pocket was artfully folded and the indispensable party badge pinned to his left lapel was in exactly the right place. He wore a gold watch on the inside of his wrist, like an aviator. His oiled hair was once again combed back flat on his narrow skull. His black shoes were highly polished and when he sat down, Rima saw that he was wearing gray silk socks with blue clocks, pulled tight over his ankles by garters.

Stutzer called her into his office, leaving Paul in the holding room alone. He ignored her for several minutes—the indispensable ritual—while he read a single sheet of paper. Then, suddenly, he struck. Decisiveness in his every movement, he wrote something on the paper with flying pen, blotted the ink, picked up the telephone on his desk, and snapped out an order. A man came in and took the sheet of paper away. Only then did Stutzer look at Rima. His eyes were peculiar. Pupil and iris were nearly the same shade of very pale blue. This made them seem colorless.

"Please do not imagine that you are under my protection," Stutzer said.

Rima had no idea what, if anything, he wanted her to say in reply. Why should she think, even for the shortest moment, that this man would protect her? From what could he possibly protect her except himself?

Stutzer said, "What was Paul Christopher's plan?"

His plan? Rima said, "I don't understand, Major."

"It is a simple question," Stutzer said. "What was his intention last night? Where was he taking you?"

"For a sail. It was my idea, because of the northern lights."

"You just went for a romantic sail under the aurora borealis. And let him stick his Aryan cock into you. Did you also suck it?"

Rima lowered her eyes and said nothing.

"Where was he taking you?" Stutzer asked. "It's a simple question."

"Truly, Major, just for a sail. No destination was discussed except a return to Rügen."

"The two of you agreed to return to Rügen?"

"Not in so many words. It was taken for granted that we would do so."

Stutzer continued to stare. This was not the answer he wanted. He began to breathe audibly. His face reddened, his eyes widened. Again he was motionless, not even blinking. Suddenly he screamed at her.

"Tell me the truth or you will wish you had! You will wish you had never been born, you. . . ."

He called her names, he described depraved sexual acts he believed she had committed, he repeated the details of her father's shaming, he recited her ancestry including the names of her great-grandparents, he described the dark-skinned men her mother was sleeping with in Buenos Aires and the things they did to her and she to them. The entire tirade was delivered while every part of Stutzer's body was perfectly motionless except his twisted face and popping eyes and his tongue, which was visible, red and narrow and making words inside his wide-open mouth. Despite the raving it was a remarkable demonstration of knowledge. He had memorized everything about Rima even though she was just one of what must have been hundreds of suspects. He was telling her that he knew everything, that he was capable of anything.

Stutzer stopped shrieking as suddenly as he had begun. One moment he was rabid, the next he was composed and speaking in a calm, even genteel tone of voice.

"Now, Miss, you must tell me the truth," he said. "This information is vital to the Reich. It is more important than you can possibly know. Where was your American going to take you?"

Rima was disoriented, nauseated. Once again she could not control her trembling body. Against her every conviction, she was overcome by the desire to placate this man. But she was struck dumb. She couldn't form words. Stutzer had cut the circuit between her brain and her tongue.

He said, actually smiling at her with small crooked teeth, "Think carefully, my dear. All you have to do is tell the truth."

2

It was midnight before Hubbard discovered that *Mahican* was missing. Paulus advised him to wait till morning before worrying. After all, it was Midsummer night, the moon was up. No doubt Paul and Rima had sailed out to look at the aurora borealis. If their minds were elsewhere, the current might have carried them quite a long way. Possibly they had come ashore somewhere else on the island and at this moment were probably leaping through a bonfire. Even if they were still adrift, the sea was calm. Paul was a good sailor, the girl was capable. Patience was the thing. By dawn the innocents would more than likely be discreetly asleep in separate rooms.

Paulus saw no need to discuss this situation with Hilde. Hubbard could think of any number of reasons not to discuss it with Lori. She would assume that Paul had been arrested again, that this time he might be gone for good. Lori was fearless no longer. How could she be, how could anyone be? They lived in a world in which all the signposts had been taken down.

Hubbard rose at first light, as usual, and when he went downstairs he found Paulus waiting for him in the hall. Paulus beckoned him outside. Paulus had already been down to the mooring.

"They're not back," he said. "No sign of the boat."

"This is not like Paul," Hubbard said.

"No, but perhaps he is a different Paul. This is the first time he's sailed out to look at the northern lights with a beautiful girl on board. I'll make inquiries."

What Paulus said he was going to do, he did immediately. He got out his army model bicycle, put the clips around his trousers cuffs, and rode off. In Paulus's opinion, sunrise was the best time of day to go calling. People were more likely to tell the truth when they had just opened their eyes. In war and on maneuvers he had always gone out to talk to his troopers before reveille. They said what really was on their minds when they were half asleep and hungry and had a useless morning erection and the urge to urinate.

Hubbard was helpless to take action. *Mahican* was their only boat. No one on Rügen would loan him another or tell him anything they knew. The local police, who for long years had been so affable, so fond of Lori and so proud of her heroic uncle and father and cousins, so tolerant of Lori's foreign husband, were no longer approachable. They had stopped looking any member of the family in the eye on the day Lori slapped Stutzer's face.

At about seven o'clock, Paulus returned. He had talked to a friend who was a retired navy captain. Word of the hilarious joke that the S-boat captain had played on Stutzer had spread through the naval community that morning before coffee was boiled.

"So the report is that *Mahican* survived being towed all night at flank speed, and that the children are wet but safe," Paulus said.

"Then where are they?"

"That's the rest of the report. They were taken into custody. Stutzer is said to think that Paul was trying to smuggle the girl out of Germany. She has a Jewish father, it seems, but for some reason she's not classified as a Jew herself, or at lest not a full Jew."

Hubbard nodded. He did not trust himself to speak.

"The navy has impounded your boat," Paulus continued. "In their log, the recovery of *Mahican* and its passengers was a rescue, nothing more. You can claim your boat as soon as Stutzer goes back to Berlin and his mind is on something else."

"I wonder when that will be."

"Soon," Paulus said. "That's the impression I got." His tone was grave. He said nothing about the exact condition in which Paul and Rima had been discovered by the delighted crew of the S-boat. Hubbard, he knew, shared everything with Lori or with his manuscript. Paulus realized how exceedingly unwise this was and how impossible it was to explain this to Hubbard.

Lori was still asleep. When she woke around eleven, they chatted while she drank the cup of tea that Hubbard brought to her. When she was fully awake Hubbard told her the news, as tersely as Paulus had told it to him.

Her voice flat, Lori said, "That wretched girl."

"It's too early in the day to decide who's to blame," Hubbard said. "The question is, what do we do now."

Lori knew immediately what to do. It was the only thing to do, and it could only be done in Berlin.

She said, "There is nothing to be done in Rügen. Stutzer will take Paul to Berlin."

"I agree," Hubbard said. "Berlin is the place. We'll get O. G. on the case. Paulus can keep an eye on things here. We should leave now—pack up and go at once."

Lori said, "It takes too long to drive. I'll take the train."

Hubbard was nonplussed. "Take the train? Why?"

"Because it's faster than the car. Because Stutzer may stop the car and confiscate it."

"But you'd be alone when you arrived. You'd have to wait till I got there."

There was little a woman could do in the Reich without the permission of her husband.

She said, "Hubbard, the train is *faster*!"

Hubbard capitulated. Minutes later Lori emerged, fully dressed in a Paris suit Hubbard had not seen before, looking beautiful apart from the dead eyes. The suit looked expensive. Hubbard wondered how Lori had saved so much out of her household purse and why she had spent what she had saved on couture. It was out of character.

On the train, Lori took a window seat in a second-class compartment—one of Hubbard's Yankee economies—and gazed out the window. She saw her own reflection superimposed on the drab landscape as it flowed by. Once or twice she thought she caught a glimpse of the Horch speeding down a country road in the distance, but she knew she must be wrong. She forbade her mind to communicate with her, but all the way to Berlin it played with the idea that no one on earth could save Paul except Reinhard Heydrich.

It was still early afternoon when Lori arrived in Berlin. She had no means of contacting Heydrich unless she chose to walk unannounced into No. 8 Prinz-Albrechtstrasse and ask to see him. He had always lain in wait for her. She, the prey, had never imagined that she would want to see him, so no telephone number or address or secret semaphore was necessary. She never knew when he might turn up. He loved to surprise her. Once while Hubbard was lost in his writing, Heydrich had called at the Christophers' apartment disguised as a municipal inspector, and in what he considered a hilarious prank, lectured Lori in a parade-ground voice on imaginary violations of various building codes. On another occasion he had had Hubbard and Paul taken into custody in the late morning, then arrived shortly afterward with an elaborate three-wine lunch packed in hampers and a squad of uniformed servants to cook and serve it. Because Heydrich always seemed to know whether she was at home and if she was not, where she was likely to be, Lori assumed that he had planted a spy in her building. Whoever was observing her and reporting her movements had to live on a lower floor. The Christophers' apartment was on the second floor, Miss Wetzel's on the first, with none below her on the ground floor and a blind veteran of the eastern front living alone across the hall. Miss Wetzel was always home, and she had nothing to do all day but listen for footsteps on the stairs and gaze through the judas hole in her door. Lori's clothing would tell the spy where she was going—riding habit meant the Tiergarten, a plain dress, shopping, a better dress a social engagement, a suitcase, alarm.

Lori went straight home from the station in a taxi. She went upstairs, sat down at the piano, and in case Miss Wetzel somehow missed her arrival, played a passage from a Liszt sonata. Then, still wearing her Paris suit, Lori clattered in high heels down the stairs, catching a glimpse of Miss Wetzel's watery blue eye in the judas hole, and strode off in the direction of the Tiergarten. Within fifteen minutes a large black car drew up beside her. A door opened. Lori got into the empty backseat. The usual pair of SS troopers occupied the front seats. Heydrich had sent a couple of underlings to collect her just as he might have sent them to make the day's fiftieth arrest. No words were exchanged. No siren or klaxon sounded, either, but the traffic parted before the Daimler on its way to the hunting lodge as if a regiment of invisible policemen were directing traffic.

3

In secret police headquarters on Rügen, Stutzer was still awaiting Rima's answer to his last question when one of the apprentices entered the room and whispered something in his ear. Stutzer broke eye contact with Rima. The look on his face, half cajolery and half naked threat, changed abruptly to naked rage. He leapt to his feet and rushed from the room. Through the thick door Rima heard the shrill noises of his tantrum.

Minutes later, Rima and Paul were released from custody. No explanation was given; in fact no one said a word to either of them. They were taken in a car to the station, provided with tickets, and escorted aboard the fast train to Berlin. Their luggage was already in their first-class compartment. So were the apprentices, fresh-faced young fellows in blue serge suits that still smelled of the flatiron. Rima had never imagined that secret policemen, trained to torture and kill, could be so young, or look so little like brutes. These two looked not much older than Paul and no less harmless. You could picture their mothers combing their wet hair in the morning and giving them pocket money before sending them out into the world.

When Rima took down her rucksack and disappeared into the lavatory, one of the young men followed her. He waited outside the door until she emerged in one of her navy-blue schoolgirl costumes, her hair in a braid down her back and a book in her hand. Paul remained as he was, where he was, until she returned.

In German she said, "Shall we read to each other to practice our English?"

She opened an American novel and began to read aloud. The apprentices gave them searching looks, then feigned loss of interest. They were undercover, after all.

With no change of tone, as if still reading, Rima said, "Let's test the English of these louts."

"Okay," Paul replied, eyes fixed on the page before them. "Do you think they're as likeable as they look?"

"They are the big brothers of your friends from the Tiergarten. In my opinion they're both Jewish. Characteristic simian skulls, and look at those noses." The apprentices made no sign that they understood these insults.

As if reading from her book, Rima said, "I think we can speak freely in this language. What happened to you back there?"

"Nothing. I was left alone in the room the whole time. You?"

"I was questioned by the madman. He was beautifully dressed."

"What did he want to know?"

"Our secret destination. He gave the impression that he already knew everything. He just wanted confirmation that we were trying to escape to a foreign country."

"He said that?"

"He was sure we had a plan."

"And what did you say?"

"Nothing. He gave me very little chance to talk. It was like watching a man have an epileptic fit. I was scared to death."

"Then why didn't you tell him whatever he wanted to hear?"

"I might have. You have no idea what he's like, red in the face, showering spit, shrieking like a stuck pig. What was he going to do next? But while I was trying to think of something that would do you no harm but not make him beat me or shoot me, someone came in and whispered in his ear. I heard some of what was whispered, just words—'Berlin, highest authority, immediately.' Obviously he was being given orders. The messenger expected death—you could see it in his eyes."

"How did Stutzer react?"

"Another fit. He leaped up and rushed out of the room. Then he started screaming in the hallway. Right after that they took us to the train."

"I wonder what happened."

"My love, don't you understand?" Rima said. "Somebody rescued us."

"Who, for heaven's sake?"

"Someone with power over Stutzer. Someone in Berlin."

Paul looked baffled. Rima wanted to say, *Think!* But she looked into his eyes instead and saw that he did not require instruction.

Paul said, "It can't be true." He turned his head and looked out the window.

Rima said, "Then there must be some other explanation."

She closed the book. They rode the rest of the way to Berlin in silence, They parted at the station. One of the apprentices followed Rima home, the other Paul. Then they vanished back into the apparatus.

4

Late that afternoon, as soon as she was set free from the hunting lodge, Lori went straight to the American embassy and told O. G. everything. The confession was a rite of exorcism. Demons flew from her mouth. She breathed naturally again, without thought. For the first time in months her lungs gave her heart enough oxygen. O. G. listened without expression, and when she was finished offered neither blame nor sympathy, but sat for a long moment with his fingertips touching and his eyes fixed on a point a few inches above Lori's head.

He said, "Forgive me for asking, but am I right in supposing that you haven't given Heydrich what he desires?"

"Of course I haven't. But in his imagination this is a courtship, and all the usual things occur. The man tries, the maiden demurs. But however. . . ."

O. G. held up a hand: tell me no more. He said, "It looks as though he's put a price on what he wants. Paul goes free, and maybe Hubbard too. You go to Heydrich."

"Clearly that's what he has in mind, but you can never be sure with him, and he would never come right out and tell me that that was the arrangement."

"He wants to hide his hand? Why?"

"Because in his own mind he's not the sort of man who pays for it. He loves me, he says. He is dizzy with love. It's an operetta. What he wants is sweet surrender. Quid pro quo would ruin everything."

"I see," O. G. said. "Then consider this. If in fact Heydrich is using Paul as a way to frighten you into making him a gift of yourself. . . ."

"If in fact he is doing this?" Lori said. "I just told you that's what he's doing."

"I heard you, and I believe you," O. G. said. "And since this seems to be the case, it seems to me there are two solutions. First, you surrender. I assume that is not a possibility. Second, we find a way to get Paul out of harm's way as quick as we can."

"In what way is that a possibility?"

"If Heydrich thought you were, forgive me, testing his love, he might let Paul just sail away."

"On the *Bremen*? It's a German ship. Paul would still be in Heydrich's power. If I didn't surrender in the four days it takes to steam from Bremerhaven to New York, they would throw him overboard."

"Yes. But he has to go on a German ship. Otherwise Heydrich loses all control."

"Precisely. Do you imagine he's going to let Paul go if he does not already have what he wants?"

"I need hardly tell you that if he has what he wants he will do as he pleases," O. G. said. "What I imagine, Lori, is that you are a resourceful woman."

"And Heydrich is a monster of resourcefulness. You have no idea."

"I'm sure you're right. But this is the best I can do in the way of advice even though I have given the same counsel several times already."

Lori said, "Is it really as hopeless as that? Surely you have ways."

Slowly, O. G. shook his large shaggy head. "I'm sorry," he said. "But I do not."

For years Lori, like many others, assumed that O. G. was chief of the embassy's espionage operations. She was wrong; despite his air of conspiracy he was, officially, as cherubic as he seemed. It was true that he was a gatherer of information, but the larger truth was that in 1939 the United States of America had no foreign intelligence service, and therefore posted no political spies in its Berlin embassy or anywhere else in the world. Diplomatists such as O. G. gathered political fact and rumor; military attachés found out what they could about the Reich's armed forces. But there were no thugs, no letters in invisible ink hidden in hollow trees, no blackmail or murder or kidnapping or even bribery. No intelligence service was rich enough to match the bribes the National Socialist German Workers' Party routinely paid to its important members in the form of property confiscated from Jews and other official enemies of the state. Secrets of the Reich sometimes fell into American laps. True, O. G. gave his dinner parties and played tennis and cards with high officials and hoped for confidences. Americans seldom went so far as to adopt the British practice of trying to jimmy locked tongues by asking rude, persistent, detailed questions of their hosts or guests. They were unfailingly polite, seemingly as neutral individually as their country was, even though they knew that war was coming and America could not possibly stay out of it.

Lori said, "If you're as helpless as you say you are, why am I here?"

"You came for advice," O. G. replied. "I've given you advice. If I didn't think it was feasible I wouldn't suggest it."

"What if they won't let him off the ship in New York?"

"A foreign ship berthed in an American port is not an embassy. American authorities can come aboard in defense of an American citizen."

"In other words, 'Trust me and don't worry your pretty little head.'"

O. G. swallowed the taunt. "Yes to the trust, no to the rest," he said. "Of course you have a right to be worried. You have a lot to be worried about, if I may say so."

"Even if Paul gets off in New York he will be out in the open, unguarded and exposed. Heydrich has men everywhere."

"True. But America is a big place, and when Paul arrives in New York he will be in the United States of America and under the protection of the Hubbards and their friends. He will be beyond Heydrich's reach."

"Nothing is beyond his reach."

O. G. made no answer to this. What Lori said was true enough, at least in theory. Heydrich was young. He was exalted by the power that ruthlessness had brought to him. He was certainly ruthless enough to kidnap an American boy on American soil and somehow smuggle him back to Germany as a way of gluing a mistress to him. But in the United States this could not happen under cover of silence. The police would tell the press, the press would tell the world. Heydrich did have superiors even if there were only two of them, and Himmler and Hitler would not be pleased by the unfavorable publicity. It would also turn Heydrich into a laughingstock—a man who tried to make a woman love him kidnapping her son.

O. G.'s sinuous mind played for a moment with that scenario. Was it actually possible to destroy or at least diminish this fat-assed monster at the cost of sacrificing his best friend's wife and the boy who was his godson? Could such an exchange be defined, if not defended as a moral action? O. G. liked moral conundrums; at Yale, ethics had been his favorite course. It instilled in him the habit of thinking like a spymaster long before he became, a few years hence, the most powerful one in the world.

Lori's eyes, therefore her mind, were focused on something outside the room.

"Lori," O. G. said, as if awakening her. He realized that was exactly what he was doing. He had to speak her name again, sharply, before she heard him and returned from wherever she had been. He decided that he must speak to her in a way that would keep her mind focused.

"We've got to agree on a plan," he said.

"So you keep saying," Lori replied. "But they can take Paul anytime. They can take any one of us, or all of us."

"I don't think they'll do that," O. G. said. "Obviously Heydrich has nothing to gain if he makes you hate him. . . ."

"*Hate* him? I'd assassinate him tomorrow if someone would show me how to do it."

"Maybe someone will. Meanwhile, there is Paul to think about. Also, if I may say so, there is Hubbard to think about. Not to mention yourself."

He looked her straight in the eye as he talked. And as he talked, she slipped away again. Her eyes dulled, the expression left her face. O. G. realized that there was no prospect of ever reviving the person she used to be. She had lost hope.

He said, "We're going to get this done, my dear. Chin up."

No response from Lori. He feared for Hubbard.

He said, "Lori, think about our talk. If you need to, come talk to me again. Come as often as you want, any time of the day or night. But confide in no one else. And I implore you, no confessions to Hubbard. It would be the end of him."

He might as well have been talking to the chair Lori sat in, her lovely legs crossed at the knees.

5

"Can they hear whispers over their microphones?" Rima asked. "Can they hear me at certain moments? Is someone in earphones writing everything down? How do you spell. . . ." Much more softly than usual she uttered the howl of joy she made when having an orgasm. "Before you, I had no idea that I had such noises in me," she said.

"What did you expect?"

"Something more ladylike," she said.

They laughed in whispers. Even if there had been no Stutzer and no Heydrich, Paul thought, Rima would have contrived this world of whispers. She was alive when they were alone together, never otherwise, she said. Now they met every morning in Paul's room. Rima came up the back stairs while it was still dark, even before Hubbard got up. Paul met her at the kitchen door, in case she was surprised by Lori, who roamed through the apartment most of the night. Rima brought oranges, bananas, tangerines, apricots. These were exotic items in Berlin. He had no notion where she found them. "I know where the lemon tree blooms," Rima said. The fruit was incredibly sweet. They kissed with sugary mouths. They licked sugar and citrus off each other's fingers. Rima took the peels with her when she left, as if Paul were a fugitive in hiding and the peels were evidence of his existence.

"It's amazing what the party has done in six short years," Rima said. "They have made this Reich of theirs into a world in which there's a reason for everything. All is explained by their theories. Soon everything any citizen of the Reich needs to know will be printed on the back of identity cards. In doubt about the Jews? Confused about Strength through Joy? Can't remember the Leader's immortal words about something or other? Just turn the card over and you will know what to think, what to say."

It was reckless to meet as they did, but they agreed that if they did not take the chance they would lose the thing they could not live without. Each wasted moment was gone forever, said Rima. It continually astonished Paul, who had imagined romantic love as something on a page of its own—bittersweet moments, lovely light falling on a fully dressed woman, chaste kisses in a garden—that physical intimacy could create such wild emotion, such desperation, such fear of loss, such joy, such moments of hopelessness. Both he and Rima were sure that sooner or later someone would burst into their room and put a stop to their happiness. Even before the dictatorship this would have happened. Parents would have done it, or clergy, or servants would have informed on them—the eternal love police and their snitches. "But until it does happen," Rima whispered, "we mustn't waste a moment. Better to remember what we've done than what we were afraid to do. Oh, far better."

Paul had no inkling that plans were still being made by those who loved him to save him by separating him from Rima forever. The fact that his parents never knocked on the door, that his mother—even Hubbard in his writing trance—could not help but hear Rima's trills of pleasure puzzled Rima.

"Maybe they want us to be happy," Paul said.

"Then they're very unusual parents," Rima said. "My father would shoot you with his Mauser army pistol if he knew what goes on in this bed."

In the week that Paul and Rima had been back in Berlin, they had heard nothing from the secret police, nor had they seen any sign of them. Stutzer had given Rima no further spy missions. But of course they were being watched. A hand in a leather glove could fall on his shoulder or hers at any time. They could be taken away separately or together. They might be released again, they might not be. They might be beaten. Rima's father had been punched in the face during the first moment of his first interview with the secret police. His nose—of course his nose—was broken. It was their way of telling him that he was no longer entitled to respect and never would be again, that he had no protection, that they could kill him if they wished and throw him into the gutter to be picked up by the night sweepers. Her father had never actually told her what had happened. The shame of it was too much for him. But she saw his smashed nose and his black-and-blue face, and she knew. Anyone would have known. They were meant to know.

Rima was back on Miss Wetzel's payroll. The coins she earned for walking Blümchen paid for the fruit she brought to Paul's room. On the day after she returned from Rügen, Rima had called on Miss Wetzel to apologize for causing her to worry about the dog. Rima already knew that Blümchen was alive and well because she and Paul could hear the little dog barking excitedly in the apartment below. No doubt, at certain moments, it could hear them.

Miss Wetzel had been afraid that something had happened to Rima. But the policeman who brought Blümchen home had explained everything—how poor Rima had witnessed a crime and was giving evidence, how she had asked that they bring Blümchen home so that her mistress would not worry about her. Such a thoughtful young lady! Blümchen missed her so! She barked her name, listen! Would Rima be interested in walking Blümchen again? At noon and in the evening, yes, but not in the early morning, Rima answered. She was studying a new subject and her mind was at its clearest when the day was new.

And now Rima and Paul had oranges and tangerines and bananas in bed, sometimes even a mango. And each other, too. Wasn't life wonderful? Rima whispered. Wasn't it lovely?

6

On Saturday evening O. G. invited all three Christophers to dinner at Horcher's, his favorite restaurant. It was also the favorite restaurant of the ruling class, and like O. G.'s dinner parties, it was thronged with women in fashionable gowns and military officers and civilian officials wearing what appeared to be the entire vast wardrobe of German uniforms. Several of the men greeted O. G. cordially. The Christophers were snubbed. Invisible.

"This place has an interesting new clientèle," Lori said. "Are we here to be poisoned?"

O. G. ordered the prix fixe menu for all along with two bottles of wine, one German, one French. He ordered the waiter to let Paul do the tasting. O. G. watched, shrewd blue eyes behind round pince-nez, as the wines were poured and Paul tasted them, chewing a piece of bread between the white and the red. The bottles were wrapped in napkins, hiding the labels.

"What's the verdict?" O. G. asked.

"I don't like Gewürztraminer," Paul said.

"Why ever not?"

"It tastes the way dried rose petals smell. But the red wine is delicious."

"Good palate," O. G. said. "Nuits Saint-Georges 1929. Drink only wine made from the pinot grape, my boy, and you'll live a happy life."

By the time the appetizer was served their table had ceased to be an object of curiosity. More important diners had more important things to think and talk about. Like all fashionable restaurants, Horcher's had its own sound—pleased with itself rather than pleasurable—few arpeggios in the bedlam of its conversation, no diminuendos. It had made a different noise when Hubbard first knew it during the Weimar Republic. No doubt the sound changed with the regime, he remarked. What did the rest of them think?

"Oh, Hubbard," Lori said.

"Strings in Wilhelmine days, saxophones during Weimar, drums and tubas now," Hubbard said, undeterred.

A rotund waiter approached. Under any regime he would have been a spy. Eavesdropping was his métier, along with taking orders and carrying plates. O. G. changed the subject as he drew near.

He said, "You're all coming to the Fourth of July party at the embassy, I take it?"

"Wouldn't miss it for the world," Hubbard said.

"I'm the official host this year," O. G. said. "The ambassador is on sick leave."

He thanked the waiter, who had been fussing with the table setting and examining the Christophers, and he went away. Behind his lenses, one of O. G.'s eyes winked at Paul.

Paul said, "I wonder if I can bring a guest on the Fourth."

"Of course you can," O. G. said. "Everyone's welcome on the anniversary of the greatest event in the history of civilization."

Lori said, "Paul, whom do you have in mind?"

"Miss Alexa Kaltenbach," Paul said, using Rima's actual name.

"You can't be serious," Lori said.

"But I am," Paul said.

He was surprised by the look of bitter disapproval on his mother's face.

"Lovely child," Hubbard said. "You'll like her, O. G. Looks like Evangeline."

"Looks like who?" said O. G.

"You know, Longfellow. 'The murmuring pines and the hemlocks, standing like Druids of eld.' "

"Oh, that Evangeline," O. G. said. "Kaltenbach? Any relation to the famous surgeon?"

"His daughter," Paul said.

"Ah. Poor fellow. He's had a bad time of it. Bring her along, Paul. She'll want a new hat. We'll be in the garden as usual, weather permitting. Hope she likes fireworks."

"Believe me, she does," Lori said.

O. G. called for the bill and signed it. He exchanged pleasant words with the waiter. Was his son well? Extremely well. He was in the Luftwaffe, a parachutist corporal serving in Austria. Lori listened with a frozen expression. O. G. gave her a warning look. You never knew what she might say. The waiter noticed. He said, "A pleasure to see you, Baronesse, if I may be permitted to say so. It has been a long time since we have received you and your husband in Horcher's." His eyes swiveled to Hubbard, to whom he said nothing, then back to Lori as he backed away, bowing.

O. G. had picked them up in an embassy car, an enormous sixteen-cylinder Packard sedan driven by a silent chauffeur. On the ride home O. G. chatted with Paul about baseball, a game Paul hardly knew.

"You should take it up next time you're home," O. G. said. "It's the most difficult of all games when it's played the right way. In fact going out for baseball is the best reason for going to school in America. Your father was a pretty handy first baseman with those long arms and legs. Hit the ball hard and far. Struck out a lot, though."

When the Packard pulled up at the Christophers' building, O. G. got out and walked them to the door. The males shook hands. O. G. kissed the air near Lori's cheeks, his hands light on her shoulders.

"Everything is falling into place," he said into her ear. "Bring the boy's toothbrush to the party."

To Paul, who was bringing up the rear, Lori said, "Run upstairs, dear, and get Schatzi. Poor dog must be miserable."

"Dear God, that's three days from now," Lori said, after the door closed behind Paul.

"Yes," O. G replied. "Chin up."

"But he doesn't know."

"Keep it that way."

Hubbard said, "He may make a fuss."

"Paul?" O. G. said. "I don't believe it."

"He's in love."

"He's in heat," Lori said.

Hubbard looked annoyed at his wife, something that happened every five years or so. He said, "Whatever you call it, Hannelore, he's not going to want to leave this girl."

O. G. said, "This is the Kaltenbach girl?"

Hubbard nodded. "She's quite wonderful," he said. "You'll see."

"She's also doomed," Lori said. "He will be too unless he wakes up to reality."

"Excellent point," Hubbard said. "We should all do that."

Lori said, "O. G., what exactly is the plan?"

"It's best you don't know the details," O. G. said. "You will leave the party, he will stay."

"Is that necessary?"

"Yes," O. G. said. "Everything has been worked out. Paul will be well taken care of, though I hadn't counted on having to rip him from the arms of the girl he loves."

"He'll be unhappy, but he's young," Lori said. "There will be other girls."

O. G. and Hubbard exchanged a glance. What hard hearts mothers had.

"No doubt you're right, my dear," Hubbard said. "But after the first it's never the same again."

7

Even before she stepped through the kitchen door into the back stairway, Rima heard Blümchen barking inside Miss Wetzel's apartment. A moment later she understood why. Stutzer's apprentices were waiting for Rima one flight below the Christopher's back door. One took her by the right arm, the other by the left. They lifted her feet from the ground and ran her swiftly down the stairs and the courtyard. Not a word was spoken. Coming out of the dark stairwell, Rima looked over her shoulder. Was Paul watching from his window? What if he decided to rescue her? She twisted her body, trying to look back at the building. Her captors, acting in perfect unison as if their brains had received the same instructions from some mother brain at the same moment, lifted her off her feet again and twisted her back into her former eyes-forward posture, then shook her, impatiently and hard, as if to snap the wrinkles from her own brain before putting her down again.

At No. 8 Prinz-Albrechtstrasse, Stutzer waited. For once, Rima was taken directly to him. He was in uniform today. It fitted him perfectly, of course. His jacket did not bulge, his sleeves did not twist. His cap with its death's head badge lay on a shelf behind him. This time he did not bother to pretend to read an important document. He was aware of Rima's presence from the first second. He stared across his desk at her for a long time. She emptied her mind and met his gaze. It was Stutzer who broke eye contact. Waving his hand as if to fan away a disagreeable odor, he sniffed loudly, sniffed again, pulled a large white handkerchief out of his sleeve—Rima caught a whiff of cologne—and held it to his nose. He called out an order. The apprentices entered and opened a small window set high in the wall, one of them giving the other a boost.

"You Jewesses never get enough, do you?" Stutzer said. "You smell like a bitch in heat." He waited expectantly for Rima's answer. She made none. She lowered her eyes, she blushed. "Hot but modest, how touching," Stutzer said. One of the boys came in again with a small crystal glass and a bottle of Martell cognac. He filled the glass to the rim. Stutzer lifted it swiftly to his lips, not spilling a drop, and drained it.

"Anti-gas measures," he said to Rima. "Tell me, when you and your American citizen are taking a rest and whispering sweet nothings to each other in your smelly bed—oh, yes, we know you whisper—does he ever tell you about the liquidation of the redskins by the American army?"

"No, Major."

"It's an interesting story. The American cavalry commander in charge of this work, a man named Custer, believed that it was more important to kill the female Indians than the warriors. In Custer's opinion Indian girls and women were far more dangerous than the braves because they were fertile, or would grow up to be fertile. They would breed and give birth to the enemies of the future. So when he and his troops attacked a redskin camp, they shot or sabered the women and girls first, then killed the warriors. Admirable logic, no? It teaches a lesson that we in the Reich should consider."

Rima, eyes still steady, revealed nothing.

Stutzer said, "So what is your opinion of the Custer solution?"

"I have no knowledge of such matters, Major."

"You don't think it would be wise to eliminate Jewesses as a means of hastening the day when in the Reich the Jews cease to be? You Jewesses are such a temptation. Look at you yourself—you are as beautiful as Bathsheba, fit for a king. No wonder there are so many Jews."

Stutzer gave her a genial smile. "You know," he said, "I sometimes think you're afraid of me." He searched her face as if looking for a sign that he was wrong. Rima remained silent. One wrong word, she thought, and I will never see the sun shine again.

He said, "The fact is, I am not pleased with you. Your work hasn't been good. You've been enjoying yourself with your American lover, but you have brought me nothing. No information whatsoever. Why?"

"There is no information, Major. This family leads a perfectly normal life."

"Sometimes no information is valuable information," Stutzer said. "Do you know why the S-boat was waiting for the Christopher's sailboat that night?"

"No, Major."

"Because we thought the entire family was aboard, trying to escape, that's why. Do you understand what that means?"

"No, Major."

Stutzer's face turned red. He shouted, pounding on the desk and showering saliva, "It means that you failed us, that you put us to great trouble and expense, and that you could have prevented this by making a simple telephone call telling us that you and your joy boy were just sailing out to stink up the ocean with your dirty business!"

Stutzer stared at Rima, eyes popping, face engorged, chin wet with spit. Then he wiped his face with his perfumed handkerchief and in the instant this took, returned to normal. He seemed to expect no answer or apology.

In a perfectly calm voice he said, "Describe this perfectly normal life."

"The father gets up very early in the morning. He makes his own breakfast. . ."

"The wife doesn't get up at the same time and prepare his food?"

"No. She sleeps longer, then usually goes riding."

"And the husband does what?"

"He writes."

"That's all? For the entire day?"

"Herr Christopher is a novelist. That is his work."

"So he is writing this novel every morning while his wife goes—let us say—riding, and you ride their son in the boy's bedroom?"

"Yes."

"What exactly is this famous novelist writing?"

"He doesn't say." This was the truth. Hubbard had never mentioned his work in Rima's presence.

"But there is a manuscript."

"I suppose there must be if he writes every day."

"Have you ever seen it?"

"No."

"So it is a secret manuscript? Where is this secret manuscript kept?"

"I don't know."

"Guess."

"In Herr Christopher's study, perhaps."

"Brava! Under lock and key, perhaps?"

"Quite possibly. He values it highly."

"Why? What's so valuable about it? It's just fiction, make-believe, is that not so?"

Stutzer's sudden affability frightened Rima. He was behaving like a friend of the family, teasing her gently, flirting with her, because she was such a pretty thing. But when she looked across the desk she did not see the genteel man who sat there motionless and smiling in his perfect uniform. She saw the screaming maniac she knew he really was. He was capable of anything. His talk of sex, his compliments about her looks, caused her to taste the contents of her own stomach. Stutzer's methodology had achieved its purpose. Rima was in his interrogation room, in his power, and nowhere else in the world or in the imagination. Nothing existed outside the present moment. He stared at her—his pale eyes were as unreadable as glass. There was no hope.

Shouting the question, Stutzer said, "Answer the question! Why does this American fool place such a high value on the useless stuff he writes?"

The answer leaped from Rima's mouth before she knew she had spoken. "I believe it is the story of their lives," she said. "He writes down everything that happens to them or has ever happened. He calls it *The Experiment*."

"Why?"

"Because it is the truth disguised as fiction."

Stutzer gave her an encouraging smile, as if he was her teacher and she had just won his favor, his gratitude, his affection with the right answer.

"Then this novel is not what it seems to be. It is actually a record, a journal."

He flicked a hand, signaling that he needed no answer from Rima. She had already told him what he needed to know. He had deduced the rest. Then his face changed into a mask of fury and he shrieked at her, "Then get it for me! Get it for me tonight! Bring it to me tonight! Why have you waited to get it for me? Do you think you will not be punished?"

Rima burst into tears. Like a small child she sobbed from the pit of her stomach. Stutzer was pleased by this. He was encouraged. He shouted more loudly, he pounded on the desk, he ran around the desk and seized Rima's braid and pulled her off her chair and dragged her across the floor. He put his gleaming black boot on her breasts and pulled on the braid with all his strength.

She was losing consciousness. She had not prayed since she was a child but she prayed now that he would break her neck. She knew that she had been tricked into the worst betrayal she could imagine. She could never be forgiven. She had become Stutzer's possession.

When Stutzer was done teaching Rima her lesson in obedience, he left her lying on the floor and strode from the interrogation room. The apprentices, who had been standing watch outside the door, immediately burst into the room and lifted her up, each one taking an arm. They rushed her down the hallway in the same choreographed way that they had danced her down the back stairway. A guard opened the back door. Without pause, without wasted motion, without losing a second, they threw her out. She fell on all fours on cobblestones, skinning her knees and the heels of her hands. Half a dozen chauffeurs, loitering beside parked cars, looked down on her without interest or expression. Her skirt flew upward when she was catapulted out the door. She covered herself, but she might as well have been dressed in a gorilla suit for all the sexual interest they took in her, or at least revealed to her or to one another. She was an object, not a human being.

8

As far as Rima could tell she was not followed to the Christophers' apartment. She could not be sure. As usual, everyone walking behind her in the same direction—or the opposite one, for that matter—could have been sent by Stutzer. Perhaps the absence of surveillance, if absent it was, was a sign of Stutzer's supreme confidence that she would now obey his orders without question. She entered from Gutenbergstrasse and climbed the front stairs to the second floor. The doorbell rang several times. When at last Hubbard opened the door, his thick eyebrows shot upward, and as he realized the condition she was in, his expression changed from delight to puzzlement to dismay. Rima had never seen the like in an adult. She put a finger to her lips before he could speak. Inside, she mimed writing with pen and paper.

Hubbard led her to a desk in the sitting room. Rima took writing paper and a pen and set to work immediately and in a few moments handed him a sheet of stationery on which she had written the details of her confession to Stutzer and his instructions to her. When Hubbard reached the end of this document, he opened his mouth to speak. Again Rima put a finger to her own lips. On another scrap of paper she wrote, *Please bring Paul to me.* Hubbard vanished, and a moment afterward reappeared with his son in tow. Paul was rumpled, sleepy-eyed. He looked like a child in his pajamas. He held her note in his hand. In a normal tone, in English so rapid that Rima had difficulty following it, Hubbard said to Paul, "Pity we don't know Indian sign language better than we do, Paul. Very useful if you're a Mahican and Mohawks are lurking in the forest, ears to the ground. Sign language was the Esperanto of the American Indians. It was a code everyone knew. No words, just concepts. Each tribe seems to have had its own private tongue that only they could understand, but they all understood the signs, from Cape Cod to the Pacific Ocean. Your great-grandfather Aaron Hubbard was fluent in it. His Mahican friend Joe, the one who was hanged for a murder he didn't commit, taught him. They were the same age, grew up together at the Harbor after Joe's people died of white man's diseases, spoke a secret language that made no sound, had no words. As a result of having this secret code they were under constant suspicion of boyish deviltry, of course, but the fun of the thing must've made up for that."

As Hubbard spoke, he leaned over the desk and wrote rapidly on a fresh sheet of writing paper. His beautiful American handwriting, sentences connected by graceful end strokes, was strange to Rima's eye, but as legible as a typeface. He wrote, *It's a lovely day for a bit of motoring. Why not take your little dog for its walk as usual? We'll have a rendezvous and go for a spin in the countryside.*

Rima nodded vigorously and whispered a few words in Paul's ear. She then left by the front door. An instant later Hubbard and Paul heard her ringing Miss Wetzel's doorbell. Blümchen barked joyfully, drowning out whatever Rima and Miss Wetzel on the floor below were saying to each other.

Hubbard and Paul picked Rima up in the Horch twenty minutes later as she walked Blümchen along Bismarckstrasse. The front seat was broad and Rima sat between them with the squirming dog on her lap. She described her half-morning in the hands of Stutzer. Her account was impersonal. She was abducted, she was interviewed, she betrayed Paul and his parents, she was dragged around the room by her braid and trampled, she was heaved through a door into the street.

"What swine they are," said Hubbard.

Rima said nothing. There was no need to confirm Hubbard in his opinion of Stutzer and his apprentices. So far the whole of Germany and Austria and half of what used to be Czechoslovakia knew them for what they were. Tomorrow, the world.

In the same dispassionate language she had used to describe the way in which she had been abused, Rima told them what her assignment was.

"They want you to steal my manuscript?" Hubbard said. "Why on earth would they want that?"

"Because I was weak and told them what Paul had told me because he trusted me."

"Never mind. They were torturing you, after all."

"The hair pulling came later. I have no excuse."

"What exactly did Paul tell you?"

"That you called it *The Experiment*, that it was a fictionalized description of everything that actually happened to the three of you and everyone you met. That in actuality it was all true."

"Paul told you all that?"

Rima nodded. "And I told Stutzer. What I did was unforgivable."

Hubbard needed no time to reflect on his answer. "Nonsense," he said. "In the same circumstances I would have done the same. So would anyone else. Don't blame yourself. Of course you must give the manuscript to them or who knows what Stutzer might do? Maybe we can photograph the pages. I only have the one copy."

Paul said, "You're talking about a thousand pages. More."

Hubbard nodded, deep in thought. Paul was examining his father as if meeting him for the first time. What would a stranger think of this man who seemed to be driven by some inner goodness he could not control?

"You can't just hand it over," he said. Hubbard, deep in thought, seemed not to hear. Paul said, "I've read it, Dad."

Hubbard woke up. "You have? How much of it?"

"All of it, as you wrote. I found the key to your cabinet years ago."

"You don't say. Including what I've written since you came home from school?"

"Not that part. I've fallen behind."

The reason why Paul had fallen behind sat between them on the vermilion leather seat. Hubbard smiled at her and then at Paul. "And you said not a single word about it till now?" he said. "You truly are a wonder. Does your mother know about this?"

"I don't think so, but who knows what Mama knows?" Paul said.

"Who indeed?" Hubbard said.

Paul said, "Dad, listen. If they read what you've written, they'll shoot you. Mama, too. Maybe Paulus and Hilde."

Hubbard smiled benevolently. But there was something in his eyes that Paul had never seen in them before. "No need to worry about your mother coming to harm," he said. "She's quite safe."

Silence fell. Even Blümchen calmed down. All three of the human beings stared straight ahead. They were deep in the Grunewald now, trees all around, birds swooping, picturesque restaurants crowded with happy people, accordions playing good German music.

9

"This is a bad figure of speech, maybe, considering the cast of characters," O. G. said to Hubbard, "but this is a heaven-sent opportunity."

Hubbard waited to hear more. The two of them, wearing tennis whites and drinking lemonade, were relaxing in the garden of the embassy after their weekly match. On this day, as sometimes happened when he had mastery of his serve, Hubbard had overwhelmed O. G.'s guile and mobility with brute strength. Now they were both in a good mood for the same reason—Hubbard's pleasure in his victory.

"It makes the psychology easier," O. G. said. "If Paul is given the secret mission of smuggling your immortal work out of the Reich, he may be less reluctant to go."

"Maybe," Hubbard said. "But he and this girl of his are in love. She's lovely, with a mind as quick as a cat's tongue." Hubbard paused. "A dark Lori."

In the depths of his being, O. G. hoped that she wasn't, really. He said, "Ah. Then we've got our work cut out for us."

Hubbard said, "I don't like lying to Paul."

"Sometimes lying is God's work," O. G. replied. "If he stays here it will be the end of him, especially if he's got a girl he thinks he has to protect. Young lovers are easy meat. Stutzer and Heydrich'll predict his every move."

"'The end of him?' you say? He's an American."

"That may not be the advantage it used to be," O. G. replied, "and if I were in your shoes, I wouldn't want to take the chance."

His tone was mild. Hubbard was cut to the quick nevertheless. He took a deep breath of air that smelled of coal smoke even on a summer day, then let it out through his nose. He knew exactly what O. G. meant "by in your circumstances." He would never come right out and say it, but both men knew that Hubbard was responsible for putting the boy in danger in the first place. His nighttime sails in *Mahican* with Lori and their fugitive friends had been romantic folly. In O. G.'s book of maxims, nothing was worse than that.

"Won't Paul be compromised by carrying such dangerous contraband?" Hubbard said. "He'll be aboard a German ship, after all."

"Everything is arranged," O. G. said. "Wrap your package."

"It will be large—seventeen hundred foolscap sheets, covered on both sides."

O. G. whistled softly—what industry! "Do you still have your cello?" he asked.

Hubbard snorted. "My cello? Yes."

O. G. had spent many miserable hours at school and in college listening to his roommate practicing chords and glissandi that he seemed to make up as he went along. Even as a schoolboy Hubbard had been so large that his cello had looked like a violin between his knees.

"Do you and Lori ever do duets together?" O. G. asked.

Hubbard said, "Jack Benny and Clara Schumann? No."

The important thing, O. G. said, a bit impatiently, was that Hubbard still had the case for his cello. Did he or did he not? He did.

"Good, then I'll send a car to your place tonight with a discreetly armed U. S. Marine at the wheel and another in the front seat beside him," O. G. said. "They will pick up the cello case, which will by then be packed with every last page of your literary masterpiece. They will bring it to the embassy, where it will be safe even from the Leader himself."

Immortal work? Literary masterpiece? Twice in a space of seconds O. G. had used a term of mockery for Hubbard's novel. Obviously O. G. thought that the chances that Hubbard's work might actually be a masterpiece were pretty remote. He was condescending to this work without having read a word of it. Hubbard was thin-skinned in such matters. He had reason to be. On the best of Hubbard's days the ratio of insult to praise for his work was five to one, or worse O. G. had had no idea that he was giving offense by his affectionate kidding, and he watched in puzzlement as he read the resentment in Hubbard's eyes. He laid a hand on Hubbard's forearm and gave it a tiny shake. They finished their lemonade. Neither wanted to end this conversation just yet, but neither knew just how to go on with it.

O. G. said, "There's still some heat in the sun. One more set?"

They played for half an hour, giving each other every chance to make the shots. By the time they quit, the embassy was almost deserted. They bathed and changed in the tennis shack.

"You remember Timberlake," O. G. said as he tied his necktie.

"I think so," Hubbard said. "Young fellow with the tall smiley wife. They're new."

"Fairly new to Berlin, arrived last fall. Yale '29, college was J. E. And so on. Hard worker. His light's still on. Let's have him join us for a martini before you go home."

O. G. prided himself on his cocktails. English gin and French vermouth stood on a side table in his office. While Timberlake and Hubbard chatted about writing—Timberlake hoped to write novels himself after he had put in his time in the Foreign Service—O. G. poured four parts Beefeater's and one part Noilly Prat into a glass pitcher, added ice, and stirred the mixture gently with a long glass rod. He strained the cocktails into chilled glasses. Then, turning his back to his guests, he removed a small medicine bottle from his waistcoat pocket, and with an eyedropper placed one drop of absinthe in each glass. This was the secret ingredient he never disclosed, not even to Hubbard.

Hubbard and Timberlake enjoyed O. G.'s martini and said so. Both knew they would get only one. O. G. believed that drinking a second martini was most unwise. Drinking a third was a sign of idiocy. Timberlake and Hubbard chatted about Yale. O. G. had introduced this third party into the conversation so that there could be no more talk of Paul. The boy must leave the Reich. He must do it now. How he felt about it did not matter.

Timberlake discovered that Hubbard had known his older brother when both were at New Haven. "Wonderful voice, sang like an angel in chapel," Hubbard was saying. O. G. smiled and sipped his martini. The absinthe really did make all the difference. As the cocktail warmed, the undertaste of wormwood was more noticeable. Hidden differences were the best things, he thought. The best fun.

SIX

1

Everyone agreed that O. G.'s office in the embassy was the only safe place in Berlin to discuss the plan. That is where the principals—all but Lori, for whom attendance would have constituted treason to the Reich—met on the Fourth of July. Once again the garden was full of men in morning coats and spats and others in splendid uniforms and plump women in summer hats, and because it was a sunny day and Berlin was famous for its exhibitionists, even a parasol or two. Hubbard's cello case, packed with the 1,786 handwritten pages of his manuscript, stood in the corner of the office, behind an overstuffed chair.

Timberlake had been given the job of explaining the plan to Paul. It was best, O. G. felt, if the details came from an official of the embassy to whom he had no emotional attachment. Timberlake recited the particulars, raising his voice a little to overcome the noise of the party outside the window. Paul would spend the night in the embassy and leave in the morning with O. G. An exit visa had been arranged.

"Arranged? How?" Paul asked.

"We have been informed of official approval," Timberlake said.

Paul did not like this young man who was so sure of himself. He wondered why this total stranger was revealing his fate to him—his puzzlement showed on his face—but he listened intently. Timberlake left practically nothing unsaid. When he was done, a silence gathered. Paul looked from one adult face to another. He was very pale, so pale that Hubbard thought he might be sick.

He said, "How do you feel, Paul?"

"Like I just fell off the Empire State Building," Paul said.

The men smiled. "I don't wonder," Timberlake said in his hearty voice. "If you have any further questions I'll try to answer them."

Paul examined his elders, studying one face after another as if checking their identity against photographs. If he was angry it did not show. If he was sad, as they all knew he must be, that did not show, either. The men saw no sign of fear. The silence seemed long, but in fact it lasted no more than half a dozen breaths.

To Timberlake Paul said, "I do have a question. Why would the secret police let me just leave the country with my father's manuscript, which they want a friend of our family to steal for them, under my arm?"

"We have reason to think they will not interfere."

"I don't understand."

"We must ask you to trust us in this matter."

A silence gathered. O. G. and Timberlake waited for Paul to speak again. Their faces were bland. Hubbard had turned his face away.

At last Paul said, "I'm sorry. I know you have my best interests at heart and that you've all gone to a lot of trouble. But I refuse to do this."

Hubbard examined Paul and as always saw in his face Lori's steely eyes and Paulus's jaw line, and kept his peace.

O. G said, "You refuse, Paul? May we know why?"

"There are a number of reasons," Paul said. On the end table at O. G.'s elbow stood a photograph of O. G. standing beside a Spad biplane. He wore an aviator's helmet and goggles, a sheepskin coat, a happy grin. The camera had caught him at a moment in which, in the midst of life, he was in a book for boys, where he had always been happiest. Paul looked up and caught his father's eyes. He expected to see the old wryness there, but in fact detected nothing but the gleam of utmost seriousness. He had seen this look before, but only when grave issues were involved and Hubbard's passions were engaged—the sanctity of art as the strong-room of truth, the puzzle of religious faith, the politics of friendship. Love, death, betrayal, the American dream.

Paul loved Hubbard. He was fond of O. G., whom he had known as an honorary uncle all his life, and for the sake of those two he felt obliged to give Timberlake the benefit of the doubt. But none of them, certainly not Hubbard in his incurable optimism, understood what a disaster could ensue if the plan they had concocted was actually put in motion. O. G. and Timberlake lived in isolation, shielded from such realities as Heydrich and Stutzer by the cotton batten of diplomatic life. They were immune from arrest, protected from insult, officially untouchable. How could they imagine being dragged around a room by the hair, how could they conceive of being asked if they considered themselves to be human beings—and if they did, being required to specify exactly how human they thought they were? Fifty percent? Twenty-five? Or full-blooded subhuman?

These thoughts produced a long silence. The older men watched Paul carefully, waiting for his next words. O. G. leaned forward and squeezed his knee. He said, "Maybe we should let the clock tick for a while longer before we get started, Paul."

Paul said, "I meant what I said."

"We know that," Hubbard said. "But we don't know your reasons."

"To begin with, Mother. How can we do this to her?"

"She also thinks you should get out of Germany at the first possible moment and by any possible means."

"I know she does, but that's because she thinks the only way out is to sacrifice herself. I understand why. But we should all get out. Especially her."

"Easier said than done, Paul," O. G. said. "Your mother is a citizen of the Reich. If you stay and the secret police insist that you are a German, too, nobody can help you. Nobody."

Paul let the words fade. Then he said, "And who would help me if I'm arrested on the quay in Bremerhaven?"

"The short answer is nobody," Timberlake said. "But no such thing will happen."

"I can't see why not," Paul said. "Forgive me for saying so, sir, but you don't know these people."

"Ah, but we do, Paul," Timberlake said with a smile.

"And you trust them just the same?"

Hubbard had had no idea that his son was capable of such brusque behavior. All his life Paul had been quiet, agreeable, pleasant, polite in all circumstances. Even as an infant he had been well mannered. There was no other term for it. He had always from his first moments on earth taken the feelings of others into consideration. It was not like him to argue; always before in case of argument he looked for something he could agree with. If that was not possible he did not resist; he withdrew. But he lost few arguments. He seemed to know what his parents and others were going to say next, what they were likely to do or not do. But when he did not want to do something, he did not do it. He did not make a fuss. He simply refused, and in such moments he was immovable. This was one of those moments.

Hubbard said, "What else, Paul?"

"You know what else, Papa. Rima. How can I leave Rima to Stutzer?"

"Rima?"

"Alexa. If she doesn't deliver the manuscript, she'll be sent to a camp. Her father, too. She was promised by you and me that she could give him the original, that we would photograph it first and then hand it over to her. We haven't done that. Instead it's safe in the embassy in a cello case and she's alone in the world. Stutzer is waiting."

To Hubbard's amazement, Paul managed to speak these words without visible emotion. His face did not change, his voice did not break. He thought Rima was a wonderful bed name for a lover. He had never been prouder of his son.

He said, "Let's go home. I don't see how we can take this any further without including your mother and Rima."

2

In the apartment, lamps burned, the Victrola played Tannhäuser. An empty glass on a side table, still wet inside, smelled of brandy. Hubbard switched off the music. Wagner was too ominous for him.

Paul heard water running in the bath. Was his mother lying just beyond the wall in a tub of scarlet water with her wrists slit? With heavy footsteps Hubbard hurried down the hallway as if he had seen the bloody image in Paul's mind. On his way to his own room, Paul looked into his parents' bedroom. When she was away for most of the day, as she had been today, she always undressed as soon as she returned, hung her clothes in the wardrobe, then took a bath. Once or twice Paul had heard her retching over the sound of the running faucets. In Paul's bedroom the scent of Rima lingered, though she had not been there today.

Paul changed from his suit into everyday clothes and sat down to wait for whatever was going to happen next. Soon he heard his parents' footsteps in the hallway, but no voices. Conversation in the apartment was impossible, of course. Hubbard got the Horch from the garage and they drove to a restaurant in the Grunewald. In their early days together this place had been a romantic destination for Lori and Hubbard. The waiters remembered them. In their long starched aprons and black livery they bowed and smiled. They looked like brothers all dressed alike by a managing mother. The house specialty was poached pink-fleshed lake trout. Hubbard ordered a large one with white asparagus in hollandaise sauce and a bottle of Mosel. The wine came in a matter of seconds. Happy memories were described by the waiter who poured it. He was an admirer of the new Germany; everything was better, especially business; the people were no longer ashamed.

Hubbard tasted and accepted the wine. They waited in silence for the asparagus to be served. Lori avoided eye contact. She was grim-faced, short of words, absent. She studied her hands as if making an effort to remember what they were and who they belonged to. She made no attempt to hide her distraction. It was unsettling to see her without humor, without expression, without intelligence. Hubbard could not bring himself to look at her. It seemed impossible to Paul that his father, who collected details as a way of life, had not guessed the reason for his mother's mood. Even though it was a Tuesday night, the restaurant was full. The talk was loud. On a small stage near the Christophers' table, an accordionist played Bavarian music while two hairy-legged young men in lederhosen danced the Schuhplattler. The Christophers had to shout to make themselves heard across the table. It was a strange sensation after years of whispers and murmurs.

On the far side of the room the kitchen door swung open and a waiter emerged bearing a load of plates. Behind him in the kitchen, Stutzer's apprentices stood side by side, talking intently to the waiters who had greeted the Christophers on arrival. The faces of the waiters were deeply serious now. They were eager to please, anxious to cooperate, careful not to smile while carrying on such a serious conversation. Paul caught his mother's eye and made a small gesture with his head. She looked and saw what he saw. So did Hubbard.

"Time to go," he said.

He left money on the table for the wine and the meal he had ordered, and they got up and left.

They had five minutes of privacy before they saw headlights in the rear-view mirror. The Horch's convertible top was down. Lori liked to ride in the open air after dark. She was sitting in the middle. Her hat blew off. She did not seem to notice. Paul had not been so close to her in a long time. He noticed differences. Her body was clenched, she did not take his hand, her hair smelled of candle smoke, the cognac she had drunk in the apartment was still on her breath.

As if he might not have another chance to do so, Hubbard hurriedly described to Lori what had happened at the embassy. She listened in silence. Then she said, "Your manuscript was smuggled out of our apartment in a cello case? This is not a plan. It's a schoolboy prank."

They drove down a dark back street. The car behind them drew closer. It was equipped with spotlights, and these were focused on the interior of the Horch. Their strong light turned Lori's face deathly white. The glare made it almost impossible for Hubbard to drive. The car weaved. The pursuers made no attempt to stop the Christophers' car. Remembering the laughter behind closed doors in No. 8 Prinz-Albrechtstrasse, Paul understood that the apprentices were just having some fun while carrying out a dull assignment. They followed the Horch all the way back to Gutenbergstrasse and lighted the

Christophers' way up the steps and into the apartment building before they switched off their spotlights and parked across the street.

Inside the building, as they climbed the stairs, Lori let Hubbard go ahead. She took Paul's hand at last, but loosely. Her hand was cold—not like her own hand at all, Paul thought. Nothing about her was as it was supposed to be.

Lori whispered in Paul's ear. "You and I must talk," she said. "Wait till you hear your father is asleep, then come to the sewing room."

Hubbard snored, loudly. It was a family joke. Paul nodded, but he was being asked to deceive his father and he was nauseated by guilt and shame as he watched Hubbard climb the stairs ahead of them, then unlock the door, then step aside to let them pass. His long face was a mask of sadness now. He went straight to the bedroom. Lori made a cold supper of leftovers for Paul. While he ate ham and cheese and apple tart she looked through an album of phonograph records and put one on the turntable. It was choral music, very familiar—Beethoven. Quite soon they heard Hubbard's first snore. Lori sat down beside Paul on a small sofa.

To confuse the microphones buried in the walls, Lori had set the Victrola's volume to maximum. Anyone listening at No. 8 Prinz-Albrechtstrasse or in Miss Wetzel's apartment—who knew who or where the listeners were?—would hear an orchestra and chorus, not living persons. Paul recognized the music at last, "Ode to Joy." Words by Schiller, who if he were still alive, would certainly not be allowed to write poetry any more than Dr. Kaltenbach could practice medicine. Softly, under the music, enunciating clearly and slowly, Lori said, "Paul, listen." He looked at her, but her face was turned away. She said, "I have something for you."

She handed him a package that had been hidden behind a sofa pillow. It was not sealed. Inside he found his American passport with its many German, Swiss, and American stampings and also a new exit visa. How had Lori arranged that? He found a bundle of Reichsmarks, two hundred dollars in American currency, and a second-class ticket to New York aboard the *Bremen*.

Paul said, "What about you and my father?"

"Not this time for us," Lori said. "On this particular day, you are free to go. Your father will be free to go on a different day."

"And you?"

"I will have my day, too."

She looked him in the eye now, but only briefly. Again he felt that he was looking at a Lori who was almost, though not quite, a different person.

Paul said, "I don't believe you."

Lori said, "What part do you think is a lie?"

"That someday you will join us."

"I'm sorry you have doubts," Lori said. "But you don't have to believe what I say. Just do as I ask."

"Why should I?"

"Because this is your last chance, Paul. If you don't go now, they will take you, and they will send you somewhere else."

"How do you know this?"

"I know, Paul. So do you. You will never come back. Nobody ever does."

Her voice wavered. Paul could not have been more shocked if she had jumped out the window. It was Lori, who hated theatrics, who had taught him, commanded him, never to speak as she was speaking now. All his life he had watched her and his father make light of things. They laughed at politics, laughed at fame, laughed at power. They wanted nothing in their lives but love and work. Hubbard often said so.

When Paul spoke, his own voice was steady. He said, "Mother, please don't ask me to do this."

"I'm asking you for your own good," Lori said.

"You're asking me to run away."

"No. I'm asking you to go on ahead, to wait for us in America."

"And all I have to do is abandon you. Abandon Rima."

"Rima?"

"Alexa."

"You have your own name for her? What does she have to do with this?"

"I love her."

At last, for a long moment, Lori looked Paul full in the eyes. "Dear God, of course you do," she said. "I had no idea."

"What did you think was happening?"

Lori started to answer, but caught herself. "It doesn't matter what I thought. I was wrong. But that changes nothing. Paul, you must go."

Paul said, "They'll kill her. Her father, too."

"They'll kill her anyway. Sooner or later they'll kill them both. That's their agenda, to kill everybody."

The music stopped. The record still turned, needle scratching in the blank grooves at the end. Neither Paul nor Lori had noticed. How much had the eavesdroppers heard? It was too late to worry. Lori rose to her feet, wound the phonograph, turned over the record, and put the needle on the disk. The singing began again:

> All men become brothers,
> Under the sway of thy gentle wings.
> Whoever has created
> An abiding friendship,
> Or has won
> A true and loving wife,
> All who can call at least one soul their own,
> Join our song of praise.
> But those who cannot must creep tearfully
> Away from our circle.

The chorus sang louder than before, or so it seemed to Paul.

With some of her old wryness Lori said, "It just occurred to me that 'Ode to Joy' may not go too well with this conversation."

"I was just thinking what a good description it is of the way things are," Paul said.

Lori said, "It's tommyrot. It always was, and the fact that it has come true as a historical joke doesn't change anything. It's still tommyrot."

For a moment, as she spoke her mind in the old way, Lori was herself again. In her flat new voice she said, "Paul, do you *want* to die?"

"No," Paul said. "But you're asking me to be alone for the rest of my life. What's the difference?"

"The difference is that I will know that you're alive. That will keep me alive."

"Alive? In what way? You've just got through saying that they're going to kill everybody."

"Alive in you," Lori said. "It's important to me—you can't imagine how important—that you carry the blood in your veins out of this madhouse and keep it alive."

Paul closed his eyes. The Beethoven rose to a crescendo, then came to an end once more. Lori seemed to have come to the end of her words, too. Paul was immersed in a silence. He put the passport, the money, and the ticket back into the package and laid it between them on the sofa. Lori neither looked at it nor touched it.

She said, "Will you go?"

"I have already refused to do that once today."

"Is that your last word?"

Paul said, "I don't know."

"When will you know? How will you know?"

The question was unanswerable.

Still whispering, Lori said, "Does this girl love you? Not what she says—what you know to be true."

Paul said, "Yes."

"Then she's the one to ask," Lori said.

3

At five in the morning Paul woke up with a start, astonished at how deeply asleep he had been. He lit his lamp as usual but Rima did not arrive. At first light he looked out of the living room window. The black car that had followed the Christophers home the night before was still parked across the street. Stutzer's apprentices, or two others like them, were still on station. Other men would be watching the back stairway. The Christophers were surrounded. Paul and Rima were separated as effectively as if they were on opposite sides of a wall. If he went out he would be followed. If she came here or if somehow they met, she would be arrested.

Paul got dressed and went to his father's study. The door was open. No one sat at the desk where Hubbard ought to have been sitting. As a child, Paul had slipped into the room and watched his father work, sometimes for hours at a time. The giant at the writing table, sometimes talking to himself, sometimes laughing, even weeping, never once realized that he was not alone. Paul listened at the door of his parents' bedroom. He heard none of the sounds that meant they were together. Knowing what he knew or thought he knew about his mother's secret, how could they possibly be together? Along the hallway the varnished doors were closed. A deep stillness filled the apartment. He no longer felt the presence of his parents in this place as he had done all his life, but rather he was seized by a sense of absence, as if everyone had been taken away in the night, leaving nothing behind, not even their ghosts. Had Hubbard and Lori put an end to themselves as Lori had tried to do at Schloss Berwick? Had they arranged Paul's escape, given him the documents and money he needed to go on living, and then taken poison? Or worse? What would he find if he opened the door of their bedroom, if he entered the bathroom? Paulus had told him stories of officers, friends of his, who had shot themselves after they had done something unforgivable. Their friends put them into a room with a loaded pistol. They were expected to do the honorable thing. *This only happens when there is no other way out, Paul.*

Paul knocked on the bathroom door. When no one answered, he opened the door and pulled the light chain. The room leapt into view—white porcelain sink and tub and bidet in deep shadows, the glittering oval mirror over the sink in which Paul had seen himself thousands of times. Three toothbrushes stood in a glass, his father's shaving brush was in its mug, his ivory-handled razor lay on the shelf, its strop dangled from the sink. Paul went back into the hallway and knocked on his parents' bedroom door. Again no one answered. He opened the door. The room was empty. The bed was made. In the wardrobes, his parents' clothes hung in neat rows. They were tidy people. They lived ashore as they lived aboard their boat, everything shipshape, with nothing more than they needed. Paul found no note addressed to himself, no explanation of any kind. He looked in all the other rooms. There was nothing there, either, except that the package that Lori had given him the night before had been moved from the sofa to a table in the sewing room. He looked inside the package. Everything was still there.

Standing back from the windows so that he could not be seen from the outside, Paul looked down into the street. It was beginning to awaken. Gutenbergstrasse was a quiet, very short dead-end street, perhaps three hundred meters in length. It had practically no traffic. It was rare to see a stranger there or an unknown car, so the apprentices' black Opel sedan was recognized for what it was by all who saw it. Nobody looked directly at the car. They passed it by with averted eyes as if it did not exist.

Paul knew that he himself could not get past the car unless the men inside had orders to let him pass. He had already decided that the same was true of the back entrance. Whatever was going to happen would happen today and it would happen somewhere else. Almost certainly it had already happened to Rima and to his parents. He half expected to see Stutzer himself in the street, in one of his resplendent costumes, waiting for him. As he watched, Miss Wetzel emerged from the building, Blümchen on the leash. The little dog dashed across the street, hauling a staggering Miss Wetzel helplessly behind her as if she were being dragged by a Great Dane. Blümchen barked furiously at the car. One of its windows rolled down. Paul recognized the face of the ex-cavalry trooper who had ridden Lori's horse back to the Tiergarten stables on the day she got into the Daimler. Smiling at the dog, he spoke cordially to Miss Wetzel, who replied just as cordially. With a series of apologetic bows, she picked up the squirming animal, clutched it to her breast, and hurried away. She was dressed for the morning in violet— matching dress, hat, and shoes. Blümchen barked over her mistress's shoulder at the intruders.

Paul ran down the front stairs and walked briskly across the street. Paul said, "Good day. I'm looking for my parents. Have you seen them this morning?"

The man grinned. "Have they abandoned you?"

"My question is, Have they been arrested?"

Another grin, showing a missing front tooth. "I have no information for you," the man said, and rolled up the window.

Paul gave him a curt nod, turned on his heel, and walked away. He expected to be seized from behind and taken to No. 8 Prinz-Albrechtstrasse, but no voice of authority called *Halt*! No hands were laid on him. He walked on. After he turned the corner, he looked behind him. The street was empty. Why weren't they following him?

Paul had no idea what to do next. It was possible that his parents were at liberty, but if Rima had not come to him at their usual hour, there was only one other place she was likely to be, 8 Prinz-Albrechtstrasse. Paul's room had been their rendezvous point. There was no other. He was assailed by second thoughts. What if Rima risked coming in daylight while he was out and the watchers let her pass for reasons of their own? What if she was waiting at the back door now, what if she had just been late? Stutzer still awaited delivery of the manuscript of *The Experiment*. Paul could not penetrate the intentions of the secret police. No one could. They were too primitive. They had awakened in themselves something that the rest of humanity had left behind centuries ago.

Paul reached the western gate of the Tiergarten. He was not far from the lawns where he had caught his first glimpses of Rima only weeks before. He sat down on a bench and tried to think systematically. There was no possibility of his finding either Rima or his parents by wandering the streets. But they might find him in the place where he was likeliest to be, the apartment. He got to his feet and walked home. The black car was gone. He half expected to find that the apartment had been searched and turned upside down in his absence, but everything was just as he had left it. "Ode to Joy" was still on the turntable of the silent Victrola. His father's manuscripts, a long row of them, were in their usual places on the shelf in rosewood boxes that looked like leather-bound books with titles and the year of writing stamped in gold on the spines. There was no sign of Rima inside the apartment. He examined his room for evidence that she had been there while he was gone, but there was none. He searched the back staircase for her, looking in all the places where she might have left a note. He went outside into the courtyard and searched there. He found nothing.

Back inside, the telephone rang, a rare event because there was hardly anyone left in Berlin who dared to call the Christophers. Paul picked up the instrument and said hello. The caller hung up without speaking a word. Paul dialed Dr. Kaltenbach's number. If Rima were there she would answer. If she was not, no one would answer. The Kaltenbach's number rang ten times before Paul broke the connection. He was thirsty. He had drunk nothing since the night before. He drank nothing now. If he was arrested with full bladder and bowels, he would give his captors an advantage. The silence in the apartment was so deep that it made a sound like the sea in a conch shell. He sat down in a chair in the music room, where he could see his mother's piano and the photographs on the table beside it. He thought of nothing. For the first time he realized that Schatzi was gone, too. He remembered the car and ran down the back stairs and looked inside the former stable where the Horch was kept. It, too, was gone.

In another time, in a different country, he would have thought nothing of these missing persons and objects. He would have read a book while he waited for his parents to come back with the car and the dog. In the here and now it was impossible to know what these signs meant. Maybe Hubbard and Lori had left him to make up his own mind about getting aboard the *Bremen*. If so, it was the first act of cruelty they had ever visited upon him. He knew that there were other, likelier explanations for his parents' absence, for Rima's disappearance. He knew that what was happening was almost surely not their fault. That did not change the fact that he had no one to say goodbye to, no one to say goodbye to him. Alone in the hushed apartment, surrounded by objects he had known by sight and touch and smell since infancy, he felt loneliness as he had never felt it before and would not feel it again in his lifetime, not even in prison.

At ten o'clock Paul took the night train to Bremerhaven. The apprentices, spruced up for the journey and smelling of tooth powder and cologne, were already in his compartment when he got aboard.

When they saw his haggard face they smiled knowingly at each other but said nothing to Paul. Nor did he speak to them.

4

The voyage to New York lasted four days. Hubbard's cousin Elliott met Paul outside customs. To be met by Elliott Hubbard was like being met by Hubbard Christopher on a day when he happened to be wearing a wig and false eyebrows. Hubbard and Elliott not only looked like twins, one blond and the other dark, they had the same gestures, the same neighing laugh, the same deep voice—and because they had gone to the same schools and been raised by fathers who had done the same, identical Yankee twangs.

"How was the voyage?" Elliott asked.

"Not bad," Paul said.

"Cabin all right? Didn't put you in with a snorer, I hope?"

"No, I was alone."

"What luck! Or was it the pariah treatment?"

As if he were still in the Reich, Paul felt the sting of suspicion. What did this person know? How did he know it? Whom would he tell? He did not answer the question.

Elliott had a chauffeur standing by to deal with the luggage—he was a lawyer in a prosperous firm and the Great Depression was still on—but Paul had brought only one small bag.

In the car, a red Packard like O. G.'s, Elliott said, "O. G. hurried by while I was waiting for you. He said he hadn't seen you on board."

"No."

"Were you avoiding each other?"

"I was in second class. He was upstairs in first."

"Then you had more interesting company than he did. I invited O. G. to dinner tonight. He thinks you may be mad at him. Are you?"

"No."

"Good. He's your friend, believe me." Elliott smiled Hubbard's toothy smile. He had been watching Paul intently. Now he handed him an unopened telegram and said, "This came for you yesterday."

It was from his parents.

"SORRY NO GOODBYES. NOT OUR PLAN OR FAULT. PLEASE FOR-
GIVE. MISS YOU TERRIBLY. SO DOES DEAR IRMA. LOVE LOVE LOVE."

He handed the telegram to Elliott. He scanned it and handed it
back.

"This sounds like they're all right," Elliott said. "O. G. is bearing
messages, too, he said. He wants to pass these on before dinner."

"I'd like to reply."

"You can phone it to the cable company from the house. But talk
to O. G. first."

Elliott did not ask who Irma was. No doubt O. G. had already told
him. As a child Elliott had fallen a year behind in school because of a
case of scarlet fever. Who else would Hubbard have tapped in the class
behind him if not his twin cousin?

Paul said, "Have you and my father ever impersonated each other?"

"Not for years," Elliott replied. "But maybe there are possibilities
for the future. Now come and meet your new second cousin."

Elliott's wife Alice had presented him with a son. The child was now
about a year old, and there would never be any doubt about his pater-
nity. His name was Horace, after his mother's father. Sitting in his high
chair, being fed liquefied vegetables, Horace was the small triplet of
Hubbard and Elliott. He had their horse face, their all-encompassing
grin, their interested eyes. Among friends and family, Alice was noted
for her wit. "I never expected to produce a child who resembles
Seabiscuit so closely," she said. "But I had got so used to looking at
Elliott that he had begun to seem quite handsome. Long engagements
dull the senses."

"Horace looks fine to me," Paul said.

The child took a liking to Paul. With a glad cry he made a grab for
him with spinach-smeared hands, leaving a stripe of green on his sleeve.

"The mark of Horace," Alice Hubbard said.

In his bedroom Paul read his parents' cable again and again. He understood everything that was written between the lines. They had been taken into custody on the day he departed, and so had Rima, so that nothing would interfere with Paul's departure from Germany. In some part of his mind, Paul had known this before he left Berlin. He had left Berlin because he knew it and understood it. Even if he remained—especially if he remained—he would not see them again. This situation made no sense. It was designed to make no sense. Senselessness was the point. Here in his cousin's house three thousand miles away, sirens shrieked outside the windows as if America was the police state, Paul lay down on his bed and forced his brain to stop its inquiries. His brain answered this command by producing images of Rima that were as elusive as her reality was becoming.

Elliott pounded on the door of Paul's room, awakening him from a deep sleep. "Awake or starve!" Elliott shouted in his courtroom baritone.

In the library Elliott and O. G. were drinking fifteen-year-old single-malt scotch whisky. O. G. was a connoisseur of scotch. As Paul entered the room, he was telling Elliott that another war in Europe was inevitable. The German army would be in France before the harvest was in.

"The experts say the Maginot Line will stop them," Elliott said.

"Generals are always preparing for the last war," O. G. said in French. "The Hun will go around those pillboxes with their Panzers and Stukas and take Paris in a matter of days." He caught sight of Paul. "What do you think, Paul? You know both countries."

"The French say that they'll win because they are stronger than the Germans."

"They do, do they? Sit ye down, son." O. G. had fresh news from Berlin, courtesy of a courier from the State Department who had crossed the Atlantic in a Pan-Am Clipper. "Message from your parents," he said. "They're unhappy that they weren't able to say goodbye to you. They were in custody."

Paul waited to hear more.

O. G. said, "The secret police came around midnight, or so I'm told, after you'd gone to bed. Apparently they weren't questioned, just held till the following evening, then let go. They're perfectly all right."

"Were they together all that time?"

O. G. paused before answering. "They were separated, I believe. Isn't that standard procedure?"

"Not always," Paul said. "What time did they let them go?"

"Soon after the *Bremen* sailed, apparently."

"They were released together, at the same time?"

Another tiny hesitation—this time, Paul thought, intended as a reproof. "So it seems." O. G. replied. His tone was neutral, his eyes vague. Hardly ever did he make an unqualified statement. Paul suspected that O. G. knew as well as he did what had really happened. Heydrich had abducted Lori for the night and locked up her husband to keep him out of the way. He had done this often enough in the past.

Paul said, "So now they're back at Gutenbergstrasse?"

O. G. cleared his throat. "At last report, yes. There's a footnote. Your young friend was also taken into custody, but they let her go."

Paul had only one young friend in Berlin. He said, "Alexa Kaltenbach?"

"Yes. Your mother saw her leaving No. 8 Prinz-Albrechtstrasse at about the same time that she and your father were released."

"Did they speak?"

"I don't know. In the circumstances they might have thought it unwise," O. G. said, "I'm sorry to bring you such news, though on the whole it's good news. All hands appear to be all right."

"You have no other information about Alexa?"

O. G. shook his head no. Behind the lenses of the pince-nez, his eyes were locked to Paul's. Then they dropped to Paul's hands, which trembled. Paul realized what his body was doing and stopped it from doing it. Obviously all was lost, just as he had warned Lori that all would be lost if he left the Reich. If this truth had been written in fire in the sky, it could not have been more evident.

"Thank you, O. G.," he said. "It's very kind of you to bring me up to date."

O. G. leaned forward and took Paul by the knee. He was surprisingly strong. He said, "I can't begin to imagine how this is for you,

Paul, but just let events take their course and all will be well, I promise you."

Paul acknowledged the advice and the absurd promise with a nod. His eyes grew cold.

"Call on me for anything, anytime," O. G. said. "Your father said to tell you to see Sebastian Laux if you need funds. And of course you have Elliott."

Later, O. G. said to Elliott, "By George, that look that Paul gave me would freeze your tongue to your sled."

The next morning Paul rose early and read the shipping news in the *Herald Tribune*. He then put on one of his suits with a white shirt and a school tie, packed his bag, and left the house. He took the subway to Wall Street, checked his bag in a locker in the station, and walked through narrow streets to a low handsome building tucked between two tall ugly ones. A small bronze sign beside the door identified it as D. & D. Laux & Company. There was no indication on the sign of what sort of business was done inside—if you had to ask, you didn't belong here. A doorman admitted him.

The receptionist, a bald expressionless man in a morning coat who had last seen Paul when he was five or six years younger, asked if he had an appointment. Paul said, "No. But please tell Mr. Sebastian Laux that Paul Christopher is here."

"Very well, sir," said the receptionist.

Paul was ushered by another solemn man—there were no women here—into the office of the chairman and president of this private bank. Sebastian Laux was a small person. As Paul entered he rose from his chair and dashed across the Persian carpet that had apparently been specially woven to fit this room to the last square inch.

"What a nice surprise," Sebastian said, shaking Paul's hand. "I had no idea that you were in New York. Your father and mother are with you, I hope."

"No, sir. They're in Berlin."

Sebastian's smile vanished. "I see," he said. "But they will be following soon?"

"I'm not sure."

"I see. Please sit down and tell me the rest of the news."

Paul did as he was asked. All his life he had been told—or had overheard his parents telling each other—that Sebastian Laux could be trusted with any secret. Therefore Paul told him everything, down to the smallest detail, omitting only his deductions about the relationship between his mother and Reinhard Heydrich. Sebastian did not interrupt. When Paul finished, he gazed for a long moment at a large portrait in oils of another elfin man, one of the two D. Lauxes who were his father and grandfather. The one in the picture looked remarkably like a much older Sebastian.

Finally Sebastian nodded, as if the situation Paul described had now been put into proper order inside his own head and he was grateful for this. He said, "Tell me why you're here, Paul."

Paul said, "I want to withdraw all the money from my account." Since birth Paul's money—birthday and Christmas checks, a small inheritance or two—had been deposited in this bank in his name.

"All of it?" Sebastian asked.

"Yes."

"May I ask why?"

"I am returning to Germany. Today, if possible. The *Bremen* sails at four o'clock."

Sebastian nodded as if this were the most reasonable answer in the world, then moved his left foot in its gleaming shoe and rang what Paul knew to be a hidden floor bell. The solemn man appeared instantly.

Sebastian said, "Mr. Paul Christopher's balance?"

Evidently the man had already looked it up. He handed Sebastian a slip of paper.

"Two thousand nine hundred seventy-six dollars and eighty-seven cents," Sebastian said. "I suggest you take five hundred in cash, two thousand in a letter of credit and leave the rest to keep the account open. Is that agreeable?"

Paul nodded. Sebastian said, "Five hundred in cash, if you please, Mr. Wilson, and the usual letter." The man disappeared. In a moment he was back with an envelope containing Paul's money in crisp new bills, together with a creamy sheet of paper. Sebastian took these. The man withdrew.

Sebastian said to Paul, "Why the *Bremen*?"

"It's the only ship sailing to Bremerhaven this week."

"Have you told Elliott about your plans? Or your parents?"

"No. Only you."

"I see. This because of the girl?"

"Yes, sir."

"Very well. The bank can make your booking if you wish. It will save you some time and perhaps will attract less attention."

"That's very kind of you."

Sebastian rang again and gave Wilson new instructions.

"It should only take minutes to book a place for you," Sebastian said. "Not much demand for tickets to the Reich these days. Our travel agent will send a messenger."

"Thank you," Paul said.

"Your parents may not thank me when you reappear in a country about to start a war," Sebastian said. "But it's obvious that you will do what you've decided to do with my help or without it and it's better for you to have a little money in your pocket. It's the girl you're worried about, I take it?"

"All of them. But yes, her especially. She has no one else to help her, nowhere to go."

"I understand. For what it's worth, you're doing the right thing by standing by her, whatever it costs. You'll find it easier to live with yourself afterward."

Sebastian uncapped a fountain pen—a much smaller and plainer one than Paul was used to seeing in the hand of Major Stutzer—and signed the paper that Wilson had brought to him. He blotted it, folded it, and handed it to Paul.

"This is a letter of credit for five thousand dollars," he said. "You understand how it works?"

"Yes."

"Good. Your mother, your father, and you may all draw on it. It instructs the banks to disregard your age. If you require more money or anything else, the bank's cable address is LAUXBANK. Mark the telegram for my attention." Paul started to speak. Sebastian held up a small manicured hand to forestall thanks. He said, "Shall I inform Elliott or your parents of your plans?"

"I'll call Elliott from the pier. It's best not to cable my parents."

"Your ticket should be here shortly," Sebastian said. "Would you like some tea?"

Before Paul could remonstrate, a young man in a double-breasted striped waistcoat under his morning coat appeared with a tray. He seemed to be in training to become as solemn as Sebastian's older employees.

Sebastian prepared the tea himself, explaining where it had come from in Japan and the history of its cultivation. It was a green tea called Sencha Hiki, from Wakayama Province. "It's sweeter than the last green tea you tried. I hope you like it better than the last time," Sebastian said, handing Paul a cup. As a child, Paul had tasted this bitter stuff while visiting with his father and had spat it out into Hubbard's handkerchief.

Paul sipped it. "I do," he said.

"Then you should cultivate a taste for it. It's good for the brain. Not to mention the appetites."

When the ticket arrived, Paul attempted to pay for it. Sebastian waved him off again—Paul's account would be debited. He gripped Paul's hand tightly. This was twice in two days that Paul had been surprised by the strength of a man who seemed old to him.

Paul said, "Have you any message for my father?"

"Only my love to him and your mother," Sebastian said. "We'll see each other soon."

They rose to their feet. Sebastian smiled up at Paul, who was inches taller than he was. The smile was a merry conspirator's smile. Oddly enough, it was not a solemn moment. Paul did not try to thank Sebastian again.

5

Aboard the *Bremen* Paul was treated as an invisible passenger. He was given the same tiny single cabin in the bow of the ship that he had occupied on the westbound voyage. The crew gave no sign that they remembered him. The passengers with whom he was seated at meals ignored him. It was no great feat to read these minds that were all alike. He was of no interest to these people. His case was in the hands of others who were high above them. Soon enough, they believed, so would his body be.

Paul sat on deck by day or lay in his bunk by night, reading Baedecker guides to north German cities. He concentrated on streetcar routes, which, like every other aspect of the country, were described by Baedecker in minute detail. Paul knew that it was possible to travel across the length and breadth of almost any country in the world by streetcar. You simply took a trolley to the opposite edge of any city, then walked a short distance to the first streetcar stop inside the next city and repeated the process until you reached your destination.

When Paul went ashore in Bremerhaven the official on duty stamped his passport but asked no questions, not even the routine ones. On the quay in Bremerhaven Paul did not see Stutzer's apprentices or anyone else who looked as if they had been assigned to follow him. He walked into the city, and at the first streetcar stop on Havenstrasse got aboard a squealing yellow trolley and began his journey across the most efficiently policed country in the world. Still no one took a visible interest in him. The secret police had no need to follow him. He was inside the Reich by his own choice, but he could not get out again unless the security apparatus permitted him to do so. For him, the Reich was a vast trap. The cheese was in Berlin. They knew where he was going and how he must get there. All they had to do was watch the bait and wait for him to spring the trap. Their routine surveillance at the Bremerhaven train station would report which train he had taken to Berlin. Their counterparts in Berlin would report his arrival. Blümchen would let Miss Wetzel know when he walked past her door on his way to his parents' apartment and she would let them know. It was summer. Paul was dressed as a Wandervögel, a youth on holiday, in shorts and knee socks and walking shoes, with the sun bleaching his dark blond hair and a rucksack on his back. He had acquired a tan during his round trip across the Atlantic. He was the picture of young Aryan manhood as imagined by the party's poster artists. The streetcar he boarded on Havenstrasse was empty except for the driver and conductor, who took Paul's pfennigs gave him the first friendly smile he had seen since saying goodbye to Sebastian Laux in New York. He got off, after changing cars, at the northern city limits. From there, on foot and by streetcar, he traveled to Cuxhaven, Stade, Hamburg, Lübeck and Rostock and Stratsund and several towns in between. He walked on country roads at night and slept in the open. He ate sausages and bread that he bought from street vendors and drank clean water where he found it. He smiled and answered the polite questions of the kindly people and the flirtatious girls he encountered, but engaged in no long conversations. No one he encountered seemed to think that he was anything but a German boy on a lark. Some found it strange that he was traveling alone; the whole point of wandering was to be part of a group, to sing, to work your way, to celebrate friendship and culture. Paul explained that he was meeting his friends farther down the road.

In Hamburg he wrote a postcard and mailed it to Rima. If she received it, and if she was free, and if she understood its unwritten parts, she would know where to find him. She would understand. He trusted her intelligence, her intuition, her knowledge of him. They had made no secret arrangements in which she might be entrapped. Rima could not confess what she could only guess.

Paul arrived in Rügen by night. *Mahican* was back, tied up at the mooring below Schloss Berwick, sails furled, centerboard and rudder stowed, with enough water and food aboard for a weekend sail. It was the dark of the moon, but this was luck. Paul had had no control over his time of arrival. He knew his destination, but even that was a short-lived secret, and he knew it. If he did not turn up in Berlin, Stutzer would know, Heydrich himself would know, that there was only one other place he could be.

Paul slept in a beech tree on an old platform he had built years before. At dawn S-boats came home and others put out to sea, trailing white wakes and rainbow spray. Moments after the sun rose, Paul caught sight of Paulus and his wolfhound Bismarck, out for their morning march along the cliffs. He wondered briefly if the dog would recognize his scent and bark him down from his tree, but Bismarck had no interest in any human being except Paulus. Paul ate some cheese and an apple, drank water from his canteen, munched on a chocolate bar. Like a scout in enemy country, he left no crumb or other sign that he had been present.

After dark, because he knew that Rima would come only after dark and would know of no place to meet him except aboard *Mahican*, he climbed down and waded to the boat. The blackout on Rügen was total. No lights showed in the windows of the schloss or any of the other houses within eyeshot. He felt the boat move as someone came aboard. The newcomer had a light step. The hull dipped only slightly. The intruder came below, making no sound, and found him in the pitch-dark space where he lay. He smelled a trace of sweat, a hint of soap, hair, and when Rima whispered in his ear, moist breath along with all the other scents that she emitted when they were together in the dark. He drew breath to speak. She put two fingers on his lips. "First, us," she whispered.

They whispered in English as usual. Rima had known that Paul's message meant that he had returned for her, and that this could only mean that he had a plan of escape, and that the only possible starting point for their flight must be Rügen. She had told no one about the postcard from Lübeck, not even her father. She knew what her escape from Germany would mean for him, but she knew, too, that he would never consent to go with her, would never break the law. He would never stop trusting his country. He still thought that Germany, his Germany, was just having a little breakdown. Soon the outlandish men from Mars, who had always before been invisible to educated people, would go back to being invisible. Germany would stop being the Reich and become the Fatherland again—hard work for all, just rewards, band music in the park on Sunday, honest boys and good girls walking together under the trees. Stern fathers and loving mothers—the real, the natural German police—would take over again. Peace and order would return.

Rima believed the opposite. Never in her lifetime would there be another Germany filled with kindly people whose stupidities were harmless.

She whispered, "Are we going to escape?"

"We're going to try, if you want to do it. But think carefully."

"Do you think it's impossible?"

"I know it is not. But the odds aren't favorable."

Rima knew this. The S-boats were still out there. No doubt Stutzer was out there, too. The secret police would be on the watch. Paul had disappeared. By now they knew that she had disappeared also. They might have followed her to Rügen. If not, it was because Stutzer knew her destination. He would certainly have deduced where they were headed next. A nice young soldier had given Rima a ride on his motorcycle all the way from Berlin to Stralsund and had not asked for so much as a kiss in payment. Stutzer would find this soldier. Someone on the empty plain between Berlin and the Baltic would have seen them riding by and made a report. Rima said nothing to Paul about the soldier. Did he know about jealousy? Rima knew all about it. She had imagined temptresses on the *Bremen*. She had fantasized rich American girls, blond and blue-eyed like himself, making eyes at him in New York.

Paul estimated their chances at fifty-fifty. He was not, after all, a novice. For the hundredth time he reminded himself that he had been present at other escapes when his parents had been in charge, so he knew that success was possible. He told Rima nothing about these secret voyages. It was dangerous for her to know. Next time, Paul knew, Stutzer's patience would be exhausted. He would take the information he wanted from them both, no more games, no more coaxing. If Rima knew a little and was forced to tell the little she knew, Stutzer would believe that she knew more than she had told him and his men would beat what she did not know out of her. No one could protect her.

The conditions necessary for escape were simple—a dark night, a good wind, luck. Hubbard in his love for simplicity had never considered installing an engine in *Mahican*. She was a sailboat, the wind was her element, and in Hubbard's mind it connected *Mahican* and everyone who sailed in her to the first human being who thought of stepping a mast in a cockleshell and hanging a piece of hide on it to catch the air. Paul and Rima had darkness and wind aplenty. A thirty-knot breeze moaned in the hollows of the chalk cliffs. The hull of *Mahican* pitched and rolled in a strong chop. The night was so black that they could not even see the schloss hovering above them. It would be next to impossible to sail into such a wind. The only feasible destination was the Danish island of Bornholm, fifty miles to the northeast of Rügen. They could run before the wind and be ashore on free territory in four hours or less.

"Unless?" Rima said.

"Unless we capsize or an S-boat finds us," Paul said.

"What are our chances?"

"Of capsizing, small if we sail by the rules, but in this weather that will be a problem. I don't know about the S-boat. It depends on where they're patrolling tonight, but they know as well as we do which way the wind is blowing."

"But how can they see us in this weather?"

"Our sails are white. They have lookouts with good glasses. There's no such thing as invisibility at sea unless there's thick fog. No chance of that tonight."

"So everything depends on their not seeing us."

Paul and Rima could not even see each other's faces. She took his face between her hands—as he already knew, her palms were slightly rough—and placed her forehead against his. "Then let's go now before they find us here," she said.

Rima remembered from their last outing how to rig the boat. She worked efficiently in the dark with Paul to fit the centerboard and the rudder and cast off. He raised the mizzen sail and the jib and as the wind pushed them out to sea, Rima could see the white triangles of canvas. The fabric glowed in the pitch dark like the phosphorescent combers into which they were now sailing. The pale cliffs of Rügen glowed also. She realized that *Mahican* would be visible as a silhouette against the cliffs. Her throat tightened with fear.

Rügen remained visible for a long time as a smudge on the horizon, and when at last the boat passed over the horizon and the island was lost to sight, Rima feared that they must be even more visible to those who were hunting them. *Mahican*, heeled over, seemed to be flying now. The mainsail ballooned. When touched it felt as tight as a drum-head. When the boat yawed and the canvas snapped, it seemed that the sound must be audible miles away. Rima had never been so frightened in her life—not by the boat or the wind, which were the angels of this experience, but by whatever else might intrude. By the searchlight that might suddenly blind them, by the smell of burnt diesel that might suddenly fill the nostrils, by the bow of the S-boat or who knew what else suddenly looming in the darkness, suddenly visible, but only for the moment that it took to ram *Mahican* into splinters.

Rima's eyes had adjusted to the darkness, but she did not look into it. She was seated on the windward rail, lashed to a cleat on the tilted deck, her body stretched out to balance the boat. Nothing it seemed but her slight weight kept it from overturning. She looked back at Paul at the tiller. His eyes were on the compass, then on the sails, then on her. He smiled. His teeth were brilliantly white like everything else in this picture that was not darkness. She was inside the picture, therefore outside the world. So was Paul. There they would remain for the rest of their lives. For an instant she actually believed in this enchantment.

The S-boat was waiting for them about a mile outside Danish territorial waters. Its searchlights found *Mahican* instantly. Its small boat, already in the water, set off with engine hammering in pursuit of the sailboat. A parachute flare ignited, signal flags were hoisted. A signaling lamp winked the command to stop. No nautical ritual was omitted except shots across *Mahican*'s bow. There was no hope of outrunning this mechanized enemy. A moment before, *Mahican* had been running before the wind at thirty knots, a giddy speed for a small sailboat. Now she seemed to be wallowing dead-slow in a bathwater sea. Paul turned the yawl into the wind and dropped the sails.

Stutzer himself and his two apprentices were aboard the small boat. Paul saw their faces clearly by the harsh light of the flare. The sailors who were operating the craft brought it alongside *Mahican* and made it fast. The apprentices boarded immediately with pistols drawn. One of them carried a large glass jug and a flare gun. Without a word or a gesture, he opened the forward hatch and hurled the jug into the hold. The glass broke, releasing the smell of kerosene. He fired a flare into the hold. Flames and smoke belched from the hatch. Blisters popped into being all over the varnished deck.

The apprentices picked Paul up bodily and threw him into the small boat. Rima, who was still lashed to *Mahican,* struggled to loosen the bowline around her waist. Paul tried to leap back aboard *Mahican* to help her but was tripped and held fast by the apprentices. *Mahican* was an old vessel, her wooden hull and decks and masts dried by seasons in the open and covered with many coats of varnish and paint. The small boat, bobbing violently in the chop, backed away from the intense heat. Rima freed herself from the rope at last. She dove overboard and swam underwater to escape the flames. The sails caught fire, then the masts. The entire hull burst into flames.

Rima surfaced several meters from the burning yawl, but the heat was still too intense to bear and she dived again. Paul fought toward the small boat's gunwales, meaning to go to Rima's rescue. In response to a small gesture from Stutzer, a tiny movement of his head, one of the apprentices pulled Paul's legs out from under him, and as he sprawled backward, the other caught him as expertly as an acrobat executing a tumbling routine. He put a forearm against Paul's throat and tightened the choke hold. Paul felt his consciousness slipping away.

"Careful with him!" Stutzer said.

The apprentice relaxed his forearm and let Paul breathe again.

One of the S-boat's searchlights was now focused on Rima. She was treading water on the other side of the burning *Mahican.* Completely alight now, masts and spars and hull outlined by flame, the yawl was being blown into the darkness as if under sail. The small boat came about, describing a circle with the girl at the center. She raised one hand to show them where she was. Her face was white, her movements sluggish. Only weeks before, the water in which she swam had been frozen solid. It was still just above the freezing point. No one could live in it for long. The helmsman steered toward Rima. A sailor clambered into the bow, a coiled line attached to a life preserver in his hands.

In a loud officer's voice, Stutzer said, "No. Leave the Jew."

Rima heard Stutzer's command—Paul was sure of this. She knew what it meant. Her eyes were fixed on Paul. He was sure of that, too, though he knew that she must be blinded by the searchlight. She continued to tread water, trying to see Paul through the blinding light. He was trying break free, trying to join her, but the apprentices, under orders to do him no harm, restrained him with remarkable gentleness, canceling his physical efforts with their own strength, as if it was their duty to keep him from making a fool of himself.

Rima raised both arms above her head in the glow of the searchlight. For a long moment she held them aloft. Then, by an act of the will, she slid into the sea as if returning to it, as if it were a place where she could breathe at last.

PART TWO
1959

SEVEN

1

Twenty years later on a winter night, as he passed beneath a streetlamp in a gray European city, Paul Christopher glimpsed, just briefly, the face of a man who was walking in the opposite direction. It was raining hard. The light was feeble, but Christopher knew at once that this person, though thinner and more gray-faced than before and dressed in threadbare clothes, was Franz Stutzer. Christopher turned on his heel and followed him. The cobblestone streets were narrow and steep, with flights of granite stairs. Stutzer wore an old fedora, a short mustard-yellow raincoat with a frayed hem, and socks with holes in the heels. Little half-moons of pallid flesh appeared above the backs of his shoes at every step. He smelled of wet wool, rank sweat, and cheap cologne. Through the rain Christopher saw his quarry indistinctly, as if he were on the other side of a smudged sheet of glass. Stutzer knew he was being followed. He glanced fearfully over his shoulder, he quickened his step.

Perhaps Stutzer did not, at that moment, realize who Christopher was. After all, he had been a boy the last time he saw him. But he feared strangers. He could not possibly remember all the faces he had ever seen, but there were people still alive all over the world who had reason to kill him. Why should this young man not be one of them? Besides, he saw by the way his pursuer moved how good he was at this game, how keen his senses were, and how used to winning he was. He was a savage, a hunter. Stutzer had just become his quarry. He was weaker than this stranger, older. He feared death. He feared pain, feared the humiliation of being caught by a stronger animal. Christopher could overtake him whenever he chose, kill him with his bare hands or take away his pistol and shoot him with it—not mercifully in the heart or the head, but in the foot or knee or intestines or all three so that pain would give him a motive to talk. He would wring him out and finish the job before anyone in this cold, damp, sleeping city woke up and interrupted him.

Christopher read these thoughts as if Stutzer were speaking them aloud, smelled his panic just as he smelled his sweat beneath the cologne. The street made a sharp turn. Stutzer disappeared from view. He began to run. Christopher knew this even before he turned the corner himself because he heard him splashing through the ankle-deep torrent that rushed over the cobblestones. Christopher himself broke into a run and, athlete that he was, was moving at full speed within two or three steps. Ahead of him, Stutzer lost his footing. His mustard raincoat billowed, his hat flew off. He fell on his back with a cry of panic and skidded downhill, hands and feet flailing. Christopher stopped in his tracks and watched. Stutzer was heading toward a flight of stone stairs that had been turned by the downpour into a waterfall.

Stutzer's momentum turned him onto his stomach. He looked at Christopher, held out a hand as if he was about to go over Victoria Falls, and shouted, "In the name of God!"

Christopher moved. He caught up with Stutzer when he was very close to the edge and seized one of his frantically waving arms. This was enough to save Stutzer, who grabbed a railing, but Christopher himself, as if on ice, slid onward toward the stairway, feet together and arms outstretched for balance. At the last moment he grasped the banister and stopped himself. Stutzer got to his feet. He stared wild-eyed at Christopher and clawed at his coat pocket. He found his pistol, but it was entangled in wet cloth and he could not draw it. He stood in front of a thick padlocked door. He kicked it, nearly knocking himself over backward, but the door did not yield. He drew his weapon at last. By now Christopher had regained his balance. He was no more than half a dozen steps away and coming fast. Stutzer fired—not at Christopher, but at the padlock. The sound was weak, not much louder and no more identifiable than a single running footstep, not loud enough to wake even a light sleeper.

The padlock, an old iron one, shattered. Stutzer threw open the door and plunged through it. Christopher, running at full speed, launched himself into the air, and hit the door with his body before Stutzer could bolt it from inside. The door, with Christopher's weight behind it, burst open and knocked Stutzer headfirst down a long flight of stairs. The stairs were carpeted. His soaked raincoat slowed him down, so that he came to rest gently on a landing. A tiny bulb at the top of the stairs shed a little light. Stutzer rolled over and lifted the pistol, aiming at Christopher. His hand shook violently. Christopher plunged down the stairs. Stutzer did not fire, but instead got to his feet and fled heavily down another flight of stairs, then another, with the cocked pistol held above his head. Christopher followed, moving faster than Stutzer, whose thin hair did not stir as he ran. Christopher remembered the brilliantine, the smell of it, and smelled it again. Because the stairs were carpeted, the two of them made very little noise. Now and then Stutzer took sobbing breaths. Once or twice his weapon slammed into the wall, but somehow did not go off. He nudged a round table and almost, but not quite, upset the tall rose-colored vase that sat upon it.

There were people in the darkened house. No one appeared, there were no sounds, but Christopher was aware of warm bodies, of locked rooms full of breath. These sleepers did not awaken—or if they did, they had no time to put on their dressing gowns and open their bedroom doors before Stutzer reached the front door. Christopher was only a few steps above him, but he did not attack or interfere in any way as Stutzer fumbled with the locks. He did not want to kill him inside this strange house. It seemed, as if in a dream, the worst of bad manners even to think of doing such a thing.

Stutzer could not solve the dead-bolt. He swore in German and pointed his pistol at the lock. In the same language, Christopher stage-whispered, "No. Turn the knob to the right." Stutzer did as he was told. The door flew open, he went through it and slammed it behind him. The noise was enormous. Christopher opened the door, showed him-

self, then flattened himself against the wall beside the door, waiting for
the gunshots. A small girl in pajamas appeared at the top of the stairs.
Christopher slammed the door shut. He heard the bullets, five of them,
strike its thick planks.

Stage-whispering again, Christopher said, "Go back to bed now,
dear."

The child nodded obediently and disappeared.

Christopher flung open the door and let himself out. It was dawn
now, or what passed for it in these sunless latitudes, but there was no
sign of Stutzer except for the empty pistol he had dropped onto the
pavement. The house stood on a square. Three streets led from the
square in three different directions. There was no way to know which
one Stutzer had taken.

The city was beginning to wake. Windows filled with buttery electric light. Alarm clocks went off, radios played. A woman dropped a
pot and cursed. These were muffled noises, but Christopher heard them
distinctly above the falling rain. Stutzer's pistol was empty, the action
locked open. Christopher picked it up by the barrel, put it into his
pocket, chose one of the streets, and set off at a run.

The street led to the train station. Had Stutzer, too, followed his
instincts, or his knowledge of the city, and gone to the station hoping
to catch a train, any train, hoping to disappear again? If so, he could
not be more than a minute ahead. Christopher reckoned that he
had now run about half a mile. He was still a couple of hundred yards
from the station. He searched the street ahead for another running man
and saw Stutzer's sticklike figure crossing the station plaza. He had
discarded his yellow raincoat and his battered hat, but even a naked
Stutzer would have been unmistakable. In front of the station he
caught his toe on something and stumbled. He staggered and spun and
seemed to be about to fall headlong, but somehow he kept his balance.
He looked behind him and saw Christopher coming fast. He looked
downward, panicked as if he had lost something irreplaceable, but then
abandoned whatever it was and ran for the doors of the station. He was
limping now.

Christopher heard the whistle of a train approaching the station.

He was only seconds behind Stutzer. Where Stutzer had tripped he saw one of his worn-out shoes lying on the cobblestones. Although train stations were heavily policed, a running man attracted little attention. He sprinted through the door into the ticket hall. It was empty except for a cleaning woman and one ticket agent inside his cage. He heard a train entering the station. Christopher took a platform ticket from the machine and went through the turnstile onto the platform. The locomotive, a coal burner, chuffed slowly down the track, half-hidden in its own smoke. This part of the station was covered by a lofty curved glass roof. Birds flew beneath the panes, some of which had been broken in the bombing and still awaited repair ten years after the war. The rhythmic noises made by the train—smoke belching, steam hissing, steel wheels screeching on steel rails—were amplified.

A dozen bored travelers waited for the train. Most of them were reading newspapers or deep in thought. No one paid the slightest attention to Stutzer, who stood behind the crowd with his back turned to the track, watching the entrance. When Christopher entered he put his right hand inside the left sleeve of his nubbled tweed jacket. The jacket was too large for him and its padded shoulders made his head look small. His pink skin showed through the soaked cloth of his thin white shirt. His chest heaved. He shivered uncontrollably—not from fear alone, Christopher thought, but also because he was chilled to the bone, exhausted, cornered. His left foot was bare, yellow nails visible. Had he, or the dandy he used to be, taken time to remove his holed sock to hide the shame of it? The bare foot twitched along with the rest of his body. He was emaciated.

The fingers of Stutzer's right hand remained hidden in his left sleeve. In a pleasant voice, Christopher addressed him by his name and the secret police rank he had formerly held. He said, "If I see a weapon, you will die immediately. Put your right hand where I can see it, please."

Stutzer obeyed. He said, "I don't know you."

Christopher said, "It will all come back to you."

In a loud but unsteady voice Stutzer said, "Papers! I want to see your papers." His tone was commanding, as if it were he who was making the arrest.

Christopher stepped forward, seized Stutzer's right wrist, then removed the knife from the sheath strapped to his left forearm inside his coat sleeve. It was a dagger, two-edged, razor sharp, a workman's tool, plain and useful with a taped handle. Christopher threw it under the train. Stutzer twisted his arm against Christopher's thumb but wasn't strong enough to break his grip. He uttered a sound—a loud whimper, the noise a spoiled child makes when frustrated. The train was almost stopped now. Another train, approaching from the opposite direction, sounded its whistle.

Stutzer's face twisted. He screamed, "Help! Help! This man is going to kill me!"

Above the noise of the trains—down the tracks, the second one was sounding its whistle again—he was barely audible even to Christopher. One or two of the passengers looked at the disturbance over their shoulders. They saw a fine-looking young man in good clothes confronted by a derelict who wore only one shoe and was screaming in dumb show, drowned out by the train. His face was twisted. Gobs of spittle shot from his mouth with every word. He was the picture of insanity. He cried, "He has a knife! He has a knife. He has a gun! He is a criminal! Help me!" No one listened.

The incoming train was still rolling, but barely. Stutzer spun around and with a desperate effort, broke free. He fell down, got up again, and made a dash for the train, arms and legs awry. Just as it stopped, he leaped in front of the locomotive and dashed across the tracks toward the opposite platform. Just as he reached the middle of the other set of tracks, another whistle blast sounded and the second train entered the station from the opposite direction. Smoke swirled, machinery howled. Stutzer kept limping toward the opposite platform. The train rolled onward, windows aglow, passengers drinking coffee in the dining car. It was a long train and though it was moving fast it seemed to Christopher that it took a long time to clear the station. When the track was empty again, there was no sign of Stutzer, no mangled body, not even a bloodstain on the ties.

EIGHT

1

The Reich and the war remade both O. G. and Christopher. After the death of Rima and the disappearance of his mother, Christopher had gone back to the United States, finished school, joined the Marines, been wounded on Okinawa, then gone to college. Days before Germany declared war on America, O. G. went from Berlin to Switzerland and there, as a member of the Office of Strategic Services, became in fact what he had previously been suspected of being. He was good at the work. Some of the German army officers he had invited to dinner in Berlin in the thirties almost succeeded in assassinating the Leader with a bomb whose silent timer (acid burned through a trip wire) was provided by O. G. Others who had come to his parties passed him information from inside the Reich. He mentioned Lori's name to people interested in murdering Heydrich, and Heydrich was murdered in Bohemia.

After the war, O. G. ran into Christopher in New Hampshire at a prep school reunion. The two men had not seen each other for ten years—not since the day in Elliott Hubbard's New York house when Christopher's chilly behavior froze O. G.'s tongue to his sled. O. G.'s greeting was cordial, but no trace of their godfather-godson relationship remained. O. G. was almost an old man. His hair was white. He had a paunch. He still wore his gold Wilsonian pince-nez and pink neckties. He displayed in his buttonhole the rosette of a decoration Christopher did not recognize. O. G. invited Christopher to lunch at a gentleman's club on Beacon Hill and offered him a job in his new organization.

Christopher accepted immediately, but the ice never melted entirely. During the recruitment lunch and ever since, O. G., calling him by his surname, had treated him as a stranger whom he scarcely knew. That was, of course, the reality.

Now that O. G. was the director of the newborn American intelligence service and Christopher was one of the handful of agents he handled personally, their contacts were fairly regular, though on a new, more formal footing. At the time of his encounter with Stutzer, Christopher was posted to Geneva on O. G.'s orders. He was engaged in an operation to recruit a high-ranking Soviet intelligence officer. The target, a KGB colonel named Yuri Kikorov, was the highest-ranking Russian who had ever, in the short life of the Outfit, come so close to defecting to the Americans. O. G. handled every detail of this project personally. Christopher was his man and acted on his orders. This break in protocol ruffled feathers in the Outfit's Geneva base. The Geneva people felt left out, unconsulted, ineligible for credit if the operation turned out well, but in danger of taking the blame if it did not.

The Russian had shown every sign that he was willing to be recruited, but for reasons unexplained he hesitated to take the final step. O. G. flew over from Washington to discuss the problem. At dinner with the chief of the Geneva base and Christopher, he remarked that what was needed to fix the problem was a fellow like Ezra Stubbins, the jack-of-all-trades who had been on call to his grandfather's cotton mill in upstate New York. "A hundred years ago my grandfather bought some fancy new spinning machines but they soon broke down," O. G. said. "Gramps sent for Ezra. Ezra studied the machines for awhile, then pulled a hunk of bailing wire and a pair of pliers out of his hip pocket and fixed 'em. Five minutes later the mill was humming again. My grandfather asked Ezra how much he owed him for the repair job. 'One hundred dollars and five cents,' said Ezra. He was asked to itemize his curious invoice. Ezra said, 'The nickel's for the bailing wire, the hundred's for the horse sense.'"

The chief of base laughed appreciatively, even though he knew that this was O. G.'s way of suggesting that he was having dinner with a slow thinker.

O. G. said, "Bailing wire, anybody?" Silence ensued. "Nobody wants to be Ezra?" O. G. said. "What about you, Christopher? You're closest to this thing."

Christopher had been the dangle in this operation—that is to say, he had attracted the interest of the Russian colonel by giving him the impression that he himself might be recruitable. After this dropping of the handkerchief, the hoped-for friendship with Yuri developed. This began with invitations to public events. Several times a year, Yuri gave fisherman's parties like the ones O. G. had hosted in Berlin, and Christopher was nearly always on the guest list. Soon Christopher was dining alone with Yuri in restaurants in the old city and sailing with him on Lake Leman. They played chess in a coffee house on Wednesday afternoons and became members of the same weekend rugby team. They discussed their wars. Yuri had fought with the partisans in Ukraine and like Christopher had been wounded in the legs. He insisted on pulling up the legs of his trousers and comparing wounds. Yuri's scars were larger. "Red Army surgery, not enemy bullets," he said. He often made little jokes about his country's backwardness. Once or twice Christopher and Yuri went together to the casino at Annecy. Yuri bet recklessly on roulette and lost far larger amounts of money than a colonel in the Russian intelligence service could handily afford. Opinion in the Outfit was divided as to his motivation. The Outfit's counterintelligence division in its deep respect for the Russians believed that it was all an act. In its opinion, no compulsive gambler could ever be promoted to colonel by the Russians. More likely he wanted Christopher, who—no offense—was no match for a Russian of Yuri's vast experience, to think he had a chink in his armor. Christopher wondered what difference it could possibly make, but held his tongue.

O. G.'s first principle in running the Outfit was freedom of speech. Everybody had it, regardless of rank, and was expected to exercise it. O. G. had gone to the trouble of enlisting the brightest young men in America, and he wanted to know what they thought. In theory the most junior officer could speak his mind to the director himself or any other superior. The principle was not, of course, always the practice where lower-ranking, less self-confident superiors than O. G. were concerned, but outspokenness was the watchword, so when O. G. asked him what was wrong with the operation, Christopher told him.

He said, "We're too hesitant."

O. G. said, "Explain that, if you please."

"Yuri expects us to ask him the question, to make ourselves clear. We don't do that because we're not sure that he's genuine. This game of cat and mouse confuses him."

The chief of base said, "But what if he's a dangle?"

O. G. turned to the chief of base. "Do you know for certain, Monty—for certain, mind you—that your wife is not a Soviet agent?"

"My wife?"

"For certain, Monty."

"No, but. . . ."

"Thank you," O. G. said. "Christopher, ask the colonel tonight, straight out, if he would like to join us."

The following evening, with Yuri already on his way to Washington on a black Outfit aircraft, O. G. invited Christopher for drinks in his hotel suite overlooking the lake. At minimal taxpayers' expense, they drank a half bottle of Mumm's Cordon Rouge, neither man's favorite champagne, and ate what the room service menu said was Iranian caviar. The room was almost certainly equipped with listening devices, so no toasts were made to bailing wire and horse sense. Christopher had simply done what he was paid to do. However, O. G. went so far as to lift his glass with one hand, give a thumbs up with the other, and say, "Well done."

They talked baseball. Christopher had in fact taken O. G.'s advice and played the game for his American school, but neither O. G. nor Christopher mentioned the many times O. G. had counseled the young Paul to take up ball and bat. Hubbard's name was not mentioned. Neither was Lori's or Rima's. O. G.'s duty as a Christian gentleman and honorary godfather placed him in *loco parentis* now that Hubbard was dead and Lori had disappeared and was presumed by everybody but her son to be dead, too. O. G.'s gaze was gentle when he looked at Christopher, but it was just as sympathetic when pigeons on the windowsill caught his eye. Christopher suspected that the old gentleman was happy enough to have, as an agent, a fellow who was reckless enough to get back on the *Bremen* in time of war and sail to the Reich. But maybe he was less enthusiastic about having him as a godson.

Christopher said, "I wonder if I could have your thoughts on a personal matter." He handed O. G. a single sheet of paper, half covered with typing.

O. G. raised his eyebrows but took the paper and read it. It was an account of Christopher's encounter with Stutzer. O. G. read at a dyslectic's pace, so slowly that he seemed to be willing himself to linger on every word. Then he read the half-page again. When he was finished he gazed through the window for a long moment at the floodlit Jet d'Eau, the famous Geneva fountain that spurted from the surface of the lake. Then he took off his pince-nez, bit his lower lip, and tapped his front teeth with his glasses, a sign of deep thought. O. G.'s eyes were watery, paler than Christopher remembered.

O. G. said, "There is no doubt in your mind about the, uh, moment of recognition?"

"None."

"Who else have you told about this?"

"No one."

It was O. G.'s turn to be chilly. "And what do you want from me, sir?"

"I just want you to know that I will be pursuing a personal matter in addition to my regular duties. Unless you object."

"In which case?"

"I will have to make a choice."

"You're asking my permission?"

"Informing you."

"You want my help?"

"No need, thank you."

"You would refuse it if offered?"

"It would depend on what kind of help was offered. As I've said, this is a personal matter."

"I see," O. G. said.

On the bottom corner of the typed page he wrote a name, David, and tore off what he had written. This scrap of paper was no larger than a thumbprint. Handing it to Christopher, he said, "This is the man to go to for information. He'll be expecting your call."

There was a little champagne left in the half-bottle. "Let's have the dividend," O. G. said. He poured what was left into their glasses in equal measure, drop for drop.

"You've read W. Somerset Maugham?" he asked.

Christopher said, "Most of him."

"Do you remember that short story of his in which a fellow stalking a tiger in the jungle goes around in a big circle and comes upon two sets of the tiger's tracks?"

"I do."

"The point being?"

"The tiger was tracking the hunter."

"Yep," O. G. said, draining his glass. "Keep your eyes open, young man."

2

"Okay, this is what we know," David Patchen said. He spoke in complete, unadorned sentences and full paragraphs. He never said *uh* or *ah* or hesitated in any way. From time to time he took a sip of water. He recited the file on Stutzer from memory without referring to notes—date and place of birth, the same for his parents and grandparents, details of his education, excerpts from his teachers' evaluations, his enthusiasms. "Essentially he was only interested in the party, to which he was fanatically loyal, and insects," Patchen said. "He was— still is, we can suppose now that we have a reliable report that he's alive—an amateur naturalist. He captured and mounted all sorts of bugs. His collection was huge, packed in special trunks with folding shelves, and he lugged it around with him wherever he was sent."

"Girls?"

"His orderly says that the troops thought Stutzer was a homosexual, but he, the orderly, never saw anything to support that idea. He never sexually molested the women or for that matter the men he interrogated. He would beat them up and sometimes shoot them, always with one nine-millimeter bullet through the left eye while they kneeled before him, an interesting detail. But no hanky-panky. Or so the orderly says."

During the invasion of Poland in 1939, Patchen said, Stutzer served as commander of several death squads whose mission was to round up and execute Jews. "He was promoted to the SS equivalent of lieutenant-colonel and awarded another Iron Cross First Class for his work," Patchen said. "According to his commendation, he was exceptionally imaginative, innovative, and enterprising. The morale of his men was high. He devised new methods that greatly increased the efficiency and productivity of his command. The methods he invented are not described. He caught the eye of Himmler, who wanted him for his own staff, but Heydrich, who had been Stutzer's patron from the start, insisted on keeping him. He went back to Berlin as head of Section A, the enemies section, of the Gestapo. He and Heydrich worked together on the most sensitive cases. According to the orderly, Stutzer procured women for Heydrich."

Christopher felt his face changing color. He began to remember the Daimler, and Stutzer directing the operation, but he pushed it from his mind. "Where does all this information come from?" he asked.

"From the files of the Schutzstaffel. We—that is, the U. S. Army—captured a lot of their archive in 1945.

And by the way, speaking of the SS archives, we found Stutzer's fingerprints, taken when he joined up. If you want, we can check to see if they match the ones lifted from the gun you took away from Stutzer."

Christopher did not respond to this offer. Patchen continued his narrative. When the Wehrmacht invaded Russia, Stutzer was right behind the infantry. He was again in charge of a formation of special groups, and this time he made an even more brilliant impression on his superiors because he found the Ukrainians even more enthusiastic than the Poles in helping him to find and liquidate Jews. He was decorated and promoted again, to full colonel or in SS parlance, *Standartenführer*, and because he had made so many valuable friends among the Ukrainians, he was placed in charge of intelligence operations and some shock operations against the local partisan movement.

"He did his usual excellent job," Patchen said. "He used the same tactics against the partisans as he had used against the Jews. Arrest them, order them to dig a mass grave and get into it, shoot them, cover them up."

"And after the partisans?" Christopher asked.

"Stutzer was captured by the Red Army on date unknown, 1944, during the German retreat from the Ukraine. He disappeared into the Gulag."

Patchen pulled himself to his feet and limped to the water cooler. He drank three large paper cups of water one after the other without pause, then sat down again.

Christopher said, "Is that the end?"

"Not quite," Patchen replied. "There are people in Z Group in Berlin. You know what that is, I believe—former German military intelligence officers, Soviet and Eastern Europe specialists, who came over to us after the war and brought their files with them. Z Group has reported some sightings."

Patchen cleared his throat. He yawned, then yawned again. It was eleven o'clock at night. He had come in to work at seven in the morning. He had eaten a sandwich from a brown bag for lunch. He had had no supper. He never drank coffee or tea. Extra weight made his old wounds more painful.

"Give me a minute," Patchen said. He took a bunch of keys out of his pocket and, holding it in his hand, leaned back in his swivel chair and went to sleep. An instant later the keys dropped from his hand. The noise woke him up. He had been asleep for no more than a second. It was Patchen's theory that a single instant of total relaxation was all that was needed to restart a deeply fatigued body and brain. He picked up the keys, put them back in his pocket, and resumed the briefing.

Patchen said, "Z Group reports tend to be bare bones, but there are half a dozen mentions of our man in their product. There were other reports, scattered over years. Stutzer in Dresden in the fifties, working as a chauffeur for the Soviet consulate and running low-grade agents.

Around this time the East German secret police were being organized as part of MfS, the ministry for state security. Stutzer applied for a job, presumably on KGB instructions, and was hired. He continued to report every week to a Soviet case officer."

"About what?" Christopher asked.

"Sorry, no information," Patchen replied. "But there's one more goodie. In 1950 Z Group heard from an asset of theirs, a Ukrainian, who had run into Stutzer in a special camp in the Urals for potentially useful prisoners of war."

"What was the Ukrainian doing there?"

"He was a guard. Anyway, he reported that Stutzer was the worse for wear after his time in Siberia or wherever—malnourished, obsequious, but still canny, still the Schutzstaffel colonel. Still insufferable, in the Ukrainian's phrase."

"But alive."

"He was when the Ukrainian saw him."

3

Of all the facts and rumors about Stutzer that Patchen had revealed to Christopher, only one offered an immediate opportunity. Stutzer had been hunting partisans in the Ukraine at the same time that Yuri Kikorov was fighting with those same partisans. Stutzer had been captured by partisans. Why had he not been shot? Had someone with a cool head recognized his value as a source of information and saved his life? Was it possible that Yuri might remember? Christopher asked for authorization to visit Yuri.

"That's tricky," Patchen said. "It breaks the rules. No stranger, especially not you, who's supposed to vanish from Yuri's life forever, is allowed to interrupt the debriefing. They have to keep him in his own little world."

Christopher said, "It has to do with Stutzer."

Patchen was expressionless. "I'll inquire. Sit for a minute."

He limped away. Patchen had been wounded by a grenade on

Okinawa. He had lost an eye, his face had been disfigured, muscles in his arm and leg damaged. Christopher heard him talking over the secure telephone on O. G.'s desk in the adjoining room. The conversation was brief.

"O. G. is concerned about Yuri's welfare, his state of mind," Patchen said when he returned. "He wants to make sure that he's okay. He'd like you to pay him a visit, see how he's getting along, judge his mood, ask if he needs anything."

"When? Where?" Christopher asked.

"Day after tomorrow, most likely. Drop by the outer office at eight in the morning on that day. Mrs. Kane-Poole will have a package for you that will include directions."

"They'll let me in?"

"Yes, you'll have a *laisser-passer* signed by the director." Patchen smiled his goblin smile. "Getting them to let you out may be another matter."

Common sense dictated that defectors should be treated well—a comfortable but isolated house, good food and wine and spirits in moderation, books in Russian that were forbidden in the Socialist motherland, a hi-fi and a record collection, newspapers, magazines and a radio and television, movies at night, no visible security but plenty of it, an atmosphere of welcome and collegiality. Anything but a woman; that was too chancy in a hundred different ways. The turncoat was permitted to go for walks under discreet surveillance, to bird-watch or collect butterflies or gather wild mushrooms if that was how he chose to relax. Tennis, billiards, chess, cards were available with partners provided. Civilized treatment encouraged cooperation. A turncoat should think that he was confiding in men like himself, not confessing to an enemy. Every spy has a story that he is dying to tell. The trick is to get him to tell the first secret. After that all the others usually spill out—except, of course, those buried personal truths that most human beings never reveal to anyone.

Christopher supposed that Yuri Kikorov was installed in some pleasant old country house with a view of the Blue Ridge mountains or the Potomac River, discovering the pleasures of life in America. The chief of counterintelligence, which was in charge of debriefing defectors, did not share O. G.'s belief in the persuasive powers of hospitality and camaraderie. In his heart he believed in shock treatment—slam the steel door on the prisoner and feed him soup and bread twice a day, watch him through the judas hole, disorient him, make him want to get out at any cost, and then connect him to a lie detector and tell him that the price of liberty was complete regurgitation of everything he knew or thought he knew. The price of silence? The silence of the grave.

As specified by the instructions in the package that O. G.'s secretary handed to him, Christopher drew a car from the Outfit's motor pool. He was issued a red two-door Pontiac equipped with whitewall tires and Maryland license plates. The Outfit's operational vehicles were nothing like the polished black Opels and Benzes and Daimlers of the Reich secret police. Their flashiness was their camouflage. They were meant to blend in, to suppress curiosity rather than invite recognition and inspire fear. Following directions included in the package, Christopher drove south from Washington through the Virginia countryside, then west toward the Blue Ridge mountains, then through dense woodland down narrow gravel roads marked *Dead End*, but seeing no dead ends until he came to a locked gate. A ten-foot-high chain-link fence topped with barbed wire stretched in both directions. A sign said *No Trespassing Private Property Keep Out Protected by Armed Guards Beware the Dogs*.

Christopher had been issued a walkie-talkie radio and given a call sign. The radio was identical to the ones he had used during the war except that it was painted in camouflage rather than plain green. He sent a series of dots and dashes by clicking the send button. There was no reply but after a few moments a man dressed in hunter's clothes the color of dead leaves stepped into the road on the other side of the gate. He carried a shotgun and led an attack dog that quivered with nervous energy. Christopher glanced in the rearview mirror. Another hunter stood behind the car, twelve-gauge pump gun at port arms. A third hunter materialized from the woods beside the car.

"I. D., please," this hunter said.

Christopher handed over the Maryland driver's license he had found in the bottomless package. The hunter examined it and handed it back. Apparently this was an all-clear signal. The hunter behind the car lowered his shotgun. The hunter inside the gate unlocked it and let it swing open. The hunter beside the car said, "Drive on, sir. It's about fifteen minutes to your destination. Do not leave the car or drive off the gravel road. Leave your walkie-talkie on."

After a mile or so Christopher emerged into broad fields surrounded by the whitewashed board fences of a horse farm. He saw no horses or other livestock, but it was winter and he guessed that the animals were in the white barns that he saw in the distance. Beyond the barns a large white manor house, verandah columned to the eaves Mount Vernon-style, stood on a low hilltop with the blue mountains behind it. A driveway lined with large trees led to the house. Christopher drove in, feeling on his skin the eyes that were watching him through binoculars.

The walkie-talkie squawked. A voice said, "Please drive around back and follow the signs to the garage." Christopher did as he was told. The garage looked like a barn, and it was fitted with several oversize garage doors. As the red Pontiac approached, one of the doors pivoted open. Christopher drove through it. The door closed behind him. He rolled down his window and remained in the car. He saw no sign of life. The garage was shadowy. Light fell in strips through high, louvered windows. He saw two Jeeps, a fire truck incongruously painted army green, several cars, and a single-engine Beechcraft airplane. Except for the pings and creaks from the Pontiac's cooling engine, the silence was complete.

A voice beside him said, "You can get out of the car now, sir."

Christopher did as suggested. Two more hunters confronted him. One asked for his ID. Again he produced the Maryland driver's license. The man looked at the license and spoke a recognition phrase: "See any deer on the way in?" Christopher supplied the correct answer: "Only one. A six-point buck." The second hunter patted him down to see if he was carrying a weapon. He was not.

"Follow me, sir," the first man said.

4

Yuri Kikorov seemed to be alone in the house. This was not actually the case. His minders from counterintelligence were just keeping themselves out of the way. They did not want Christopher to see their faces or hear the fictitious names they were using on this job. He had no need to know what they looked like or who they were or what they were doing. They were the most secret of the secret and wanted the world to know it.

Yuri, dressed as an American in a plaid shirt and corduroy trousers and hunter's boots, met Christopher at the front door. He had grown the beginnings of what promised to become a luxuriant black mustache and beard. He was very much at home. He led his guest to a greenhouse room in which a small orange tree and several large tropical plants grew in pots. A small round table was laid with a teapot under a cozy and sandwiches and a large chocolate cake.

Yuri said, "We have Russian tea and peanut-butter-and-jelly sandwiches. Are you hungry? The sandwiches are excellent."

As they ate, Yuri described his outings. He had been to the movies, *The Far Country* with James Stewart, *East of Eden* with James Dean. He preferred Stewart, a serious actor. Dean should be punished for his mumbling, his twitches. He had dined in restaurants, always ordering southern fried chicken and mashed potatoes, followed by apple pie à la mode. He had gone to a basketball game. He had asked to be taken to a dance hall, but his minders told him that there were none closer than Richmond. They gave him instead a copy of Playboy. A Civil War battle had been fought nearby and he had visited the battlefield and studied the historical accounts. "Lee should have been a general in the Russian army," he said. "He loved frontal assaults. Thousands died to entertain him. Charge the cannon, make corpses." In the Great Patriotic War, at least in sectors where Yuri had fought, the Red Army had driven crowds of prisoners from the gulag ahead of itself into the German machine guns on the theory that the enemy would run out of ammunition before the real armed Russian troops charged. Sometimes the victims were equipped with pitchforks or scythes to encourage the

Germans to take them seriously. "The slaughter was amazing," he said. "But the enemy always had more bullets than we had ziks."

For dessert they had the chocolate cake—in Yuri's case, two pieces. Yuri said he had never in his life eaten so many sweets as he had done since coming to this house. "I have tremendous energy," he said. "Of course you get the same amount of sugar from vodka, but vodka makes you unconscious. It is quite clear to me now. History will be decided by this struggle between vodka and chocolate cake."

Both men knew that every room in the house was wired. Microphones were hidden in the table, in the orange tree, in the fichus in the far corner. Yuri may well have assumed that one was hidden under Christopher's clothes.

Christopher said, "Is it possible to go for a walk?"

"We'll see. Usually there's no objection, but usually I have no one from outside to talk to like today. The men in brown are all over the place with their shotguns, and everyone knows I certainly have no wish to escape this paradise, so let's go. Do you want to empty your bladder first?" Christopher shook his head.

The day was bright, the sky cloudless. A sharp wind blew, rearranging the thin snow that lay on the ground. For his outings Yuri had been provided by his hosts with a bright-red woolen deer hunter's coat and cap. "From Abercrombie and Fitch," he told Christopher. "The wool is very fine." Now that the sun was warmer, horses, some of them mares with colts, had been let out of the barns. Yuri said, "Many, many horses were killed in the war. We ate them, ours and the Germans'. So did the enemy. A dead horse is sadder than a dead soldier. Can you make a poem out of that line, my friend?"

Christopher thought of his father, driving across Pomerania in the Horch and telling the woeful tale of fallen German war horses. Had Hubbard been present, he would have told them the precise nutritional value of horse meat. Yuri's reference to writing poetry caught Christopher's ear. In theory Yuri did not know Christopher's true name, let alone that he had published poetry. But there was no guessing what he might really know.

"This was in the Ukraine?" Christopher asked.

"What?"

"Eating the dead horses."

"We preferred wounded horses—fewer worms. The Ukraine, yes. But everywhere was the same," Yuri said. "Your army had no horses?"

"Only for parades," Christopher said. "Did you ride horses like the partisans in books?"

"Sometimes, but in the end we always had to eat them. We foraged for our food in a country where everything, every kernel of grain, every turnip, all animals wild and domestic had already been eaten, raw sometimes, even the dogs and cats and the rats and mice. The American army would have sent a hundred airplanes and parachuted hot dogs and chocolate cake to the boys. But we were on our own."

They sauntered along a forest path. A hunter walked a few yards ahead of them, out of earshot, and another followed them at the same discreet distance. A couple of others drifted through the woods on either flank. Yuri said, "The others, up at the house, call these guys Daniel Boones. Did you know that?"

Christopher shook his head no. "If you were that short of food, what did you do with prisoners?" he asked.

Yuri said, "We conversed with them, then we shot them. We seldom ate them."

"You always shot them?"

"We couldn't feed them."

"Shooting them was the rule, even when you captured a German officer who might have important information?"

"Such prisoners were rare, no pun intended."

"But not unknown."

"No. My friend, come to the point, please."

Yuri paused and lit a Russian cigarette with a Zippo. He did not offer a cigarette to Christopher, who, as he knew, did not smoke. The Zippo's large smelly flame flared in the fresh breeze. "A deer or a peasant could smell this thing on the wind a kilometer away," Yuri said, having an anti-American moment. "It is also very hot in your pocket."

Christopher said, "I'm interested in a particular officer of the Schutzstaffel, a colonel, who was captured by partisans in the Ukraine in 1944."

"An SS *Standartenführer*? He probably was shot in both knees and the testicles and left to die."

"This man lived."

"You're sure of that?"

"I saw him in the flesh quite recently."

"Name?"

"Stutzer, Franz. A thin man, about your height. Very well dressed."

"That certainly would have made him stand out in the Ukraine in 1944."

Christopher produced a photograph of Stutzer as he had been in Berlin. Yuri studied it for a moment, then handed it back with no show of interest.

"Why are you interested in this man?" he asked. "The war is over, the Germans are your friends, he is nothing today."

Christopher said, "I think you know him."

"Do I? Tell me why you are interested."

"This is personal, nothing to do with your situation or your debriefing by the people up at the house."

Yuri inhaled smoke, drawing so hard on his cigarette that the burning of paper and tobacco was audible. His eyes bored into Christopher's. This was no prisoner, but a man who was as used to being in absolute control as Stutzer once had been. In his brand-new Abercrombie & Fitch coat and hat he even looked faintly dandyish.

"Personal in what way exactly?" he asked.

Christopher told him as much as he needed to know. He left his parents out of the story and said nothing about his round-trip to New York and he gave Rima another name, but he related the facts of their encounter with the S-boat and her death.

Yuri said, "I can understand why you might want to find this person. You're right, I know him a little. What I know I will tell you. For your ears only. An extra, just for you. Agreed?"

Christopher nodded. Yuri pinched out the coal of his cigarette and put the butt into his pocket, a prisoner's economy. He said, "You'll owe me a favor for this, you know." Christopher nodded.

They walked on. The hunters fell in step.

5

Just after the war Yuri was posted to Berlin as a Russian midwife to the East German intelligence service. The Nazis had killed so many German communists before the war that there was a shortage of qualified operatives to man the embryonic Ministry of State Security. "The Americans were having success in West Germany with former Abwehr types and worse," Yuri said, "so Moscow decided we should rehabilitate some Nazis of our own."

Yuri fell silent for perhaps a hundred steps as he and Christopher continued along the forest path. Christopher did not ask for a reason. He had learned when he was still very young that if he kept quiet, the other person would fill the silence. It began to snow. Plump snowflakes clung to Yuri's scarlet costume and lodged in his beard and mustache and his thick black eyebrows.

"This was in the early nineteen-fifties," Yuri continued. "The war had just ended. I still hated the Nazis. I had many reservations about this policy of inviting them inside to work with us side by side. These people remained what they had been. There is no such thing as an ex-monster. However, Moscow had made up its mind to find them useful. It was pointless to raise issues that had already been resolved."

Another hundred-step silence followed this brief speech. Clearly Yuri was having difficulty with the subject at hand. He stopped for a moment and looked back at their footprints on the snow-dusted path. The air was still, the light milky. Snowflakes were falling faster now. "The answer to your unspoken question is that I never knew Stutzer in Ukraine," Yuri said. "Somebody else captured him. However, I did hear something at the time about a big Schutzstaffel fish being taken, then shipped east for processing. It was remarkable how much gossip floated around in that no man's land. I assumed that this criminal would be wrung out by our interrogators, then shot."

Nevertheless, as the years went by Yuri kept this particular prisoner of war in mind. Who had he been? What had he known? Why had he been shipped to a camp instead of being shot in the back of the neck? As Christopher already knew, Yuri forgot nothing. Finally, sometime in 1950, Yuri was introduced to an emaciated German who was being held in a jail in East Berlin. "It was the man in the photograph you just showed me," Yuri said. "Until today I never knew his true name. He was captured under a false name. Even that was taken from him by the routine. He became a number. Today I will call him Stutzer for your sake."

Yuri and Stutzer met in an interrogation room. "On the wall of this room, which was used by the Gestapo before we took it over, was an old bloodstain left by somebody who had been shot through the head, judging by its height on the wall," Yuri said. "The stain looked like an upside-down map of Italy. It had been left where it was to encourage prisoners to cooperate. They were made to stand on a mark on the floor so that they were looking directly at the bloodstain and the bits of brain and skull that were stuck in it."

This prisoner was not fazed by the bloodstain. He stared at it calmly, in the detached way in which a connoisseur will examine the work of an unknown artist. Yuri wondered if the man was trying to date and classify the bloodstain. German or Russian? Jew or counterrevolutionary?

Yuri's task was to evaluate the prisoner. Was he or was he not a candidate for recruitment? What Yuri saw before him was what he had seen many times before—a half-starved, half-mad zik dressed in the layers of rags that were the uniform of the gulag. This man had lost everything but his physical existence and he held on to that by a thread. All ziks had once been more than they were now, but this one managed to convey that he was still a somebody. Though he attempted to conceal it, he had a certain force of personality. He had perfected the role he was expected to play—submissive body language, eyes downcast in the presence of his betters rather than staring into empty air like a soldier's or meeting another's eyes like a man. But this was a role he had chosen to play, nothing more. Within himself he still believed, even after six years in the worst kind of captivity, that he was born to dominate. What he had been suffering since 1944 was a mere interruption in his destiny to rule over lesser mortals. He looked like a broken man, he acted like a broken man, but in Yuri's judgment, formed in a matter of seconds, he was not a broken man.

"Usually I avoid such flights of fancy about first impressions," Yuri said. "But it was obvious that this one had not conquered his pride, whatever his act. I asked him a question. He answered in a servile tone of voice. I said, 'Speak to me in your own voice, Number Whatever-you-are.' He snapped to attention, even slapping his heels together in their felt boots and of course not making a sound. He stared at the bloodstain on the wall and answered my original question again. This time his voice was very loud—a Schutzstaffel bark. We were speaking Russian, but nevertheless what came out of his mouth was a sound that only a German officer could make."

The file on Stutzer told Yuri little that was useful. He had cooperated from the first with Soviet interrogators. He understood from his own past experience that resistance was pointless. In the end, everybody broke, everybody talked, everybody begged for mercy. His captors knew that he knew this. In Yuri's opinion Stutzer had lied to his interrogators about nearly everything, including his identity. His papers identified him as a member of the fighting SS, rather than as the secret policeman he really was. The rest of his testimony was a cover story backing up his papers. True, he commanded a *kommando* that hunted down Soviet partisans, but that was war. The partisans conducted the same type of operations against German forces, as his capture and the immediate summary execution of all his men demonstrated. All questions about the German order of battle he answered truthfully. He had no reason not to cooperate. The Red Army already knew what units of the Wehrmacht they were fighting, who commanded them, what their strength was. Besides, the German armies were in full retreat. Chaos was queen. Communications were disrupted. Even the German High Command did not know exactly what units were left or where exactly they were or how effective they might be. The war was lost. Everyone knew this. Stutzer had done his duty in the greatest war in history. Now that the war was over except for the final skirmishes, his duty was to preserve himself and the wisdom he had gained to fight the next one. Of course Stutzer never said that, but Yuri knew that it was true.

Yuri said, "He said the same thing about the Soviet victory as Hitler did later on. In his first session with an interrogator Stutzer said, 'The eastern people have shown that they were stronger than the German people, therefore they are the superior race.' Whether he actually believed this or was just telling a stupid Russian peasant like me what he thought I wanted to hear is an open question."

Throughout his many interviews with Yuri, Stutzer conveyed his admiration for the Red Army, for Communism. The war, he said, had taught him that the wind of history was blowing the Soviet Union toward world rule. If Germany had been overwhelmed—not merely defeated but subjected to apocalypse—what chance could the bankrupt English, the French who had been erased from history, the soft Americans possibly have? Communism, which was just another name for imperial Russia, had already prevailed in China and in half of the old Europe. The rest of mankind would soon surrender, too.

"All this was a subtle performance at first," Yuri said, "conveyed through rueful smiles and words that seemed to escape from him rather than being spoken by a conscious effort of the will. As time went on he became more forthright. It was all lies, of course, but he was a good actor and he gave a masterly performance. In the end it was the performance that opened my eyes to the value of this fellow. After all, I wasn't looking for an angel. I had been asked to decide if Stutzer might be useful to the Ministry of State Security of the German Democratic Republic. By every measure—Stutzer's training, his skills, his experience, his accomplishments, his intelligence, his guile, his gifts as an impersonator, his fluency as a liar—it was obvious was that he was wonderful material. The fact that he was also a psychopath was no impediment—quite the opposite."

Still Yuri hesitated about signing him up. With Yuri's blessing, Stutzer was controlling the interviews, and, in his own mind at least, controlling Yuri. How could such a megalomaniac be controlled? Even the Schutzstaffel, which Stutzer had loved and still loved, had not been able to control him. Also little by little, Yuri was drawing from somewhere inside Stutzer a truer, if not entirely true, record of his past. In every assignment he had ever been given, this monster had exceeded his orders, exceeded his mission, exceeded his authority. He had also exceeded the expectations of his superiors in nearly everything he did, and because he worked for an organization that had abolished the very idea of excess, he had been richly rewarded. Promotion, decorations, reputation, favor from on high had all come his way. Stutzer was supremely confident that this would happen again if only he could persuade Yuri—condition him—to recommend him to his superiors in the Soviet intelligence service, who were the most powerful secret policemen in the history of the world.

"All of this was mind-reading on my part," Yuri said. "But he was too clever by half, so he was not all that hard to read."

Rising out of his silence, Christopher said, "You liked him."

"I couldn't bear him," Yuri replied. "But I thought he was qualified. My assignment was to render an opinion on his potential as a servant of the Communist Party of the German Democratic Republic. I was in a position to do great harm if I made a bad decision. I was being pressed to make up my mind on this case. I was accused of dawdling."

"He was your only case?"

"No, there were others, but he was by far the most interesting one. Usually the answer was obvious. Maybe one in every fifty candidates got a yes. Even the yeses were almost always gumshoe material. Stutzer was different. If he was chosen, he would succeed, he would rise, sooner or later he would be trusted. Then what? That was the question."

Yuri decided to put Stutzer through a series of practical tests. This required putting him on the street. He was outfitted with a new suit and everything that went with it. "He hadn't been dressed like a human being for six years, but you could see the disgust in his eyes when he put on these ugly cheap clothes made in the USSR and looked at himself in the mirror. It was a two-way mirror, needless to say, and I was on the other side of it. The heavy wool suit with its elephant-ears lapels, the clumsy shoes, the hat, even the baggy socks—everything revolted him. He buttoned the coat, he tilted the hat, he turned this way and that like a girl in front of the mirror. His vanity was astonishing, especially since he was a professional who knew all about mirrors in police stations and therefore he understood that he was almost certainly being watched by me from the other side. These clothes had been cut and sewed by chimpanzees. He preferred his gulag rags. No one could question his taste and social rank for wearing a prison uniform. Contempt was written all over his face and of course that expressed his true opinion of the Soviet Union."

Yuri's acuity was already well known to Christopher, but he had never before seen it on such open display. Always before the Russian had concealed a portion of his cleverness—he was too good at what he did to invite something as useless as admiration—but now he was fascinated by what was emerging from his own memory. Christopher was tempted to interrupt, to confirm Yuri's intuition with descriptions of Stutzer the dandy, but Yuri was switched on now and Christopher knew better than to interrupt a man who was trying to tell him something that he desperately wanted to know.

Stutzer was given a number of exercises in tradecraft—follow this man, suborn his wife into informing on him, study his contacts, build up a profile, make a case, nail him even if he was innocent—as he probably was. For Stutzer this was child's play. More complicated exercises followed. He succeeded in them all. He worked quickly, efficiently, without distraction. As his masters in the Schutzstaffel had discovered, he was endlessly resourceful, he found new ways to do things, he improved on old methods. He had forgotten nothing in the six years at hard labor he had already served. He had even learned from the experience. His captors took brutality into new dimensions. They had perfected humiliation as a form of punishment that had no ending, even for those who were eventually released from captivity. His camp in the Urals had had no barbed wire. It wasn't even necessary to lock the cells. There was nowhere to go except into a worse emptiness. The USSR itself was a vast prison of space from which no escape was possible. Even the rags in which he was clothed had a meaning that was, for Stutzer, next door to metaphysical. Appearances were meaningless. The people he had tortured and shot in his day as a secret policeman were always properly dressed for their date with death. Even in Nazi death camps the condemned wore clothes that were in such excellent condition that prisoners were required to take them off and fold them neatly before they were executed. The communists had eliminated such niceties from their own methods. Of course few Soviet citizens owned clothes that anyone else would wish to inherit.

"Stutzer won top marks in everything he was instructed to do," Yuri said. "He would turn what was supposed to be a mere exercise into a real case. Two of his subjects—the man he followed and his treacherous wife—went to prison and another man was actually shot due to his work. He discovered and was able to prove—at least to the satisfaction of my superiors—that this second subject, a former Nazi, was working with the French. In those days it was possible to cross over quite freely from one part of Berlin to the other. Stutzer followed the subject and photographed his meetings with a Frenchman we knew to be a member of the Service des Renseignements. It was Stutzer who broke this man, who extracted his confession."

Yuri broke off and walked on in silence. The snow was ankle-deep now and his cap, his coat, his beard and eyebrows were white. It did not give him a Santa Claus look. His small brown eyes, set deep and wide apart, burned. He stopped and stared at Christopher. He said, "The snow is getting worse." He seemed to expect a question.

Christopher said, "He interrogated this man?"

"Yes," Yuri replied. "It was his final test. I watched through the two-way mirror. Some of my superiors were there, too, because Stutzer had aroused their curiosity. They were already impressed by his feats, and the way in which he conducted the interrogation impressed them beyond their dreams. He was a master, one minute a kindly uncle, the next a madman, quick as a weasel, smart as a whip. The subject had no chance even though he had been in the Gestapo himself and was now a member of the police—an underling, yes, but nonetheless somebody who knew what to expect. It did him no good. Stutzer made him stand for an hour with his arms above his head, he made him drink liters of water. The man wet himself. After that Stutzer really went to work on him. In less than an hour he was signing a confession to crimes he had never committed. Never have I seen a man so much in his element as Herr Stutzer. That was what my colonel called him when they were introduced, Herr Stutzer. My chief was so pleased that I thought he might let him shoot the prisoner himself. But he didn't."

Yuri had not looked at Christopher as he talked, but walked along with his hands clasped behind his back, his eyes fixed on the Daniel Boone who was in the lead. Now Yuri turned around and headed back toward the house. "Without our guides we would be lost," he said. "Tell me, did Stutzer ever interrogate you?"

"Yes," Christopher said.

"How was he dressed?"

"Sometimes in his uniform, sometimes in a civilian suit. He was very well dressed. A dandy."

Yuri said, "On the day he broke the man who wet himself, Stutzer wore his zik rags. He insisted on it. It was very impressive, that, to dress as a prisoner and yet in a matter of minutes establish absolute authority over a policeman."

After this virtuoso performance, there was no real question about Stutzer's future. He would be offered a position in the secret police. He would be given work—lots of work. His talent was needed. The German Democratic Republic swarmed with counterrevolutionaries, with enemies of the people, with former Nazis, with men and women who had treason in their hearts—though like the policeman Stutzer broke they might not know this about themselves until they had spent an hour alone with Stutzer.

"Stutzer knew, of course, that he had made a fine impression, but he was not a man to leave any stone unturned," Yuri said. "In our final interview, the one that would determine my recommendation to my superiors—who had of course already made up their minds—he took me into his confidence on an important matter. I had given him a cigarette, the first one I had ever offered to him, and his eyes watered when he inhaled the first drag. Clearly he had not smoked for some time, if ever. Was he a smoker when you knew him?"

"I never saw him smoke, but yes," Christopher replied.

"Then how did you know?"

"I smelled it on him, and sometimes he left a pack of Dunhill cigarettes on his desk."

Yuri nodded, as if he were the investigator instead of Christopher and he had just gained an important piece of information that he could file away for future reference. He seemed to be following a new line of thought.

Christopher said, "You were saying something about the last interview."

"Yes. He told me he was a communist." Yuri waited for Christopher's reaction to this revelation. Was it staggering, comical, or what? Christopher did not react. Yuri said, "I asked myself, How can a Nazi, a Schutzstaffel officer, a man who swore a personal oath of loyalty to Adolf Hitler, be a communist? I asked him this same question. Naturally he had the answer on the tip of his tongue. He had converted in the camp. One day the scales fell from his eyes and he realized that the ideals of the revolution were the ones he had always believed in his heart. He was the child and grandchild of workers, all his ancestors had been miserable peasants. 'Workers of the world unite' was just another way of saying 'Tomorrow the world.'"

"He said that?"

"Of course not. He wasn't a fool. But that was what I thought as I listened to his first confession. He became the earnest novice. I was the wise old Jesuit."

"You didn't believe him."

"No, my friend, I didn't. But his audacity made an impression. Anyway, by now the decision had been made. He was in. All that remained was to put it in writing, as my colonel expected me to do. I wanted to ask Stutzer how many Jewish Lutherans and Catholics he had handled in his former life, and how many of these converts he had considered to be genuine. But the question was pointless. Stutzer was an opportunist because he was a survivor, and vice-versa. Now he had decided to become an upside-down Maranno, a hidden Nazi instead of a hidden Jew, lighting candles on the Sabbath in a secret room in his house. In its way this was hilarious. He was so sly, and this made him so predictable."

Through the falling snow Christopher saw the windows of the house, filled with yellow light, as if to guide Yuri home. They trudged on, Daniel Boones on the alert all around them, their boots crunching in the snow. Christopher's socks were soaking wet. Yuri's feet in his Abercrombie & Fitch boots must have been as warm as toast. Now the house loomed, its roofline visible, its bulk still obscured by the snow but just discernible. Hubbard, had he been present, might have said that if Turner's palette had been smeared with the colors of ice instead of the colors of fire, this scene would have resembled a Turner painting.

Yuri and Christopher were now too close to the house to finish their conversation before reaching it. Christopher stopped in his tracks. Yuri paused too. Christopher said, "So what was the outcome?"

"I recommended recruitment with permanent precaution."

"Meaning what?"

"Castration," Yuri said. "It gave us some small hope that we could control him."

Christopher stared. "Your recommendation was accepted?"

"He met the surgeon soon afterward." Smiling through the snow, Yuri said, "It's an ancient precaution in the orient. We Russians are an oriental people. We learned from the Tatars that taking a man's testicles makes him dependent on those who have done this to him—grateful, even. He becomes a pet—loyal, affectionate. This is a great paradox, of course—you'd expect undying hatred—but thousands of years of experience with eunuchs have proved that it's true. Stutzer was no exception. The fact that he is a madman may even have heightened the effect."

"He didn't protest?"

"He wasn't told until he woke up from the anesthetic. But why should he protest even if he knew what was in store? Sex meant nothing to him. His vocation was everything. He was born to be a secret policeman. He had little to lose and everything he ever wanted to regain."

Yuri nodded brusquely, as if he had now explained everything, not only about Stutzer but about the whole human race.. He walked on to the house. He stamped his feet on the veranda to knock the snow from his boots. Christopher remained where he was. Through the window he could see a wood fire burning on a hearth. Surely Turner would have made that the heart of his painting.

NINE

1

A month or so after Christopher's talk with Yuri, he and Patchen and Patchen's Doberman Pinscher, Rudi, were walking down the Mall in Washington. "Amazing!" Patchen said. He was enthralled by the city at night. The illuminated buildings—Capitol at one end, Lincoln Memorial at the other, and all the others in between—took his breath away. The classical architecture suggested to him the timelessness of power and civic virtue. New as it was to history, America was the consequence of Athens, the reflection of Rome, the future of the world just as those bygone empires were its past. Like Christopher, his best friend and Harvard roommate, he had been wounded on Okinawa. His injuries were far more serious—he had lost an eye and most of the use of one arm and leg. He loved the country he had bled for. So did Christopher, but because America was something new in the world, he thought that Washington's public architecture should be new, also—less imitative. It should gleam. It should consist of skyscrapers and towers instead of temples and obelisks. He disliked imitations.

However, he did not argue the point. Patchen was almost as silent by nature as Christopher was, so they talked very little about anything but business. They threaded their way through a shantytown of ugly temporary buildings that had been erected on the Mall during the First World War to house an overflow of bureaucrats, and then expanded for the same purpose during World War II. Many of these leaky structures—unpainted, warped, and askew—were now occupied by various operational branches of the Outfit, which had no central headquarters.

O. G. believed deeply that it should never have one, that being scattered all over Washington under a hundred fictitious names and titles kept it from becoming a hive. He wanted it to be anti-bureaucratic and therefore creative, energetic, realistic. Its people, by golly, ought to use their imaginations and do useful things instead of killing time in pointless meetings and otherwise running around in circles, impressing each other. Like Christopher, with whom he had never discussed the matter, he thought that Greek temples bred pride and folly and a sense of inheritance, the seeds of disaster. The greater the privilege, the humbler the home. That was his maxim, or one of them.

Patchen unlocked the door to one of the shanties, identified on its weather-beaten sign as the Center for Language Studies, and turned on the light. They were in a small windowless foyer furnished with a desk and chair and several chairs for visitors. There was no guard, no alarm system, no security at all except for two ordinary Yale locks, one on the outer door and one on the massively thick inner door that Patchen now opened. It led to what appeared to be a radio studio, soundproofed and thickly insulated, but otherwise unfurnished except for a battered oak library table and half a dozen chairs.

Christopher said, "No microphones?"

"Not even in the walls, which is the point," Patchen replied. "You can say anything you like in here and nobody can overhear, unless of course, the Russkies are lurking in the sewer that runs underneath this shack."

"And if they are?"

"That's Rudi's job. He's checking right now."

Patchen released the Doberman from its leash. It trotted around the room, ears up, sniffing the carpet. Then the animal sat down in front of Patchen, awaiting orders. Patchen gave the dog a treat that he took from his pocket and said, "Take a nap." Rudi gulped the treat, lay down with his muzzle between his paws, and closed his eyes.

The two men sat down at the table that was the only furniture in the room. With a sigh Patchen pulled his pistol from its shoulder holster and laid it on the table. It was heavy. He disliked carrying it. Notwithstanding his time as a U. S. Marine, he had been raised as a

Quaker and disliked guns as a matter of principle. Also, its weight was painful because it hung from his wounded right shoulder, which had never healed entirely and never would. But the weapon was an excellent instrument of self-defense. It was so powerful that just one of its soft-nose bullets would paralyze an enemy no matter where it hit him. A man shot in the big toe by a .45 slug was just as helpless as if mortally wounded.

Apart from his chats with Patchen and Yuri, Christopher had been idle since the operation in Geneva. Before that, Christopher had been working eighteen hours a day, weekends included, for more than a year. Like a major league manager, O. G. was giving his star a few days off to heal the invisible injuries that the game inflicted. Christopher was just back from a vacation. Because he had lived abroad most of his life, he wanted to see the America he had only read about. He took the train to Utah, bought a horse to ride and a pack mule, and went camping alone for a month in the mile-high desert of southern Utah. After three weeks of solitude he sold the horses, bought a rubber boat and paddled alone under a chalky daytime moon down the tequila-colored San Juan River. The stream raced through the goosenecks of its narrow canyons. For a week, soaking wet the whole time, Christopher saw only brown water, brown rocks, and a thread of china-blue sky hundreds of feet above him.

"Do you feel rested?" Patchen asked.

"Reborn."

"Good, because I've been asked to pass along one of O. G.'s suggestions."

O. G. never gave orders. He floated ideas, he found gold dust in the opinions of his subordinates, he made what he called suggestions. Sometimes these instructions baffled, sometimes they took the breath away. In O. G.'s mind nothing was impossible. He was loved for this. After all, to be told you were capable of doing the impossible was a rare kind of flattery. Christopher waited to hear what was coming. He had to wait. Patchen rose to his feet, turned his back, gripped the back of the chair with whitened knuckles, and faced the blank wall. For a long moment he seemed to be gazing through a non-existent window. He was subject to sudden attacks of excruciating pain—the nerves down the right side of his body had been damaged by the grenade that almost killed him—and Christopher realized that he was having a seizure now. Patchen was hiding his face. Rudi lifted his head and watched his master. Then the dog, the blackest, sleekest, most muscular animal Christopher had ever seen, fixed his attention on Christopher. He made no threatening movements, but the message was clear: Do not move until Patchen does.

As white-faced as if his skin had been bleached, Patchen sat down again. He said, "O. G. wants you to go to East Germany."

Christopher accepted this information without comment. He knew from experience that this might be the entire instruction. A year or so before he had been given an airline bag full of hundred-dollar bills and told to go to Africa. The colonial powers of Europe were bankrupting themselves supporting their colonies, and it was obvious, at least to O. G., that Britain and France and Belgium would soon be forced to grant these primitive countries independence. The United States was pressuring them to do so. They were looking for a way to lay down the burden of governance without losing the revenues that had been the reason for stealing these godforsaken lands and inventing names for them in the first place. American intelligence, and therefore the rest of the U. S. government, knew very little about what were soon to be called the emerging countries of Africa, and next to nothing about the politicians who were soon going to take over the reins of government. Christopher had deduced that his assignment in Africa was to meet, evaluate, and by doing the favors that his satchel of money made possible, make friends with as many of these future leaders as possible. That is what he did, entirely alone and on his own. O. G. was delighted with these results. "We can be a presence in Africa now, by golly," he exclaimed. "All these benighted colonies are going to be full-fledged members of the United Nations in less time than it took Stanley to find Livingston!"

Now Patchen said, "Your mind is elsewhere."

"Sorry, yes."

"Would you like to know more, or do you plan to make up the

German Democratic Republic as you go along, like you did in Africa?"

"I'm all ears."

Patchen said, "Berlin has picked up some interesting stuff on KGB plans for certain Arab countries, or at least certain Arabs."

"Such as?"

"Such as support and training for guerrilla movements."

"The Berlin base picked this stuff up on their own, or their Germans picked it up?"

"Mostly Z Group. Wolkowicz, is following up."

Barney Wolkowicz was the current chief of the Berlin base. Christopher said, "Tell me the interesting stuff."

"At first it was vague, a report from a minor source, possibly reliable, that the Russians had decided to make use of East German expertise in paramilitary operations in Arab countries."

"What German expertise would that be?"

"There are some former SS and Gestapo types in the East German Ministry of State Security with the necessary experience. Assassination. Bombs. All like that."

"And the East Germans are charged with this."

"Others are involved—Bulgarians, Romanians, Poles. But the Jerries seem to be up front. The Russians hang back, but they provide the plans, the tactics, the money, the guns and explosives."

"Is there a training center, a camp, in East Germany?"

"We think so. We have U2 photographs of an installation that might be it. The analysts made out people in turbans. Somebody on the ground got close enough to smell couscous. There are rumors, again from Z Group, of an office of dirty tricks in East Berlin. Mostly we have the usual suspicions and suppositions. O. G. thinks the motivations add up. Nazis hate Jews, Stalinists hate Jews, Arabs hate Jews. When O. G. was in Berlin before the war he knew Gestapo and SS people who spoke Arabic. He also met anti-Zionist Arabs who were passing through. Even then the Nazis and certain Arabs had a common cause. So it seems possible that old relationships are being reawakened."

"So we don't know much for sure, except that most of this stuff seems to be happening in the German Democratic Republic."

Christopher believed that Patchen was holding something back. It was difficult to read his face. As a practical matter he had no expressions—his wounds again. His artificial eye was unreadable, of course, and so was the good one because it was doing the work of two and always looked tired. Christopher had not known the unwounded Patchen, so he had no idea whether he had always been inscrutable, but he was now as bland as wax. Nevertheless a smile tugged at his lips and there was a brief flash of teeth as he digested what Christopher had just said.

Patchen said, "Z Group, by the way, thinks this is a one-man show. Just one German officer is running this operation."

"Who?"

"Unknown. But he seems to know a lot about irregular warfare."

"And he's doing all this alone?"

"Or with a very small staff. Theoretically, that makes the op all but impenetrable from the top down or the bottom up, because no Arab will ever be told who this guy is or where he comes from."

"Interesting," Christopher said.

"I thought you might think so," Patchen said. "I think O. G. has some idea that you know this man, that you have a personal interest in him."

"Really? Why?"

"It's Stutzer."

"You're sure of that?"

"Yes. O. G. may even be trying to help you out in some godfatherly way, though I'm not sure of that. But watch yourself."

2

Whenever he could, Christopher traveled by train. He liked the solitude of a sleeping-car compartment, the chance to read while the countryside flashed by, the mechanical sounds and the sheer inertia of the experience. In Paris, after his flight from New York, he booked a place on the night train to Berlin. At dinner he was seated by the head-waiter with a young woman who was also dining alone. Her eyes were fixed on the menu. She wore a wedding ring. The choices were mushroom soup or grapefruit, roast chicken or "sole" (meaning flounder), salad, and caramel custard or cheese.

The woman put her hands in her lap and studied the menu card. "Chicken or fish, how dreary," she said in French. "What do you think?"

"The flounder," Christopher replied.

She had not yet looked at him. Now she lifted her eyes, which were large and brown, and examined him without smiling. The waiter arrived with his pad. She put her hands back on the table. Her wedding ring had vanished.

"The soup, the fish," she said. "A small carafe of Muscadet. Cheese."

She looked something like a photograph of Virginia Woolf. She had a long aristocratic face, one of the least symmetrical of the seven or eight faces allotted by evolution to the French. But she had vitality. Her eyes were intelligent, with thick lashes. It was impossible to judge her hair because it had been combed and sprayed into one of the large stiff helmets that were in style. She had good teeth and a quick smile. She dressed modishly, a jacket over a blouse with a many-stranded necklace of beads at her throat. She was tall for a Frenchwoman, slim, well-kept. Christopher did not take this inventory. With little gestures she presented it to him item by item. She was an amusing talker. She spoke French with a faint Niçois accent, lifting her voice at the ends of words and adding a final Italianate vowel that was not present in the written word.

They talked about the Côte d'Azur. She recommended restaurants in Nice and Cannes and their surrounding villages. She recommended Provençal dishes as if he had never heard of them, especially sea bass with fennel and bouillabaisse. She liked swimming, sailing, and in the winter, skiing in the Maritime Alps and sometimes in Cortina and Megève.

"Do you sail?" she asked.

"Not as much as in the past. I don't live close to water."

"You live in Paris?"

"For the moment."

"But you ski, surely."

"Why surely?"

"You look like a skier."

Christopher talked with her about skiing in Switzerland and Austria as he finished his food and arranged his knife and fork on the empty plate. She asked about movies. What did he like? Mostly American movies, he said. Why American films, of all things?

"Because the girl never takes off her clothes and dies in the end."

"Which part of that French cliché do you object to?"

Christopher smiled and drank the rest of his Evian water. Hubbard and O. G. had taught him when he was young to drink good wine or no wine at all. He understood that this was a rule for snobs, but he didn't like bad wine. On a train, which was a giant overheated cocktail shaker, there was no such thing as good wine no matter what the label read. The Muscadet had brought a flush to the woman's cheeks. She was talking more rapidly.

"Me, I prefer French films," she said. "Sometimes Italian, if they're funny. I adore Gérard Philipe—*Fanfan la Tulipe, Les Liaisons Dangereuses*, everything."

"Not Fred Astaire?"

"Tippety-tap. 'Isn't it romantic?' I don't know what Ginger sees in Fred."

The dinner, rapidly served, was not bad. They ate their cheese. The waiter asked if they wanted coffee. The woman said yes, Christopher declined.

"It keeps you awake?" she said.

"Yes."

"Me, too," she said, drinking. "Sometimes all night." Her eyes were wider now and shining.

Christopher had brought a book to the dining car. It lay face-down on the table, dust jacket removed. "What are you reading?" the woman asked. Christopher showed her. It was a novel in English. She turned the pages until she came to the one she was looking for. She rummaged in her purse and found a pencil. With it she drew a circle around the page number, closed the book and handed it back.

"Hide and seek," she said, and rising to her feet she walked down the aisle, swaying with the train and the wine. Her legs were slender like the rest of her—a cyclist's legs, with visible muscles. At the door she looked over her shoulder, a glance full of meaning.

It was bad form for an agent of the Outfit to permit himself to be picked up by a stranger on a train. Even if this had not been the case, Christopher did not sleep with married women. He went back to his own compartment, undressed, and started to read his novel—Joyce Cary's *The Horse's Mouth*. Soon he came to the page whose number the woman had circled in pencil. It was, he knew, the number of her compartment. He put the book down for a moment and remembered Lori's hand without her ring. The Daimler, the Tiergarten, a different train. No. 8 Prinz-Albrechtstrasse. He did not attempt to erase the penciled circle. He read on, but there was no place he wished to go tonight with the mad painter Gully Jimson, and at last he turned off the light and lay in the dark, listening to the train.

3

Christopher met Barney Wolkowicz in a safe house near the Olympic stadium, in the far west end of Berlin. The apartment, small and cramped and dark, was on the top floor of a prewar building that had somehow escaped bomb damage. Nearly every other building Christopher had known as a boy, including the one in which the Christophers had lived in Gutenbergstrasse, had been obliterated by allied bombs. Walking past a certain address he would remember people who had lived behind brick walls and stone façades that were now heaps of fire-blackened rubble. Some of them—Miss Wetzel, perhaps—must be buried under the debris. He did not mention this, or anything else that did not have to do with the business at hand, to Barney Wolkowicz.

He and Wolkowicz had known each other for a long time but even though they liked each other, neither would have described the other as an old friend. Wolkowicz was that rarity in the Outfit, a birthright

member of the working class. His father, born in Russia like Wolkowicz
himself, was a steelworker. His ancestors were serfs. Wolkowicz was a
thick-bodied man with a squashed Slavic face and small eyes that never
wavered—liar's eyes, said Patchen, who had Wolkowicz for an enemy.
Wolkowicz looked older, but he and Christopher were both in their
thirties and not far apart in years. They had a history. During the war
Wolkowicz served in the OSS in Burma under one of Christopher's
cousins by marriage. Later he worked for Hubbard Christopher, who
became head of OSS operations in Berlin after the war. Wolkowicz had
been present when Hubbard was run down and killed in the
Grunewald by a speeding car. It was murder. The murderers, presumably Russians or Germans controlled by the Russians, were never identified. Before being posted to Geneva, Christopher had worked for
Wolkowicz in Vienna. Their operation, located in an abandoned sewer
beneath the Russians' communications center, had been discovered and
invaded by Russian shock troops. Christopher had pulled a wounded
Wolkowicz to safety, shooting down commandoes as he withdrew, then
blown up the sewer. Wolkowicz's German wife had had an affair with
a British agent who was part of the team. Wolkowicz nearly killed the
man, then nailed him for treason. Wherever he went, things happened—bad things as often as good. But his operations usually succeeded, gunfire and moments of rage notwithstanding. He was brave.
No man in the Outfit had been so often decorated. Few were closer to
O. G.'s heart. Only Dickens could have invented such a wondrous
character, said O. G., who was in fact the man who invented him. The
Moloch—that should be Wolkowicz's funny name, said Patchen.
Wolkowicz, who hated most people, had loved Hubbard. Because he
had not prevented Hubbard's murder, he felt responsible for his son.
Because of the episode in the Vienna tunnel, he felt that he owed his
life to Christopher.

Climbing the steep staircase, Christopher heard a piano. The door
to the safe house—apartment, really—was unlocked. Christopher let
himself in. Wolkowicz was playing an old upright that must have survived the air raids, too, but was nevertheless in tune. Christopher wondered if Wolkowicz had smuggled a piano tuner into the safe house,

and if so, what had happened to the piano tuner afterward. The music was Bach, who was Wolkowicz's favorite composer—because of the math, he said, not the melodies. He had gone to college in Ohio on a mathematics scholarship but had minored in music. Hunched over the instrument with his hat jammed on his large head, blunt hairy fingers moving over the keyboard, he looked like an ape in a secondhand suit, but his touch was exquisite. He played as well as any amateur Christopher had ever heard, including his mother. Wolkowicz's musicianship was only one of many unlikely things about him. He spoke half a dozen languages, English and Russian like the native that he was, and had often demonstrated that he could learn any other tongue in a matter of weeks whenever the need arose. He was intensely romantic. In Viennese restaurants on scraps of paper he had written love poems in German for his German wife—very good ones, Christopher thought. In Christopher's opinion he was probably the smartest officer in the Outfit and certainly the most ruthless. He was the rudest person Christopher had ever known. He talked like a thug and pretended to be one and sometimes behaved like one. He went nowhere without a loaded pistol and a blackjack on his person. Because of the cowardice of Christopher's cousin, who had run away from a firefight in Burma and left Wolkowicz alone to be captured by the enemy, all of his teeth had been pried from his jaw by a torturer equipped with a bayonet. He hated the Yale men with whom the Outfit abounded because Christopher's cousin was a member of Skull and Bones and because, in his opinion, all Yale alumni thought that they had done everything that could ever be expected of them in life simply by being admitted to Yale. He felt the same, with less facial expression, about the rest of the Ivy League. His own alma mater was Kent State College.

Christopher made almost no sound opening the door of the garret apartment but Wolkowicz's hearing was keen and so were his other senses. He knew that someone was standing behind him. He knew—did not guess, knew—that the newcomer was Christopher. He finished the piece he was playing, spun around on the piano stool, and said, "For sixty-four dollars, kid, name that tune."

Christopher was surprised that Wolkowicz did not have a pistol in his hand. He liked practical jokes that involved firearms. "One of Bach's fugues for harpsichord," he said.

"A genius. Here's the jackpot question. If Johann Sebastian Bach had been a junior what would his middle name have been?"

"I don't know," Christopher said.

"Ambrosius. What did they teach you at those fancy schools?"

Christopher smiled. He could not help himself. Wolkowicz was a man he did not like unless he was in his presence. When he was, amusement wiped out all the bad moments that Wolkowicz had brought down on him and his family.

"So why are we here?" asked Wolkowicz.

He wasn't playing innocent. He had been told that Christopher would be in Berlin on a certain date and that he was acting under the director's orders as usual. No one had told him that Christopher would want to see him because Christopher had not mentioned this to Patchen, the only man to whom he had spoken at headquarters. Wolkowicz being Wolkowicz, he might have sniffed out something more, or guessed something, or collected fragments of information from some of his many sources. But the three people who knew what Christopher's assignment actually was—O. G., Patchen, Christopher himself—certainly had told him nothing. Even they did not know the whole scenario, and even Christopher would not know until it was over. In operations as in war, plans had a short existence. The future did not issue warnings to the present.

"I've been asked to look into something that interests O. G.," Christopher said.

"What would that be, exactly? Everything interests him."

"Whatever it is, it should have no effect on your interests."

"Right. You're always such a soothing presence. Give me a hint."

"I'm just letting you know as a matter of courtesy that I'm going to be around for a while. I can't go beyond that."

"Why not? You're on my turf. That makes me responsible for you."

Christopher did not say, You know the rules. Wolkowicz cared nothing for the rules. His only rule was to know everything. He demanded to be trusted absolutely. He browbeat anyone who denied him information or trust until he got what he wanted. He was never going to be left behind again. "No more jungle dentistry" was Wolkowicz's motto.

To Christopher he said, "You're here to tell me I've got no need to know what you're up to, and I'm supposed to swallow that and say, Okay, kid, go right ahead and burn the Reichstag, I just love fires. Is that it?"

Christopher knew that there was no point in answering Wolkowicz's question. It wasn't a question. It was a provocation. Force a man to justify himself, make him argue, just get him to speak, and you're halfway home.

Christopher understood Wolkowicz's technique. He broke in to his line of questions and said, "How did you get the piano up here, Barney?"

Wolkowicz glowered. "Stick to the point."

"No, seriously. The windows are too small. The last flight of stairs looks too narrow."

"It was here already. Maybe the Krauts took it apart before the war, carried it up the stairs, and put it back together."

"It sounds like it's in perfect tune."

"To you, maybe."

Wolkowicz emptied his lungs with a mock sigh of impatience. "Cut the crap," he said. "Why are you here?"

Christopher said, "Would it be okay if I stayed in this place until dark? I'd like to do some thinking and take a nap and I don't want to check into a hotel just yet."

Wolkowicz looked at Christopher in silence for a long interval. Christopher knew he was counting his breaths. That was how he had got through the interrogation by the Japanese in Burma, by counting inhalations and exhalations between bursts of pain and thinking of other things—in that particular case, his escape across the steppes as a small boy carried on his father's back. He had used breath-counting as a timing device ever since.

After half a dozen breaths Wolkowicz said, "Sure, why not? Are you armed?"

Christopher said, "No."

"What a surprise. Do you want something now?" Christopher was notorious in the Outfit for his disdain for weapons. In Wolkowicz's view, his refusal to carry arms was demented.

"No, thanks."

"Okay," Wolkowicz said. "If need arises, and if you just happen to be in East Berlin, take the U-bahn to Klosterstrasse, go to the Red Orchestra Inn in Littenstrasse, and ask for Sepp Bauer. He won't be there. Ask to use the bathroom as a matter of very great kindness—use those exact words—and then unbuckle your wristwatch and drop it in the left-hand pocket of your suit coat."

"Wow."

"Shut up and listen. You'll find what you need under the windowsill above the toilet. Push the board toward the window, hard, and keeping the pressure on, lift up. When you hear the click, it's open. Don't force it. Be sure to put it back together before you leave."

As he talked Wolkowicz dressed himself against the bitter damp Berlin winter in a heavy scarf and a thick loden overcoat with a button-in lining that must have weighed ten pounds.

He said, "You're not going to tell me anything, are you?"

Christopher shook his head no.

Wolkowicz fished a key from the thumb of one of his fur-lined gloves and tossed it to Christopher. "Lock up when you leave and throw away the key before you go through the checkpoint," he said. "Don't ditch it in this neighborhood, and not too close to the check-point."

Christopher nodded his thanks.

With his hand on the doorknob Wolkowicz said, "Don't put beans in your ears."

He left, but as Christopher listened to him descending the stairs at a heavy trot, he knew that he would be seeing more of Wolkowicz. Or of people Wolkowicz knew.

4

When Christopher left the apartment at about ten that night he looked for surveillance but saw none behind or ahead of him. He wasn't surprised. This was a desolate neighborhood with practically no cover. Anyone attempting to following him would stick out like a sore thumb. Wolkowicz would have stationed his scouts farther away, somewhere between here and the checkpoint Christopher was likeliest to use when crossing the line that separated the two Berlins. Christopher understood this and had expected it. If he would not tell Wolkowicz where he was going and why, Wolkowicz would put a team on him and find out for himself. If Christopher ran into trouble in the East, then in the worst-case scenario the Outfit would know at least that he had been taken hostage. In the best case, Wolkowicz's men would help him in case of need.

At this time, the Berlin Wall and the long period of quarantine it symbolized were in the future, though not very far in the future. With the proper papers almost anyone could walk across the frontier from west to east. Christopher had all the documentation he could possibly need, all of it false and all of it forged in the Outfit's shop, located in one of the temporary buildings on the Mall. Patchen had handed it over. "You are an obscure toiler in the vineyard of world socialism," he said. "You are an employee of the Ministry of State Security. How's that for chutzpah?" Christopher gazed at his own picture on an official Stasi identity card and tasted bile.

Wolkowicz's sidewalk man picked up Christopher in the Kochstrasse U-bahn station. Two of his friends were posted outside and fell into position as soon as Christopher emerged. All were shabbily dressed and of average size. All were gray-faced men of a certain age, war veterans probably, Z Group possibly. They wouldn't know who Christopher was, only that Wolkowicz was interested in him. As Christopher walked briskly toward Checkpoint Charlie, they followed him, working with tired efficiency like figures from a mechanical clock, changing positions at every crosswalk. They could do this with their eyes shut. Their eyes, thought Christopher, might as well be shut.

At the checkpoint, no one on the American side paid attention to Christopher—the job of the young military policemen was to watch people coming from the other side, and besides they spoke almost no German. The Vopos on their side of the neutral strip looked at Christopher's Stasi ID and asked no questions. The whole process took perhaps three minutes, and then he was walking down Friederich-strasse, but not too briskly because only two of Wolkowicz's men were following him and he did not want them to lose him before the third joined up and he could ditch him, too.

Patchen's had shown Christopher pictures of his target—the building in East Berlin that Patchen called the Mosque, a place where Arabs came and went. Some of these images were mystifying high-altitude aerial photographs. A handful were snapshots taken at ground level. The Mosque was not actually a building, but rather something that used to be a building, a bombed-out wreck whose missing top stories resembled a row of ragged triangles scissored from a sheet of cardboard by a small child. It appeared that two or three rooms on the ground floor of the Mosque had been cleared of rubble to make a sort of cave. Tons of shattered masonry rested on top of this space that was, according to the Outfit's hypothesis, the trigger mechanism of a coming explosion of terrorism in the Middle East. The snapshots were badly underexposed, taken perhaps by a miniature camera hidden under an agent's coat, so that they were not much more informative than the U 2 photos. Nearly everything about the building had to be deduced. Not even its exact address was known, only the street on which it stood and the name of the nearest cross street. Christopher had long since ceased being surprised at how little the U. S. espionage service, and presumably all other such agencies in the world, knew for certain. Their wasteful methods—photographs taken through buttonholes by furtive cameramen trembling in fear of arrest and torture—were so cumbersome that the smallest scrap of knowledge was treated as the bluest of diamonds. Combined and rightly arranged with some of the millions of other scraps of information that rained down daily on headquarters, and with the right luck, this speck of knowledge might someday become a treasure trove. At least that was the theory. Christopher wanted to see the Mosque, which lay near the River Spree, not far from the Ostbanhhof, with his own eyes.

By now it was almost midnight, late to be out in East Berlin, and other pedestrians hurried past, trying to catch the last train from the Underground station a block away. In minutes, if he did not hurry like the others, Christopher would be the only figure on the most patrolled street in this half of the city. Only one of Wolkowicz's men was still behind Christopher. The second had overtaken him and was now bustling ahead, on his way to cover the entrance to the Underground station on the next corner. The third man, easy to spot because he wore a tightly cinched trench coat, had disappeared.

Christopher hung back. The other pedestrians were not numerous enough to make a crowd, but just the same it would be hard to single him out. He wore dark clothes, a dark hat, an end-of-the-day stubble on his chin. He carried a worn briefcase that contained that day's party newspaper, a piece of hard cheese, a half-eaten sausage. He walked with self-importance, like a German who in his youth had been taught to march and stand up straight. He looked and moved and smelled like any other citizen of the German Democratic Republic hurrying home after a long day at work or an evening in a beer hall. When he was close to the station, perhaps twenty steps away, he felt the train rumbling beneath the pavement. He broke into a run. Wolkowicz's lookout waited at the top of the stairs. Christopher stamped on the arch of his foot as he went by, felt limber bones bending under his heel and heard the man gasp in pain. He ran headlong down the stairs, flashed his Stasi ID at the ticket-taker, who saluted, and at the last possible second wriggled sidewise through the closing doors of the crowded car. All eyes were on him for the first second. Like the Stasi man he was pretending to be, he glared back at these inquisitive nobodies, ostentatiously studying their faces as if he intended to recognize them if ever they met again. After that no one met his eyes. He got out his newspaper and read it until it was time to get off. Actually reading the mind-deadening thing was a sign of loyalty to the regime. No one else seemed to have a copy.

He got off the train at the Frankfurter Tor station. There were few streetlights in this bleak quarter of the city. The night sky was overcast.

Christopher was in darkness, and as far as he could tell, alone. This had been a squalid neighborhood even before the bombing by the RAF and the shelling of the Red Army. The damage had been so great and the local population so scattered that the Russians had not even attempted to clean up the damage, except to clear the streets. Because property had no commercial value in a socialist economy, no one else had done so, either. Fires that had burned here fifteen years before could still be smelled on the stones, as if like fossils of the Nazi regime they had colonized the pores in the brick and granite.

Before the war there had been an indoor public swimming pool nearby and on winter Saturdays he had come here with Hubbard, who as a sailor and a former member of his school's swimming team set great store by water sports. He taught Paul the Australian crawl, the breaststroke, the backstroke, the butterfly, even a muscle-twisting, breath-burning Civil War era stroke called the trudgeon that sent water flying for many meters when Hubbard slammed the surface with his long arms and legs. The two of them had always walked back to the streetcar with wet hair smelling of chlorine, stopping along the way at a coffee shop for hot chocolate with whipped cream. Christopher had studied maps to refresh his memory of this neighborhood, to pinpoint the Mosque, but as he walked through the streets leading from the railroad station, he remembered them even though the landmarks had vanished.

The Mosque was on a short street close by the River Spree. By the time Christopher reached it—the way was roundabout and he reckoned he had walked more than a mile—his eyes had adjusted to the darkness. The glow of West Berlin, just across the river, cast a helpful light. He saw that the Mosque in the photograph was not the only one that was occupied. Caves in the rubble had been made in two or three others. On closer inspection he saw that all these were empty. The people who had lived there, perhaps for years, had been cleared out. Stronger doors, clearly brand-new, had been installed and padlocked. Windows had been bricked. Signs had been posted: *Entry Strictly Forbidden.*

It began to rain, softly. Outside the blacked-out Mosque Christopher saw no light but knew that lights burned inside because he heard the putt-putt of a small electric generator and smelled its exhaust. He heard the faint clatter of a typewriter being operated by a fast typist. He looked for a place to conceal himself but spotted no cover. The pad-locked caves, let alone the Mosque itself, would be checked regularly by whoever from the Ministry of State Security was responsible for guarding them. He decided that the best observation point was the roof of the Mosque.

By now his night vision was good, and all around him, wet and gleaming, he saw hillocks of rubble. It would be difficult, he knew, to climb them without dislodging stones and making noise, but after studying the vertical face of the building he could think of no other way to hide himself and see what he had come here to see. Gingerly, he began to climb. The mountain of rubble to which he clung was a land-slide waiting to happen, but as on a real mountain there were solid bits to hold onto—old cornices and sills and beams and fragments of chim-ney. Christopher groped for these handholds and footholds, and mov-ing as slowly and cautiously as if he had been climbing the rock face of a peak in Austria, made his way to the roof. He perceived, rather than saw or heard, some of the scores of feral cats who made their home on the roof bounding soundlessly into the darkness. The smell of cat urine and feces was overpowering. Where there are cats, he thought, there are rats, but what do the rats eat? He took up a position between two of the saw-tooth fragments of wall atop the roof and watched the street below. He was directly above the entrance to the Mosque.

Hours passed. The rain stopped. He heard what he thought might be a pack of rats scurrying across the roof. The smell of the cats' droppings nauseated him. He thought about living the life of a librarian in a small New England town—the harmlessness of it, the seasons, the scent of old books, the walk home under elms that fil-tered the afternoon sun. A wife, a child who liked to listen to stories, iced tea and soft American sandwiches on a screened porch. Rima. He hadn't pictured her in years. He forced her from his mind now. Two uniformed men on bicycles came by and checked the doors of the Mosque and the padlocked caves. They shone flashlights, too feeble for the job, on the rubble and stirred up some cats. One held his torch on a scampering cat while the other pegged stones at it, missing every time.

Shortly after three in the morning, two new figures approached. They shared an umbrella. One of them carried a flashlight. Clearly they knew where they were going, but they did not move with the assurance of Germans, who in this part of town were still conditioned to make an impression even when they were not being observed. Talking incessantly, these fellows sauntered carelessly, following the bull's eye of the flashlight beam as it moved before them over the pavement. The light turned them into silhouettes so that it was difficult to make them out in detail. They were bundled up in heavy coats and what looked in the dimness like knitted ski caps. One of them clapped his gloved hands together. As they drew closer Christopher could see their breath in the beam of the electric torch and wondered about the visibility of his own exhalations. When the two were directly below him, he made out the throat-clearing sounds of Arabic, and even understood a few words. They were talking about women, German women, and the hasty way in which they made love instead of waiting, instead of enjoying the prospect of pleasure, instead of letting themselves be brought to a proper pitch. They were interested only in themselves, they just lay there and waited for the pop. What was wrong with them? As they studied their watches with the flashlight, waiting for the minute hand to move, Christopher glimpsed their faces—dark men, young, one of them bearded. They knocked on the door of the Mosque—two loud bangs, a pause, four taps.

The door opened. No light shone outward. In German a man said, "You are exactly on time. Good."

The door clicked shut. A key turned in an oiled lock. Christopher looked at his watch. It was thirteen minutes past three. The voice he had just heard was a bit thinner, a trifle higher than before, but the tone, the placement of words, the undertone of regal aggrievement as if like Louis XIV he had only just escaped waiting—all those were the same as they had been the last time he heard this man speak.

Climbing down a mountain is more difficult than climbing up it.

Even the cats sent bits of masonry bouncing when they leaped by squads and platoons across the rubble. Christopher swung over the edge of the roof, and pressing his body against the damp wall which was slimy with mildew, found a foothold, then a handhold, then another foothold. He missed the next foothold and fell half a meter or so before grabbing a windowsill, swinging for a moment on his painfully stretched arms, and finally continuing the descent. He put his ear to the door. He could hear men speaking inside the mosque, but so faintly that he could not make out words.

He walked away from the Mosque and at a curve in the street half a block away, pressed his back against a saw tooth of wall that was still standing, and waited.

The Arabs left the Mosque at four-thirty, while it was still dark. They walked away in the same leisurely way in which they had arrived, talking animatedly to each other. Christopher caught no words—the men were too far away—but from their hoarse laughter he imagined that they had resumed their conversation about the sexual behavior of German women. One of the men walked with a slight limp. The other, who swung an umbrella, did not hurry him. From the relaxed way in which they moved, the unguarded way in which they talked in half shouts about things that could do no harm even if overheard, Christopher decided that they were probably not so young as he had earlier supposed. These were men on the brink of middle age, old enough to become the leaders in whom their handlers would naturally be interested. On behalf of their masters the Russians, the East Germans were building a network, designing an instrument. The reckless youths, the ones who were willing to die, would come later. The limping man and his friend with the umbrella were being trained to find them, to recruit them, to set them in motion.

Half an hour later a woman departed, letting the door of the Mosque slam behind her as if she wished to make a point to whoever remained inside. If she was the typist he had heard, she walked as rapidly as she typed and as confidently as though she were moving from streetlight to streetlight instead of plunging ahead into pitch darkness. She was out of sight in moments, heels clattering on the pavement, a sturdy figure in an ankle-length raincoat, carrying a man's furled umbrella at shoulder arms.

Still Christopher waited. He was not being patient in any conscious sense. He was not aware of being wet and miserable. He did not feel his wounds, as he usually did in weather like this. Concentration had put him into a kind of trance. The same thing happened to him when he was writing poetry. In a sense he was enjoying himself. He had seldom in his life been so interested in what he was doing as he was now. All five of his senses were working. Cat stink and the acid smell of long-dead fires lingered in his nostrils. He heard tiny noises in the rubble—the cats again and the rodents. In the velvety darkness he apprehended movement, shapes, the first signs of first light. He tasted and felt a fragment of sausage lodged between two of his teeth. He felt the rough ground beneath his feet. His head itched.

His eyes were fixed on the door of the Mosque. Little by little the light increased as the rays of the rising sun grew stronger on the other side of the thick clouds that sealed off the city. The dimly perceived hillocks of brick and stone, the shells of buildings changed gradually into silhouettes, then into visible objects. Christopher waited to see what he expected to see, the matchstick man he had pursued through the rain. He knew Stutzer was inside because he had heard his voice. This was his place of business. Was he waiting for the light because he did not want to go out into darkness in which an enemy might be hiding? Sooner or later he would have to come out, unless he never came outside, or came and went by some other route.

Christopher had focused so hard on the door of the Mosque that he had shut down all but the particle of intelligence that was needed to imagine a thin man with a large head, the last man from Mars, opening a door and walking through it. He had seen the whole picture, detail after detail, in the developing fluid of his imagination. All that was needed was for Stutzer, who had already stepped out of the past, to step out of the real world into the one in which Christopher was waiting for him. Now he heard a dog bark, heard a sharp human voice speak a single word to the animal. The sounds were distant, distorted. He realized that dog and man were in another valley of rubble on a street parallel to this one. Suddenly Christopher understood the reason for the padlocked doors on the vacant caves. Stutzer wanted no neighbors. The one room in these smashed buildings that would still be intact would be the cellar. A man who wanted to come and go in secrecy would find a way through this labyrinth of cellar rooms, old sewers, and who knew what hidden passages. There might be a dozen exits. The ones to look for would be those that were not padlocked from the outside.

Christopher set off at a run in the direction of the sounds. He felt his cold muscles, his aching bones, the scrapes and scratches he had gotten while climbing the mosque. Would the new Stutzer, a eunuch who dressed in rags and believed in the puritan virtues of socialism, be met by a polished black car at the end of his daily labor as in the old days or would he take a streetcar? Christopher ran harder, and finally, rounding a corner, he glimpsed far ahead of him a man with grasshopper limbs who was being pulled along by an Alsatian dog. A large black car followed them at walking speed. It was not so big or so shiny as the Daimlers of a different time in Germany, but its symbolism was the same. Christopher's heart raced, he panted, he trembled and perspired. All this, he realized, was Pavlovian. He smelled the diesel fumes of the S-boat, saw *Mahican* afire and sailing into the blackness. He had not expected this. Even on the night he had pursued Stutzer through the rain, he had remained in the present. More than he wanted to kill him, irresistible though that urge was, Christopher wanted to talk to him, to make him confess, to see if he even remembered what he had done. That was his objective, to make the monster explain.

Christopher watched Stutzer and his dog out of sight, then turned back and began the search for a way into his lair.

5

In West Berlin, Christopher recovered his suitcase from the left luggage at the railroad station and in the men's room changed back into his usual clothes. He rolled up the damp, made-in-the-Eastern-bloc garments he had worn the night before and packed them in a canvas satchel that he carried in the suitcase. The ill-made, ill-fitting shoes stank of cat droppings. He cleaned them, wrapped them in newspaper, and put them into the canvas bag with the clothes.

When he emerged from the booth, Wolkowicz said, "Nice cologne."

He stood at a urinal. Christopher was not surprised to see him. He had detected no surveillance after he passed through the checkpoint. Wolkowicz must have posted a lookout at the checkpoint, then deduced where Christopher was headed. The two men had met in this facility before. Wolkowicz favored public toilets as rendezvous points. True, the police kept an eye on men's rooms but, knowing this, Wolkowicz's contacts were uncomfortable and anxious to escape and would usually tell him what he wanted to know in the fewest possible words.

For the moment he and Christopher were alone. Wolkowicz said, "Last night you broke that guy's foot, you know. Shattered—*shattered* I say—the metatarsal and mangled a couple of other bones. He barely made it back across the line. He had to answer a lot of Vopo questions about his brand-new limp. He's in a cast. Gumshoeing is all he knows. How's the poor chump supposed to make a living? He gets paid by the hour. He's got a family. How come you've got no pity for the great unwashed?"

Christopher held an electric razor in his hand. He plugged it in and shaved by the faint natural light that was the only illumination in the big room. His beard was light, the stubble almost invisible. Moving closer and peering at Christopher's chin, Wolkowicz said, "That's a full day's growth?" Christopher nodded. Wolkowicz said, "Jeez. Some people are farther up the evolutionary tree than others, I guess." His own face, shaved only a couple of hours earlier, was blue with stubble. Christopher put his razor away.

Wolkowicz said, "So where did you go last night after you shook the surveillance?"

"I visited a neighborhood I knew when I was a kid," Christopher said.

"Which neighborhood?"

Christopher told him.

"That's where MfS is, on Frankfurter-Allee." Wolkowicz used the German acronym for the Ministry of State Security. "What was your plan, to climb the wall like a human fly and break in and photograph everything?"

Christopher noted the reference to a human fly and wondered if one of his lookouts had watched him climb the Mosque. Not much was accidental where Wolkowicz was concerned. He said, "My father taught me to swim at the public pool next door to the velodrome."

"So you got dolled up like a member of the proletariat and danced all night in cat poop just for old times' sake?"

Christopher knew that this conversation would not be over until Wolkowicz knew more about Christopher's mission—however much he might know already. He said, "Why do you care?"

"This is my town. I'm the mayor. You're my responsibility."

"I am? How did that happen?"

"Everybody is my responsibility when they're on my turf—even the ones who went to Hahvud. I've got a need to know." He poked Christopher's biceps with a stiff forefinger. "Confusion kills, pal."

They heard a train arriving. Christopher moved away from Wolkowicz. In moments the room filled with passengers. Wolkowicz, pretending to wash his hands, recognized one of the newcomers in the mirror and abruptly departed. His toes pointed outward when he walked and he held his arms stiffly at his sides. He swayed. From the rear in his tight coat he resembled a penguin in a travelogue. He frequently looked like something he was not.

After checking the canvas satchel back into left luggage Christopher took a taxi to the Kempinski hotel and checked in. He ordered breakfast from room service and after eating all of it—canned fruit, cheese, ham, bread and butter, jam, coffee—showered and went to bed. Now that he was safe and relaxed he felt his weariness keenly, but he could not sleep. At last he drifted off and began to dream. In his sleep Hubbard and Lori danced in the ballroom of the old Kempinski, Paul stalked imaginary Indians through the beech groves of Rügen, Lori galloped a horse, not her Lipizzaner, across a pasture with snowy peaks in the background.

The phone rang. Even while rising from his shallow sleep Christopher knew it could be no one but Wolkowicz on the line. He did not answer. The phone continued to ring insistently. Christopher picked up the receiver and replaced it, breaking the connection. The phone rang again and went on ringing. The Kempinski operator, he knew, would never ring more than a half dozen times unless the caller insisted and had some sort of authority. Christopher got out of bed, dropped to his knees, and unplugged the phone. Next would come knocks on the door, Christopher knew, and after that, if Wolkowicz asked his friend the chief of police to make a call to the manager, an expression of regret from the hotel management that his room was no longer available. Sleep was now impossible. Christopher, nauseated by fatigue, got up and put on his clothes. His idea was to get out of the room before the hammering on the door began. It was raining hard and the rain was mixed with hail. The soaking cold of the north European winter radiated into the overheated room through the window glass.

It was too early in Berlin to do anything interesting, and in any case too wet and cold to go outside. The lobby was crowded with the hotel's clientele, mostly American businessmen in expensive suits and the neckties of British regiments. Christopher waited until one of them departed, then sat down in his warm chair and read the Paris edition of the *Herald-Tribune*.

The chair beside Christopher became empty. Wolkowicz sat down in it. "I've been thinking about what you said about the Indians," he said.

"What was that exactly?"

"That they were all spies."

"Which Indians?"

"The Sioux, the Cheyenne, the Mohawks."

Christopher, who also forgot little or nothing, recalled this conversation about Indians, but it had taken place years before in Vienna.

Wolkowicz said, "Your theory was that they had a culture of espionage. Always sneaking around but leaving no tracks, eavesdropping, assassinating people, stealing the other tribes' horses and women instead of secret documents."

Christopher said, "Was that the way I put it?"

"Maybe I missed the subtleties," Wolkowicz said. "So tell me what makes you so interested in Arabs all of a sudden?"

Wolkowicz's shrewd small eyes bored into Christopher's. He was looking for a spark of surprise, a hint of annoyance, any all-but-undetectable sign that he had hit the mark. He saw none of these things. Christopher, silent, waited for Wolkowicz to make the next move. If he was true to form he would offer a morsel of information and hope to get better information in return. He worked like a smart lawyer, leading the witness, playing dumb, pouncing at the right moment.

"I did some checking," Wolkowicz said. "A couple of weeks ago we got a cable from One-Eye asking for everything we knew about a certain officer of MfS, and then we got another cable asking for information about MfS contacts with bad-guy Mohammedans, and what d'you know, there was a connection. And then all of a sudden O. G.'s fair-haired godson pops in to say hello but won't say anything more than that. If you were me, pal, what would you think?"

Christopher said, "If I were you, Barney, I'd probably leap to conclusions."

"Yeah, probably. But you're not me. You're a whole lot smarter than me to begin with and you're in full possession of the facts. How come you're so, uh, unforthcoming?"

Wolkowicz spoke the long word in a parody of a Saint Grottlesex drawl. Although he was surrounded by potential eavesdroppers, he was talking of these clandestine matters in a normal tone of voice, as if he and Christopher were alone in the lobby. Better here in a crowd, according to Wolkowicz's modus operandi, than head-to-head in a room that might be bugged. An operative who acted like himself instead of impersonating an honest man was less likely to attract attention, and that the louder one talked in a public place the less likely others were to pay attention to what you said. Acting like a boor caused people to look away. It made them stop their ears. It was furtive gestures and whispers that raised suspicions.

Wolkowicz said, "So?"

"So what don't you know?"

"I don't *know* anything. I'm just rubbing snot on the windowpane, watching you rich folks enjoy your dinner."

Christopher yawned. He was having trouble staying awake. Except for Wolkowicz, the people in the lobby were sitting so still that they might have been posing for a photograph. Christopher had not slept on the train from Paris, he had not slept on the plane from New York, he had not slept last night.

"Wake up," Wolkowicz said. "Are you going to go back across?"

"Probably."

"When?"

"After you let me get some sleep."

"Why are you doing this?"

"Old times' sake, like you said."

"Right. But what's the operational reason?"

"The life-and-death struggle between good and evil for the soul of mankind."

"I'm going to give it to you straight, pal. I'm very uneasy about this."

"You, Barney, uneasy? That's a twist."

"It's not funny," Wolkowicz said. "Broken Foot—that's the Indian name of the guy you tromped on—said that you used Stasi credentials to get through the checkpoint last night. Is that true?"

"Really?"

"Did you flash any such document at the Vopos? Please tell me."

"How would your man know what paper I showed unless the Vopos told him? Think about that."

Christopher yawned again, deeply and uncontrollably. Wolkowicz glared.

"I'm not yawning on purpose or because I'm not enjoying the conversation," Christopher said. "I can barely stay awake."

"You *did* use Stasi ID, didn't you?" Wolkowicz said. "Golly gee, what a nifty idea that was. Who thought it up, your one-eyed buddy? I know you're not that stupid."

Christopher yawned again.

Wolkowicz said, "I read somewhere that yawning is the body's way of inhaling more oxygen. It helped our caveman ancestors stay awake when they were being stalked by predators."

"No kidding."

"You should watch out for predators. I've got something for you."

Wolkowicz handed Christopher an envelope sealed across the point of its flap with a short piece of Scotch tape. He could feel what was inside and knew what it must be, but he opened it anyway, so as not to spoil Wolkowicz's pleasure. It was a well-worn East German identity card bearing Christopher's photograph, also well-worn, and a false name. He was described as a translator.

"Use this ID from now on," Wolkowicz said. "It's genuine-false in the true name of the holder, who's a secret heroin addict we've been helping."

Christopher nodded his thanks. He put the card in his pocket and handed the envelope back.

"So tell me, Gabby," Wolkowicz said. "Are you going to be commuting to the GDR or what?"

"Why do you ask?"

"Because if you're going to stay over there for a while you're really going to be sleep-deprived. It's not a country where you can travel anywhere you want. There are very few discreet hotel keepers in the GDR. Cops outnumber civilians. Whatever they call the country now, it's still the Russian zone and Russians are all over the place. You might need a friend."

Christopher said, "A friend. All right. What name, what place, what words?"

"The person in question will be introduced when you pick up your weapon at that place I told you about. The words are, 'Does the Museum of Natural Science have dinosaurs?' What you say is, 'Yeah, but they're nothing but skin and bones.'" Wolkowicz lurched to his feet. "Watch your fanny," he said. "It's a jungle over there."

TEN

1

Nobody in East Berlin seemed to be interested in Christopher. He took a long walk along Wilhelmstrasse, all the way to Parisier Platz, where the American embassy had stood in O. G.'s day as a diplomat. He saw no one behind him. This half of the city was gray and subdued and quiet, with much less automobile traffic than before the war. Little dogs like Schatzi and Blümchen that were once almost as numerous as human beings had vanished with the elegant shops and restaurants of another time. Pedestrians scuttled along the sidewalks as if in a hurry to get out of sight before their permits to be seen in public expired. He remembered a snatch of a Marlene Dietrich song, *Berlin will always be Berlin.*

It was mid-afternoon when Christopher reached the Red Orchestra Inn. It was a guesthouse really, wedged between two larger buildings. Inside, the light was dim. As he entered, the young woman at the desk lifted her eyes from the book she was reading by the grimy daylight that fell through the glass above the door. She wore round steel spectacles. She waited, inert, until he spoke.

He said, "Sepp Bauer?"

The woman shook her head. "Not here."

Christopher smiled. "Then I've missed him. But as I am already here, I wonder if, as a matter of very great kindness, I might be permitted to use the lavatory."

Still smiling, feeling like a fool as he always did when engaged in such stage business, he unbuckled his wristwatch and dropped it into the left-hand pocket of his jacket.

"Second door on the left," the woman said, and went back to her book. It was a novel in Russian, *Days and Nights* by Konstantin Simonov. Christopher had read it in an Armed Forces edition English translation when he was in the Marine Corps. It was an intensely patriotic work about the Battle of Stalingrad, written while the war was still going on, a sort of Eisenstein movie set in type, not quite propaganda, not quite art. He had thought that the text must be poetic in the Russian.

Everything in the w. c. was as Wolkowicz had described it. Christopher put his weight—all his strength was needed—against the spring-loaded windowsill and it slid back smoothly, clicked, and came loose in his hands, revealing a hidden compartment that exuded the odor of blued steel and gun oil. He found three fully loaded Makarov pistols wrapped in oiled paper. The Makarov was a powerful, dependable, accurate military weapon of simple design—Wolkowicz's kind of gun. One of the pistols had been manufactured in East Germany, the others in Bulgaria. Christopher took the one made in East Germany, which felt better in his hand, along with three eight-round clips of ammunition and a large folding pocket knife, then closed up the windowsill. He tucked the Makarov into his waistband at the small of his back, put the knife in his jacket pocket, flushed the toilet, and walked out.

At the front desk the young woman's nose was still in her book. She did not look up, so what he saw was the top of her head. Her hair, almost blond, was pulled tight into a chignon. The ruler-straight part in her hair, her ears, her hands holding the book and her nails were scrupulously clean. Her body, or what he could see of it, was narrow, the back straight. Christopher said thank you as he walked by.

As he reached the front door, the woman said, "One moment, please."

Christopher stopped and looked back.

She said, "I am wondering something. Does the Museum of Natural Science have dinosaurs?"

Now she was looking straight at him. Her eyes were unsmiling but friendly. She looked even more immaculately clean now that he saw her entire face.

Christopher said, "Yes, but they're nothing but skin and bones."

The woman said, "You shouldn't be outside in daylight with such things in your pockets. We have an empty room."

"Who else is staying here?"

"At the moment, no one. But we get a simple clientele here. Mostly men who travel and, sometimes in the afternoon, couples who want privacy."

Christopher waited for her to say something else. She understood what he wanted—her eyes showed her amusement—but she did not oblige.

He said, "What's the rate?"

"Ten marks-fifty a night, breakfast included, supper available, alcohol extra. There is a bar, also for simple people."

"How long can I stay?"

"Until you make a disturbance." She took a key from the rack. "Come, I'll show you the room."

He followed her up the steep narrow stairs. She had pretty legs, a lithe body. At the top she gave him a look to let him know that she realized this.

The room lay under the sloping roof on a blind side of the building. There was no number on the door. It was small and spartan—a bed, a dresser, a straight chair, a washstand with a small round mirror. There was no window. A small bulb screwed into a ceiling fixture provided the only light. The woman pointed to the lavatory and bathroom down the hall. "There is no hot water," she said. In that case how could she be so clean, Christopher wondered. Again her eyes were amused as she read his thought. She said, "Do you snore?"

"No one has ever complained," Christopher replied.

"If you do snore or talk in your sleep, no one will hear you in this room. It's out of the way. It's a clean room, a quiet room. I take care of it myself."

As the woman spoke she stood in the open doorway, well away from the bed. She had excellent posture and a voice that carried without being loud. Christopher guessed that she was about thirty. She dressed to conceal her figure, in a baggy sweater and a long skirt, and her utilitarian eyeglasses and the way in which she did her hair and the drab colors of her clothes deprived her face of softness. Her eyes were notice-able, which may have been why she had been so absorbed in her book. If she wasn't striking, it was by choice.

"My name is Heidi," she said. "Please stay inside the room. I'll bring you something to eat around eight o'clock. We can go out at about ten. The streets are busier then."

"We can go out?"

"Of course, we. A couple attracts less attention. This was not explained to you?"

Christopher looked around at the blank walls and understood that he was a prisoner of this woman if that was her desire. The large brass key to the room dangled from her hand. She could if she wished slam the door and lock it from the outside and leave him to starve to death. It was a heavy oak door. The lock with its massive deadbolt was from the time of the kaisers. Like most things made by the artisans of that era, it did what it was designed to do. Any lock could be picked, of course, but picking this one without specialized tools could be the work of hours. As these thoughts passed through Christopher's mind the woman watched him solemnly, as if puzzling out a note in handwriting she had not seen before.

She handed him the key. "If you want to rest in peace"—another flash of smiling eyes—"I recommend you to lock the door and leave the key in the lock," she said. "That way the door cannot be locked from the outside."

"Is there a way out from this floor?"

"Down the stairs is easiest." Now she was openly amused.

"In case of fire, then."

"There's a window at the back—that way." She pointed. "A circus performer could go over the roof, then over the next roof and down the wall of that building balcony to balcony. Both the U-bahn and the S-bahn are nearby, in opposite directions." She pointed to show him where the rail lines were.

Christopher said, "Thank you, Miss. You're very kind."

"Always on Saturdays. My name is Heidi."

"Heidi, then."

"Supper at seven o'clock. We eat simply here. Soup and bread. Then we'll go out and pretend to be in love. Everyone in Berlin has at least one lover. It's for the privacy, a way to avoid the Stasi for an hour or two."

Heidi's voice was lighter than it had been, her manner more relaxed. She gestured. She kept her glasses on, though, and stood well away from the bed. In his mind he had begun to call her by name. He had given her no name for himself, but nevertheless she said, "Until later, then, Paul." Wolkowicz had told her his true first name. Who else knew it? A joke, a wink, an elbow in the ribs.

After she left, Christopher locked the door and disassembled the Makarov. Everything was in working order. He put the weapon back together, failing on the first try because he did not know that the hammer had to be cocked in order to fit the slide back onto the frame. He chose a cartridge at random and pried it open with the knife. It, too, seemed to be everything it should be. With the weapons on his person he reconnoitered the rest of the top floor and found two unmarked doors, one of them a closet, the other locked. The single window at the back swung open easily. It looked down on a tiny enclosed courtyard four stories below. As Heidi had said, the only way out was over the steep mansard roof.

In the wardrobe he found a sports newspaper that was badly out of date and a stack of paperbound books, some in German, some in Russian. He chose a book of poetry in Russian, Simonov again. One of his admirers must have spent a few days here and left this library behind. Christopher lay down on the bed, rolled onto his side in order to take as much advantage as possible of the tenuous light, and began to read—to study, really. His Russian was workmanlike but shallow. Simonov's verse read, to him, like Longfellow or Whittier—entertaining, sentimental, with technique and the ideal reader more in mind than the work. He wondered if there was more to it than he thought. After a while he closed the book, put the pistol under his pillow, and fell asleep.

He was awakened at seven o'clock exactly by a knock on the door—a single sharp rap that was in no way a signal. Obviously Heidi had no time for the frills of tradecraft. He was glad of that, and glad of her punctuality because it confirmed that his new cheap watch kept accurate time. Holding the pistol behind him in his right hand, Christopher unlocked and opened the door with his left. The hallway was dark. There was no sign of life or movement. A tray covered with a white cloth had been left outside his door. Under the napkin he found a bowl of potato soup, a chunk of dark bread, a piece of cheese, and a bottle of beer lying on its side. He ate the bland soup, which was heavily salted, and the tasteless cheese and the dense dry bread, but left the beer unopened. When he was finished he covered the tray and put it outside the door where he had found it.

He waited for Heidi to knock on his door again. He had no idea what might occur later tonight. He had no plan. He hardly knew what his own intentions were. Nothing he could do would change the past. Nothing could make him understand it better. However, he was already in motion. An operation was like a poem in progress. It came from nowhere, it wrote itself, it changed itself, its existence was a matter of indifference to the world and even to the poet to whom it had been given so that he could asphyxiate it like a butterfly and mount it on a pin. He thought, I'd better stop reading Simonov.

2

Holding hands and flirting, Christopher and Heidi rode the S-bahn along the River Spree. Heidi seemed to be enjoying the charade. She had changed for the evening into a shorter skirt, heels, a necklace, lipstick. Her hair was looser, her face softer. She wore perfume. Christopher found it easy to smile at her, to squeeze her hand when she squeezed his. Watching their reflections in the window of the train, Christopher had to admit that her expert performance made them look like a couple on their way to bed.

The night was dark, and on the other side of the Spree, a block or two away, the glow of West Berlin was bright—skyscrapers with every window ablaze, thousands of lights of all kinds burning. They got off at Ostbahnhof. It was Saturday and there were more people in the streets than usual. Heidi led the way to a street of cafés and bars. Nearby a door opened and the sound of an accordion and violins playing "Falling in Love Again" drifted into the street. Dietrich was everywhere. Heidi said, "Shall we dance?" She took Christopher's hand and pulled him to her. They danced half a dozen steps along the sidewalk, Heidi pirouetting at the end. Her skirt ballooned prettily to reveal her knees. She smiled provocatively.

Inside the bar where the orchestra played, Heidi had many friends. A large party of people made room for her and Christopher at their table. Coughing on smoke that rose from scores of burning cigarettes, Heidi introduced Christopher, calling him Horst, and between coughs put names to her friends, all of whom were more than a little drunk. Christopher was an object of curiosity to the women. "Dear God, Heidi, where did you find him?" one of them shouted. It was almost impossible to hear spoken words above the din of the orchestra and the noise of customers singing along with it. One of the men went to the bar and returned with a glass of wine for Heidi and a beer for Christopher. Just as he arrived the orchestra started playing "Whistle While You Work," the Disney song that had been a great hit in the Reich before the war. Heidi leaped to her feet and led Christopher onto the small round dance floor.

She danced expertly, like a teacher, eyes sparkling with enjoyment. "You're pretty good," she said. "You've got a little German accent in your dancing." The music changed. She said, "Can you tango?"

Christopher said, "Why else are we here?"

She slid a hand down his back and touched the Makarov in his waistband. "The other girls may ask you to dance," she said. "Better say I'm the jealous type."

They danced for a long time, jostled by other couples. Now that they were off the street she had stopped flirting. Even in the slow numbers, during which she closed her eyes, Heidi danced discreetly, keeping space between them as if they were in a dancing class. Christopher studied the faces of the other dancers. They, too, danced with their eyes closed. These were working class people who had not always been working class people. Most were about his own age. He wondered who they used to be and what they were now. Had he had known any of them in school, in the swimming pool or on the football field, had he seen them in the Tiergarten?

The orchestra played a waltz. As they whirled around the floor, Heidi said, "Look behind you. At the end of the bar."

Christopher turned her and looked over her head. Stutzer stood at the end of the bar, his Alsatian at his feet, drinking a glass of brandy.

"He will have three brandies, the first two straight with chocolate that he carries in his pocket, the last one with soda, and then he will go home," Heidi said. "He comes here every Saturday night, always alone except for the dog, always at this hour."

She felt Christopher's body grow tense. "No," she said. "Not now, not here. Dance with me, look at me. Be a good boy. He's not really alone. There are others here, his people, watching out for him. Stop staring. It isn't safe."

On the way home Heidi told Christopher more about Stutzer's habits. Soon after dusk every evening he traveled on foot, moving at marching pace, from MfS headquarters to the Mosque or sometimes to another safe house, and then walked back to headquarters in the early hours of the morning. Heidi thought that he slept and ate at the office, for he never went anywhere else. In public he dressed simply, in Old Bolshevik fashion, usually wearing a worker's cap and a leather jacket. He seemed to like the illusion of being alone, seemed to enjoy the sensation of being exposed, but the people who looked after him were never far away. Though he rarely rode in it, his Volga sedan was always near at hand, inching along at walking speed, sometimes right behind him but usually keeping abreast on a parallel street. Bodyguards, both men and women, mingled with the other pedestrians if there were any, and if there were not, were posted in concealment at intervals along the way, muttering to one another over two-way radios. He was never alone, never unprotected—at least while he was on East German territory.

He could be hunted, Heidi said. But not captured.

"Hunted?" Christopher said, "You mean assassinated?"

"What a mind you have," Heidi said, looking up into his face. "What would be the point, to kill him? That would be a childish thing to do."

They were walking toward the Red Orchestra Inn on a wide, deserted street that paralleled the S-bahn tracks. She held onto his arm, tottering slightly in her high heels. Without her glasses her eyes seemed larger and bluer and much more serious.

He said, "How do you happen to know so much about his habits?"

"It's a game," Heidi replied.

"For what purpose?"

"To know what is interesting."

"That, or to take chances for the fun of it?"

"You're a good one to talk about that," Heidi said. "I was told you were the silent type, a man who never asks questions. Apparently I was misinformed."

Christopher was probing for information, but there was no need for this. Heidi was providing all the answers she was prepared to give without benefit of being questioned. Obviously she was a trained and experienced operative, but who had trained her and then deployed her? The first and most likely possibility was that she worked for MfS, perhaps directly for Stutzer, and Wolkowicz was so hungry for a source, any source, inside East Germany that he had taken recklessly whatever bait was offered and signed her up, just to see what happened. In his book of rules it was better to make a mistake than to do nothing. The second possibility was that she was what she seemed to be, an honest traitor. The final possibility was that she worked for a third party that had reasons of its own to be interested in Stutzer and wanted to know who Christopher was and why he was getting in the way.

Heidi stumbled on a patch of broken pavement but quickly recovered her balance, tightening her grip on Christopher's arm. She was strong—not just strong for such a small woman, but strong.

"Anyway," she said, "I'm the only person you know in this part of town, so who else would tell you these things?"

"Who indeed," Christopher said.

"Did you have a good time tonight?"

"Wonderful. I haven't danced in years."

Christopher wondered where she had learned to tango. Germans of her age and older usually performed the dance as a variation on the goose-step, see-sawing back and forth as the man took a step forward while bending over backward while the woman leaned forward, then the movement was reversed. The others on the dance floor had danced the dance that way. Heidi, however, tangoed as if she had grown up in Argentina, all sinuous legs and sultry come-ons and brusque refusals.

"You tango amazingly well," he said.

"You noticed!"

"How did that happen?"

"A gramophone, a lonely room, a pillow for a partner, an old book of instructions. I am a tango autodidact."

They rounded a corner and the Red Orchestra Inn came in sight. She cocked her head as if she heard something, let go of Christopher's arm and in her clattering heels dashed over the cobblestones and up the steps as if she had never stumbled in her life. She opened the front door with her key, let him in, then locked the door behind them—first with the key, then by throwing two deadbolts. Christopher was incarcerated again. Heidi put on her glasses, an unmistakable signal that their make-believe date was over. A car drove by and the headlights made her lenses glitter.

"Go upstairs," she said. "Good night. Sleep well. I have work to do to get everything ready for tomorrow."

What, he wondered, was everything? No lights burned anywhere in the hotel.

Into the darkness he said, "How do you happen to be called Heidi?"

Her glasses glittered as she turned her head. "It just happened. Everything just happens."

He climbed the creaking stairs and went to bed. Alone in the dark he wasted no time wondering about Heidi or who or what she belonged to or what her intentions were. Often enough he had entrusted his life to strangers who had no reason to trust him and no motive to let him live and he had always come out all right. He liked the girl. He smiled to himself at the memory of her on the dance floor. Heidi was the first of his caretakers who could tango—and the first whose German, when she had drunk a little wine, had the faint, almost inaudible accent that he had heard in it tonight.

3

Heidi unlocked the front door every morning at seven o'clock precisely. The morning after her night out with Christopher was no exception. As soon as he heard the turning of the key he went down the stairs two at a time and strode past the unmanned reception desk and into the street. Heidi would know immediately that he was gone. The stairs squeaked like a nest of rats, the loose glass in the outer door rattled no matter how softly the door was closed.

It had snowed during the night, and though the pavement had already been trampled bare, the roofs of high buildings were still frosted. He joined a knot of workers who walked silently toward the S-bahn station. A few drew on cigarettes as if smoking in their sleep. Their clothes were drab and alike. No Miss Wetzel clad in shades of violet, shoes and hat to match, walked among them. No one talked to an animal as she had chattered to Blümchen. Christopher saw no one behind him, certainly not Heidi, but that did not mean that no one was there. For all he knew the man beside him was following him. In this Berlin, unlike the last one, the secret police drew no attention to themselves, and because they kept the entire population under continual surveillance, they had plenty of opportunity to perfect sidewalk skills. No one in the crowd paid Christopher the slightest attention even though they knew perfectly well that he was a stranger. Like airline passengers, but with better reason than fear of boredom, Berliners started no conversations in which they might be trapped for an entire journey. As was the German custom, Christopher carried his lunch in his briefcase. The cheap bag sagged a little under the weight of the Makarov pistol and the extra clips of ammunition that were also inside it, beneath the newspaper-wrapped bread and cheese and cold sausage of his uneaten breakfast.

Christopher took a train headed in the direction of the Mosque. He

got off at the first station after the Ostbahnhof at which a large number of other passengers also dismounted. He stationed himself at the
back of the crowd, a step or two behind the slowest walkers. After a few
blocks he split off by turning down a side street that ran parallel to the
street in which the Mosque was located. The others trudged onward.
He was alone. He did not walk onward into the street, in which the
snow was fresh and undisturbed and without tracks of any kind. This
was better luck than he had expected. He had come here early because
he thought it possible that the Mosque was closely watched, front and
back, and strongly protected only when Stutzer was in residence.
Because Stutzer arrived at dusk and departed at dawn, the day shift
must be a skeleton staff, if it existed at all. Locks and alarms—and for
today, the snow—were likelier sentinels than armed men. Because of
the snow he could go no farther today. All he could do was wait for the
snow to melt. Half of secret life—more than half—consisted of waiting. Christopher was an expert killer of time. He read, he wrote poems
in his head and composed imaginary conversations in one or another
of the languages that he knew. He remembered his life, he dozed when
daydreams tricked his brain into perceiving that he must already be
asleep.

He went shopping. He wanted a flashlight, a ball of string, a pair of
rubber boots, a bicycle. It was wearisome to shop in a city whose stores
had almost nothing to sell. It wasn't a question of bargaining. What the
state stores offered for sale was what they had and what they displayed
was all they had. It was pointless to ask if the store might have a particular item in the storeroom or whether it might come in sometime in
the future. The clerks had no idea what they might have next or when
they might receive it. Whatever they offered, no matter how shoddy,
people lined up to buy.

Having found nothing that he was looking for, he went back to the
Red Orchestra Inn. "A ball of string?" Heidi said. "You think there is
such a thing in this country as a ball of string? Or in the name of God
a flashlight? A bicycle we already have. It's the hotel bicycle. The next
time you want to take French leave, just borrow it."

Except for tone of voice, Heidi did not reproach Christopher for his brief escape. She did not even mention it. Nevertheless she wished him to know that she was annoyed. There were spots of color on her prominent, almost Slavic cheekbones, and behind the circular lenses of her glasses her eyes were wifely in their cold resentment. She had more reason than most real wives to expect and demand good behavior from Christopher. He was safe with her and with no one else. She was utterly responsible for him to whomever she worked for, no matter who that was. If he got himself into trouble in a country where trouble was a very dark business, she would be in trouble too. For the rest of the day they did not speak.

Before going out the following morning, Christopher put the Makarov and its ammunition back where he had found them. The hidden compartment in the lavatory was empty—no Bulgarian Makarovs, no ammunition, no weapons of any kind. He wondered if his Makarov would disappear, too, and hoped that it would. It was a great inconvenience, heavy and difficult to conceal. In case of an encounter with other armed men he could not fire it without being riddled with bullets. He had no use for the thing, no plans to shoot anybody under any circumstances. He had other plans than sudden death for Stutzer.

Just after dawn Christopher rode the hotel bicycle down Stalinallee in the general direction of the Mosque. The streets, even this broad main thoroughfare, were virtually empty at this hour and the city was so quiet that he could hear the bike's tires humming on the pavement. The note was high-pitched and steady and pleasant to hear; no doubt Wolkowicz could have told him its key and other musical particulars. A few blocks farther on he saw in the watery light another cyclist riding ahead of him. Christopher drew a little closer. The other rider was a youngish man and like Christopher he was dressed for the soaking cold in a heavy overcoat, but instead of a fedora he wore a black fur cap. He rode in an unselfconscious way, slumped in the saddle, paying no attention to his form, not like a German at all. Christopher fell back. His bicycle had no mirrors, but while circling the Strausberger platz roundabout he glimpsed a second bicycle behind him. Its rider also wore a fur cap—brown rather than black like the other rider's, but similar in shape. Instead of turning into the continuation of Stalinallee,

Christopher left the roundabout at the next big thoroughfare and
farther on made a right turn into a narrow street that ran parallel to it.
After a couple of blocks he saw ahead of him the slumped rider, who
had exchanged his fur hat for a Red Army field cap with the red star
removed and the earflaps tied under his chin. At the next intersection
the second rider, still wearing his fur cap, again fell in behind.
Apparently the other cyclists wanted him to know that they were there.
Christopher speeded up a little. So did the other bikers. He slowed
down with the same result. The maneuvers were executed with something like a sense of humor. This was not the behavior of secret policemen, who were either invisible or putting their hands on you.
Christopher rode on. He pedaled past streets leading to the neighborhood where the Mosque was located, then made a series of left turns.
Now he was only a short distance from the Mosque. The cyclist ahead
of him, accelerating, turned off into the first cross street. The other
rider turned into the same street, but in the opposite direction.

Up ahead, in the next block, Christopher saw Stutzer and his
Alsatian. Three men with two-way radios stood on the sidewalk. Two
or three more were posted beyond Stutzer. Christopher heard radio
static and distorted voices. Stutzer unleashed the Alsatian, which stood
beside him, ears and tail raised, awaiting orders. Christopher heard a
car behind him and smelled its exhaust—Stutzer's Volga, he presumed,
but he did not look back.

Pedaling steadily, Christopher swept by the first three men and out
of the corner of his eye saw the last one produce a submachine gun
from beneath his coat. There had been no signal from Stutzer, so no
one made a move to stop him. Stutzer, standing erect—more than
erect, actually bent slightly backwards—watched him approach. Like
his human protectors, the Alsatian, still awaiting orders, was frozen in
place. Christopher looked directly into Stutzer's eyes. He saw in them
everything he already knew about the man and new things besides. He
was acquainted with his own vulnerability now, and for an instant
Christopher saw it flicker. In their last encounter, in the rain, it had been
too dark to see so much. Stutzer's face was thinner now, his eyebrows
almost invisible, his lips less girlishly pink. His chin quivered slightly,

also the hand that was not holding the leash. No spark of recognition showed in his eyes for a long moment, and then he remembered Christopher's face.

As in their last encounter, memory resembled dream. The moment was curiously peaceful. Had Christopher brought the Makarov, if he had believed in guns, if Stutzer's death could have been payment enough for him, this would have been the perfect moment to make the kill—a single shot to the heart. Instead, as though he had never seen Stutzer before and had no idea who or what he was, Christopher nodded politely as he rolled by, and rode on. He expected the black Volga to overtake him, or the men posted up ahead to dash into the street with drawn weapons, or the dog to attack. But none of these things happened. He pedaled onward at the same steady speed, in the same gear, hearing the same purr of the tires, until he was out of sight.

4

Among the things Christopher had carried into East Berlin to simulate innocence was a cheap German wallet stuffed with the cards and tickets and snapshots that Patchen's forgers had supplied. In his room at the Red Orchestra Inn he extracted a passport-sized photograph of Yuri Kikorov that he himself had added to the collection, and on its back, in German, he wrote a date, a time, and a place in the angular Teutonic script he had learned as a child. He sealed the picture in an envelope and put it into his pocket. At midnight he went out. It was another pitch-black night. The cold was too saturating to be borne without exercise and there was no place to get warm. With hours to kill, Christopher walked. In his mind he reviewed what he knew—not much, but more than he had known only a couple of days before. He knew from Heidi some of Stutzer's habits—how he divided his hours between MfS headquarters and the Mosque, where he went on Saturday night and what he drank. From his own observations he knew where Stutzer walked in the morning and who stood guard over him, what he wore when in public. By the sound of their voices he knew two of the people who visited Stutzer at the Mosque. He knew that Stutzer rewarded them with women. He knew that Stutzer could be surprised. He was beginning to know larger things, the largest of all being that the new Stutzer was different from the old one. At the core the creature was the same but it no longer believed itself to be immune from harm. It could be startled, perhaps even frightened. Possibly it could be controlled—or if not actually controlled, then influenced to behave in a predictable way by playing on its old illusions and its new doubts.

He walked through the silent city like the native that he was, knowing when to turn before a street ended, avoiding parks, stopping to listen for voices, for footsteps. The Berlin his brain had mapped in his youth still existed. Landmarks may have vanished but for the most part, the streets were the same. In the dark it made no difference that their names had been changed or that monuments and steeples had been demolished. The neighborhoods and their parks were still there. In the absence of dogs and horses the smells were less recognizable than before. It was strange to hear so little noise. But even though it was half dead, Berlin in some respects did remain Berlin, as the song promised.

By three in the morning Christopher had worked his way back to the street on which the Mosque was located. He took up a position and waited. He heard the Palestinians talking long before he saw them. Their topic was the same as before—the sexual behavior of German women—and they were discussing it at the top of their lungs. Christopher's grasp of their speech was far from perfect. The only Arabic he knew was a dialect spoken in the Maghrib. In childhood he had learned it in fragments from a Berber friend of his mother, who during long visits to Gutenbergstrasse and Rügen had taught him words and phrases and rewarded him with dollar bills when he remembered them and made sentences of them. The difference between the dialect he half knew and the one these men spoke was the difference between the English spoken in York and New York.

He followed the men by listening to them. He could not see them. Even though rain was not yet falling, its chilled moisture was present in the air. It soaked its way through Christopher's woolen overcoat, jacket, sweater and shirt, then through his pores and all the way to the bone.

Perhaps these men thought and talked about fornication as a way of avoiding thoughts about the miseries of the German winter in the way that a Christian ascetic might do the opposite. In and of themselves they were of no more interest to him than their conversation. His mission to identify them and neutralize them was a fiction. O. G. had sent him out to rid himself and the world of Stutzer. He was interested in these Arabs because they were on their way to Stutzer. Christopher wanted them to deliver a message to him. When they were close to the Mosque, he opened his clasp knife and uttered a loud hiss. This sound stopped the Arabs in their tracks. He was near enough to see them now, darker shapes in the seamless night, and they froze as if a shot had been fired into the pavement behind them and they were listening to the ricochet. They did not turn around.

Christopher had rehearsed the words he wished to say to them. He pressed the point of the knife against the neck of the man on the left and said, "Take off your right glove and hold your hand behind you. I am going to give you something."

The man did as he was told. Christopher pressed the envelope into his hand. He said, "Give this to the skinny German you are going to see. Don't fail." The Palestinian took the envelope. Christopher said, "Go." Then he walked backward into the dark, and when the door of the Mosque opened to admit them, he watched them go inside. Then he turned around and walked rapidly away.

ELEVEN

1

The ruins of No. 8 Prinz-Albrechtstrasse lay against the demarcation line just inside East Berlin. Christopher had already scouted the neighborhood from the other side of the line. Now he reconnoitered it again. There was little to see. The buildings had been bombed during the war, then further demolished afterward. The name of the street had been changed. Obliteration of the site had proved to be impossible, but almost nothing remained above ground. Underneath the rubble on both sides of the demarcation line, cells still existed in which Stutzer had done his work and Christopher and Hubbard and Rima—though never Lori, who on Heydrich's orders was always kept in a room that had a window—had been held for questioning. No plaque or stone commemorated the wraiths that lingered here. It was because of these spirits, perhaps, that this neighborhood was so lightly patrolled, especially at night. Free Berlin was only steps away. It was possible to slip across the frontier in either direction without being challenged. Over the years, as part of his work, Christopher had done it a dozen times, sometimes in daylight, without being accosted or so far as he could tell, even noticed. Tonight he had stood in the ruins for the better part of an hour without seeing a single patrol.

It was dark now and in the emptiness of the site Christopher felt the ghosts. Often, in dreams, he was one of them and met his parents again, and Paulus, and Rima and Dr. Kaltenbach and others he had known in his boyhood. Sometimes in dreams the phantoms of his childhood summers were also present. He had encountered them at the Harbor, the homestead of the Christophers and the Hubbards in the hills of western

Massachusetts. Generations of the two families had been aware of these beings, whom they called the Cousins. There were many stories about the Cousins and Christopher had heard them all. One of them followed living relatives around the attic, breathing coldly on their necks. Another climbed the wooden back stairs on Christmas Eve, scuffling up and down, up and down. Some of them had actually been seen by the living—male ancestors in the uniforms of half a dozen American wars, a drowned maiden, a hanged Indian and a murdered bride, children lost to disease. He knew them all by name from family legend. All had died before their time and were believed to resent this. They were treated with affection by the living family, and the belief that these visitors so badly wanted some sort of relationship with the living was a poignant one. One patient ghost stood at the foot of Christopher's bed night after night, waiting to be seen. Paul never opened his eyes and looked at it because he was sure that such an act would make the visitor visible, perhaps empower it in some unknowable way. As a child Christopher had formed the opinion that the dead were not happy.

The sense of kinship with the dead was strong in Prinz-Albrecht-strasse, too. He fancied that he walked through an invisible crowd, rudely bumping into beings he could not see and who could not see him. He was sure that they were present, but they did not seem to notice him. He was irrelevant. They were waiting for something—who knew what?—but not him. He realized that these were wildly inappropriate thoughts for someone who did not believe in an afterworld, but he had them nevertheless. While he waited he was once again chilled to the bone, but that was the rain, the winter.

Christopher chose a sheltered spot close to the demarcation line and waited. It was after midnight. His watch did not have a luminous dial and there was no light, so he wasn't certain of the exact time. On the back of Yuri's picture he had scribbled 1:13 as the time of the meeting. This was Soviet practice. Communist intelligence services nearly always held clandestine meetings at an illogically precise minute after or before the hour. Even the most stupid agent was expected to be exactly on time. It seemed to be a principle of Leninism that punctuality was the mother of discipline. In the early days of the revolution, when clocks were erected by the party on factories and collective farms but few workers and peasants could tell time, the tardy were sometimes shot as an example to the others. The Outfit and most other Western services met agents on the hour or half-hour, or at least hoped to do so. Agents were more often late than not, or appeared at the wrong time or on the wrong day or in the wrong place or not at all.

Christopher did not expect Stutzer to be late. Depending on what he believed or suspected when he saw Yuri Kikorov's picture and read the instructions on the back, he might not come, he might send someone else, he might surround himself with bodyguards. But whatever was going to happen would happen on time.

At 1:13, prompt to the second, Stutzer or his decoy appeared, more sensed than seen. Whichever he was, the man paused as instructed on a certain spot and lit a cigarette. In the flare of the lighter Christopher saw a face that might be Stutzer's, a marionette body that might be his. He smelled cigarette smoke, not his elegant tobacco of yesteryear but coarse stuff, stronger than a caporal, a cigarette for a street sweeper. No doubt this was part of Stutzer's new persona. Just as Stutzer's wardrobe was different, so were his habits—he now drank raw brandy in a worker's bar instead of aged Martell from a crystal goblet, smoked ditch-digger's tobacco instead of Dunhill's. In his earlier life he had impersonated an officer and gentleman. Now he played the lowly worker. Alone, unprotected, slouched instead of soldierly, he waited, smoking the reeking cigarette as if he enjoyed it, inhaling deeply so that its coal glowed red.

Christopher could make out not only Stutzer's stork-like figure but also the outlines of the rubble and the reconstructed buildings across the street. He saw no movement. He himself did not move. He and Stutzer were no more than fifteen feet apart and if Christopher had wanted to assassinate him he could easily have done so. Stutzer could have killed him with equal convenience had he been able to see him. The fact that Stutzer had come alone, or seemingly alone, suggested ... . what? That against all logic he believed that he was meeting Yuri Kikorov? That he knew after seeing Christopher's face earlier in the day that it was he who lay in wait for him? Christopher remembered Yuri's words about Stutzer: He was so sly that he was predictable.

Stutzer flicked away his cigarette. It spun across the rubble, shedding sparks. Christopher knew immediately that this was a diversion but before he could react he was caught in the beam of a flashlight. At first he heard no shots and because he was blinded by the flashlight, saw no muzzle flashes, but he heard bullets slam into the wall beside his head and then heard others ricocheting off the rubble. He heard the popped-cork sound of the silenced pistol.

Christopher was unarmed except for his clasp knife. He dodged to his left, then to his right, in and out of the beam of the flashlight. He picked up a piece of masonry the size of a tennis ball and threw it hard at the flashlight. Stutzer fired twice more and Christopher felt one of these rounds strike his head. He saw stars as if he had been punched and felt warm blood gushing from the wound. He was conscious but his ears rang from the impact of the bullet and his head filled with pain, as if pain were a syrup being poured into his skull. He was running straight at Stutzer. This surprised him. He had no memory of having willed his body to do this. Despite the ringing in his ears he heard the sound of a magazine being ejected and that of another being snapped into place.

The flashlight wavered, beam wandering, while Stutzer inserted the fresh magazine into the weapon and pulled back the slide. Christopher was quite close now. He had a larger chunk of rubble in his hand but did not know how it had got there. He threw it at Stutzer with all his strength and heard Stutzer shriek as it hit him. The flashlight spun away. Stutzer put a hand to his face and with his other hand fired his pistol blindly into the darkness. Christopher was approaching Stutzer from the side. Then as later Christopher did not understand why he did what he did next, but he launched his body into the air in a football block and clipped Stutzer at the knees. Stutzer's body collapsed as if it his legs had been severed from his torso. His head hit the pavement with another sound from football, that of the pigskin being kicked. The pistol flew into the darkness. The flashlight lay in the street, its beam spreading over tar pavement and reflecting from bouncing raindrops.

Christopher retrieved the flashlight and shone it on Stutzer's unconscious face. There was no question that this man was Stutzer. Blood ran into Christopher's eyes. It was salty. It felt like soap in the eye. He could not wipe it away fast enough to keep it from blinding him. Stutzer was wearing a woolen scarf. Christopher pulled it off him, wiped his eyes with it, and then wound it around his head like a sweatband. He could not believe that Stutzer had come alone. There must be others, the black Volga parked around the corner, the thugs posted nearby waiting for a radio signal. If they received it they would come. If they did not receive it after a stated interval, they would come. How could they not have heard the sound of gunshots, silencer or no? Christopher stood Stutzer on his feet. He was alive—Christopher could see his breath— but the head lolled, the knees buckled, the face bled, the jaw hung loose. Christopher wondered if the second rock he had thrown had broken Stutzer's jaw. He thought, *He can't talk with a broken jaw*. He patted Stutzer down and found a handheld radio. He made sure it was switched off, then threw it into the rubble. He found a second pistol and threw that away, too.

He slung Stutzer's body over his shoulder and headed toward the demarcation line. The burden was so light that Stutzer might have been a very large insect instead of a man. Christopher hurried, counting his footsteps, lighting his way through the rubble with the flashlight. In seconds he had crossed into West Berlin. He had no real sense of where he was or what was the correct direction, so he scuffled toward the nimbus of electric light that hung over the western zones of the city. To keep himself going he counted cadence in German. When had he done this before? He knew that he had and that he had been wounded on that occasion also, but he couldn't remember where or when, though he realized that on that occasion he had been carrying a different man through a night lit by explosions. He saw headlights, a taxi. He turned and waved. The taxi steered around him and sped by. Blood ran into his eyes again. He wiped them with the back of his hand. He felt the scarf he had wound around his head. It dripped blood. He had seen scalp wounds before and knew that this one would not kill him, but he was losing a lot of blood and he knew that he was going into shock.

He began to tremble violently. He moved forward on rubbery legs. Stutzer, who had until now been as inert as a corpse, began to stir. Ahead of them the lights were much brighter. Christopher heard traffic. Stutzer uttered a wordless burst of sound, as if he were trying to talk through a gag instead of a mouthful of blood. Christopher shouted, "Silence!" Stutzer replied with another incomprehensible gargle, as if attempting to scream underwater.

They came to a small park. Among trees, Christopher staggered across its muddy lawns. Stutzer squirmed weakly on Christopher's shoulder. He seemed to be searching his clothing for his extra pistol. Perhaps he had other hidden weapons. He was so heavily dressed, ankle-length overcoat over suit or uniform, sweaters beneath, that he might well have had a knife or a blackjack. At the edge of the park they came upon a watercourse and Christopher briefly thought that he had walked in a circle back to the River Spree and they were inside East Berlin, but there were too many lights for that to be true. He was standing on the bank of the Landwehr Canal. Christopher was tempted to dump Stutzer into the frigid water and watch him drown. The impulse was momentary. Instead, he went back into the park and shrugged the insect—in his mind he had begun to call Stutzer that—off his back. Stutzer fell heavily, with a loud tongue-tied grunt. He sprawled against a lamppost, arms and legs limp and twisted. Soft light filled with slanted rain shone down upon him. His eyes were the same eyes Christopher had seen many times before—filled with rage but this time with that new something in them as well. Stutzer was afraid. He thought he was going to die, and very soon, at the hands of someone who was unworthy of the honor of murdering him.

Christopher hauled Stutzer to his feet. He searched him again, peeling off the long overcoat and casting it aside, patting him down. He found Stutzer's MfS credentials and put the folder into his own inside pocket. He found a short stabbing knife inside Stutzer's left sleeve, a small glass bottle of liquid inside his right sleeve. He threw the knife into the darkness. He took the cap off the bottle, watching Stutzer's eyes, in which terror suddenly appeared, and dribbled a few drops onto the sleeve of his jacket. Instantaneously the liquid burned holes in the fabric. Christopher smelled sulfuric acid. He held the bottle under Stutzer's nose, then tossed that away, too.

All this happened in silence. Christopher would not speak, Stutzer could not speak. It was now obvious that his jaw was broken and that his knees had been damaged. The pain must have been excruciating. This, too, showed in his pale eyes, so that expressions of distress and rage and fear succeeded one another. Christopher himself was deeply tired. He could hardly stay awake. His head throbbed. Blood ran less freely from his wound. He was thinking more clearly now and assumed that it was beginning to clot. He held his palms and face up to the rain, which was falling more heavily. The streetlamp glowed at the top of its post. Christopher looked at his watch: 1:24. All this had happened in a mere eleven minutes. This seemed remarkable to him.

He pulled Stutzer to his feet. Stutzer uttered a loud gargle of pain, staggered, and collapsed. By the streetlamp Christopher saw that Stutzer was indeed wearing a uniform. He could not make out the insignia of rank on the shoulder boards. He assumed that Stutzer must have been wearing a military-style cap at the beginning of the evening and that now it lay somewhere between this spot and what used to be No. 8 Prinz-Albrechtstrasse. Was one of Stutzer's men finding it even now? Had he also found Christopher's lost hat, perhaps with a bullet hole in it? Was he radioing the news of his discoveries and their awful portent to the swarm of thugs who were supposed to keep this insect from harm? Were the ghosts of Prinz-Albrechtstrasse following along behind Christopher and Stutzer to see if things might come out differently this time?

Christopher stood Stutzer up, bent over, and slung him onto his shoulder again. He seemed heavier now, though he must actually have been kilos lighter now that he had shed his heavy rain-soaked overcoat. He shivered as if from a malarial fever and moaned his blubbery word-less cry of pain as if appealing for help to the ghosts. These giddy thoughts made Christopher aware that he was not himself and that he must soon find a place to keep his prisoner. He had no destination in mind. He kept walking west. Now that his scalp had stopped bleeding into his eyes he saw more clearly, and he was beginning to recognize landmarks. He crossed the Potsdamer Bridge. The lights ahead were brighter now. It was not so late in West Berlin that the streets were deserted. Automobile traffic was steady. Soon Christopher was walking among pedestrians. Some stopped and stared at the spectacle of a man covered in blood carrying another, blubbering person. Some gave him a wide berth, others laughed at the spectacle. One man with a hearty voice, a Christian evidently because he called Christopher brother, asked if they had been in an auto accident. The question sounded like an accusation, as if Christopher's objective in going out that night had been to wreck a perfectly good car, or perhaps two. Christopher shook his head. The man said, "Someone must call the police." But there were no public telephones nearby. Christopher said, "Thank you, but we are almost home."

He turned into a darker street. No one followed. Up ahead he found a telephone booth. He tumbled Stutzer from his shoulders again and again Stutzer cried out in pain as he hit the pavement. Christopher reasoned—his thought process had never seemed to him to be smoother, better oiled—that the pain would immobilize Stutzer while he made the call. He put coins into the phone and dialed a number that came into his head. He knew, but did not know, whose number this was.

He heard the thick-tongued voice of a man awakened from sleep. He told this person who and where he was, but used a false name. He spoke English, so he reasoned that he must be talking to someone for whom English was a native language. He had stopped shuddering, but Stutzer, curled in the fetal position, twitched uncontrollably. Christopher approached him, meaning to pick him up and continue on his way, but then realized that he must stay where he was if he wished to be found in time.

Found in time for what? By whom? His mind was clouding again. He felt a stab of embarrassment. He did not know whom he had called. Or rather, he knew but could not retrieve the mental records for the person in question. Stutzer writhed, shuddered, moaned. Christopher felt weak. He leaned against the phone booth and waited for the feeling to pass. It did not pass. Nausea welled up in him. He leaned over and vomited. The vomiting was convulsive. He could not stop. His legs failed him. He felt that gravity had been reversed, that he had dived into a bottomless abyss—dark, dark. He let himself fall. He could neither help himself nor save himself. He could not breathe. He heard himself gasping for breath. He believed that whatever was happening to him was the last thing that would ever happen to him. He lost consciousness.

2

Christopher awoke in a hospital room. There was nothing to be seen through the window except a blank brick wall across an alley. His watch had been removed and there was no clock on the wall. Except for a hospital gown he was naked. By the angle of the light he guessed that it was mid-afternoon. The smell of the room and the furniture and equipment were American and could be nothing else. Transparent intravenous tubes ran into both his arms. He was connected to a monitor that registered what he supposed were his vital signs. He could feel and hear a strong pulse throbbing inside his skull, but he had no pain even though the presence of pain was the first thing he had expected to feel when he opened his eyes. His ears rang loudly. He touched his head. It had been shaved and was covered with stubble except for a strip of gauze, fastened by adhesive tape, on top of his head. He felt stitches beneath the bandage. He touched his face and estimated a two-day stubble. He turned his head to the side and felt the rush of vertigo and nausea. He turned his head back to its original position so that he was again lying flat on his back. The vertigo passed. He remembered everything that had happened, including his last moment of consciousness, but nothing after that. A bell-call for the nurse was pinned to the sheet near his right hand. He did not touch it. He knew that no nurse or doctor could tell him the only thing he wanted to know: Where is Stutzer?

A half glass of water with a bent straw in it stood on the bedside table. Christopher picked it up and sucked water through the straw, then put it down. Almost immediately he fell asleep again and dreamed that he was at a picnic with a lot of people he didn't know and their children. A large poisonous snake slithered into the dream. Christopher killed it with a rock, beating its head to a pulp. The other guests watched in silence, glasses at their lips but not drinking. No one spoke to Christopher or even seemed to notice him until a self-righteous little girl said, "Everyone hates you!" Christopher asked why. "Because you killed that snake," the child replied.

The dream woke him. Dusk filled the room. A nurse entered and switched on the lights. Christopher was dazzled by their brightness and was now certain that he was in the hands of Americans. "Ah, we're awake," said the nurse. She moved his hand back to his side and checked to make sure that his IVs were still stuck firmly in his forearms, then took his pulse, temperature and blood pressure and noted these on the chart at the foot of the bed. She wore captain's bars on her collar. Her name tag, half hidden beneath the stethoscope draped around her neck, told him that her first name was Krista and her last name began with a K. From her accent he guessed that she was from the Middle West. She said, "Do you know where you are, Colonel?"

Colonel? Christopher wondered what name had been manufactured to go with this manufactured rank. He said, "No."

"You're in the U. S. Army Hospital in Frankfurt, Germany," the captain said. "Until midnight I'm your nurse."

"What time is it now, Captain?"

"Twenty after five. Do you know what day it is?"

"No."

"It's Thursday. You're going to be fine. Your injuries are not, repeat not, life-threatening. Major Sadlowski, the physician on duty, will tell you the details. I'll notify him that you're awake."

She filled his water glass and held it while he drank through the straw. By her manner, professional but aloof, she created a distance between them. She was a fine-looking woman, slender but buxom. Oddly for an American girl she had not smiled once. She studied his face but avoided his eyes. She made no small talk, not even the standard where-are-you-from. She had made up her mind about him. Clearly she thought that he was not a real colonel, perhaps not even a real American. She would have been far more friendly to a genuine superior officer. A good many Outfit people had passed through this hospital and no doubt she had learned to recognize the type. Christopher wore no dog tags. Almost certainly he had arrived naked, with no personal effects. He wore no wristband with name, rank, and serial number. He was an exotic, an impostor, a mystery.

Major Sadlowski was as distant in manner as the nurse had been. He was an enormously tall, rawboned man, taller even than Hubbard had been, who had to bend double over the bed in order to use his stethoscope and carry out the rest of his examination. His questions were brief and to the point. He called Christopher sir, not Colonel. He did not call him by name. At the end of his examination he stood upright and looked down from his great height on the supine Christopher and asked if he had any questions. Christopher asked about the vertigo attacks. He did not call it that because he did not yet know what it was, but described the symptoms.

"Vertigo, probably," Major Sadlowski said. "Have you ever had these symptoms before?"

"No. They began the night I was shot."

"What makes you think you were shot?"

"Because someone was shooting at me. Am I wrong?"

"No, sir. How's your hearing?"

"A bit muffled, as if I had cotton in my ears. It comes and goes."

"That's interesting. I'll ask an ENT man to have a look at you. The inner ear, which controls balance, can be affected by a blow to the head. Or the vertigo could be the onset of Ménières syndrome, which sometimes results in hearing loss. Try to lie still, flat on your back, with your head slightly elevated. Don't look down or you'll feel like you fell down a mineshaft. The nurse will bring you extra pillows."

"What about the wound?"

"It's a gunshot wound, all right. Did it knock you unconscious?"

"No. Just a headache and a lot of blood. And the dizziness and nausea."

Major Sadlowski nodded as though this information was deeply interesting to him. He said, "You went on functioning normally?"

"I could walk and talk. I was somewhat disoriented. How deep is the wound?"

"Superficial. It dug a furrow in your scalp and blew away some bone fragments but it didn't penetrate the skull. We cleaned it up and sewed it up. You have a concussion, which is never a good thing, but the pictures show no other damage. Had the bullet struck at a slightly different angle or a millimeter lower, you'd have been in trouble. You also had symptoms of exposure. It took us a long time to get your temperature up to normal, but that's over now. Apart from the wound and the vertigo you're okay, but we were told that you inhaled some vomit and could have died if the person who found you hadn't stuck his finger down your windpipe and whacked you on the sternum."

"Do you happen to know who that person was?"

"No, sir, but whoever he was, he was a quick thinker," Major Sadlowski said, "All I know for sure is what I see."

What he really meant, Christopher thought, was, What I see is all I want to know. Major Sadlowski busied himself with the chart, frowning and scribbling.

"If this is Wednesday, I've been unconscious for more than twenty-four hours," Christopher said. "Why?"

"Not exactly unconscious," Major Sadlowski said, without looking up. "Asleep. You were given a heavy sedative before you got here."

"What sedative?"

"We don't know for certain. One of the opiates, probably. Morphine, maybe heroin. Maybe a combination of drugs."

"But whatever it was put me to sleep for twenty-four hours?"

"Longer than that," Major Sadlowski said. "It was an overdose. There were people around here, sir, who wondered if you'd ever wake up."

3

Instead of simply telling Christopher what time it was, Wolkowicz unbuckled his wristwatch—cheap, black, and Japanese—and tossed it onto the bed. Christopher reached for it, feeling a touch of vertigo as he bent forward. It was 4:24 A. M. He offered to give the watch back.

"Keep it," Wolkowicz said. "I've got more."

Using operational funds, Wolkowicz bought digital watches and ballpoint pens and cheap cameras in job lots. Such items were scarce in peoples' democracies and like a trader in Indian country, Barney handed them out as a way of making friends and influencing people behind the Iron Curtain.

He had shown up unannounced in Christopher's room. "We should talk," he said. "Patchen is on his way to spirit you away, so this is a preemptive strike."

Sarcasm was Wolkowicz's way of disabusing Christopher of any idea that he was capable of a corporal act of charity like visiting the sick. Christopher smiled.

Wolkowicz said, "Let's make this simple. Tell me what you thought you were up to in Berlin and I'll answer a question from you. Any question. There must be something you're dying to know."

"How did I get here?" Christopher asked.

"That's your one big question?"

"No."

"Let me know when we get to it. You remember making a phone call?"

"Yes. To your home number."

"Correct," Wolkowicz said. "We sprang right into action, and here you are."

"Who's we?"

"Me and some of the guys."

"What guys?"

"The ones who were on call that night. You were lying on Bülowstrasse in a pool of vomit, covered in blood and not breathing. Somebody cleaned out your windpipe and gave you the kiss of life. Puke and all. Imagine. Most people would have held their nose or given you a tracheotomy with a Swiss army knife. Not this guy. He must really love his fellow man."

"He must have got there pretty quick," Christopher said. "Usually people who breathe in their own vomit die in no time."

"Not you, apparently."

"So why am I here?"

"Well, for one thing you were full of dope and we couldn't wake you up, so our doctor in Berlin thought you should be in an American hospital. For another thing headquarters thought you should get out of Berlin. I agreed."

"How did I get full of dope?"

"Search me. And that's your last irrelevant question. I've got a few of my own."

"You think this is the best place to talk?" Christopher said.

"If it's not, then it's too late to start worrying," Wolkowicz replied. "But everything's fine. This room is like a medical safe house. It belongs to the Outfit. We own all the equipment. We use the room when we need it and the army keeps it under lock and key the rest of the time. It was swept last night before you woke up. It's clean as a whistle. The door is bazooka-proof. The window is bulletproof. There're guards outside the door. It's like we're in Action Comics."

This may or may not have been the truth. It was standard reassurance, page one of the agent-handler's manual. The case officer always told the agent that everything was fine, that he was safe and protected by an omniscient employer who loved him, that nothing could possibly go wrong.

Wolkowicz said, "Sadlowski—our guy, by the way—tells me you remember everything up to the time you passed out. I know from Heidi that you can do the tango like Valentino and that you took a lot of crazy chances with Stutzer and the Stasi, like riding by him on a bicycle and letting him see your face. I know that you slipped out of Heidi's hotel in the wee hours of the morning in question. I know you'd be dead if it wasn't for my timely arrival."

"Now you're boasting."

"I'm not a WASP, I'm allowed. Tell me the rest."

Christopher gave him a step-by-step report of everything he had done in East Berlin. Wolkowicz listened intently. He took no notes. A stranger to his ways might have supposed that he was relying on hidden microphones and a tape recorder, but Christopher knew that Wolkowicz would remember every word he was hearing, probably for the rest of his life.

When Christopher finished his narrative, Wolkowicz closed his eyes for a long moment and whistled a tune through his teeth. Then he said, "So after you were shot in the head and while you were bleeding like a stuck pig, you bashed Stutzer with a rock and carried him across the line, across the Potsdamer Bridge, and down Potsdamerstrasse into the heart of West Berlin?"

Christopher did not reply. Wolkowicz had heard what he said. There was no need to tell him again.

"And nobody followed you?"

"I saw nobody behind me."

"Were there any witnesses?"

"Yes. I talked to some of them." Christopher described the encounter with the Christian and the others.

"Okay. So tell me what happened when you found the telephone."

"I put Stutzer on the ground and called you."

"And then?"

"And then I passed out."

"All of a sudden you conk out, after this superhuman fireman's carry through the ruins. Why?"

Christopher said, "I couldn't stay conscious. I thought I was going into shock. The world spun around. Everything went black."

"Where was Stutzer while all this was going on?"

"Lying on the pavement, propped up against the phone booth."

"In other words, he was right where you dropped him. Was he conscious or unconscious?"

"Immobilized. He couldn't talk or walk. He made a noise. His jaw was broken. I think I tore up his knees when I clipped him."

"But his face was the last thing you saw before you went under?"

"Yes."

"And he was alive."

"No question."

Wolkowicz inhaled, bit his lower lip with his impossibly perfect false teeth. He covered the teeth with his upper lip and again whistled the same unrecognizable tune. "That's amazing," he said. "Because your call came in at one minute after five and my first man, who just happened to be in the neighborhood, was on the scene at five-oh-four, and when he got there, there was no Stutzer. Just you, out like a light and choking to death."

No Stutzer? Christopher was so startled by this information that he moved suddenly—plunged toward Wolkowicz, who stood at the foot of the bed. This triggered a vertigo attack. Nausea rose into his throat, his mouth, his nostrils. The hospital bed turned upside down and he seized the rails to keep himself from falling out.

He put his head back onto the pillows. The attack passed. He said, "You didn't find Stutzer's Stasi ID in my inside pocket?"

"No. No sign of him whatsoever."

Another man, hearing what Wolkowicz had just told him, might have said, "That's impossible." But Christopher knew that in his vertiginous world and Stutzer's and Wolkowicz's, the possibilities were unlimited, so he held his peace.

4

Christopher was slow to recover from vertigo and even slower to reconcile himself to the reality that he had had Stutzer in his grasp and then lost him or had him stolen from him. The episode in East Berlin faded in everyone else's memory, if not in his own. On O. G.'s orders the capture of Stutzer was never put into writing. No one outside the original circle of knowledge was ever briefed. Nothing about it was recorded, nothing remembered. No one but Patchen ever discussed the episode with Christopher, and Patchen himself spoke about it only once. This conversation took place as the two friends walked once again across the campus of Georgetown University. They had dined on limp pasta in a bad Sicilian restaurant that Patchen liked because it was always nearly empty. The night was damp, mist rising from the Potomac. Patchen was recovering, as he often was, from a lung infection. Every few steps he coughed, one sharp dry bark after another, and the paroxysm stopped him in his tracks. The Doberman sniffed his coat sympathetically and licked his hand.

"O. G. ordered me to make no file and to keep knowledge of the operation strictly quarantined—his word," Patchen said to Christopher. "On our side of the fence, only he and you and Wolkowicz and I know what happened and only you know everything—except of course for the most intriguing things, namely what happened while you were unconscious and what happened to Stutzer. Apparently O. G. wants to preserve the ambiguity."

"And do we know what is known or believed on the other side of the fence?"

"All is darkness," Patchen said. "Even the Israelis don't have a clue, and needless to say they're at least as interested in Stutzer as you are. We assume that Stutzer's absence was noted by MfS. The accepted hypothesis is that MfS people found the two of you in the nick of time and spirited Stutzer away before Wolkowicz and his goons came on the scene. Do you agree?"

"No. If that's what happened why they didn't spirit me away, too?"

"Everyone wonders about that, except Wolkowicz. There's not a doubt in his mind. According to his hypothesis, they tried to kill you with an overdose of something instead."

"That was Stutzer. Who else could it have been? He was draped across my back, he had every opportunity and every motive."

"You didn't search him?"

"I did, and found all kinds of weapons, but I guess I missed the syringe."

"How?"

"I wasn't looking for it. I thought he was trying to kill me, not keep me alive. But I should have remembered what he is—an interrogator. I had aroused his curiosity. His plan would have been to knock me out, take me to a safe house, break me. The dose was never meant to be fatal."

"So why didn't his men throw you in the trunk of the getaway car so he could question you?"

"Because there were no such men. His priorities changed. After I made the phone call all he wanted was to get back home. He crawled away on his own or had other help."

"Excellent point. But then there are a lot of nice debating points in this case. Consider Wolkowicz's hypothesis."

"Which is?"

"That you were hallucinating. That the slug that split your scalp addled your wits. That you imagined the whole thing, and that what you think happened never actually happened. It was all a crazy dream."

"How did he arrive at that?"

"For one thing, you told him you had Stutzer's papers in your pocket when you passed out. But the pocket was empty."

"True but irrelevant. Anybody could have picked my pocket. What else?"

"Barney submitted the sterilized facts—no names, no place, no time, just a hypothetical situation—to our best forensic shrink and that's what he came up with. It made all the sense in the world to Barney. Stutzer got away from you. But nobody gets away from Wolkowicz."

Patchen's lip curled. His disdain for Wolkowicz was well known, especially to Christopher, to whom he spoke frankly at all times. Apparently he felt that he should say a good word for his enemy. He continued, "In justice to Wolkowicz and the shrink, you were shot in the head. And in both versions, yours and the shrink's, everything follows from that. However, the questions remains, if there was no Stutzer, who shot you and why would they bother?"

Patchen had another fit of coughing. Refusing to yield to it, he walked on, the sound of his cough echoing from the portentous architecture.

When he had recovered his breath, Christopher said, "So what do you believe?"

"Let's just say I believe you to be perfectly capable of carrying a wounded man a couple of miles on your back while wounded yourself."

"And O. G.?"

"It's my job to tell him everything that's in my mind," Patchen said, "not to read his mind. But he is, I believe, your godfather, and he's the one who put you into this situation, so he's got to give you the benefit of the doubt."

Christopher was tempted to say more, to tell Patchen what O. G. knew about Stutzer, to tell him what Stutzer had been to the Christophers in the past. He had never told anyone—not O. G., not Hubbard, not Lori, not Paulus—what had happened to Rima. None of them—and not Patchen either—had had a need to know or a right to know. That did not mean that they hadn't guessed the truth. What mattered was that Stutzer had taken everything but Rima's own death away from her. She had a right to keep that for herself, and keep it she had, stored in the mind of her lover.

TWELVE

1

For two years there was no news of Stutzer. No one was looking for him, and thanks to the way in which O. G. had erased him from the Outfit's archives, no one ever would except by mistake. This did not mean that there was no Stutzer still in the world, whatever his reinvented identity might be. Christopher's life, like everyone else's, was a map of coincidence and he believed in its power. He went from assignment to assignment, always expecting that at the next turning of a street in Cairo or Hue or Leopoldville he would glimpse the matchstick man again, just as had happened before, and that this time Stutzer would either kill Christopher by treachery or Christopher would have his revenge. But what revenge could cause the sea to give up Rima, could cut the loop of image and sound and scent that haunted him— Rima's arms in her last moment curved above her head, the glare of the searchlights, *Mahican* aflame and running before the wind into the night, the Baltic taking the girl, the unbelief. The briefness of it. Maybe when the moment for retribution came, it would simply happen like a poem that was ready to be born running onto paper out of a pen. This frozen zygote he had been carrying within himself for half a lifetime would somehow at the last moment turn into a complete being and tell him what to do and how to do it.

After a long uninterrupted time in the field he took a month's leave. A year or two before he had moved to Rome. One night as he waited for his supper in an open-air restaurant in Trastevere, Heidi slipped into the empty chair across the table. He had not seen her since Berlin.

She was no longer the unsmiling hotel manageress in a green apron that she had been in East Berlin. Now she wore sunglasses after dark, a jumble of cheap beads around her neck, rows of bracelets on both arms and slacks and sandals and a bright red shirt that perfectly matched her painted toenails. Her hair, formerly twisted into a bun, now hung to her shoulder blades. She shook it back so that Christopher could see her face. "Fancy meeting you here," she said in English.

In her new costume she seemed smaller and prettier than he remembered. "This is a surprise," he replied, also in English. "What brings you to Rome?"

"Curiosity," Heidi said. The waiter brought pasta. "And hunger," she said. Christopher told the waiter to divide the pasta into two portions and bring another glass. Heidi ordered the same main course as Christopher—grilled sea bass. "Everything in Italy tastes so wonderful," she said after her first mouthful of pasta, "and olive oil is so much better for the digestion than lard."

While they dined, two mimes in clown suits and white greasepaint performed in the street near their table. Their routine was to do everything in mirror image. They were very good. Each gesture, each expression was an exact duplicate of the other man's. One of them was rotund, the other thin, but this difference only made the synchronization funnier. Christopher came often to this restaurant but he had never seen these performers before. Looking over Heidi's shoulder, he studied them. Greedily, Heidi ate her tortellini con funghi and sipped Frascati and studied Christopher as if waiting for him to do some particular thing she knew he must do. Finally he recognized the mimes. When this happened Heidi must have seen some change in his eyes because she said, "You've identified the suspects, am I right?" Her English was American, and unlike her German, entirely free of accent.

"The bicyclists in the fur hats on Stalinallee," Christopher said.

Heidi said, "You are good, aren't you?"

"*They* are. Are you part of the act?"

"Sometimes, but I'm just décor. They're the artistes."

"This is their hobby?"

"No, no, they've studied with the best. It's what they want to do when they grow up."

"Work in the streets?"

"Not forever. World fame is their goal, Marcel and Marceau. It might happen, don't you think?"

The mimes were passing the hat, going from table to table. Christopher gave them a thousand lira. They paid him and Heidi no particular attention.

"It's amazing how much money they can make in an evening," Heidi said. "Sometimes a kilo of coins. Cheapskate tourists give them foreign coins which are useless because they can't be exchanged."

The mimes wandered away. Heidi paid them no further attention. Christopher said, "You're traveling with them?"

"Always."

"Then you are an act."

"Sort of. Sometimes."

Heidi changed the subject to movies. Marcello Mastroianni grew up in this neighborhood, she said, and was sometimes seen dining with friends at one of the restaurants in the piazza. "He wears sunglasses at night, just like his character in *La Dolce Vita*—just like me, when in Rome et cetera," Heidi said. "Nobody bothers him when he materializes. He's just Marcello from the neighborhood. He eats his pasta and talks to his friends and walks home to his mama's house. How do the Romans do it—live so naturally?"

Heidi herself hadn't the knack. Her conversation, her costume, her expressions were as studied as the mimes' had been. In Berlin she had played a hotel manageress. Now she was playing an American girl in Rome. Christopher wondered if really she was an American girl, and if she was, who had set her on his trail and what she wanted. He suspected Wolkowicz.

The waiter brought the check. Heidi took it from his hand and paid for their dinner with a ten thousand lira note the size of a page ripped from a book. "Another thing I like about Italy is the money," Heidi said. "It's just the right size."

They walked along the Tiber for a few blocks, stopping at a bar to have coffee. Heidi said, "Add cappuccino to the list of things I like about Rome." They crossed a bridge. She seemed to know where she was going. Christopher followed along, and finally she led him into a tiny street and then into a necktie shop. It was closing time and the shop seemed to be empty, but after a moment a man wearing a beautiful necktie and a suit with the jacket cut short in the Italian style bustled out of the backroom, and paying Heidi and Christopher no more attention than he would have done if they were tourists here to waste his time and buy nothing, went outside and cranked down the metal shutter that covered the door and the display window. They were locked in.

Heidi smiled a bright American smile.

The shop was separated from the back room by a bead curtain. Heidi parted it and stepped through the doorway. When Christopher did not follow she held out a hand, her body on one side of the curtain, her slender arm with its many bracelets on the other. Because there was no way out the front door it was pointless to stay where he was, so he followed her into the back room. It was as large as the shop, boxes stacked everywhere. The space was better lighted than the rooms in the Red Orchestra Inn, but dim all the same. In one corner an electric ring glowed red beneath a teakettle. A very small man, little more than five feet tall, sat in a frayed chair with his feet dangling. He was elderly and bald. Tufts of gray body hair protruded from his shirt collar. He held a glass of tea in his hand. With a gesture he offered Christopher a chair that had been drawn up to face his own. Behind him Heidi worked with swift efficiency and handed Christopher his own glass of tea. Then she sat on the floor at the old man's feet, her legs crossed, her expression intent. Christopher sipped the oversweetened tea. He could taste the sugar on his tongue many seconds after he had swallowed it.

The little old man lifted his glass to Christopher and speaking English with a heavy accent said, "I am happy to see you again."

Christopher had already recognized him. He was not a figure who, once encountered however briefly, was likely to be forgotten, but Christopher had other reasons besides his unforgettable appearance to know who he was.

The small man said, "Do you remember the last time we met?"

"Yes," Christopher said, "in Rügen. We were introduced on the beach. You went sailing with my parents. I was left behind."

"You were what in nineteen thirty-four, nine or ten?"

"About that."

"You were tall for your age, about my size, I remember that," said the small man. "That sailboat burned, I hear. A shame, it was so beautiful."

Christopher was not in the least surprised that this man knew this detail. He specialized in details.

Christopher said, "Am I to understand that you're still working, Mr. Stern?"

"From time to time, off the books, when the job is interesting. Call me Yeho. You're old enough now."

In his writings Hubbard had called Yeho Stern, who had been his friend, the hidden man. Yeho was hiding now. He was polite, deeply so, but it seemed to Christopher that this was an impersonation of politeness, just as Heidi's role for tonight was an imitation of Americanness. It was Yeho who had planted in the minds of Hubbard and Lori the idea of smuggling Jews who had no other hope of getting out of the Reich. Yeho had asked them for help and they had given it. In asking for help he asked them to put their own lives on deposit as well as the lives of the people they rescued. They had paid the price. What did he want now?

Expressionless, Yeho watched Christopher as if he had no need to read his thoughts—as if he already knew them by heart, having read the same kind of thoughts in other people so many times before. He finished his tea. Heidi took the glass from his hand. Yeho never took his eyes from Christopher's face.

Finally he said, "I have some information." Christopher waited. Yeho said, "You're much more like your mother than your father, did you know?" In spite of himself Christopher reacted to these words— something in his eyes, a slight movement, a half smile. Yeho said (was he making a little joke or did he think that Christopher might mistake his meaning?), "What I just said to you is not the information." Eyes fixed on Christopher, Yeho accepted another glass of tea from Heidi.

He said, "This is the information. We have located this subject in whom you are interested, this Stutzer."

These were startling words but once again Christopher was not surprised that Yeho should know something that almost nobody else in the world knew, or that he should share this secret with him. Yeho made no altruistic gestures. He wanted something in return. But what?

Yeho said, "You have nothing to say?"

"I was waiting for the rest of the information."

"Good," Yeho said. "Very good. Everyone says how good you are. The abduction of Stutzer, excellent. Foolhardy but excellent. One man against the Stasi and such a target, this Stutzer, such improvisation. Forgive me, it's too late to critique, but you should have waited a minute. You should have let Heidi and the boys help you. They wanted to help you."

"And now you want to help me."

"I want to make it possible for you to do something you want to do."

This was O. G.'s formula. Christopher wondered which old man had plagiarized the phrase from the other, or whether experience had planted the same maxims in both their minds.

Christopher said, "Ah. And what would that something be?"

"You have to ask? You want Stutzer. You have a right to him. I will help you take him, and this time keep him. No more hypodermics at the last minute."

"In return for what?"

Yeho lifted a forefinger, teaching. "Again you have to ask," he said. "What can I tell you? Maybe I want what you want and this is a way for both of us to get it. Maybe I can't do what I want without you. Maybe vice-versa. Maybe I owe you something and I want to pay the debt. Maybe you owe me something without knowing it. Maybe it's just opportunity that has put us together."

Christopher felt exasperation rising into his throat. He pushed it down. Yeho was an Oriental to the marrow, and Christopher realized that the little man was trying to exasperate him. He was dickering as though they were in a bazaar and the price of a carpet was at stake.

Exasperation is the most valuable tool a bargainer possesses. Exasperation makes the other man give up, it makes him say have it your way! Yeho wasn't trying to cheat him. Like a woman trying to manipulate a man, he was trying to see how well Christopher held his own, what he was made of, how strong he was. How otherwise could he know? He hadn't seen Christopher with his own eyes since he was nine years old. The rest was gossip.

Christopher said, "I will need more information."

"Okay, why not, what could be more reasonable," Yeho said. "Here is some information. Tomorrow, thirteenth August, early in the morning, something is going to happen in Berlin. Something big. At breakfast, listen to the radio. If it's big enough to make you curious, come here tomorrow night at closing time and I will know that the son of my old friends wants to be my friend, too."

2

The next morning, Sunday, August 13, 1961, East Germany sealed the frontier between the two Berlins and began to build the Wall and rip up streets that connected East and West. At eight o'clock that evening Christopher appeared in front of the necktie shop in Rome. It was closed. From inside the shutter was rolled up with a clatter, but only halfway. Heidi's beckoning arm and hand, clinking bracelets and vermilion fingernails, appeared in the gap. No passerby could possibly understand such a signal as anything but a lover's invitation. Christopher ducked under the shutter and went inside.

In the back room Yeho sat with his feet on an ottoman, his head reclined on the back of the chair, his eyes closed. Without opening his eyes he said, "So what do you think?"

"I think they've got balls."

"Sad but true." Yeho opened his eyes. He said, "Maybe this is all your fault. Maybe the way you kidnapped their secret policeman was the last straw. Don't laugh. George Washington started the War of the Spanish Succession—a world war, my friend—by shooting a few

French soldiers in the woods in Pennsylvania. Everything starts small."

Christopher said, "You're in a world-historical mood today, Yeho."

"You're right. I apologize. Next time I'll give a signal when I'm kidding you. But I'm not kidding when I say that Stutzer is as now safe as a war criminal can possibly be as long as he stays inside East Berlin."

"I agree."

"You do? Good, because there's a however."

Now Yeho assumed a crafty look. Christopher chuckled. He was charmed by this homunculus, this terrorist and mastermind who had probably shot a hundred enemies between the eyes with the cumbersome .45 caliber Webley revolver that folklore described as his weapon of choice. Christopher understood that he was supposed to be amused. Yeho was doing his routine.

Christopher said, "A however?" And he thought, *What a surprise.*

Yeho said, "A big however. But first, are you with me in this thing? I'm offering you a chance to do what you want to do. We will get him, I promise you. Personally, because of what's going on in Berlin, I think this is going to be your last chance. But if you want to refuse, refuse. No hard feelings. However, I can't tell you the information till you tell me yes, you want to help, yes, you will help, yes, you are in the game. Now is the time to walk away if you want, before I give you the information."

"What about afterward?"

"Afterward, no walking."

Christopher said, "Three yeses, Yeho. Tell me."

Without so much as a pause for effect, Yeho said, "Believe it or not, Stutzer is on the island of Rügen."

This information literally took Christopher's breath away. While his heart beat wildly, his lungs shut down for the space of five or six breaths and for that brief interval his body seemed to forget how to breathe involuntarily. He turned his back to Yeho, wrapped his own arms around himself, and tried to remember how to draw air into his chest and then expel it. For the first time in his life he was unable to have two thoughts at the same time, so he blacked out Stutzer and the cascade of images that had chased Stutzer into his mind—the schloss, the chalk cliffs, the beeches, the bone-white houses of the island, the gulls, the sloshing gray sea, *Mahican* aflame—and commanded his lungs to breathe. Then he was all right.

All this consumed a second, perhaps less. Yeho said, "It must be soon. Can you get away?"

"I'm already on leave. When do we depart?"

"Today, now, this minute, before you get ordered to Berlin. The Outfit will send everybody to Berlin, it's only natural. You can't go home where the phone might ring. We've got for you everything you'll need, the right kind of toothpaste, everything. The business in Berlin is a big diversion. It gives us our moment, our chance. MfS's attention will be on that. They're hypnotized by their own folly. They're scared, their pants are full because they can't believe the Americans are going to let them get away with this."

"But we will."

"I don't like to say it, but yes, you will. Your new president has no balls. Now go with Heidi. I'll tell you everything on the ship."

"On the ship?"

"A ship is the best way to get to an island and leave on your own schedule, no? Go, go."

"And you?"

"We will meet on the ship, we will do everything together. Don't worry, I'm right behind you."

That promise, coming from Yeho, might have been enough to make many men worry but Christopher took him at his word. Christopher and Heidi, traveling as a happy couple, Heidi now dressed in a demure suit and pumps, caught an Alitalia flight to Copenhagen. Heidi had provided Christopher with a suitcase and a Canadian passport, along with a wallet stuffed with lira and Canadian dollars and the usual poker hand of fabricated identity documents. In Copenhagen they boarded a freighter registered in Liberia. The name painted on the stern and bow was *Olaster*. It was a Victory ship, a tramp, but its hull was only slightly rusted. The crew—only a few men—were dark-haired, olive-skinned, young, and voluble in an Eastern language Christopher did not understand but knew to be the Hebrew, whose murmur he had heard in Heidi's German.

One of the crew, silent and incurious, led Christopher to a cabin. He unpacked the suitcase. Inside it he found the right toothpaste as promised and also a suit, a blazer, shirts and ties, a sweater, underwear, socks, work trousers, turtlenecks, a waterproof jacket, a knitted watch cap, tennis shoes. Everything fit because everything belonged to him. Heidi and/or the mimes had removed it all from his apartment.

The two mimes were already aboard. When Christopher passed them in the corridor they greeted him, deadpan, then disappeared into their cabin. He looked for Yeho but did not find him. He locked his cabin door, lay down on the bed and read a book, a Sybil Bedford novel that he had found in his suitcase. He did not bother to check the room for listening devices or cameras or other hidden apparatus as all good spies were supposed to do. He wasn't going to talk to himself while he was aboard, he would be sleeping only with Mrs. Bedford, and if Yeho wanted to take his picture he would find a plausible excuse.

Christopher dozed off. He roused when the engines started and the ship moved under him as it left port. He drifted off again. When next he woke to a knock on the door, Hubbard's old shave-and-a-haircut-two bits, he felt beneath him the rolling swell of the Baltic, unlike any other sea he had ever sailed upon and as familiar as the jaunty knock that had awakened him on thousands of mornings.

3

Farther out, after the wind died, the Baltic was placid. The *Olaster* sailed smoothly through the calm waters. At dinner, taken in silence, quickly, Yeho ate everything on his plate. Heidi and the mimes followed suit. The mimes seemed to time their chewing to Yeho's, and finished their supper at almost the same moment as he did. In Christopher's hearing at least, Heidi had not spoken a syllable in Yeho's presence. The mimes were just as quiet. In filial silence they listened intently to his every word, eyes shining with admiration as if he had just stepped out of the Torah. Even Christopher had no trouble imagining him as a biblical figure in a cloak—Eve's adviser, David's secret agent, Solomon's conscience, Joshua's tactician. Christopher left half of his bland food uneaten, and the atmosphere of deference to the patriarch was so noticeable that he would not have been surprised if Yeho had reproved him for wasting eggs and cheese in a world in which children went hungry. Heidi and the mimes cleared the table. With his eyes closed—his signal, Christopher guessed, that the talking lamp was not yet lit—Yeho waited for them to finish.

The captain joined them. Yeho introduced him: "This is Simon, the captain. Simon, an American friend." The two men, about the same age, nodded to each other. Like the rest of the crew Simon wore ordinary clothes. His badge of rank was an old blue officer's cap without insignia.

Heidi and the mimes returned to the table. Yeho opened his eyes and said, "Here is a significant fact. This American is the only living witness to Stutzer's crimes. Otherwise there are no survivors because he either killed all his victims or they died in the camps or afterward. Did you know that?"

"No," Christopher said. He wondered how Yeho could possibly know this himself, given the scale on which Stutzer had murdered people, but Yeho gave him no opportunity to inquire.

"Besides that," Yeho continued, "as we know, you have seen Stutzer very recently, and up close, so you can make sure we get the right person."

Christopher said, "So has Heidi seen him."

Yeho, talking through this interruption, looked him benevolently in the eye as if to say, *Wait and you'll know everything.* He said, "Also, you used to live in the house in which Stutzer is hiding."

Startled again—evidently Yeho liked surprises—Christopher said, "Stutzer is staying at Schloss Berwick?"

Yeho held up a hand—wait!—and said, "So that means you know the house, the trees, the ground, the beach, the waters as none of the rest of us possibly can. Also, as we know, you have unusual skills."

He fell into a short silence as if to see if anyone would interrupt him again, then turned to Christopher and said, "The answer to your question is yes, we believe with good reason that Stutzer is inside the schloss.

The house and grounds now belong to the state, of course, and it's being used as a place for Stutzer's Arabs to be inspired and trained. It's a good place for that. Hardly anybody in the world knows that there is such a place as Rügen. It's deep inside the GDR, a long way from Berlin and all other windows into this country, so by the MfS it's secure. That's why Stutzer's here. He thinks he's safe. For us, that's good luck."

Christopher said, "We go tonight?"

Yeho nodded.

"To do what, exactly?"

"What else?" Yeho asked. "Go ashore, burgle the schloss, snatch Stutzer, bring him back. Sail away."

Christopher said, "What about the Arabs?"

"Not tonight. Tonight, only Stutzer." He put a hand on Christopher's forearm. "Please listen for a minute, my friend, to what I'm trying to tell you."

Christopher subsided. A steward brought tea in glasses. It was scalding hot. Yeho drank his tea through the usual sugar cube without bothering to cool it and with no sign that it was anything but exactly the right temperature.

To the captain Yeho said, "What time will we reach Rügen, Simon?"

"About two o'clock in the morning. Roughly eight hours from now."

"That's when the team gets off."

"Yes. Then we sail on for an hour, come about, and return to our original position off Rügen."

"So you'll be there, waiting, right on schedule at four o'clock more or less."

"That's the plan."

Yeho went on with his briefing. The others had rehearsed the landing together. There had been no time for Christopher to participate, and even if there had been time it would have been insecure. "Don't worry, when you have good people, improvisation is better," Yeho said.

He went on. They would go ashore in a Zodiac, a very fast type of boat with a big outboard motor. The landing party would consist of the mimes, Heidi and Christopher. Heidi was the leader. Yeho did not justify this. The mimes did not seem to see anything unusual in the arrangement. "We've only got one pair of night-vision goggles," Yeho said. "Heidi will have them, so inside the house she'll be the eyes of the team." There would be a moon tonight, so they could see while they were outdoors. Christopher was the guide, he would go first. Each of the four would be armed with a silenced pistol, a knife, a blackjack, and a stun gun. Also a grenade apiece. They would go silent as soon as they were on land—no talking, hand signals only, a hiss in case of dire emergency. They would have no radio because radios made too much noise. A fifth person—Yeho did not name this operative—would go ashore with them and stay with the boat. He would have a radio with which he could communicate with the ship. The others would signal him, if necessary, by flashlight.

"Do this quietly, on tiptoes," Yeho said. "Stutzer's friends should wake up in the morning and ask each other, Where is he? Not wake up in the night and reach for their guns. Silence, prudence, speed—those are the words."

"And if we're discovered?" Christopher said.

"Don't be. But if you are, nothing changes. Do what's necessary. Grab Stutzer, come home."

Christopher looked at him. Yeho read the question in his eyes. He said, "You make me say it out loud? Okay. No rescue if you get in trouble."

4

On time to the minute and moving dead slow, the *Olaster* arrived off Rügen. Even by full moonlight the island was not visible except for the pulse of its lighthouses reflecting from low clouds. Christopher knew that this meant that they were miles offshore. Yeho told Christopher—he addressed all his remarks to him, presumably because the others already knew the facts—that they were in international waters. This meant a long run back to the ship from the shore, and an almost impossible one if the East Germans had patrol boats in the water, as they almost certainly did given what was going on in Berlin. Yeho, who had no taste for the obvious, did not mention this hazard.

Heidi and the mimes stood somewhat apart. Christopher studied them closely so as to be able later on to recognize their silhouettes in moonlight. Like him, they wore watch caps and turtlenecks and dark baggy trousers. Their faces and hands were blacked. He did not like this last bit of theatricality, and if he had been in command he would have ordered them to clean up. The ship's crew worked wordlessly and within seconds had lowered the Zodiac into the water. The team rappelled down to it, mimes first, then Christopher, then Heidi, who bounced elastically from point to point on the ship's side as if trying out a new thrill in an amusement park. The last man, the boat driver and lookout, was lowered in a bosun's chair. It was Yeho. The mimes had already started the outboards—there were two of these, enormous Evinrudes—and Yeho opened the throttles and headed for shore. The flat bottom of the Zodiac slammed the water. According to its speedometer the boat was traveling at forty miles per hour. This was faster than Christopher had expected. The *Olaster*, showing running lights, moved slowly eastward.

As the Zodiac drew closer and the island came up out of the sea, it snapped into place in Christopher's memory. Yeho beckoned Christopher to sit beside him. He piloted the boat to shore not far from *Mahican*'s old mooring. Christopher knew the cliffs and the other landmarks by heart and he was sure, within a meter or two, where the Zodiac ran aground. The team went ashore, leaping from the bow of the boat to the sand to keep their shoes dry.

Christopher led them to the cliffs, which were more than one hundred feet high at this point, and immediately started climbing, using the cavities in the chalk as foot- and handholds. The smell of chalk and the gritty way it felt on his hands, the stink of guano and rotting nests reawakened his memory of this place just as its silhouette, seen from miles away, had done. In moments he reached the top of the cliff. Heidi and the mimes were right behind him. He led them into the beech grove. A deep cushion of rotted leaves lay underfoot, moonlight dappled the ground.

Christopher walked upright through the grove at a normal pace. A man moving swiftly at night was easier to see. The others kept pace, spread out like an infantry patrol in diamond formation. They seemed to trust him. He wondered if they really did. How could they? They had no idea what he might do, what he might lead them into. Nor did he have any idea what their intentions were toward him.

The schloss was bathed in moonlight, tall windows on the west side aglow with it. The roof was crowded with antennas of all shapes and sizes. To Christopher's eye this spoiled the comeliness of the house. Instead of the tender nostalgia he had expected in himself and guarded against, he felt annoyance at this vandalism and wondered if the ghost of Paulus was beside him, hoping that he had come to blow the place up. The grounds were patrolled, as he had been sure they would be. A guard with a submachine gun slung across his chest sauntered across the open ground between the trees and the house. After four minutes a second man slouched by in the opposite direction. They were so unmilitary in their baggy Russian-style uniforms that Paulus would not have believed that they could be Germans. As soon as the guard turned a corner and disappeared behind the schloss Heidi gave a hand signal. She and the mimes dashed across the open ground and faded into the shadows next to the house. Christopher waited till the next guard passed by and then walked across.

What, he wondered, did Heidi and the mimes plan on doing next? His question was answered when they drifted around the corner, following the guard. A third man was posted at the front door. His back was turned. Heidi made another hand signal. Without hesitation, moving swiftly and silently, the slender mime moved toward him and struck him on the head with a blackjack, then rolled him into the shrubbery. The chubby mime took off in pursuit of the guard who had just passed. The other mime went in the opposite direction, on the hunt for the second remaining guard. Heidi tried the great front door, found it locked, took tools from her pocket, and efficiently picked the lock. The mimes returned. Heidi donned her night-vision goggles and went inside. In a moment her hand and forearm appeared, signaling the others to come inside, just as she had beckoned Christopher into the necktie shop.

Christopher was the last to enter. Enough moonlight filtered into the hall to reveal its familiar features—the double stairway, the great stone fireplace, the empty spaces where the pictures had hung and where the suits of armor with their peculiar pewterlike sheen of old German steel had stood. Heidi made a deferential gesture to Christopher to lead on. She seemed to assume that because he knew the house he would know where Stutzer could be found. Christopher made an assumption of his own and led the others toward Paulus's old room. It was the baronial chamber, three times as large as any other bedroom in the house, with frescoes of nymphs and knights on the ceiling and pillars surrounding the elevated platform on which the bedstead stood. Surely this was the room that Stutzer, as man in charge, would commandeer for his own use. The door was locked. Heidi knelt and swiftly picked the lock. The tiny noises she made were enough to alert a husky young sentry on duty inside. He flung open the door. He did not immediately see Heidi kneeling before him, and he may never have seen her before she pressed a stun gun against the front of his trousers and released 600,000 volts of electricity into his private parts. He froze, then dropped to the floor unconscious.

Christopher stepped over him. The mimes followed, he could feel them behind him. A man sat up in Paulus's and Hilde's old bed with its tall carved headboard and fringed canopy. Hilde hissed, the signal for danger, and Christopher guessed that the man was armed. He took another long step, meaning to attack, but the sturdy mime, who was surprisingly quick on his feet, had already reached the bed. He punched the man hard in the stomach. The man gasped and bent over double. Something dropped to the floor. Christopher picked it up—a cocked pistol. He lowered the hammer and put the weapon on what used to be the commode in which Paulus's wash basin and chamber pot were stored.

Heidi handed Christopher her night-vision goggles. He realized that she wanted him to verify the identity of the prisoner. He put them on and in the green night-vision field saw Stutzer in striped old-fashioned pajamas, clutching his stomach, mouth agape, his emaciated body bent at queer angles.

Christopher said, "It's him."

The slender mime, who had been waiting with a syringe in his hand for Christopher's answer, immediately gave Stutzer an injection. He twitched, opened his eyes wide in what seemed to be terror, then went limp. For an instant Christopher thought that an execution had just taken place but then Stutzer moaned and moved and he knew that the plan really was to take him alive.

The mime removed a hank of climbing rope from the other's day pack. Heidi pulled back the curtains and opened a window. The mimes bent the rope around a pillar, then threw one end out of it the window. While the mimes held the belay, Heidi went out the window and rappelled down the wall of the schloss. The heavier mime followed her, with Christopher helping the other one to bear his weight. As soon as his strain was off the rope the slender mime tied a bowline on a bight at one end, leaving a long tail which he attached to the other half of the rope with a taut-line hitch. This permitted a slow descent by controlling the flow of the rope through the taut-line hitch.

Christopher and the mime slipped the two loops of the bowline over Stutzer's legs. The mime secured him to the rope with two slipknots. They sat Stutzer on the windowsill, legs dangling outside, then threw the long end down to the others, who were waiting below the window. By the light of the sinking moon Christopher watched as the mime told him in dumb show that he would take Stutzer down and Christopher would follow and pull the rope down after him. His message could not have been plainer if he had written it in block letters on a placard.

They carried Stutzer to the chalk cliff in relays, then swung him down on the rope, snubbing it around a beech tree. While he waited for the team's return Yeho had taken the Zodiac out to sea. Heidi signaled him with her flashlight. Christopher read the dots and dashes. The message was *OK*, simplicity itself, just like the rest of this operation. He looked at his watch. The entire raid had taken twenty-three minutes.

Yeho brought the boat in more quietly this time, at low revolutions, but the wind had risen at his back and as he approached they could hear the whine of the outboards.

Yeho expressed no surprise or pleasure at the sight of Stutzer's unconscious person. The team had done what it was supposed to do, so who was he to offer congratulations? "We've got a little time to kill," he said. "You're early."

With the unconscious Stutzer in his twisted flannel pajamas stretched out in the bottom of the boat, they motored out to sea at no-wake speed. Gradually, light by light, Rügen sank beneath the horizon. When they got to the rendezvous, the *Olaster* waited for them, lights lit for all the world to see.

THIRTEEN

1

Yeho was in a chatty after-picnic mood all the way from shore, reminiscing light-heartedly with Christopher about his long-ago visit to Rügen and Schloss Berwick and his sail to Demark aboard *Mahican*. Now, as they waited for lines to be lowered, he said, "My brother-in-law from Berlin arranged that meeting with your parents. He was a man, a Social Democrat, a friend of Friedrich Ebert all his life, close to him even when Ebert was president of the Weimar Republic. From the start he handled Berlin for us, very risky work. He and my sister and their boy Norman made it to Palestine before they got caught because Hubbard and Lori gave him a sailboat ride. Were you along on that one?"

"No," Christopher replied. "Usually I went along only if I stowed away. But I knew Norman and his parents."

"I'm not surprised. They and your parents were friends for years. My brother-in-law was a literary man like your father, he wrote political books, every one of them burned, no doubt. When he made the suggestion that your parents might help us I said, What? An American two meters high and a baronesse, you must be joking. But as soon as I met them I knew they were going to be all right, even though your father had this look in his eye like he was going to suggest we go into the ventriloquism business together, me in a smoking jacket sitting on his lap. I've got to admit it would have been good cover. We could have gone anywhere, me in a suitcase, him on a U. S. passport."

Yeho reached up and squeezed Christopher's shoulder, a vice-like grip despite his size and age. "I know you've got memories," he said. He pointed to Stutzer's inert form, his first acknowledgment of the prisoner's presence. "Thanks to him, so do a lot of people." He heard a winch and looked upward. "Here come the ropes," he said.

Stutzer lay at their feet, unconscious and shackled but not senseless, apparently, because he shivered in the chill night air even though the mimes had covered him with a blanket. There was no compassion in this. Stutzer was cargo to be protected. In the bow of the Zodiac, Heidi sat with her legs folded under her, looking into a hand mirror and removing the black from her face with tissues that she threw into the sea.

Except for Heidi, who was still working on her face, Christopher was the last member of the team to be lifted back aboard the *Olaster*. By the time he reached the deck the others, including Stutzer, had vanished. Simon the captain was nowhere to be seen, either, and Christopher knew it was pointless to put a question to the crew, who spoke no language other than their own, at least in his presence. The winch whined and Heidi came into view, holding onto the rope with one hand and with one foot in a loop in the rope, a star of the circus rising to the trapeze. Her face was still smudged. When she drew closer Christopher was taken unawares by a perverse little rush of sexual interest. Quick as ever, she detected this, or so he thought. Anyway something made her smile a woman's tight, knowing smile like the one she had given him after he had followed her up the stairs in the Red Orchestra Inn.

Christopher said, "Where is he?"

"Which he?"

"Stutzer."

"Below, I imagine. Sooner or later Yeho will want to talk to him."

"Where below, exactly?"

She hesitated, but only for an instant. Then she turned to a man in an officer's cap who seemed to be in charge of the crew that had lifted them aboard. She spoke to him in Hebrew. Busy with other things, he answered brusquely.

To Christopher Heidi said, "Come."

She led him at her usual half run through an open hatch in which he supposed the Zodiac was going to be stowed. Then she scampered down a ladder into the bowels of the ship and through several cargo holds connected by open watertight doors. The holds contained crates and barrels and bales and in one of them a small airplane with its wings removed and an oddly shaped vehicle of some kind, covered by a tarp, were lashed to the deck.

Heidi opened the waterproof door of the last compartment in the stern of the ship. She said, "According to the first mate, this room is called the lazaretto."

A large packing case stood on end at the center of the compartment. Like all the other packing cases in the hold, this one was made of rough scrap lumber. Unlike any of the others, it was wired for electricity. Light —very bright incandescent light—showed through chinks in the boards. Heidi slid open a bolt and then a small panel, revealing a judas hole the size of a saucer, and stepped aside. Christopher looked through the hole and by the light of a hundred-watt bulb in a wire cage, saw Stutzer, stripped of his pajamas, slumped on a rough lumber bench. Apparently the heat from the bulb was enough to keep him warm even though he was naked, because he had stopped shivering. He was still unconscious, or pretending to be. Christopher saw without deliberately looking for it that Yuri had been truthful about the castration. Stutzer was not bound to the bench or restrained in any way, except that there was just room enough in the box for a man in the sitting position. If Stutzer woke up and attempted to free himself he would realize immediately that there was no hope of this happening and that if he was not able to stop himself from struggling, he would be scraped and bruised as he came into contact with the unplaned lumber.

Heidi said, "Yeho will talk to him later."

"Where?"

"Here, I suppose," she said. "The box is nailed shut."

2

"Don't get sugar on the cards!" Yeho said. He was dealing and the cards were sticking together. The team was playing gin rummy and drinking sweet tea in the dining room and by each player's place the table was marked by rings of sticky moisture left by the tea glasses. Yeho was by far the shrewdest player in the game. Even Heidi, who played to win, could not get ahead of him.

It was late afternoon. After the raid the entire team had napped or at least remained in their cabins for several hours while the ship steamed eastward. Christopher, unable to sleep, passed the time by reading Mrs. Bedford's novel. Her characters, insouciant aristocrats down on their luck, resembled the people in Hubbard's novels except that disappointment rather than doom awaited them after the end of the story.

Neither Yeho nor anyone else at the card table spoke of Stutzer. Presumably he was sweltering below decks in his illuminated wooden box. Christopher supposed that Yeho was softening the prisoner for interrogation, but what could Stutzer confess that would add anything useful to what was already known about him?

Heidi cried "Gin!" and laid down her hand on the sticky table, catching Yeho with a large fan of cards in his hand. He glared at her, then grinned. "And to think I loved you like a daughter," he said. After that Yeho could not win. After a couple of hands Christopher, who remembered every card that Yeho and everyone else discarded, realized that he was contriving to lose. Heidi also seemed to understand what was happening. No doubt she had seen this behavior before and since the deception spoiled her one small victory, she ended the game. She cleared the tea glasses and started to scrub the table. The others disappeared.

Christopher went to the stern of the boat and watched the sun go down. It was a pallid sunset, half faded blue and half salmon, then shades of gray. He smelled tobacco smoke and looked behind him. Heidi stood at the rail, drawing deeply on a long thin cigarette. Her eyes were fixed on nothing. She knew that Christopher was there, of course, but she paid him no mind.

Christopher said, "Finished your K. P., I see."

Heidi frowned. "My what?"

"Kitchen police. You seem to get stuck with it quite a lot."

Her face was blank. "You noticed," she said. She was annoyed, withdrawn, unfriendly. By the way she smoked her cigarette she warned Christopher that she didn't want to talk.

Nevertheless Christopher said, "May I ask you something? What's the silence all about?"

"Silence? What silence?"

"About Stutzer. Why is everyone avoiding that subject?"

"Wait a while," Heidi said. "The conversation will get livelier."

"When?"

"Soon. Probably tonight. Catching one of them always has this effect on Yeho. He thinks whatever thoughts he thinks about the past, about all the murders, about the lost six million, about what might have been—the books, the science, the music, the wealth, the kids—if everybody had gone on living, and while thinking these thoughts he talks about the weather. Then for a while he doesn't talk at all. Then he spoils a card game or something. And then he goes back to being Yeho. And then he becomes the Memuneh."

"And when he's the Memuneh, what does he become?"

"Memuneh as you no doubt know means 'big boss.' The term was invented for Yeho when he ran everything. Now he's retired, in theory, but once a year he's the big boss again, at least on this one operation."

"You're saying he only runs one operation a year?"

"That's the arrangement. He gets a team, he gets whatever he needs, he picks the target. Usually he goes after some forgotten loathsome creature from the past like Stutzer. Tidying up. Usually, not always, he leaves our current enemies to the people now in charge. He doesn't step on toes."

"And this year he picked Stutzer. Why?"

"I guess he heard that the target had become available. A cast of thousands still tells him things. He heard something, he saw a possibility, and here we are."

"Including me."

"Obviously you're the reason for everything, my dear. Are you blind? He's doing this for you, for your family. Whatever sentence he's going to impose on Stutzer is an extra. He owes you something for what you lost. He knows it was his fault. He wants to pay the debt."

Christopher's back was turned to the bridge. Looking over his shoulder, Heidi saw something. Christopher turned and saw the mimes standing together. Heidi made a gesture of acknowledgment.

"Yeho calls," she said. "He wants you, too." She sucked the last smoke from her cigarette, burning it down to the filter, and flicked it overboard.

3

Because none of their cabins, including Yeho's, was large enough to contain five people, the team met in the hold, in the space next door to the lazaretto. Before a word was spoken, in response to two fingers lifted by Yeho, the mimes closed and locked the watertight doors at either end of the compartment, sealing in whatever words were about to be spoken.

"By now this man we captured last night has been wondering for many hours where he is and who's got him," Yeho said.

His air was professorial, reasonable, judicious. He was explaining to a class what to expect when the imaginary curtain behind him was opened and the monster in his shackles was revealed to them.

He continued, "He may even have guessed the truth. However, no matter who's got him, he knows his situation is not good. Because of the heat from the bulb inside the box, which is not very big, he will be very hot. He will be thirsty. He may have fouled the box. None of this comes as a shock to him. He knows we're trying to scare him, to break him down, to make him admit he deserves worse than he's going to get. He's an expert, one of the most experienced people in the world when it comes to processing suspects. He probably thinks we're amateurs compared to him. Nevertheless, now come these amateurs, who've got the power to set him free and also the power to torture him. He's been expecting us. He probably expects torture. He tells himself he's prepared for the worse but he knows he isn't, because while he himself has never been tortured he has tortured many others and he knows that no one can stand up under torture. He may defy us, he may tell us what we want to hear, he may say nothing. Naturally he won't tell us the truth under any circumstances. His truth is not our truth. You've got to realize he doesn't think he ever did anything wrong. To him, being nailed in a box with a hot electric bulb shining on him, shining in his eyes, is a crime against humanity. To him, the only thing he ever did in his life was enforce the law. He followed a virtuous calling. He was a good policeman. This person is an idealist. He has always been an idealist. He likes himself, he admires himself because he has ideals. Why else should a person have ideals? That's the most important thing about him. Remember that. Now come with me."

In the lazaretto the silence, except for the thump of diesel engines deeper in the ship, was almost as complete as the darkness. The box, glowing through its many cracks and fissures as if light were seeping through the very pores in the wood, seemed to be suspended in midair. Christopher wondered if Yeho had staged this *trompe l'oeil* as a mock religious experience: Lucifer imprisoned and giving up his light.

Followed by Christopher, whom he ignored, Yeho strode across the deck and flung open the judas hole. A wave of heat came out of the aperture. Stutzer uttered a little groan as if grateful for the cooler air that flowed inward. Christopher laid a hand on the outside of box. It was hot to the touch. It had not occurred to him that one light bulb burning in an unvented space could produce such scorching heat. Through the judas hole he saw that Stutzer was wide awake, with intelligence in his eyes. He dripped with sweat, some of it faintly bloody where his skin had scraped against the rough wood or come into contact with one of the bent-over nails that protruded from the boards. He covered what was left of his sexual organs with cupped hands. With his ravaged face, his disheveled hair, his suffering eyes, his protruding rib cage, his all but fleshless bones, his flaccid muscles, his hairless skin, his seeping wounds, he looked like anyone but Lucifer.

Yeho, standing well back in the darkness and off to the side where the light from the box could not reveal him, studied Stutzer at length. Then he closed the judas hole and taking Christopher by the arm, drew him away from the box. In a voice so low that Christopher had to bend over to hear the words, he said, "This is something for one person to do. Two is no good."

What did Yeho mean? That one person should talk to Stutzer, one person should shoot him, one person should set the box on fire? Christopher had no notion of Yeho's intentions, except that his fundamental purpose still seemed to be to exasperate. Christopher took a deep breath, then another. His patience revived.

He said, "Fine, Yeho. Go first."

"Go first?"

"Talk to him, but leave something for me to talk to when you're through."

Yeho jumped in his skin in surprise or indignation or both, or something else if he was acting again. "What kind of a remark is that?" he said. "That's something you should say to a Stutzer."

In a flat tone of voice Christopher said, "Yeho."

Mimicking the tone Yeho said, "Paul." He loaded the name, speaking it for the first time, with resentment. What had he ever done to deserve such a sting of the serpent's tooth?

As if speech was no longer to be considered as a way of communicating with Christopher, Yeho turned his back on him and strode back to the box. He stopped before it for a long moment, collecting himself. Then he rapped sharply three times on the top of the box and opened the judas hole. By its light Christopher saw that a low chair had been placed in front of the box. Yeho sat down in it so that the light shone directly on his face. He let Stutzer look at him for a long moment.

Then he said, "Life is long, Herr Standartenführer. You are in the hands of the Jews."

4

Standing in darkness behind the box, Christopher could see Yeho's face by the light from the judas hole, but not Stutzer's. The two were talking to each other in German, Yeho's voice soft and reasonable, Stutzer's changing by stages from shrill anger to bluster to a reasonableness so studied that it seemed to be mockery. Finally only Stutzer talked, a long soliloquy in which he told the story of his life—his parents, his childhood, his schooldays, the unjust discrimination he had suffered as the son of a man who was small in the world, everything but the parts that had nailed him into the box.

For a long time Yeho did not interrupt. Finally, hours after the conversation began, he began to confide. He spoke in low tones, confidentially, and Stutzer replied in kind. Christopher caught a word here and there. In the final hour, Yeho and Stutzer whispered to each other, parties to an understanding so secret, so delicate that no one else on earth could be privy to it.

At last they shook hands through the judas hole. Yeho pointed a finger at the box. Before stepping into the light Heidi and the mimes covered their heads and faces with black hoods and offered one to Christopher. He said no. The mimes, perfectly rehearsed, took the box to pieces in instants, first the top and then the four walls, which fell to the floor all at once like the panels of a magician's box. The bulb, lying on the floor now, provided the only light and with the whole locker to fill, it was no longer its former blinding self. In its weakened glow Stutzer stood up, naked and gleaming with sweat. His face was in shadow. As before he covered his mutilated parts with a cupped hand. In the last twenty-four hours he had not stood up or moved more than an inch or two. Now he lost his balance and staggered. Yeho did not touch him—in fact he drew back avoid contact—but in a solicitous tone he said, "Careful of the nails, Franz. Don't move."

The mimes vanished. Heidi shined a flashlight into Stutzer's face. He blinked and raised a skeletal arm to shield his eyes, but he wore a pleasant expression—the vestige, Christopher supposed, of the look of deep sincerity he had been wearing to win Yeho's trust. Christopher heard water being drawn into tin buckets offstage. The mimes returned, each lugging two large slopping pails. Yeho pointed another finger and the mimes poured the water over Stutzer, emptying three buckets over his head and flinging the last bucket at his fouled buttocks and groin. Some of the water splattered onto the electric bulb and it popped and sparked. By the smell of it, the water was warm and in the darkness Stutzer gasped softly in pleasure. Heidi and the mimes surrounded him and trained flashlights on him. One of the mimes threw Stutzer a large white Turkish towel. After he had dried himself he tied the towel around his waist. Another towel flew through the darkness. Stutzer snatched it from the air and draped it over his head and shoulders like a monk's hood.

With all his attention concentrated on Stutzer, Christopher had lost track of Yeho. Now he felt a hand on his arm. Yeho said, "Come, we'll talk for a minute."

Christopher said, "What about him?"

"He's yours now, a promise is a promise, but you should know what's what before you talk to him."

Yeho was being an uncle to Christopher. His voice, his manner, even the pressure of his hand suggested affection, trust, a special connection. He seemed to be telling Christopher that whatever resentment he might have felt earlier, whatever cross words may have been spoken, were now forgotten.

Christopher said, "So what is what?"

"Not here," Yeho said.

"Why not?"

"He has ears."

"Me too, but I couldn't hear what you said to him or what he was saying to you when I was six feet away."

"He was telling his story. Everybody has a story he wants to tell."

"So they say. But what were you whispering to him? What promises have been made? I don't want to turn my back and have him disappear."

Another impertinence. It was too much to bear. Yeho shrugged and threw up his hands. It was too dark to see this, but Christopher sensed the gestures. Yeho sighed heavily. He said, "You're telling me you don't trust me?"

"Nothing personal, Yeho. I just want to talk to him."

"Look who's talking about personal. So what do you want to do first, listen to me or talk to him?"

"I want to hear what you've got to tell me. I don't want to hear it down here. We can do it on deck."

"What about him?"

"We'll take him with us."

"In the towels?"

"He looks like he could use some fresh air. So can I. Yeho, I don't want to be in a confined space with him, where I can smell him. Not for another minute."

Across the room Heidi and the mimes continued to hold Stutzer in the beams of their flashlights. Wrapped in his white towels, his face obscured by the cowl, he looked a hundred times less sinister than he had looked twenty years before as a tailor's dummy.

In a voice heavy with resignation, Yeho said, "You want to go upstairs, we'll go upstairs."

It was a long way up. Heidi led the way at her usual scamper. The mimes handled Stutzer. In his bare feet and weakened state he had trouble with the ladders and by the time they reached the deck he was badly out of breath. The moon was full again tonight. A torpid sea sparkled in its light. Christopher found the North Star. The ship was moving westward now, but very slowly. The usual stream of shipping flowed by in the distance, lights burning. A mile or two to the north he saw an island and recognized its silhouette—Bornholm, the Danish island he and Rima had almost reached.

They were on the foredeck. On the deck above, officers and seamen were at their stations on the bridge, but the rest of the deck was deserted. Heidi and the mimes tended to Stutzer. After his climb he was wheezing asthmatically.

To Yeho Christopher said, "I don't think he's going to overhear us."

Yeho, unresponsive and glum, waited until Stutzer was a little quieter, then snapped his fingers and made a gesture. The mimes walked Stutzer, who now seemed to be too weak to do anything without assistance, to the bow of the ship and helped him to lower himself to the deck. Rather than sitting he fell to one knee. The others, standing in a semicircle, still wore their black hoods. Stutzer tugged his white cowl into place and bowed his head. They looked like mummers posing for a Lenten procession.

Yeho took Christopher's arm. "We'll walk while we talk," he said, "I'm stiff after all that sitting."

From the moment Heidi and the mimes put on their hoods Christopher had believed that Yeho was going to let Stutzer live. If he was going to die, why protect their identity? Let him live for what purpose, live where, live how, live why?

Yeho had the Eastern habit of lightly holding hands with a confidant while they talked. Fingertips touching, he and Christopher walked back and forth across the deck. For the first few transits, Yeho seemed to be gathering his thoughts. He kept silent or at least wordless while making small, apparently involuntary noises—clearing his throat, muttering to himself in whatever language he happened to be thinking in at the moment, coughing.

At last he said, "I guess you've figured it all out, but I want to be sure you understand what's happening and why it's happening." He looked up brightly into Christopher's blank face. "Also why it's for the best."

Christopher waited for him to go on. Yeho had been speaking German to Stutzer most of the night and he spoke German now. He spoke guardedly, so that Stutzer could not overhear. The wind was rising, so some of his words were blown away.

In English Christopher said, "Can he understand English?"

"I don't think so," Yeho said. "Why would he? Did he ever speak English to you or your mother and father or"—he paused—"anyone else you knew?"

"No."

"So what's your point?"

"If we speak English you can talk louder and I'll be able to hear you."

Christopher steered Yeho to the narrow stairs that led to the bridge deck. They sat down together, Yeho perched two steps above Christopher so that they could look into each other's eyes.

"What we need now is tea," Yeho said. He pointed a finger at Heidi. Even in the dimness she picked up the signal and when he made a drinking motion, went inside to fetch what he wanted. As though things could not go on without her, they waited in silence for Heidi to come back. Although Christopher could hear diesel engines idling and smell their exhaust, the *Olaster* was not moving under power, but was being carried along on the current. At last Heidi came back with a tray of steaming tea glasses. Yeho took one and drained it. Christopher handed him his own untouched glass.

Yeho said, "You don't want it?"

"He doesn't like it," Heidi said.

"Is that true?" Yeho asked, amazement in his voice. He said, "To tell you the truth I've got a little sore throat, all that talking to the Standartenführer. The tea helps. Why don't you like it?" He was making small talk. He seemed loath to come to the point.

Christopher said, "To me, sometimes, the tea seems a little too sweet. Yeho, it'll be morning soon."

Yeho said, "Okay. I'm going to tell you everything. You can ask questions, but if something is missing it's because I don't know what goes in that pigeonhole or I forgot it. Okay?"

"Fine. But please remember that I already know the story of his life.

There's no need to go over it again."

"So what interests you?"

"His future."

"Easy," Yeho said. "He thinks we're going to put him back on shore. He's going to work for us—make that *pretend* to work for us."

"Why?" Christopher asked.

"He says he hates the communists because they castrated him."

"You believe him?"

"What is truth? It's a temptation to go let him think we believe him. We could put him in place, let him work for us for a while, then tip off MfS, and bingo he'd be back in the gulag being whipped and starved and worked to death, his worse nightmare."

"Just how tempted are you, Yeho?"

"What I want to do is try him in open court. But as I already told you, the problem with Stutzer has always been that he cannot be tried for his crimes. When he was a Nazi he killed everybody he ever met in his life except you, even his own men by leading them into a trap. Hubbard is dead, who knows what happened to your mother. You're the only witness. As far as we know, nobody else who ever saw him lived to tell the tale."

Christopher said, "So my role as you see it is to identify him in a court of law?"

"We both know that can't happen," Yeho replied. "Anyway, what charge would be enough? What sentence? Would hanging or a firing squad or tying him covered with honey to an anthill in Africa be enough?"

Christopher said, "Yeho, stop. If nothing is enough to even the score, tell me, please, what you plan to do with him."

Yeho said, "I'm going to let you talk to him some more. Then we'll decide. Right now it's your turn." Yeho hissed and when Heidi looked up, pointed a finger first at Christopher, then at Stutzer. To Christopher he said, "Go. Take your time."

In the bow of the ship, Stutzer was crouching now instead of kneeling. Christopher stood over him. He said, "Stand up."

Stutzer rose painfully to his feet. Swaying a little, he stood at attention, heels together, back rigid, eyes straight ahead. His posture was a confession that he wished to make a good impression. He was at his captor's orders. However, now that the moment for interrogation had come at last, Christopher had no questions for him. He did not care what Stutzer remembered or did not remember or whether he understood that Christopher was who he was.

In loud German Christopher said, "You remember this place?"

Even louder, as though he had a greater right to the German language than this impostor, in English, looking Christopher straight in the eye, Stutzer replied, "Everything!" He pronounced the diphthong as if it were the German *z*. His tone was prideful. Yeho was right: this man liked himself. He was proud of his memories.

Christopher had had no intention of doing what he did half a second later, no inkling, even, that he was going to do it. As if someone else were using his body, without forethought, without emotion, Christopher picked Stutzer up and threw him over the side of the ship. Stutzer weighed so little that Christopher half expected that he would drift on the wind like a big insect. Instead he fell like the bag of bones that he was, white towels fluttering away in the night, and made a phosphorescent splash when he hit the water.

No one cried man overboard. A searchlight came on and swept the water. Christopher expected to see nothing. But the circle of bluish light found him and blinded him.

Stutzer was alive, thrashing as if trying to swim the trudgeon. His movements, wild and uncontrolled, resembled the gestures he used to make when having one of his tantrums. If he was screaming, no one could hear him. The thrashing, frantic at first, slowed as the cold took hold of him, and after a few seconds, not longer than that, he sank beneath the surface, creating a dimple in the water that sealed itself almost at once. No one but Christopher had moved or spoken. For several minutes the light stayed on the spot where Stutzer had drowned, but no boat was lowered, no life preserver flung. No effort whatsoever was made to rescue him. At length the searchlight went out. The diesels throbbed, the screw bit into the sea. The *Olaster* shuddered and made way.

Not much had happened. Not much had changed.

Paul, from whom Christopher had not heard in years, said, "My God, how I loved her."